PE

Dangerous to Know

Please return/renew this item by the last date shown.
Items may also be renewed by the internet*

https://library.eastriding.gov.uk

* Please note a PIN will be required to access this service
- this can be

By the same author

Mad
Bad

Dangerous to Know

CHLOÉ ESPOSITO

PENGUIN BOOKS

PENGUIN BOOKS

UK | USA | Canada | Ireland | Australia
India | New Zealand | South Africa

Penguin Books is part of the Penguin Random House group of companies
whose addresses can be found at global.penguinrandomhouse.com.

First published 2020
001

Set in 12.5/14.75 pt Garamond MT Std
Typeset by Jouve (UK), Milton Keynes
Printed and bound in Great Britain by Clays Ltd, Elcograf S.p.A.

A CIP catalogue record for this book is available from the British Library

ISBN: 978-1-405-92884-7

www.greenpenguin.co.uk

For Richard

Contents

Contents

What good is it for someone to gain the whole
world, yet forfeit their soul?

Matthew 16:26, The Bible,
New International Version

I am in blood
Stepped in so far that, should I wade no more,
Returning were as tedious as go o'er.

Macbeth, **William Shakespeare**

Beware for I am fearless, and therefore powerful.

Frankenstein, **Mary Shelley**

Prologue

I'm flawed. Aren't we all? What's *your* fatal flaw? Mine? I love too much. I do *crazy* shit for love, mad and bad and dangerous . . .

Whoever said time heals is a fucking liar.

It's been *a year*.

My dark prince, I'll make it up to you.

I loved him and I killed him. Yeah. *Biggest mistake of my life.* We were star-crossed lovers, like Romeo and Juliet, except I'm still alive. Nino was the first person I loved and the first one to love me (apart from Channing Tatum, obvs, but that was more *one way*).

It's all my fault Nino is dead. I miss him every day.

Judge not lest ye be judged. That is Jesus Christ. So don't go getting all *judgemental* because I shot some guy.

Listen, I'm not saying I'm *perfect*. I'm saying I made a *mistake*. You'd have done the same in the same situation, wearing my (fabulous) shoes.

I close my eyes and he's in there, *whispering*. His voice sounds like the wind. Nino speaks to me, ever present: '*Alvie, Alvie, Alvie.*'

I love him like an opiate, a drug that you taste once and then you're hooked for life; nothing will ever feel so good or hurt so much. That's love.

Now it's up to me to make it right. I know what I have to do.

Perhaps two wrongs will make a right?

I'll do ONE LAST HIT for Nino.

He said the billionaire, Ed Forbes, was responsible for the death of his father. Eddie, Ed, you bad, bad boy. Your time is up, sunshine.

One more hit and then I'm done. I'll hang up my gun.

(Haven't you ever done something wrong, but for the right reason?)

Then no more mistakes. No more *train-wreck* Alvie. I'll leave behind the old me. I'll transform like a butterfly. I'll be different. *Awake.*

There's no point in being *alive* if you are not *awake.*

The unexamined life is not worth living. That is Socrates.

And Socrates knew his shit.

Parados

I roll over on my bunk bed. Grab my Birkin bag. I pull out my fake ID and study the girl in the passport. There's a photograph of me. It was taken a year ago in a photo booth in Rome in a place called Trastevere. I have pink hair and a brand-new nose (I had an emergency nose job to make myself unrecognizable to the authorities). I'm wearing one of my sister's old Balenciaga T-shirts and have what can only be described as a criminally good tan.

I sigh and stroke the cheek of the girl in the photo. Her face is familiar but at the same time she looks alien, strange, as though she wasn't me. The pink hair dye has long washed out and the fabulous tan has faded. And the passport says it isn't me: Miss Alvina Knightly. It says my name is *Siobhán*. Siobhán *Faelan*. (I don't know how to pronounce 'Siobhán'. Is it SEE-OB-HAAN? Or SHUH-VAWN?) I study the dates in the burgundy book: now I'm three years younger and *Irish*. Apparently I was born in Cork on 22 August and, according to the stamps, I've visited the Bahamas.

I'm not going to lie: I don't remember most of the past year. It is a blur, like a Monet painting or some other Impressionist's. There are flashes of red: a *Smirnoff* bottle,

3

Nino's blood on the bed sheets . . . But other than that there are muted colours: the grey of the London sky, the off-white ceiling in the hostel seen through half-closed eyes, the dirty beige of the carpet and the white of a railway line that stretched for miles and miles to nowhere. A pale face. Was it mine? Stuff happened. I blacked out. Cocaine . . . That's all I know. It's like that movie, *The Hangover*, when these guys wake up in Vegas the morning after a party and they don't remember a thing because their drinks were spiked with 'roofies' – it's that, but for *a year*.

(How the hell did Elton John and Keith Richards write their autobiographies? They must have used creative licence, that's all I can tell you.)

It is time to become *Siobhán*. I'll go out in a blaze of glory. One more hit. The hit of my life. The hit of the fucking century. I have wasted too much time in this god-forsaken *pit*. I'll do something bold and romantic. I'll do it for *him*.

I close my eyes and lie back on the bed with one hand down my knickers . . . Bob's on the bunk bed down below and Roxy's snoring over there, but I could give a fuck right now: I need to *come*.

I ride the waves of my orgasm and picture Nino's dick. *So. Fucking. Beautiful. Why did he have to die?*

Nino can't kill Ed, so I will. *An eye for an eye. A tooth for a tooth*. It's the *least* I can do, you know, after murdering him in the face. (I still feel bad about that . . .)

Ed Forbes isn't just the guy who killed Nino's father. He also happens to be *rich,* which might come in useful . . . Of course, the fact he's a *billionaire* is quite irrelevant. I'd kill him if he were as poor as a church mouse. It's not about the

4

money. But if I can get my hands on his cash, I could buy myself a new life. With a billion pounds I could even purchase my own private island! I could buy Kylie Jenner's face and use it to replace my own (like Nicholas Cage and John Travolta in that movie *Face/Off*). I could do that thing that Michael Jackson did and change my skin colour from white to black, then black to white, then white to black again. I'd confuse the hell out of the cops. They would never find me. I'd get away with all the murders and theft and arson, etc.

Yes, yes, with *money* comes options. It's the only way.

I grab my phone and download a new app called Basecamp. It's a project management tool that I am going to use to help to keep me bang on track with my new quest. I type in my to-do list. It's basic, but to the point:

1. Become Siobhán.
2. Find Ed.
3. Kill Tiff (his wife).
4. Seduce Ed.
5. Marry Ed.
6. Kill Ed and spend all his money on clothes and hide from the police.

Yes, that's *very* professional. Nice and organized. I shove my phone back in my bag. I really need to pee. I jump down from my top bunk and head down the hall to the bathroom.

I glance through the double doors. There is a *cop* at reception. I freeze. I stare. He looks my way. We make eye contact for a second, then he looks away. I leg it into the toilet, lock the door and climb on the seat.

'Fuck. They've finally found me,' I say, as I squeeze out

through the window, the brickwork scraping my shins, my heart exploding like ammo and my breathing as loud as an asthmatic's in crap scuba gear. I drag myself up off the grass and an *enormous* squirrel cuts me up. I trip and fall face down into the mud.

'*Bastard.*'

I run across Archway Road, the buses cursing at me, and stand in the window of Greggs watching the entrance to the hostel. I wait, sweating and panting, with my breath fogging up the glass. I can't buy a sausage roll. I really, *really* want one, but I don't have any cash. I consider *nicking* one . . . The hot, delicious smells of pastry and processed meat fill my nostrils. I whimper softly, aware that these could be my last moments of freedom.

'I'm dead meat,' I say.

Of course the police are looking for me. It was only a matter of time. I killed a bunch of people last year on holiday in Italy.

The woman at the desk asks me if I am OK.

I nod. I can't speak. I can't look at her. I look at my hands: they're shaking. My hangover progresses to *nine*. Sweat snakes down my back as the bile rises up my oesophagus.

Eventually I see the cop come striding out of the hostel. He looks both ways down the road and frowns then climbs into his patrol car. I wait until he's driven off, then sneak out of the pie shop. I take a deep breath and steel myself then sprint back to the hostel. What if he's left a trap for me? A bug? A hidden camera? But I need to go back for my phone, my cash, my fake passport . . .

'What was that all about? With the cop?' I ask Darragh at reception.

He looks up from the game he's playing.

'Why are you covered in mud?'

I brace myself and tense my jaw, expecting him to say 'He was asking after *you*. I don't know why, but it seemed important. He checked the bedrooms and everything. He's coming back tonight.'

But instead he says: 'I called the cops because there was a belligerent squirrel bothering some of the residents.'

I blink. 'I'm sorry, what? A belligerent *what*?'

'A belligerent squirrel loitering around the entrance. A couple of people have complained.'

I study his face. He looks serious, but there is a chance he is taking the piss. 'You called the cops about a *squirrel*?'

'I did, yeah,' he says. 'I thought about calling the RSPCA or Rentokil, but I thought the police should know what kind of anti-social behaviour the local wildlife are displaying. It's very intimidating.'

I am at a loss for words and our conversation is over. Darragh is back to *Black Ops 4* or whatever the hell he is playing, so I turn slowly on my heels and head back down the corridor towards the communal bedroom that I share with five other slobs.

Urgh, I hate this place. It *smells*. I've been here nearly a *year*, after flying back from Rome on Siobhán's passport. I climb back up to my top bunk, lie down and stare at the ceiling. I'm getting mud all over the sheets, but I have other problems. I retch over the side of the bed, but nothing comes up. Not yet. Bob's still passed out down below: he snores like he's being strangled and I can see a dirty foot poking out from beneath his blanket.

My heart rate slowly returns to normal. I had a lucky

break. This time it was a stroppy squirrel, but next time it would be *me*. They're coming for me soon. I know. I feel it in my bones. I'm hunted like a common fox by a pack full of old Etonians. I am not *imagining* it. I'm not *paranoid*. I'm telling you, this is *my life*. If you can call it that. I've been living quietly, laying low, no drama. But hiding isn't going to help. I need to take serious action.

But first I need to get out of here. It's not safe. I need to keep moving. I'll go and grab my cash and *run*. Let's get this show on the road. I clamber down from my top bunk and stub my toe on the ladder. I grab my hoody from the floor and drag myself along the hall towards the hostel lockers, glaring at the too bright lights and trying not to vomit.

I open up my locker and remove the false back to reveal . . . *nothing*. I'm completely out of cash. *Shit*. Where has it gone? Instead of piles of cash, there is a Hubba Bubba wrapper, the crumbs of what had once been Pringles, a G-string I'd forgotten I owned and a crumpled-up receipt for six bottles of Tesco's Imperial Vodka. Where are all the banknotes?

'Balls.'

I am almost broke. I pick up the remaining coins: £9.58. Surely one of the residents – Bob or that guy with the spider's web tattoo across his face and neck – have nicked my stash?

But *no*. It slowly dawns on me that I've spent it. A year ago, I sold my sister's diamonds for two hundred grand, and I've been living off that ever since. Until *now*, that is . . . I had to pay the rent for the hostel. There was all that money I spent in Gucci, Prada and Louis V. (Looking this good is *expensive* . . .) And then there were all the lottery tickets I've bought recently. (I won ten quid on Saturday night, but I'd spent twelve quid to buy the tickets, so it was bittersweet.) I paid a grand for some customized trainers. Manicures. Pedicures. Handbags. Shoes. (I really like shoes. And bags.) I splashed out on a gorgeous vintage Hermès Birkin bag. I get a lot of compliments; it was worth the hundred grand. I get a lot of Deliveroos and Uber Foods and Just Eats. And then there are all the brunches and lunches: avocados on toast and flat whites.

This is bad. This is Very Bad. I won't be able to *eat*. This is a massive kick up the ass. This is an *invitation*. It is time to sober up. The universe has spoken.

First Episode

The first thing on my Basecamp list is: 1. *Become Siobhán*. It has taken me *all week* to get used to the fact that I'm *Irish*. I mean, it's fine. Of course I have no problem with being Irish. It's just a little *bewildering* after twenty-odd years of *not* being Irish. It's disorientating, that's all.

I have done extensive research into how to be Irish. I've watched a lot of *Father Ted*, all six series of *Ballykiss-angel*, and developed a, frankly unhealthy, obsession with the young Colin Farrell.

I've been taking my new identity *very* seriously. If the 'intelligent' men and women at the nation's intelligence services, at Interpol and MI5 and MI6, etc. are going to believe that I'm Siobhán and *not* Alvina Knightly, then I have got to believe it myself. I have to be *convincing* in the manner of a top method actor: Michelle Williams as Marilyn Monroe, Natalie Portman as Jackie Kennedy, or Christian Bale as Batman. Otherwise it won't work.

The pink hair in my passport shot is clearly *not* a natural hue, and any member of Her Majesty's constabulary who believes that it *is* needs to have their head examined. My research into the Irish race on Google has revealed that

Ireland has the highest number of red-haired people per capita on the planet. The key thing here is that the hair is *red*, not *pink*. It's different. I've decided that an authentic colour for Siobhán's hair would be *carrot*: see Florence Welch from Florence and The Machine or any of the models painted by Dante Gabriel Rossetti and other members of the Pre-Raphaelite Brotherhood. After three days of dying my hair and eyebrows and pubic hair *orange*, I can honestly say that I feel like a ginge and can empathize with Prince Harry and Geri Horner, formerly Halliwell, aka *Ginger Spice*.

At first I was worried I'd have to learn Irish. Imagine my relief when I discovered that, in fact, most of the people of Ireland speak English but with an Irish accent. This has saved me a lot of time and effort and money on lessons and language apps like Rosetta Stone, which is *great* because I can't be arsed. I have very much enjoyed perfecting my Irish accent and practising on unsuspecting members of the public. A couple of times I forgot I was Irish and slipped back into my English accent, or Gloucestershire with a London twang to be more precise. I was chatting to a girl in the line for the soup kitchen when she said, 'Huh? I thought you were *Irish*?'

'Oh yeah, *shit*,' I said. 'Yes! I mean, *no*. I mean, *yes*. I'm *half* Irish.'

She nodded as though this explained my fluctuating regional accent. To be honest, I panicked. I recited the popular Irish phrase 'May the cat eat you and the devil eat the cat'. I'm not sure what it means, but I think it might be rude because she didn't speak to me after that, which I can't say is a shame.

My favourite thing about speaking Irish is saying 'wee' all the time, not 'wee' as in 'pee', like 'I need a wee', but 'wee' as in 'small'. You can make anything sound nice by using the prefix 'wee'. For example, 'Oh, I'm just having a wee hysterectomy. It's nothing serious. To be sure. To be sure.' Or 'Oh, I'll just pop a wee bit of ricin in your tea. It will only kill you a wee bit, I promise.'

Incidentally I've discovered that the Irish *love* tea and believe it fixes everything. 'Poisoned? Have a cup of tea!' 'Beheaded by ISIS? Have a cup of tea!' That kind of thing. Since becoming Siobhán, I've been drinking six or seven cups of Barry's per day and, personally, I've found that it fixes fuck all, but it makes you wee a lot.

I've been watching a lot of *Riverdance* on YouTube. I've decided Siobhán loves singing and dancing and The Corrs and was subjected to years of punishing Irish dancing classes as a child. I've been practising dancing like Michael Flatley in the communal toilets of the hostel when I think no one's around. I play Irish music on my phone at full volume and tap my feet and keep my hands and arms very still and close to my body. If one of the other residents comes in, I very quickly pause the video and pretend to be exterminating ants with the soles of my shoes. 'Bloody ants,' I'll say, or something similar, and this throws them off the scent. I have almost perfected the first five minutes of the *Riverdance* routine and feel confident that, should I ever encounter an Irish dancing expert, who demanded to see my Irish dancing as proof of my Irish nationality, then I would successfully dupe them.

Siobhán is three years younger than Alvie and, as a result, has amazing, glowing, wrinkle-free skin. On Tuesday

I pawned a pricey bag (a patent burgundy Lady Dior) then visited a health spa for a chemical peel. I also had something called 'microdermabrasion', a procedure whereby the dead skin cells on your face are scraped off by tiny razor blades and then vacuumed away. I am now Botoxed and filled and plumped to within an inch of my life, so that I can no longer move any of the muscles in my forehead, which is a good thing.

As Siobhán is so much younger than Alvie, you might assume that she would be fitter and healthier, with iron glutes, a flat stomach and absolutely no muffin top whatsoever. And yet, until now, Siobhán has neglected her physical fitness, thereby ageing prematurely. She has refused to visit any kind of gym. She has consumed only Guinness and potatoes, her tipple of choice being a shot of whisky and cream inside a pint of Guinness.

In fact, this concoction is the perfect 'hair of the dog' to help her get over the regular bouts of 'Irish flu', otherwise known as a 'hangover'. According to the World Health Organization, the Irish have the second-highest level of binge drinking in the world, second only to Austria, a ranking that I'm sure the people of Ireland could surpass with sustained practice and enough ibuprofen and fry-ups. I mean, these people add whisky to *coffee*. They can do anything.

According to the 'satellite' function of Google Maps, Cork is in a green bit of Ireland that I assume to be remote and tranquil, unspoilt countryside. As Siobhán is a country girl, it follows that she will love nature and horses. I have studied the indigenous flora and fauna of Ireland and can name all two hundred varietals of potato. (Potatoes are indigenous to Peru, not Ireland, but you can't be too careful.)

Siobhán is a *very* strict Catholic and *extremely* religious. I therefore attended mass every day this week at my local Catholic church, St Joseph's in Highgate, and am now on first name terms with the vicar (Sean. *Hot*. A 9/10!). I also make a point of wearing a rosary and praying loudly to the Virgin Mary whenever anyone enters the communal bedroom at the hostel and catches me wanking over Colin Farrell.

Finally I thought it would be appropriate to purchase a small plastic figurine of a leprechaun to attach to my mobile phone. This very tasteful lucky charm is holding a gleaming pot of gold while crouching at the end of a rainbow. It has, so far, been effective in bestowing me with 'the luck of the Irish', since I have yet to be apprehended for any of the twenty-odd murders I have committed or arrested for any of my other transgressions, e.g. blowing up a hotel.

My metamorphosis into Siobhán is, at last, complete. I have nailed the Irish 'ting' and sound like Saoirse Ronan. I've even opened a bank account under my new name. It is time to turn my attention to the next thing on my list: 2. *Find Ed*. Hmm, this is the tricky bit.

I call up Google on my phone. (The hostel's Wi-Fi is *terrible*. The internet is so fucking slow that I might as well walk to a library and ask for a book from the back of the vaults with black-and-white pictures in.) Eventually – once I've been on Facebook and scrolled through the posts about Brexit, politicians talking shit and new mums' pictures of their kids – I google-image 'Ed Forbes'. (I've done this *many* times before, but I don't believe you can internet-stalk someone *too much* as a rule.) The first hit is a *silver fox*. He looks fifty, but he's actually *sixty*, a clean-shaven George Clooney type. He is crazy hot, but *old*. Like Harrison Ford but fitter. I click the Wikipedia page for Edwin Forbes. Another picture. I zoom in. He has pale blue eyes and a winning smile. It says he made his fortune in funds in something to do with 'hedging'. He's one of the world's leading art collectors and has his own gallery in Mayfair. Ed is married to Tiffany (born 9 August 1985 in Chelsea, UK). First wife, no kids. They've been married for seven years, so it's time for their seven-year itch . . .

I type the URL for Tiffany's website. She is famous for being Ed's wife, like Melania, Kate or Coleen, but more talented. Tiffany was a catalogue model before she married Mister Bling. Now she does lots of charity work; there's a link you can click for the Dogs Trust. But the reason I *immediately* love her is because of her AMAZING vlog, *Breakfast with Tiffany*. It's like *Oprah* crossed with Goop with a bit of *I'm a Celebrity* and the crazy glamour of *RuPaul's Drag Race*. It's my new favourite show. Tiff posts every single day about spiritual things like love eggs, kale and Dzogchen meditation. I watch her vlog all the time. (I know that people use that expression 'all the time' and don't mean it. Like maybe they do it twice a month, or every week or something. But I actually watch it *all the time*. Like, that's all I do. I don't have a job, so it's just me and Tiff on my Samsung phone.) It's weird, but I feel like I *know* her. I feel like she knows me too.

Watching Tiff's vlog is also helpful for my Basecamp quest: it will be *easy* to win Ed's heart if I learn to act like his wife. I mean, he clearly has a *type*. If I can become more like *her*, then once Tiffany's dead and buried I can bag my man.

Breakfast with Tiffany is also Siobhán's cup of tea. She is *very* spiritual and, between you and me, it's *obvious* that Siobhán needs to sort herself out. That girl is a *mess*. Quit the drink and drugs and get on to the kale and kombucha. Meditation and yoga would help. Her body must be a temple. To pull off this hit Siobhán must *transform*, like that guy who turned into a beetle.

I click into Tiffany's vlog and play the post about shamans. This video is my favourite. Tiff goes on a vision quest in a cave in the Amazon Jungle; she's in a trance, sitting on the floor banging drums with a Peruvian. They reach an altered state of consciousness. *It's so fucking spiritual*. Then Tiff and the Peruvian have a cup of tea and he gives her a special gift: his ancient shaman's pouch. It's fashioned from the snouts of foxes stitched together with twine and a fibre from coca plants. It's really, *really* nice. I wish I had a bag like that. I'll have to look out for a roadkill fox on the Archway Road so I can make myself one.

I click into Insta on my phone and find the page for Tiff Forbes. I sigh. She's fuck-off beautiful. It's a shame she has to die, but needs must, I suppose. She is collateral damage. In the picture, she's posing with Ed outside the Savoy. There's the shiny silver sign and the golden statue of some guy. I scroll down past some more photos. There's another one of them there. And another. And another. They check in regularly. It's easy to recognize the hotel. The black and white tiles. The roundabout. I've never actually been *inside*, but I've walked passed a ton. It reminds me of the Ritz. (I stayed there once. Didn't like it.)

I accidentally 'Like' one of Tiffany's pictures from ten months ago.

'No.'

Shit.

I 'Unlike' it. Wow. It's lucky I noticed. That would have looked *really weird*. She'd think I was a *weirdo*.

If I got a job at the Savoy and worked there long enough, then Tiff and Ed would be sure to show up sooner rather than later. I'd be able to earn some dough and keep all my beautiful bags. Yes. Yes, that's what I'll do. It's a *great* idea.

> *Put on your big boy*
> *Pants, Mr Forbes. Siobhán*
> *Is coming for you . . .*

I hear Taylor Swift (my ringtone) and my phone vibrates. I grab the phone from inside my bag. 'Mavis' flashes. *Mum.* Ever since my sister died, my mother started calling *me*. I guess she misses Beth (don't know why) and I'm the next best thing.

'Hello, Mum. What are you up to?'

'I did a spot of laundry and then I watched some daytime TV.'

'Ooh, sounds *fun*. How's Ernie?'

Ernie is my sister's son. He's two years old (I think). I was going to adopt him when my sister died. I would make a *wonderful* mother, there's no doubt about that, but it wasn't safe for him with me, what with all the shoot-outs. I wish I could have him, though. I think a child would suit me. (I had a handbag dog in Rome and I imagine it's similar.) Ernie and I have a special bond. For starters he looks like

me, and I can tell he prefers me to *Beth*. I am his cool auntie. But I'm hiding from the cops and kidnapping is a
crime I'd rather not add to my list. Mum's been looking
after Ernie ever since I killed his folks. Poor thing. He's
going to need *a lot* of psychotherapy.

'And you've been doing *nothing* as usual?'

'Not true. *I wrote a haiku.*'

'Why don't you let me call a friend and arrange a job
for you?'

'A job! That's rich, coming from *you*. You haven't worked
since the eighties.' She probably wants me to *work in an
office*. Or become *an accountant*. 'I don't need help to find a
job. I can get one myself.'

'I have a friend,' she says. 'He's rich. He could sort you
out. His name is –'

'Wow, look at the time. I'd better get going,' I say. 'I'm
working on something *big, actually*. It won't be long till I'm
done.'

'Don't tell me. Another poem? Wasting your life away.
Wasting your time on *poetry* instead of *procreating*.'

'No, it's not a *haiku*.' *Bitch*. 'It's a lucrative job opportunity. Was there a reason for your call or was it just to
annoy me?'

'I was going to update you on the trial.'

'Uh-huh.' I stifle a yawn.

Last year my mother was arrested on suspicion of the
murder of my father, Alvin, in the early nineties. When I
first heard, of course I was shocked, but now I think about
it it's very much in character. I'm not surprised at all.

'As you know, I am pleading "not guilty". The whole
thing is *preposterous*.'

She pauses and waits for me to agree. I don't say anything.

'The trial's set to begin next month. My lawyer's optimistic that the jury will see sense and give me the all-clear.'

'Right. Well. Good luck with that. I'll talk to you later,' I say.

She has as much chance as O. J. Simpson. Less chance, probably. She's been out on bail for *months*; it is time they locked her up and threw away the key.

I hang up and stretch and yawn. Now, what was I doing? I find a Pringle under my pillow and eat it: BBQ flavour! Oh yes. Ed, Tiff, the Savoy, etc. I lick my fingers one by one, sucking off the deliciousness. If I'm going to get a job at London's poshest hotel, I will need to clean myself up . . . take a shower at least. And it would probably help if I wasn't permanently wasted.

Monday, 1 August, 7 p.m.
Archway, London

'My name is Siobhán and I am an alcoholic.'

'Hello, Siobhán,' everyone mumbles.

'Welcome,' a few people say.

The legs of my plastic chair scrape the floor. I glance round the circle. There's no one I know. Most of the faces are gazing off into the middle distance, but some people nod and smile, encouraging me to go on.

'Is this, er . . . *confidential*?' I ask.

The group leader says, 'Yes. We protect your anonymity; that's why it's called "anonymous".'

'Alcoholics *Anonymous*. I get it. This is my first time.

So whatever I say, you can't repeat it, not to the cops or anyone?'

The group leader shakes his head.

OK, here goes nothing . . .

I take a sip of disgusting coffee and spit it out on the floor. I have the hangover from hell, plus I'm drunk as well.

'Actually, can I start again?'

I sit down and then stand up. I hold on to a chair's back for balance. The room spins round like a carousel and I want to get off. (I downed a bottle of Malibu on the bus on the way to the meeting. I thought if this is my *last ever drink*, then I might as well enjoy it. Now I think I'm in the Caribbean at some kind of carnival, not stuck in a prefab in Holloway that smells of cabbage and mould.)

I study the floor. The floorboards are swaying. I wobble a bit, then stumble and trip. I grab on to a chair.

'What do you want me to talk about?' I focus on the leader, but there now seem to be *two* of him. Perhaps he's a twin, like I was?

'Maybe you could tell us a bit about why you are here?'

I stare at him. My mind has gone blank. I don't know why I'm here. I can't remember how I got here. Something about a bus?

'Why are you here, *Siobhán*?' comes a voice.

But I got *nothing*.

Eventually, when I don't speak, the group leader continues. 'Usually people like to share what alcohol has done to their lives and what actions they took to deal with their problem.'

'Right. Makes sense,' I say.

I glance round the ring of strangers. Everyone's eyes are on me. It's fine. They haven't noticed I'm hammered. I let out a high-pitched squeak: hiccough.

'I'm sorry,' the leader says. 'You're not allowed to come if you're *drunk*.'

'Drunk?' I say. 'I am not *drunk*. I'm on medication for . . . hay fever. It makes me very horny. And *drowsy*. I thought you weren't allowed to interrupt? Isn't *that* one of your rules?'

'Please go on,' he says with a sigh. 'My mistake.'

'What alcohol did to my life is that . . . I got drunk and murdered my twin. Then I pretended to be her, so that no one would know she was dead. It worked really well . . . for a while. We were *identical*.'

The group leader frowns. I study his face. Will he interrupt? He opens his mouth, but then shuts it again. I guess I'll carry on.

'My sister's husband realized that I wasn't *her*. So I had to kill him as well. I had drunk quite a lot of champagne.'

A couple of people in the circle nod as though they get it. Alcohol makes you do mad things. It's the devil's drink, or something. No one speaks, so I go on. I am on a roll now. I'm sure they've heard it all before and it's not that bad now I say it out loud. A crazy week. It's *nothing*.

'But . . .' My voice breaks and I can't get the words out.

'It's OK,' someone says. 'You can do it.'

I feel a warm hand on my back. I look up and frown. The room is suddenly blurry with tears. I take a deep breath. Try again.

'When I murdered my fiancé, I wasn't drunk. I *promise*.'

The group leader raises his eyebrows.

'Really. Really, I wasn't. I had had quite a lot of cocaine, but that doesn't count here, does it?'

'Umm . . . it's frowned upon,' he says.

'I have to quit drugs too?'

That is going to be challenging. Coke is my staple diet.

'What about cigarettes?' I ask.

'I mean . . . they're *bad* for you. But one step at a time . . .'

'Fine! The fags are going too.'

In for a penny, in for a pound. I'm going to do this *properly*.

I take the Marlboro Lights from my pocket and chuck them at the guy next to me.

'All right, cheers,' he says with a smile.

'That'll be a tenner.'

The woman with the stopwatch waves. My three minutes are up. Phew. I'm glad that's over with. I did *not* want to talk about Nino.

I down the dregs of my now cold coffee and my stomach growls. I'm peckish. I wonder if there are any biscuits? I head for the refreshments.

The stopwatch woman smiles at me. 'How long have you been sober?'

I glance at the clock and squint my eyes to read the dancing numbers. 'Twenty minutes. Give or take.'

'Every minute's a milestone.'

I grab a handful of custard creams and shove them in my mouth.

The leader says, 'Er, right, who's next?'

Good luck following *that*.

> *Three days sober! It's*
> *Been . . . fun. (I would crawl over*
> *Broken glass for rum.)*

I jog down the road through the smog and the heat, wheezing and coughing my guts up. The sun beats down on to my skull. This city is hotter than *hell*. What is going on with the weather? It's global warming, *obvs*. The polar ice caps are going to melt and we'll be snorkelling. This town will be under the sea, like Atlantis, and only the fish will survive.

I run all the way to town, dodging the deluge of tourists that clog the city streets like fatty plaque in arteries.

'Move it. Watch out, Jeez.'

I photobomb a few people's selfies in Trafalgar Square and swat down selfie sticks like flies.

'Stop taking pictures.'

I swipe someone's bottle of Volvic before they can take a sip.

'Hey, you! Come back! Give me that!'

Ha ha. I'm faster than he is.

I glug the water and pour cool liquid over my head. That's better. I never drank water until I went sober, but you know what? It's all right.

I spot a cop walking down the street and I can't help it. I freeze. I watch and wait till he turns a corner. *Alvie, sort yourself out.* It's just some guy in a uniform. He's not even that hot.

I couldn't afford to take the bus, so I ran all the way here from Archway. That's *five miles*, give or take. My cheeks are burning up. I'm hot. My top is sticky, smelly.

I take a deep breath and stand up tall as I approach the Savoy. The doorman spots me and hesitates before he opens the door. I shoot him a murderous look then pick the *revolving* door. I push through the brass and glass panels and step into the spacious hall.

I stand and blink. It's a whole new world, like that *Aladdin* song. Wow, this place is *beautiful*. The stuff that dreams are made of. There's the scent of lily of the valley. The taste of bankers and trust funds. And it's the perfect temperature: much cooler than outside.

'*Ciao*,' I say to the girl at reception. 'I'm here about a job.'

She looks blank, so I try again, as I wipe my brow with my top.

'I'm here to speak to the hiring manager. Where's the HR office?'

She gawks at me. Takes in my clothes. I guess I'm a bit underdressed, but it's OK. Strong is the new skinny and active wear's all the rage.

'Nikita's office is down the hall. Do you have an appointment?' she asks.

She watches me wring out my shirt.

'Yeah, of course. *Dur*. As if I'd just *show up*.'

'I'll call and let her know you're here. What's your name?'

'No need. I've already called,' I say. 'I am extremely efficient.'

I look in the direction she's pointing over the black and white tiles. Now she probably wants a tip. I know what these places are like. I sigh and reach into my Birkin and rummage around through all the crap inside. I have a few banknotes now from pawning my Chloé Nile bag, but I don't want to give her a *fiver*. I need that money to *eat*. I find a dirty five-cent coin left over from Italy.

'Here,' I say. 'That's all I've got. You can probably change it at Lloyds and get about fifty p. Or probably more . . . because Brexit.'

The woman looks at the filthy coin and then back at me. She doesn't pick it up or say thanks, she just leaves it there on the counter. I shrug and jog off down the hall. Some people are *so* ungrateful.

I clock a stunning china bowl overflowing with tropical fruit. I help myself to some apples, bananas, a mango and pineapple. I shove the fruit into my Birkin. Pineapple leaves stick out. I'll have to watch myself on those. They are as sharp as daggers.

I find a door marked 'HR', knock once and then walk in.

A woman sits at a messy desk eating a bagel. She is small with curly hair that looks like a 'before' photo for one of those magical hair-styling brands like Frizz Ease by John Frieda.

'Oh!' she says, looking up.

'Nikita?'

'Yes?'

'I'm here.'

'I see. And your name is . . .?'

'Siobhán.'

I sit down at the desk in a spinning chair and spin round a bit.

She frowns. 'Do you have an appointment?'

'Of course I do,' I say. Then I remember I'm supposed to be Irish. 'Bejeebus. To be sure.'

She frowns then turns to her computer. 'There's nothing here in the schedule.'

'Really? Huh. That's strange. Oh well, I'm here now. Might as well.'

'Are you *sure* that you have an appointment?' she asks.

'You don't remember me?'

'Er . . .'

'We scheduled this *last week*. I can't believe you forgot.'

I pull my most wounded face. Think last puppy left at the pound. I start humming 'Father and Son' by Boyzone – it gets me every time . . .

'How can I help you?' she says. 'I'm so sorry. I was having lunch.' She wipes her mouth with a napkin then shoves her food into a drawer.

I watch her chew and then wait till she's swallowed. How rude. So unprofessional.

'I'm here for a new job.'

She frowns. She eyes my Birkin bag.

'You need a job?' she asks.

I stare. Am I speaking Mandarin? Must be the Irish accent. 'I want to work *here*,' I say, slowly. 'It is my favourite hotel.'

'How nice. Are you a regular?'

'I've never been here before. I was thinking *security*. I'm very good with *guns*.'

'*Guns?*' she repeats. Her face falls slack. 'Were you in the army then?'

'No. Why?'

She swallows. 'Er. Do you have a CV?'

I roll my eyes. 'Nikita, *please*. No one bothers with those any more. Seriously.'

If I *did* have a CV, then there would be a gap for about the last year after it said *Vengeance*.

'What was the last job you had?' she asks, jabbing away at her keyboard.

I won't mention cold-calling. I don't want to do *that* again. That job was about as much fun as a cervical smear test. I once had a job in a Japanese restaurant, but they won't remember me. That was *ages* ago now. No way I could ask for a reference . . .

The woman frowns and pushes her glasses further up her greasy nose. 'So, what have you been doing for the past few years?'

I shift in my seat. 'You know, just chilling. Writing haikus mostly.'

She doesn't need to know that I'm an international hitwoman.

The woman reaches into a drawer to extract a boring-looking file.

'Do you have any qualifications?' she asks.

'Er.' I rack my brains. 'I have a Level 1 Food Hygiene certificate from ten years ago, but . . . I lost it.'

I won't say I was expelled from school for harassing the headmaster. (It wasn't anything *sexual*. I just burnt down his car.) My twin was the one with the GCSEs and the master's degree from Oxford. She was the one that made Mummy proud: vaccinated, breastfed, *loved*. I was the embarrassment.

'Don't worry,' the woman says. 'Plenty of jobs are low-skilled.'

Ha. Low-skilled. If only she knew. I can kill with my bare hands.

Her fingers click away at the keyboard. How long is this going to take? I keep on spinning round in the chair until the spinning-thing breaks.

'I could be your new doorwoman. Your current doorman is *shit*.'

She looks up and gives a tight smile, but doesn't say anything.

The doorwoman job would be *great*, actually. I'd be sure to spot Tiff and Ed.

'Or maybe a receptionist? I'm a *people person*.'

'OK, here we go,' she says at last. 'I've pulled up our vacancies but we only seem to have *one* match. It's for a pot wash,' she says.

'Pot wash? What is that?'

'You wash the saucepans in the restaurant kitchen.'

I swallow. I wouldn't want that job if it was the last job on earth.

'Nicky? Nora?' I say, leaning in. 'That sounds *perfect*.'

I find the Savoy Grill restaurant. I guess it's better than *nothing*. At least I'll have some money. Some food. A regular income. I can lay low while I look out for Ed and the gorgeous Tiffany. It shouldn't be long before they show up for a date. And I'll be ready for them. I glance around the dining room. It's pretty here as well. The air is filled with the scent of peach melba. Well-dressed ladies are having lunch. There's the mellifluous sound of laughter. They look like they're having fun. They look up as I pass by.

'What's the craic?' I ask.

I Irish dance across the floor and push through the doors to the kitchen and into a wall of heat. People are shouting and something is burning. The chef has his back to me.

'Ahem,' I say. 'AHEM. AHEM.'

The chef turns round and glares. There's a frying pan in his hand and the frying pan is *on fire*. I study the blaze. It looks really cool. The flames are dancing orange. *Ooh, it looks beautiful.* My eyelashes singe.

'Who are *you*?' asks the chef.

I tear my eyes away from the blaze. If I were a moth, I'd be screwed.

'My name is Siobhán,' I say. 'I'm here for the pot wash job?'

I take in the chef's white coat and tall white poofy hat. I don't know how he can wear all that, this kitchen is fifty degrees. A bead of sweat slides down my neck. My cheeks flush, my face burns. London doesn't cope with heatwaves. We should all just leave.

'The sink is over there in the corner.'

He turns his back again.

'Oh. Is that it? Did I get the job?'

He doesn't reply.

Ed: 0. Alvie: 1. This is happening!

'*Slàinte!*' I say. That means 'cheers'. It's a popular Irish phrase.

The sink is on the far side of the room. It's piled high with pots. I pull on some gloves and run the tap. Shit, that water's *hot*. I scrub at the stains at the bottom of a pan, but they won't go away. I scrub and scrub and scrub and scrub. My mind begins to stray. I remember the last time I did this I was scrubbing *blood* . . .

It was midnight in Taormina. My knuckles were red-raw. I had a bucket filled with water and a sponge. I was trying to remove every trace of my brother-in-law from the amphitheatre stage. I'd had to smash in his brains, you see, with a large rock. (He'd discovered that I was *not* my twin while we were having sex . . .)

I pour in some more detergent. Let the cold tap run. Scrubbing blood was more fun than this, and blood is a bitch to get out.

I watch the clock. The hands don't move. OK, so they're moving *slowly*. I could be here for weeks. Or months. Who knows when Ed's going to show? Soapy suds rise up. I sigh. I sink into a depression.

'All right?' comes a voice. It's one of the cooks. 'How is your first day going?'

I don't bother looking up.

He laughs. 'Aww. You'll get used to it.'

I scowl. Rinse out a ramekin.

'Oh yeah? No, I don't think so.'

I look up for the first time and study the cook.

Hello. Ooh, look it's Henry Golding. (It's not, he just looks like him.) The cook is tall and slim and Asian. He has a dreamboat smile. He's wearing black-and-white checked trousers and a hair-net covers his head, but somehow he pulls it off, like this is the latest style.

'*Ciao*, I'm Siobhán. Nice to meet you,' I say in my sexiest Irish accent.

'Hey, I'm Jack. Cheer up,' he says. 'This is a nice place. I've worked here for three years.'

I watch as he tastes some nigiri.

'But you're not doing *this*.'

I grab a ceramic dish and scoop out gratin dauphinois. The creamy goo plops in the bin. I shove the dish in the sink.

'At least you're doing it *here*,' he says. 'This is the best place in town. We get a lot of celebs.'

'Like who?' I say. 'Channing Tatum?'

'Channing who?' he says.

'Doesn't matter. Do you get Ed Forbes?'

Jack stops cooking. His face lights up.

'He comes to eat here sometimes, yeah. He might be here tonight.'

I smile. I move in closer to Jack. 'Oh yeah?'

He doesn't reply.

I must be doing a scary face, because Jack looks back, afraid. He looks down and starts to slice up a fish. He slips and cuts his thumb.

'Ah, no,' he says. 'That hurt.'

Bless his cotton socks.

He shoves his finger in his mouth and sucks it.

'Get a plaster on that,' says Chef, materializing from nowhere.

'Yes, Chef,' says Jack, still sucking.

'Fucking muppet,' says Chef.

I can taste that blood from here. I lick my lips. *I miss it.* What am I doing here stuck in the kitchen? Why am I *washing dishes*? I roll my eyes and pull off my gloves and pick up Jack's knife from the board . . .

I finish slicing the tuna into beautiful even chunks. When Jack gets back with a thick blue plaster wrapped round his finger, the fish is cut into perfect slices. Even *I'm* impressed. The flesh is gorgeous ruby red with a shiny, glossy finish. All it needs is a dash of soy sauce and a soup-çon of wasabi.

Jack gawks. 'Did *you* do that?'

'No, Jack, it was a *goblin*.' I still have his knife in my hand. He blinks at me, astonished.

'Where did you learn to cut like that? How did you do it so quickly?'

'I used to work in the kitchen of a Japanese restaurant.'

Jack just stands there, staring at me.

'What's going on?' says Chef. 'What is pot wash doing?'

'Er, nothing,' says Jack. He lowers his voice. We make eye contact. 'Fuck me, that was *awesome*.'

I reach into the ice and grab another hunk of fish. I lay it out on the chopping block and slice that up as well. The knife moves up and down, up and down, like I'm Edward Scissorhands. The blade makes a pleasant drumming sound against the chopping block; it reminds me of Tiff and the shaman drumming in the Amazon. Thud, thud, thud, thud, thud, thud, thud.

'Wow,' says Jack under his breath. (I think I'm turning him on . . .) 'You are *really* good at that.'

'Yes,' I say, holding his gaze. 'Yes. Yes, I am.' I keep on chopping and let the knife do the talking.

Chef appears standing next to me. 'Pot wash.'

'My name is Siobhán.'

'I don't give a *fuck*,' he says. He thinks he's Gordon Ramsay. 'Why the fuck aren't you scrubbing pans?'

'I *was* scrubbing pans, but then this muppet decided to chop up his finger instead of chopping up the fish. I don't want to hold up the service.'

'Bullshit,' he says. 'You were showing off.'

I shrug. I suppose I *was* showing off. 'If you've got it, flaunt it.'

'Jack?' says Chef.

'Yes, Chef,' says Jack.

'You are our new pot wash. Pot wash?'

'Chef?' I say. 'It's *Siobhán*.'

'You're our sushi chef. Now, get on with it.'

Chef leaves and Jack gawks. 'What the hell just happened?'

I pick up the Marigolds and throw them at his face. 'I just got promoted and you got my job. Sorry not sorry, mate.'

I smile and stab another fish. Perhaps I'll like it here?

I remember my first job, the one that proved so useful today . . . I left home when I was sixteen and ran away to London. I couldn't stand another day with my family in The Slaughters. Beth and mum were driving me *mad*. It was mostly Beth, though: always being *nice* all the time and *good* at everything. I slept rough for a couple of nights until I found a hostel. Then I got the job chopping up fish. I was a natural. The head chef was an ancient man called Mr Tomohiko. He had a wispy long white beard and glinting grey eyes. He was easily eighty years old. Probably closer to ninety. He had a calm smile, a twinkle in his eye, the patience of a Zen master. He was the one who gave me the knife. (He didn't know how much I'd like it.)

The place was on a backstreet in Soho downstairs from a brothel. Everybody else who worked there was Japanese. The dining room was tiny but pretty, with bamboo shoots and ebony screens. Delicious smells wafted from the sizzling robata grill. I watched the charcoals glowing white, yellow, orange, red . . .

I remember it like it was yesterday, I walked through that door and it felt like home. It was a sanctuary from the outside world. I couldn't understand a word that anyone was saying, but that didn't matter. I didn't care. I actually kind of liked it. No one there made me feel stupid. Nobody mocked or criticized me. No one there knew I was a twin. It was like being my own person.

The first time that I entered the kitchen, Tomohiko produced a chunk of raw fish. The tuna was skinned and filleted, a gorgeous rosy red. He handled it tenderly as though it were his newborn son and asked me to demonstrate my skill by chopping the fish into slices. He reached into a wooden box and handed me a brand-new knife. I felt a tingle down my spine as I reached out to take it. I grasped the sashimi knife; the steel glowed like polished silver. It had a single bevelled edge, sharpened to a point at one side – I ran my thumb along the blade – the other side was flat. He said it was a *Yanagi ba*. *Yanagi ba* means 'willow-shaped'. The knife was set at a special angle for use by a left-handed chef. The blade was very, very thin, so it wouldn't tear or bruise the fish. It could cut a block of flesh in two with a single stroke.

Tomohiko spent hours teaching me how to cut fish, how to make smooth, glossy surfaces that were shiny and even. I knew how to cut the perfect texture that would maximize the flavour. 10mm for sashimi. 6mm for sushi. I learnt the art of slicing from him. I was bloody good. That was many years ago now, but I'll never forget it. I loved that knife like I'd never loved anyone or anything in my life. Until Nino, that is. Yes, knife skills have served me well. They have come in useful. And something tells me they will come in handy in the future . . .

Friday, 5 August, 12.02 a.m.
The Savoy, London

The clock on the wall reads two past midnight. I just worked *two minutes* for free. I can't believe I stayed so late when *Ed Forbes* might be here. What if I've missed him? What if he ate and left and *muggins* here was slicing salmon all night long? I'll be so pissed off. I chuck the knife into the sink and wipe my hands on my apron. Urgh, I feel like Cinderella and I smell of *fish*.

'See you later, Siobhán,' calls Jack.

'Bye, Jack. See you later,' I say.

'Will you be in tomorrow?'

'Oh yeah, for sure,' I reply.

He winks at me and I wink back. (If he's annoyed he doesn't show it.) Some low-level flirtation never did anyone any harm and he is all kinds of tasty. I grab my Birkin bag and push out of the steamy kitchen. I'd love to stay and flirt, but I've got bigger fish to fry.

I'm knackered from my *twelve-hour* shift (twelve hours and two minutes, but who's counting?), but nervous excitement spreads through my body and my skin is tingling.

The restaurant is empty now. I knew it. I'm too late. As if I'd find him on *my first night*. No way. No one's *that* lucky. But I head out to find the bar. I'll check in there, just in case . . .

I stride down the corridor to the sound of laughter and

voices. The American Bar is heaving. Packed. I look around for Ed. I scan the bar. It's nice in here. A 1930s feel. Black-and-white photos on the walls of Elizabeth Taylor and David Bowie. Someone's playing something jazzy at a grand piano. I perch on a leather stool at the bar and admire the drinks display – shiny bottles sparkle like diamonds and stretch to infinity. I've never seen so many different types of gin or vodka or brandy. No wonder Hemingway liked it here; apparently he was a regular. Marilyn Monroe came too. (I've heard it all from that chef . . .) I think of the sobriety coin tucked inside my wallet. I've been sober since AA. I am counting the seconds.

A bartender in a smart white suit strains a cocktail into a glass. I breathe in deep: that's rum and lime. I'm getting drunk on the fumes. A golden bottle of Southern Comfort seems to call my name:

> *'Alvie! Alvie, come*
> *On. Drink me. I want to be*
> *inside you.' SHUT UP.*

'Yes, madam,' the barman says. 'What can I do you for?'

I grab the cocktail list: *Manhattan*, *White Lady*, *a Corpse Reviver.* I study the virgin drinks, but they all sound boring. They are basically just *juice.* I'd kill for a margarita. I guess if I'm going to do this thing, I've got to do it *sober.* It's too important to mess up. I mutter to myself.

'Are you all right, madam?' asks the barman.

Oh God, I was probably drooling. 'I'll just have a tap water, but in a martini glass.'

'This way, Mr Forbes,' comes a man's deep voice.

I nearly fall off my stool.

A high-pitched woman's voice squeals, 'Eddddddd.'

I can't believe my luck. But I'm not ready. I need more time to work on my Basecamp plan. It's *very* basic at the moment. It needs fleshing out.

I watch as a butler ushers a crowd towards the exclusive royal circle, a private area with a table and gleaming mirrored columns.

By the pricking of my thumbs, something wicked this way comes.

I knock back my tap water and slither off my bar stool. I creep over to the group and make like a spy, like George Smiley. Ed Forbes and another man are surrounded by a harem of the most stunning women that I have ever seen. I stop dead in my tracks and stare. I can't believe I've found him. It's him. It's *definitely* him. I recognize his watch. It's gold: a Patek Nautilus. I saw it on Insta this morning. I gawk at the girls as they enter the bar. None of those girls look like Tiffany, the Brigitte Bardot body double with the killer smile. My eyes trail their barre-toned-bodies. They all look like finalists on *America's Next Top Model*. They're hookers, of course, but they look expensive. I, on the other hand, look like a hobo and smell of pickled eels. I can't meet *Ed Forbes* like *this*. What am I going to do?

One of the girls breaks away from Ed's table. I trail her into the ladies', stand at the sink and run the tap. Perhaps if I can scrub up quick, then she can introduce me? I splash some water into my kisser and untie my hair. I check my reflection in the mirror. Not Tyra Banks, but better. I'm wearing a plain white shirt and boring black work trousers (they gave me a work uniform when I showed up in jogging bottoms). I shove my neon orange sweater into my Birkin bag. One of the cubicle doors swings open to reveal the six-foot glamour model. I gawp. Up close like this, she's really pretty. Intimidatingly so. I take a deep breath. *You can do this, Alvie. Always doubting your potential. Imposter syndrome can fuck off. You are an accomplished killer. You put the* bad *into badass.*

'*Ciao*,' I say in my best Irish accent.

'How are you doing, honey?'

That's a drop-dead gorgeous voice. She sounds like she's from Birmingham but her husky dulcet tones make her accent sexy.

She washes her hands and I stand here, staring. She smells of Chanel. I move in a bit closer and sniff. That is Coco Mademoiselle: patchouli and tonka bean. She peers into the bathroom mirror and applies a slick of scarlet lipstick. I admire her bandeau outfit: skintight Hervé Leger. Her long black hair reaches down to her ass. She's wearing six-inch Louboutins with peephole toes and studs on.

'Wow, I like your shoes,' I say. 'No, I don't like them. I *love* them.'

'Thank you. The boys like heels,' she says, laughing.

'Well, they look *great* on you. You have the feet of a Victoria's Secret model.'

She smiles. She likes the compliment. She leans against the sink.

'To be honest, they're *killing* me. I wish I had some flats.'

I glance down at my Prada pumps.

'You can borrow these, if you like? We look about the same size.'

I try my least scary smile.

'Really? You don't mind?'

'Honestly,' I say, 'not at all. I know what it's like when you've had a long night and I'd love to take *those* for a ride.'

She laughs. 'We can't.'

'Of course we can. We'll swap back at the end of the night.'

Ha ha. Yeah, right. They're mine. All mine.

We remove our shoes.

I strap on her killer heels and she pulls on my pumps. I strut around the bathroom, beaming.

I am invincible.

'My name is Venus, by the way.' She giggles as we shake hands.

'Like the goddess of love?' I say. 'My name is A-A-A-Amazon.'

Nice save, Alvie. That was close. *Amazon?* I like it. It somehow feels appropriate. I'm a girl going into battle.

'Could I borrow some of your lipstick?' I ask. 'I feel a bit bleurgh.'

She hands me the red and I have a go.

False face must hide what the false heart doth know.

We head out into the bar and stop by the grand piano. The pianist's playing ragtime jazz; it's all very *La La Land*.

'Who are you here with?' I ask.

'My girls and a couple of guys. Who are *you* here with?' she asks.

'No one. I just finished work.'

'You're not here all by yourself?'

'I am.' I make a sad face.

Venus touches me on my arm. I look down at where her hand is. 'Join us for a drink?'

'Oh no. I couldn't possibly.'

Wow, that's great acting, Alvie. You're the next Meryl Streep.

'You *must* join us. We have magnums of Cristal. Come on, it'll be fun.'

I do a fist pump in my head. This is going *well*.

She grabs my hand and pulls me along. I follow willingly. Her skin is as soft as Italian leather. I bet she uses posh hand cream. I find my phone inside my Birkin. I want to take some pics. I don't know why, but I get the feeling photos could come in useful. If Ed is being a naughty boy, some snaps could be handy. I need all the dirt I can get if I'm going to take this asshole down. I take some sneaky photos as we enter the private room.

'Forgot to say, *no phones*,' says Venus. I put my phone away. 'I have to use this shit old Nokia when I'm on a job. Camera phones are trouble,' she says. 'They make clients nervous.'

Ed is sitting at the table with some Saudi prince and four other glamazons. The girls all look like they're under twenty. Ed looks like their hot dad.

'Eddddd,' squeals Venus. 'I made a new friend.'

'Oh. Well done,' he says.

Ed moves up along the bench so Venus and I can sit down.

I sit down right next to Ed. I get a 'watch out' vibe. I tense. I don't speak. My heart is pounding. This is the man who screwed Nino's dad so badly he *killed himself*. Ed looks like he can take care of himself. I shouldn't mess with him. No one gets that fucking rich without being a

40

badass. I start to sweat. I study Ed. I can't take my eyes off him. He's more handsome in the flesh. When does *that* ever happen? I've never been this close to a billionaire and it's all I can do not to lick him.

'*Ciao*, I'm Amazon,' I say, offering my hand.

He shakes it. 'Ed. Your name is *what*?'

'Amazon,' I repeat.

I'm surprised he double-takes. Don't tell me '*Venus*' is legit. I give myself a mental shake – *get your act together.* My eyes move down from Ed's tanned face to the platinum chain at his neck.

I feign a sip of the champagne that he's just poured for me. It smells of elderflowers and honey. I bet it tastes delicious.

'Thank you, *Ed*,' I say.

Don't get drunk. Don't blow it, Alvie. Just pretend to drink.

'Amazon like the online retailer? That's an unusual name. Jeff Bezos is a friend of mine . . .'

Here we go with the name-dropping.

'No, like the female warriors.' Ed looks blank, so I carry on. 'You know, the daughters of Ares and Harmonia? They live on Themyscira? Haven't you seen *Wonder Woman*? Gal Gadot?'

Watch out, Ed. I know my shit. I'm not just a pretty face. What you've got here are brains *and* beauty. That's one lethal mix.

Ed picks up his glass and we clink. 'It's a pleasure to meet you, Amazon.'

I study his glacier eyes. They're as cool as Daniel Craig's. I'm getting a James Bond vibe. Ha. Look on your nemesis. But all of the Bond villains are *men*, which is weird if you think about it. I bet Bond's pissed off *lots* of girls. He can't keep his snake in its cage.

I can't tear my eyes away. Ed notices me staring. We hold eye contact for too long. He's hot, but I'm not sure I *fancy* him. Perhaps if I wasn't going to *kill him*, I'd be interested? But there is something *electric* about him. Plus he smells really nice.

'Amazon let me borrow her shoes. Isn't she cute?' Venus says.

'Did she really? Yes, she's cute.' Ed looks at my shoes.

I stick out my foot and wiggle my toes. His eyes light up. They linger. That's a foot fetish, if ever I saw one. I've found his Achilles heel.

'This is Cherry, Lola, Angel and Brandy,' Venus says, interrupting us to introduce the other girls. 'And this is Prince Abdul from Jeddah.'

'How do you do?' says the prince but whatever.

I move up along the bench, a little bit closer to Ed.

2.55 a.m.

'And that's why currency hedging is crucial to safeguard my risk-adjusted portfolio returns,' says Ed. 'But, of course, that's obvious.'

Oh my God, what time is it? I sold Beth's Omega watch last time I was low on funds, so I have no idea. I pick up Ed's left hand and study his Patek Phillipe. Wow. It's nearly 3 a.m. Time flies when you're having fun.

'Mr Forbes, would you care for another?' the waiter asks, pointing to the Cristal.

'No thanks,' says Ed. 'Just the bill.'

The prince stands up and says, 'Bedtime.'

I follow the crowd back through the bar. I can barely walk in these shoes. We stagger down the corridor and pile into a lift. I slip in just as the doors are closing and lean against the mirror. I catch Ed's eye and he holds my gaze for a split-second too long. All the blood rushes to my face. What is going on? I suddenly feel light-headed and it wasn't the alcohol.

The lift pings at the top floor and we spill on to the landing. Ed leads the way with the Saudi prince. I try to think. Be *strategic*. What am I going to do now I've got him? I'm not thinking straight.

I keep towards the back of the group. Wasn't I supposed to be *filming*? All this with the girls is incriminating. Ed's a married man. I glance at Venus, but she's not looking. I grab my phone and click, hiding the thing in my Birkin with the lens peering over the top like a makeshift periscope. I feel like a paparazzo.

The girls fall through the door to the suite and I get a close-up of Ed. I'm about to zoom in on his crotch when Ed turns to me and says, 'Come on, eBay.'

I shove my phone back in my bag and step through the threshold to the suite. Ed's eyes are on the back of my neck. I can feel them burning.

The first thing I notice is the view. Windows all along the wall frame London's sparkling skyline. At this time of night the Thames looks black, but reflections of the city lights all twinkle like stars on the water. The London Eye is lit up in pink. Headlights shine on Waterloo Bridge. I take a breath; it's beyond exquisite. I am literally speechless.

London's pretty when
You're rich and the city lights
Up like diamonds.

Then I take in the spacious suite. It is fucking *massive*: *two* bedrooms, *two* bathrooms, a living room and a dining room. Lamplight casts a golden glow. Luxurious golden curtains flow. The furniture is all antique. The wallpaper shimmers like gold dust.

'Are you OK?' asks Ed with a warm hand on my shoulder.

'Yup. Uh-huh.' I think I was staring. 'Nice crib. Really bling.'

'They really are *lovely* shoes,' says Ed and my heartbeat quickens.

Oh God, I wish I had a plan. I mean, a *better* one. I'm supposed to kill *Tiff* before I shag *Ed*. He's my victim, not my lover. I'm getting confused with all the adrenaline coursing through my veins and now Ed's staring at my feet like they are Helen of Troy. Anyway, I can't do it *here*. Not with all these people around. Argh. I need to buy some time . . . I need to get my head straight.

The girls are pulling off their clothes and piling on to the four-poster bed. It's like the Playboy Mansion in here. Ed helps himself to a drink.

'Want one?' he asks.

I decline.

He stands by the bar and sips the dark gold liquid. If he's wasted, I can't tell. I plop down on a red chaise longue. One of the girls – is that Angel? – pulls the prince's trousers off. I hug my Birkin on my lap and slyly begin filming.

Ed turns to me and I smile a tight smile. I hide my phone in my bag. Have I got enough footage? Then I notice my finger – *it's bare*.

My heart stops beating. I don't breathe. My engagement ring is *gone*. It's the ring that Nino gave me. What have I done with it? It can't be missing. It can't be. I get down on my hands and knees and check the thick pile carpet.

'No, no, no, no.'

That was the last trace of Nino.

My stomach sinks. I'm trembling. My world is crashing down. I start to hyperventilate. Oh God. I've got to get out of here. I need to find that ring. I can't – I can't live without it. Ed Forbes is going to have to wait. It's a life-or-death situation. I glance at the writhing mass of bodies on the double bed and stand up slowly, silently. Ed's gone – to take a whizz?

I tiptoe back across the room and sneak out of the suite. I definitely had the ring this morning before I started my shift. If I retrace my steps, I might find it. I'll check every inch.

I step out into the corridor, my whole body shaking. I know the ring is *worthless*. It is from a *hand grenade,* but it has sentimental value. It is irreplaceable. I see his face in my mind's eye. '*Alvie, will you marry me?*' I refuse to cry.

I crawl down the corridor on my hands and knees, searching every millimetre of carpet. It isn't in here, is it? The lift pings and I crawl in. The ring is on the floor in the middle of the lift. I grab it and slide it on. The doors swish shut.

Oh God. Thank God.

I lean against the wall, clutching my hands over my chest where I think my heart is. (My heart is on the *right*, not the *left*. I have *dextrocardia*: a mirror image of my twin.

She was right. I'm wrong.) I take a deep breath then haul myself up and open the lift doors again.

I sprint back down the corridor towards Ed's suite. I try the handle. It's locked. Of course. I knock. I bang. I shout, 'Ed? ED?'

But there's no answer.

Have they all fallen asleep? Or they're all at it so damn hard that they can't hear me yelling. I press my ear against the wood, but can't hear anything. I knock once more, but it's useless. I'm on my own. Again.

I ride the lift back down to the lobby and find the girl at reception.

'Good evening, madam,' she says with a smile.

'I got locked out,' I say. 'Can you ring Mr Forbes' suite so they can let me in?'

'Of course,' she says, picking up the phone. 'Who shall I say is calling?'

'Amazon,' I say. She frowns. 'I know . . . My parents were *hippies*.'

She winks at me. 'I get it,' she says. 'Check out my name badge.'

Sunshine.

'I wish *my* name was Sunshine,' I say. 'That would really suit me . . . because of my sunny disposition.'

'Sorry, there's no answer,' she says.

'Try again,' I say. 'What am I supposed to do? Sleep in the fucking *lobby*?'

Sunshine gives me an icy look. 'I'll try one more time,' she says. 'But Mr Forbes might be sleeping and I don't want to bother him . . .'

'*Jesus. Just call him,*' I hiss.

I watch as Sunshine punches the buttons on the telephone.

'He'd better answer this time.'

She wrinkles her nose.

I glare as she listens to the dial tone. Eventually, she hangs up.

She shrugs. 'I am really sorry.'

'No shit, Sunshine,' I say. 'You've been *really* helpful.'

I turn on my heel and skulk over to a lounge area. I knew it was going too well. Ace. Now what? I sit in the lounge and hide behind a copy of the *Financial Times*. The pink papers cover my face. I'll just rest my eyes. I slump down in the armchair. They got through *four* magnums of Cristal. Ed was *wasted*. He'll forget about me. He'll be balls-deep in Venus by now or one of those other girls. But what if that was my only shot to waste him and now it's too late?

Nino's face appears in my mind. I squeeze my eyes tight shut.

'I'm sorry, my dark prince . . .'

I hear a voice reply.

'Sorry, pet, but you can't sleep here.'

I awake with a jolt.

I look up and see that doorman standing in my personal space.

'Urgh. I got locked out,' I hiss.

'Move along then, please.'

I haul myself up and stagger through the revolving doors. The streets are wet and empty now. I'm *knackered*, too tired to walk anywhere in these stupid shoes. I wander down the Strand. I'll just wait right here until morning. Ed will have to come out.

I cross the road. A bus beeps and swerves when it sees me coming. I glare at the driver and flip him the bird.

'Learn to drive, asshole.'

I sit on the street opposite the Savoy. It's raining cats and dogs; it's one of those tropical monsoons you get when it's really hot. I shelter inside the doorway of a high-end jewellery store. I'm probably in some tramp's favourite spot and he'll try to fight me for it. I peer in through the window, but there's nothing there to see. All the jewels and the diamonds have gone, stored in a safe overnight. All that's left is the velvet display case and the tiny price tags. The air is priced at thirty thousand pounds plus VAT.

I hug my knees into my chest and wrap my arms round myself. I shiver. I yawn. *I'm all on me tod.* It's just me and my leprechaun.

I find my phone and click into the pictures in the gallery. I scroll through the footage again and again. That is clearly Ed's face. I have undeniable evidence that billionaire art mogul Ed Forbes went into a hotel room with no less than *five* hookers. I'm willing to bet that *Tiffany* would find this interesting. Yes, if wifey sees these snaps, then there'll be trouble in paradise . . .

Saturday, 6 August, 9 a.m.
The Strand, London

I wake to the sound of a key clinking in the jewellery shop's lock. A woman has tiptoed over my body so as not to disturb me. Damn, I shouldn't have fallen asleep. I'm supposed to be keeping watch. I am Adam Carter in *Spooks*. Ethan Hunt in *Mission Impossible*. What time is it? I check my phone: 8.50 a.m. Hopefully Ed is still asleep. Oh man, what if I've missed him? I stand up and stretch it out. My joints *crack*. I am aching. Those paving slabs were worse than my bunk bed and *not* conducive to sleeping.

I cross the street – looking out for that doorman, but I can't see him yet – then push through the Savoy's old-fashioned spinning doors. I glance through the glass inside the brass panel and spot Ed Forbes coming out just as I'm going in. Wow. What are the chances? I keep on pushing the door round. Ed climbs into a taxi.

Then the doorman reappears. It's the one with the attitude.

'*You* again?' he asks.

'Yes *me*. I work here, damn it. Give me a break.'

(My shift starts in three hours. I'm going to miss it, aren't I?)

I fall out of the revolving door and run towards a taxi. It seems to be driving the wrong way round the Savoy's roundabout.

'Follow that car,' I say to the cabbie, jumping into the back seat. 'Follow that car. Don't lose it,' I say. I've always wanted to say that.

'Of course, madam. No problem at all. Would you like a Polo mint?'

The cabbie passes the sweets to me.

I eat the rest of the packet.

Ed's cab finally slows to a stop on the Bishops Avenue. I watch Ed pay and get out of the car.

'Keep going. Take the next left.'

The cabbie passes and takes the next turning.

'OK. Now stop. This is good.'

'That will be nineteen pounds and ninety pence,' the driver says.

How much?

I give him a twenty. It's my last twenty.

I wait for my change.

I'm still waiting.

Still waiting.

'Hey, dickhead, where is my ten p?'

He gives me a coin. I climb out of the cab and slam the door shut behind me. I head back round the corner then stand and gawk at Ed's mansion. Oh. My. God. Seriously? Now I know how Lizzie felt when she first saw Pemberley. The colossal house is visible behind black gates and topiary. There's a driveway with a marble fountain and room for twenty cars. The place is *huge*; I'd guess twelve bedrooms. Maybe even more. Along the facade, towering columns support a pale grey tiled roof. The plot itself is easily the size of Selfridge's.

There's an oak tree in the garden opposite Ed's fuckoff house. There's a wall I'll have to scale, but it's a good place to keep watch. I check the street, but no one's looking. I try to jump on to the wall, but it's tough in Venus's six-inch heels, so I kick them off. I shove them in my Birkin then climb the wall and tree. I straddle a branch and look over the road, with the grace of a gold-medal gymnast. I study the house with its battlements. Ed's place is like Fort Knox. Razor wire stretches out all along the fences. Security cameras are fixed to the posts at the side of the wrought-iron gates. A large sign says 'BEWARE OF THE DOG', with a picture of a pit bull. His teeth look big and sharp and pointy. I wish I had my old dachshund. I can't see a way inside without an invitation. It might be slightly easier at night. I could launch a stealth attack . . . but still, I bet those are night-vision cameras. It isn't worth the risk.

A BMW approaches and pulls on to the drive by my tree. I shrink into the foliage and hide as a woman steps out. I keep very still so I'm invisible, hold my breath and close my mouth. I wish I was wearing a khaki top, not this neon sweater. (Orange is too conspicuous for undercover surveillance.) The woman walks across the lawn towards me and I freeze.

'Hey, you,' she says. 'Get out of my tree.'

Perhaps she's not talking to me? My whole body's tense. I don't move a muscle. I glance round the shrubbery. Perhaps there's somebody else here? Perhaps she hasn't seen me?

'Did you hear what I said?' she yells.

I sigh and climb back down the tree. My Birkin catches on a twig. I crash on to the lawn.

'I thought I saw a cat,' I say.

She doesn't look convinced. 'Do I need to call the police?'

'Oh no, don't do *that*.'

I strap my shoes back on again and stomp off down

the road. I need somewhere else to hide. *Where? Where? Where?* I look around for a bus stop or phone box, but the people who live here don't take the bus and all the old red boxes are gone, converted into coffee shops like that micro-café in the village. How to be invisible? How to be surreptitious? I need to keep an eye on that house. I need to befriend Tiff or Ed.

There's an abandoned Boris bike leaning against a wall. It's black with red Santander ads on the frame and the wheel. I jog over and grab it. This thing looks like a death-trap, but I'm a pro. I hop on and ride. I haven't ridden a bike for *years*, but you know what they say: it really is like riding a bike. I only hope that the same thing applies to *murder*. It's been a while and I am rustier than this bike. I'm in need of some lubrication.

I cycle up and down the road. Pretend I'm going somewhere. After what feels like forever but is actually ten minutes, my knees are stiff and my bum has gone numb and the gates to the house sweep wide open. A sleek black Bentley pulls out. Is that Ed? I can't tell. All the Bentley's windows are tinted, so I can't see inside. The car turns right and then speeds down the road. I'm going to follow it.

I swerve off the kerb and down the street, Jason Bourne style. I spot the Bentley up ahead, approaching the Spaniards Inn. The road narrows to just one lane and the Bentley has to wait to pass through. It gives me the time I need to catch up. I pedal as fast as I can.

I reach the Bentley and slam on the brakes. I don't want Ed to see me. I let my hair cover my face and I'm camou-flaged by my mirror shades. I'm getting used to cycling in heels, even these six-inch ones. I bet Jason couldn't do *that*. He always has sensible shoes. I look up and the car has *gone*. I double my speed and cycle along Hampstead Lane. I spot the car up ahead. It makes a turn by Jack Straw's Castle. That's one steep-ass hill. I stand and push down on the pedals. *Come on, faster, faster.*

We head through Hampstead into Frognal, down to London town. Hot blood pumps around me like a steam train. I'm sweating like a paedo. My fingers grip the handlebars. My thighs are agony, but my eyes are glued to the Bentley's plates. I'm not going to lose him again.

1 p.m.
Christie's, St James's, London

The Bentley stops outside Christie's on King Street. I slam on the brakes. The tyres on the Boris bike screech and a Prius behind me beeps. I lean on the handles, sweating, panting. I must look a *state*, but at least I didn't lose the car. I never thought that I'd be grateful for London traffic.

I study Christie's auction house. It's an imposing building with a billowing red flag. Wrought-iron railings line the walls. Its large windows sparkle like silver. I imagine the riches that pass through its doors and the treasures locked in its vaults. I wonder how much priceless art is stored beyond those walls. Do they have any Caravaggios? I bet they do. They'll have *loads*.

I watch as a driver steps out of the Bentley and opens the passenger door. How will I explain if Ed spots me? This looks odd. It looks dodgy. Hopefully he was wasted last night and won't remember Amazon . . .

But it's not Ed that gets out of the car. It is *Tiffany*. I gasp. *Christ on a bike*. It's *her*. I am beyond star-struck. It's her. It's really, really her. It's all I can do not to shout, 'TIFF! TIFF! IT'S ME! ALVIE!' I bite my bottom lip.

> *Glorious goddess!*
> *Heavenly creature! You shine*
> *Too bright for this world.*

Seeing her for real like this, she seems so alive, so full of life. Like I say, it's a shame to kill her . . . but it's fate. It's written. I watch to see if Ed will get out too, but the driver shuts the door and then drives off along the road. It's just me and Tiff.

Tiff is wearing tight black slacks in what must be faux leather. She'd never wear an *animal*. #FURISMURDER. I spot the pouch the shaman gave her draped over her arm. (It's OK to wear a *fox,* but only if it's been upcycled by a medicine man.) Her T-shirt skims her perfect figure. I check out the slogan. It's Dior: *We should all be feminists*. She's political *and* spiritual. She sports a Caribbean tan; her skin is the colour of *Baywatch*. I recognize her knee-high boots. She modelled them on her vlog. They're made from recycled plastic bottles. I would *kill* for those shoes. I watch as she crosses the road, her head held high, her pace brisk. She skips the queue lining up outside. The doorman lets her in. If Tiffany is going *there*, then that's where I must go.

I chuck the bike against a bin then jog across the road.

Hundreds of people are queuing up. There's a long, long line. Christie's must be hosting some kind of exclusive art event. A red carpet stretches as far as the eye can see, but life is way too short to queue; I should know, believe me. I take a deep breath and stand up tall, ignore the knot in my stomach and stride towards the double doors. It is *showtime*, baby.

The doorman is dressed in a charcoal suit with red lapels and tie. Neat cap. White gloves. Shiny black brogues. 'CHRISTIE'S' on the doormat.

'What's the craic?' I say, as I whip off my mirror shades and flash him a smile.

'Good afternoon, madam,' he says, glancing at the guy at the front of the queue. 'And you are . . . ?'

'Siobhán Faelan. I'm a guest of Tiffany Forbes.'

He hesitates, so I scale the steps as fast as I can. *Nice work.* I skip inside and scan the room. There's no way I'm *queuing.* The scent of centuries of art. The taste of family money. The room is vast and bright and spacious with towering columns and white walls. A widescreen TV shows pictures of sculptures. Classical music plays. I think that's Mozart, *The Marriage of Figaro.* It's all very civilized.

A young woman stands at the front desk. She checks her PC.

'Welcome to Christie's, madam,' she says. 'Your name please?'

'Siobhán Faelan,' I announce. 'I'm here for the art thing today. Did you see where Tiffany went? Oh yeah, there she is.'

'Are you here to bid?' asks the woman, frowning at my outfit.

I'm taking nonchalant déshabillé to a whole new level, like Woody Harrelson wearing pyjamas to a movie premier.

I nod. 'I am!'

'I'll need to see some ID to create your account.'

'Of course,' I say. I find Siobhán's passport in my bag. 'Hurry up,' I say. 'Chop-chop.' (I don't want her to see that it's fake.)

'And we need to take a photo, if you don't mind.'

I glare at the camera on the computer. It clicks. It's fine. It's an excellent fake. I reclaim the passport and leave the woman at the desk. Where is Tiffany? I catch a glimpse of myself in the mirror. *Look at the state o' you.* I just cycled the Tour de France and spent the whole night sleeping rough . . . time for a makeover, me thinks. I head for the cloakroom. *Urgh.*

There's a young man at the desk. He looks about *eleven:* acne, braces, a failed attempt to grow a downy beard.

'Hello,' he says.

'*Ciao,* darling,' I say. 'I am *ever so* sorry, but I just left my jacket in there . . . *that one. There it is.*' I point to a jacket hanging on the rail just behind him. 'Silly me, I've lost my ticket. Blonde moment.' I laugh.

He frowns at my hair. Oh yeah, I forgot I've dyed it *orange.*

'It is *strawberry* blonde,' I say. 'You *do* remember me, don't you, darling?' I give him my warmest smile. 'I just dropped that jacket off. Can I have it back? I'm cold.'

'I'm not supposed to . . .'

'It's *chilly* in here with all this air conditioning. I thought I wouldn't need it, but . . . could you just grab it for me?' I point at the jacket. He looks where I'm pointing. 'It's just that one, there.'

He reaches towards it slowly, but then he turns round again.

'I can't. Not without the ticket.'

'*Darling.*' I roll my eyes.

I lean in towards him and make eye contact over the desk. 'You do know who I am, don't you?'

'Er . . .' He looks away.

'This is *ridiculous*,' I shout, banging my fist on the desk. 'I *demand* to speak to your manager. I can't believe that *Christie's* treats its VIP clients like this. Really, what a fucking *disgrace.*'

A few of the people in the room stop talking and look our way.

'OK. I'm sorry. I'm sorry,' he says. 'My apologies. Please, take your coat,' he says. 'My mistake. Just . . . just keep your voice down.'

I snatch the jacket and pull it on. It's a Chanel tweed with logo buttons and silk lining. It probably cost ten grand.

'Ooh, that is *lovely*,' I say, stroking the arms of the jacket and doing a little twirl around. 'How do I look? You like?' I fasten the golden buttons. 'Do you think they're *real* gold?' I give him a wink and walk off. I look a million dollars.

I wander over to reception and spot a copy of *Harper's Bazaar* lying on a coffee table. I have an idea. I pick it up and flick through the pages. There must be a sample in here. Somewhere. Somewhere . . . Yes, here's one. I rip a sachet of Valentino's perfume from the page, open it up and rub it on my wrists, behind my ears, on my cheeks and under my chin. A little bit down my cleavage. It's bergamot and orange blossom. Now I smell like an Italian heiress, not like a post-coital tramp who's been scoffing Polos.

I tie my hair in a *chignon* then make a beeline for Tiffany. I've spotted her on the far side of the room and I am *ready to roll*. My mouth is dry, my neck is rigid. *Watch out, Alvie, don't scare her.* First impressions are priceless. This is my big moment.

Tiff is browsing a display case. A sign says 'Real Estate'. I pretend to be interested and sidle up to her. There are glossy brochures with photos of houses; they're modern and minimalist. There's a house that looks like a giant golf ball and one made entirely of glass. She flicks through pages with pictures of places that I would give my right arm for. I notice Tiff's the same height as I am and we are a similar build. Her eyes are more *blue* than *green*, but the difference is negligible.

I swallow. Hard. This is it. This is it. I feel like I'm meeting the Queen. I'll try not to call her *Ma'am*. I really hope I can say *words* . . .

'*Ciao*,' I say. 'I like your face.'

I can't think of anything else.

'Oh. Thank you,' she says, turning round and examining me.

'Is it by Dr Sebagh?' I ask.

'No,' she says. 'It's all my own.'

'Wow,' I say. 'Just really wow.'

'Wow *yourself*.' She laughs.

We keep eye contact for a second. I'm the first to look away.

'Go way outta that . . .'

'I'm sorry?'

'It's a popular Irish phrase.'

Tiffany's voice surprises me. It's sweet and clear, not

high-pitched. It's the same voice on her vlog, of course, but it seems different in real life. I stand and stare and grin. *Come on, Alvie: WORDS. Stop being an idiot.* Stop *acting the maggot.*

Tiffany eyes my vintage Birkin. 'I like your bag,' she says. 'I used to have one just like it . . .'

'We're bag twins!' I blurt.

'But I donated it to a raffle for Great Ormond Street Hospital.'

She gives me a lingering look up and down my body, then smiles and turns her back on me. That went well, I think. I'll try again in a little bit. She's not getting away that easily. I am nothing if not tenacious. I'm dogged. Resolute. I make Macbeth look under-ambitious and Lady Macbeth look nice.

I follow Tiff up a flight of stairs with curving banisters. I let my hand run over the smooth polished mahogany. I think killing will cheer me up. I've been stuck in a rut this past year. I miss murder. I miss arson too. I enjoy a bit of stealing. And if this is my last hurrah, I want to go out, guns blazing. I'll kill Tiff and Ed in a blaze of glory. It will be *magnificent.* This will be my opus magnum. Or is it magnum opus?

There are bouquets of flowers in beautiful vases and cabinets filled with golden clocks. I sigh. I miss my cuckoo clock. I had a great one in Rome. I wish I could steal one of those, but I'm not here for ornaments. No, I have a job to do. *A little focus, Alvie.*

Upstairs there are abstracts of faces. I trail Tiff into a room filled with arty types: well dressed, expensive shoes. There's a waiter with a tray filled with flutes of pink champagne. I take two and shadow Tiff down a dimly lit hall.

At the end of the corridor is what looks like a shrine. A security guard stands by a rope that stretches along the wall, but there only seems to be one picture hanging on display. The painting is illuminated, framed in black and gold. It's striking, an ancient portrait of Jesus. He has a pale face and calm eyes. Christ is in a dark red robe with a blue sash draped over one shoulder. I read the sign; it's by Da Messina. Tiff and I study the art.

'I like the way he's done the *nose*. I can never do noses. They're hard.'

I offer her a glass of fizz, then pretend to start on the other one.

'Oh, thank you,' she says. 'That's kind.'

She accepts the drink.

I pour mine into a pot plant. The sacrifices I make . . . It's not like me to refuse free booze. Nino had better appreciate it. I watch the fizz sink into the soil. Do pot plants drink champagne? Or have I just killed it? Oops.

I turn my attention to Tiff. I'm about to tell her that I love her vlog and that I'm also very spiritual, when I'm distracted by a couple talking loudly as they approach us. It's two young men in sharp grey suits. They look like finance types. Maybe they're professional investors. Perhaps they work for an art fund.

'I bought a six-hundred-year-old Ming dynasty vase made for the emperor for twelve million dollars. And to think it was used as an umbrella stand.'

Tiffany walks away.

I hang back so it isn't obvious. I don't want her to freak

60

out. She might complain that I'm stalking her and then I'd get thrown out.

I watch Tiff enter another room and disappear through the door. I wait twelve seconds then follow her. Those suits are still bragging.

I slip through the door and on to a balcony. Tiff sits down at the far end. My eyes trail round the auditorium. It's crowded and buzzing with energy. The room is packed with hundreds of people chatting excitedly. The men are carbon copies in suits. The women are all dressed in black with gleaming strings of pearls. They clutch this season's statement bags. I cradle my Birkin. There are people on phones with black curly wires, here to bid for their clients. Photographers stand with lights and cameras ready to film the action. Nervousness bubbles up inside me; this is my first auction.

An old man in a charcoal suit and a pink cravat stands on the stage behind a lectern. Behind him a screen shows the values of different currencies: yen, dollars, euros. He bangs his hammer and the room grows quiet. A screen flicks on; it shows the painting of Christ that we have just seen.

'Lot One today is the magnificent Antonello da Messina, *Christ Blessing*, ladies and gentlemen. Da Messina was truly the first of the moderns. A fine example of the union of Italian simplicity with Flemish ecstatic realism. We're starting the bidding at one hundred thousand pounds.'

Bloody hell.

A man on a phone opens the bidding on the far side of the room. He has dark glasses, a black suit and a receding

61

hairline. He raises his hand to make the bid. He looks like the baddie from *The Matrix*.

Moments later, Tiffany bids one hundred and five. Neither of them want to back down, and silence fills the crowded room as they bid against each other. People are filming on their phones. The cameras click and flash. This goes on for quite a while until Tiff says, 'Two hundred!'

'About to sell. Two hundred might take it,' says the auctioneer.

No one speaks. No one moves a muscle.

'Two hundred and ten!' I say.

Tiffany turns to look at me. We lock eyes. I smile.

'Two hundred and ten. Thank you . . . Siobhán!' says the auctioneer, reading my name on his laptop screen.

'Two hundred and fifty,' says Tiffany.

'Three hundred,' I say.

An excited murmur spreads through the room. The auctioneer raises an eyebrow.

'Three hundred thousand is bid,' he says. 'And we're still not done.'

Tiffany fans herself with a flyer. 'Four hundred,' she says.

'At four hundred thousand now,' he says.

'Five hundred,' I say.

'Give me six,' says the auctioneer. 'Do I have six hundred?'

Tiffany pauses. I start to panic. I don't actually want to *buy it*. I couldn't even if I wanted to. I'm down to my last fiver. The auctioneer sips a glass of iced water. I begin to freak out.

'I'll have to hurry you,' he says.

Tiffany nods.

That was *close*.

'With you, Tiffany,' he says. 'Do I have seven?'

'Seven hundred.' I raise my hand. I've always liked pushing boundaries.

'Thank you,' he says. 'We're with Siobhán.'

The room is deathly quiet. Shit. Have I gone too far?

'Not with you, Tiffany. With Siobhán,' he says. 'Seven hundred could take it.'

Tiff waves. Thank fuck for that.

'Eight hundred. With you, Tiffany,' says the auctioneer. 'Are we done? Fair warning.'

I clear my throat. 'Nine hundred thousand.' My palms are clammy with sweat. I can hear my heart beat like some kind of techno rave.

'Nine hundred thousand with you, Siobhán,' says the auctioneer.

Tiffany turns to me and stares. I shrug and mouth, '*It's nice.*'

Seriously? What the hell am I doing? If I win this thing, I'm screwed. But I want her to *notice* me . . . I need to get her attention somehow.

'One million pounds,' says Tiffany.

Oh my God, that's cool.

Noisy excitement spreads through the room. One of the journalists faints.

'One million pounds,' says the auctioneer. His chest puffs up with pride.

He turns to me. I shake my head. *Slightly above my price range.*

'At one million, ladies and gentlemen. You heard it. Thank you, Tiffany. It's yours. Selling to Tiffany Forbes for one million pounds.' He knocks his hammer into the block. The room erupts into cheers.

I am feeling slightly nauseous. I finger my leprechaun. Yes, that was a *lucky* break. I fan myself with a flyer.

Tiffany stands and walks towards me. I'm blocking her path to the door. I can't let her get away. Not yet. I stick out my hand.

'Congratulations on your purchase.' Tiff and I shake hands. 'I'm sorry,' I say, 'if I tripled the price.'

'Oh please, don't worry about it. Have I seen you here before?' Her eyes trail my body.

'No, it's my first time,' I say. 'I was bidding for someone else.'

'Oh, and who is that?' she asks.

'A client. It's confidential.'

She smiles then tries to walk past me, but I block her way.

'I don't buy art personally. I spend all my money on dogs.' She turns round to look at me. 'I *love* dogs,' I say. 'I don't have one, but I give all I earn to the Dogs Trust.'

'Really?'

I nod. There's no point in being subtle when I have *seconds* to reel her in. She beams at me. Oh good, it worked. 'And I'm a *big* fan of yours,' I say. 'I love *Breakfast with Tiffany*.'

'Aww, thanks,' she grins. 'What did you say your name was?'

'I didn't. It's . . . it's *Siobhán*.'

'Isn't that pronounced SHIV-AWN?'

I shake my head. 'It's SEE-OB-HAAN. I pronounce it the *English* way. I'm only *half* Irish,' I say.

'Ah. I see.'

I suddenly remember that I'm from Cork. I switch to my Irish accent. 'May the road rise up to meet you.'

'I'm sorry, what?' she says.

'It's a popular Irish phrase. Who did you say you were buying for?'

'I'm buying for myself,' she says. 'Well, really for my husband. He has a soft spot for Da Messinas. He started his collection with one.'

A tingle spreads along my spine. I step in a bit closer.

'Come on then,' I say with a grin. 'Let's go and get some fizz. This calls for a celebration. No hard feelings. The best woman won.' I open the door for her.

'Like I said, I'm a *massive* fan of *Breakfast with Tiffany*.'

We reach the bar and I grab another couple of flutes of champagne. I hand a glass to Tiff.

Tiffany blushes. 'You're too kind. It's just a hobby.'

'I'm also *very* spiritual.'

'Oh, you are?' she asks.

'Uh-huh. VERY. Like Russell Brand. I can even read *auras*.'

'Really? Wow. Can you read mine?'

'Mmm. It says "butterfly".'

She frowns. 'Isn't it supposed to be *colours*?'

'Yes, that's what I mean.' *Damn*. 'You aura is *butterfly* colours . . . in the *shape* of a butterfly.'

Tiffany looks confused. 'Oh, right.'

I panic. I carry on.

'This bit by your ear is a kind of purple with glittery bits, and down here, by your arm, it's luminous turquoise. And over here you've got red-and-white check, you know, like tablecloths. And this bit here is an orange disc in the shape of a barn owl's eye.'

I point at her boob.

'Amazing,' she says, giggling like a six-year-old.

Oh God, I wish I could have some booze, but right now I need to focus. The sooner she's *dead,* the sooner I can marry her hot rich husband, then it's vintage Veuve Clicquot for breakfast *every single day.*

'I'm so fucking spiritual that I actually live in a wigwam.'

'A *wigwam?*' she says. 'You mean you're *homeless?*'

'No, I live in a *wigwam.* In Archway. I used to live in a yurt.'

'A *yurt?*'

'But that burnt down. Before that I lived in a tree house in Jeremy Corbyn's allotment.'

'Oh wow. That sounds . . . nice.'

'It wasn't. It was *awful.*'

I pretend to sip my drink. Oh God, it smells *delicious.* I somehow manage to resist. I deserve some kind of medal.

'I'm so fucking spiritual that I have killed my ego. I dissolved it through meditation and now I'm a hologram.'

Tiffany widens her eyes. 'You don't *look* like a hologram.'

'I know. It's good, isn't it? You can touch me. Try my arm.'

Tiffany reaches across the bar and squeezes my wrist. 'There you are!'

'I'm a *three-dimensional* hologram projected from 2D light sheets at the edge of the universe. Clever, isn't it?'

'But you feel *warm*,' she says, laughing.

'I know. It's the light. It's hot. I may seem like a human being, but actually I'm not. I'm a hologram. You know, like Elon Musk?'

'I wish I were a hologram,' says Tiffany, joining in, 'but I have too much of an ego.'

'Egos are the *worst*,' I say, encouraging her to go on.

'I tried to kill it by meditating, but it doesn't work.'

I grip on to Tiffany's arm and look deep into her eyes. 'I could kill it for you?'

We both burst out into laughter. Some champagne shoots from Tiff's nose.

I reach for the canapés and choose something pink. It smells weird.

'Hey, you,' I shout at the waiter. 'What's this?'

He approaches and clears his throat. '*That* is a gluten-free blini with lobster mousse, dill air and scallop foam,' he says with a subtle nod of the head that I think was a tiny bow.

I shove it in my mouth and chew. 'Tastes like fish,' I say. 'Want one?'

Tiffany giggles and shakes her head. 'No. *I'm* so fucking spiritual that I don't eat *food*. Food is bad for the environment. I'd never hurt a plant, so I'm training my body to photosynthesize. I have never felt better.'

'Oh yeah? You eat mouthfuls of *light*?'

Tiffany downs her champagne. 'No! I'm just kidding!'

I grab another fistful of lobster. 'Have you bought anything else recently?' I ask with my mouth full.

The longer I can keep her talking, the more likely we are to be friends. (The more that people get to know me, the more they like me. I'm ace.) I'll wait a bit before I kill her. I want her to open up. I need to learn how to be *Tiff*, that way I can win Ed. I need to know her deepest secrets. Every. Last. Detail.

'Oh yes,' she says, her face brightening. 'Last week in Vienna, I bought a cabinet for Ed.'

'Shopping is *very* spiritual.'

'It wasn't any old cabinet. I bought the Badminton Cabinet.'

'For storing your badminton rackets?' I say.

Tiffany shakes her head.

'The Badminton Cabinet,' says Tiff, leaning in for full effect, 'was made in 1726. It is *priceless*.'

'OK, right, so now I get it. It wasn't from IKEA.'

She laughs. 'It was an investment for Ed. Art has no correlation to the stock market, so it's one of the ways he diversifies his investment portfolio.'

'Huh? Tell me about the cupboard.'

Tiffany sips champagne. 'It's set with lapis lazuli and gold and precious stones, like rubies.'

She shows me a picture on her phone.

'Well, hot damn,' I say.

I zoom in on the photograph. That's one fine-ass piece of wood. It's covered in hundreds of sparkling jewels, like my snatch when I got that vajazzle. If only I had posh furniture, then my life would be *epic*.

'What's Ed like? I've heard of him, of course. I mean, who hasn't?'

She smiles. Her blue eyes sparkle like the sapphires

on that cabinet. 'Oh, he's just like any guy, but with a massive –'

'*Yes?*'

'With a massive *bank balance*.' She blinks at me.

'Oh God, I thought you were about to say *dick*. A massive *dick*,' I say.

She laughs. I laugh. It feels like we're friends.

'Money has its perks,' says Tiff, 'but I don't care about that. The material realm is meaningless. We are spiritual beings.'

'I bet your wedding was pimp as fuck.'

'I'm sorry, what?' she says.

'I bet your wedding was . . . slick as a duck.'

'I wanted something simple . . .'

'Where did you go on your honeymoon?'

'Ed insisted we do a world tour.'

'Holy shit,' I say (I can't help it). 'You didn't fancy the moon then?'

'Richard says we're top of the list for Virgin Galactic's maiden flight, but I said *no*, I didn't want to go because of the carbon dioxide.' She downs her champagne. 'I've got to go. I'm volunteering at a soup kitchen.'

'Is it the one on the Archway Road? They do a great minestrone.'

She stands up.

'No! Tiff, don't go. It was *so* nice to meet you.'

She touches my arm. I look down at her hand. 'It was nice to meet you too, Siobhán.'

She remembered my name!

Tiff goes to leave. I jump up too. I grab on to *her* arm. 'What are you doing tomorrow?' I ask. 'I'm working later on, but I'm free in the morning? We could do . . . something nice?'

She pauses. 'I'm going to CrossFit,' she says.

'Amazing. I *love* CrossFit.' (I don't.) 'Can I come with you?' *Please?*

I watch her face as she hesitates. I look into her eyes. I think she's going to brush me off . . .

'Why not? It might be fun!'

Sunday, 7 August, 8 a.m.
CrossFit, Holloway, London

I shove my phone into my Birkin: Lucozade, sweatbands, towel. I jog down the hall and out of the hostel and down the Holloway Road. It's only a ten-minute run, but by the time I reach the 'box', I'm choking on the pollution and beyond destroyed. I collapse against the wall. *Damn those pints of Guinness.* I have a stitch in my abdomen like a stab wound stab-stab-stabbing and there are blisters on my feet from my customized trainers. I am bending over double cursing at the pavement, when I hear the purr of a car's engine. I look up and gasp.

Tiff emerges from the Bentley looking like a cross between somebody from Little Mix and Camille Leblanc-Bazinet, CrossFit champion athlete.

'Wow, you look *amazing*,' I say.

I take in her tie-dye top and lilac cycling shorts. I have sweated through my top and I can feel my trainers ripping through the skin on both my feet. They weren't designed to *run* in.

'You look lovely too,' she says. 'Have you done CrossFit before?'

'Of course I have. *I love it*. Like I said, it's my favourite thing. You know, CrossFit and dogs.'

I lean against the wall and wheeze.

'Let's take a photo for Insta,' Tiffany says, holding up her phone and smiling into the camera lens.

'No,' I say, ducking down.

'Aww, go on,' she says. 'Don't be shy.'

'I can't. I'm . . . too spiritual.'

She frowns. Insta is her religion. She posts twelve times a day. But I don't want a record of me with Tiff on social media. No. No way. That could be my downfall. It could be my undoing.

'Every time someone takes your photo, you lose a little piece of your soul,' I say.

She shoves her phone into her pouch. It's the one she got from the shaman.

'Fine. Shall we go in?' she asks. 'I take too many pictures anyway.'

I nod and follow her through the door. She looks better from behind. Her ass is something from an ad for shapewear by Jennifer Lopez.

'Hey,' calls a man who must be the coach. He's wearing nothing but shorts and his abs make Ryan Reynolds's torso look like an ironing board.

'Hey,' says Tiffany with a wave.

Yum. Who is *that*?

He crosses the gym to give her a kiss on the cheek.

'Er. HELLO,' I say.

'Hi,' he says with a grin.

'Matt, this is Siobhán,' says Tiff. 'She's joining me today.'

I resist the urge to flirt or, you know, mount him.

I copy Tiff as she grabs some kettlebells and does some box jumps. I pull the muscles in my legs by doing a dozen squats. Soon I'm ready to pass out.

'Is that it? Are we done?'

Tiff laughs. 'That was the warm-up, honey.'

OMFG.

The room is full to bursting and the workout finally starts.

'All right, everyone,' says Matt, shouting over the music. 'Hungry' by Rob Bailey is playing at maximum volume. 'Let's do this, people. We're going to *smash* it.'

Rob is singing about killing and working and money. I like that song.

Everyone gets into position. Tiff and I are first up. You have to do the workout in *pairs*.

I look at Tiff. She's beaming.

The timer beeps and it is *on*. The workout is a combination of excruciating movements assembled in a sadistic sequence by a psychopath. It involves pull-ups, burpees and – my least favourite – dead lifts.

'One, two, three . . .'

COME ON.

I push through the pain. My back is on fire and my legs shake. The skin on my palms is ripping. I'm dizzy. I smell sweat and blood. This is beyond *torture.* 'Eight, ten, twenty!' I say, dropping the weights on the floor.

'That wasn't *twenty*,' says the coach.

I glare at him.

'OK. *Twenty,*' he says.

'Might have been *twenty-one.*'

I write my score on the whiteboard with a red marker pen. Honestly, the things I do . . . Nino'd better appreciate it.

Tiffany does *thirty* reps. She makes it look *easy.*

Tiffany makes a grunting noise, but it sounds kind of sexy, like a lady volleyball player reaching for a smash.

She drops the weights and we high-five. Tiffany wipes her brow, but she doesn't even *sweat.* She just kind of *glows.*

Tiff beams at me and I beam back. I'm the first to look away. Man, I wish she was my twin. (I kind of wish she was my *date.*) She's the coolest girl I ever met. She's almost as cool as *me* . . .

We watch the other guys compete, but no one else matches our score.

The coach adds up the reps and times scribbled on the whiteboard.

'OH MY GOD, WE WON,' I say. 'We make a *great* team.'

Unlike me and *Beth* . . . Beth and I were like chalk and cheese.

I don't know why but I think about my twin. It's not something I like to do. Ever since I murdered her I try to forget that she ever existed. But she did. It's a fact. Beth was always showing me up by being *great* at everything. But Tiff would make an *awesome* twin. I wish I were her. It would have been so nice to have a twin who

73

was a *friend*, someone who *cared*, someone who had my back in hard times, someone who . . . I stare into the middle distance and imagine how things might have been.

'Congratulations,' says the coach, coming over and giving us both another round of high fives. I get a warm fuzzy feeling inside, like I love Tiff and the coach.

'Tiff,' says the coach, 'that was your PB. You're really nailing those dead lifts.'

'Thanks,' says Tiff. 'I feel super fit. I'm ready for the marathon.'

'Holy fuck. A *marathon*?' I say.

'Yes,' she says. 'Siobhán, are *you* training for the marathon too?'

I nod. 'You bet I am!'

No. No. No fucking way. Now I *definitely* have to kill her . . .

Tiff emerges from the shower in a cloud of steam like the goddess Aphrodite born from the sea spray.

I pull on my pants.

Tiff's staring at me. Her eyes trail my body.

What's that?' asks Tiff.

'What's what?' I ask.

'All those little patches?'

I look down at my naked body. 'Oh yeah. I forgot about those. I just quit smoking,' I say. 'They're nicotine patches, you know, Nicorette.'

Tiffany stares. I have about fifteen patches stuck all over my stomach, waist and back. There are little squares all over my body; I look like a patchwork quilt.

'I haven't smoked in a week.'

'Oh wow, well done,' she says. 'That's amazing.'

'It *is* amazing, actually. I was on sixty a day.'

Tiff's phone rings in her bag. 'Get that for me, would you, Siobhán? My hands are all wet.'

I rummage through her bag and grab her phone. 'Nanny' flashes up.

Hang on a minute, *nanny*? I thought she didn't have kids? That's what it said on Wikipedia. A kid could mess up my plans . . . Ernie's face flashes in my mind's eye. Poor kid. I've ruined his life. Perhaps she's only just had a sprog and hasn't updated her web page? I check her stomach. No stretch marks, hmmm, but maybe she's had them lasered?

'Hello?' I say. 'This is Tiffany's phone. Tiff is wet and naked . . .' I hear sobbing down the line. 'I think you'd better take it.'

Tiffany wipes her hands on a towel. I pass her the phone. I would have noticed her being knocked up on *Breakfast with Tiffany*.

I smile. 'I hope it's nothing urgent.' I don't want her to go.

'Hello?' says Tiff. 'What do you mean, *you've lost him*?' she says. 'My baby? You've lost my baby? Where? How?' Her voice is shaking.

Wow. So she really *does* have a kid. Perhaps she had a surrogate?

Tiffany looks like she's going to cry. She hangs up and turns to me. 'I think I'm going to be sick. It's my nanny. She . . . she . . . she . . .'

Tiff's phone starts to ring again. She looks at me with wide eyes.

She takes the call. 'You found him in a *bush*?'

I get dressed and eavesdrop the rest of the conversation.

'Take him home *immediately*. And then you're *fired*,' she says.

Tiff hangs up. 'I need to sit down.'

I clear a space on the bench.

'My baby. My poor baby,' says Tiff. 'I think I need to go home.'

'What happened?' I say, with my hand on her shoulder. I do a 'poor you' face.

'What will I do? Now I don't have a nanny?'

I think on my feet.

'I might be able to help you,' I say.

She sniffs. 'Really? How?'

'I'm an executive assistant, that's why I was at Christie's, and I've been working for a number of high net worth individuals. I can't name names because obviously discretion is very important, but I might have some leads for you for the nanny job!'

'You do?'

'Absolutely I do.'

By leads, of course, I mean *me*.

She sips her bottle of alkaline water and studies me carefully. Her beautiful eyes are brimming with tears.

'Oh, thank you, thank you,' she says.

11 a.m.
The Bishops Avenue, Hampstead, London

I step out of the Bentley on to the drive. White pebbles crunch underfoot. The driver clicks the door shut behind me. That was one sweet ride. I follow Tiff to the front door and gawk at the towering columns. I feel like the Fresh Prince of Bel-Air; I really don't belong here.

'I think Ed's still asleep,' says Tiff. 'He's just back from a business trip: Tokyo, I think. Or it might have been Silicon Valley. Usually he takes some pills and sleeps till the jet lag's gone. He'll get up just in time for his nightcap. James, Ed's butler, always brings it in at 10 p.m. on the dot. Then he'll sleep again.'

Hold on a minute. *Sleeping pills?* They could come in handy for my Basecamp quest. I make a mental note of that.

A housekeeper opens the door. 'Hello, Mrs Forbes,' she says with a curtsy.

'Hello, Fifi,' Tiff says. 'How are you today? I bought a new painting. I think you'll like it.'

'Oh, that's nice,' she says. 'Is it another Da Vinci?'

'No, a Da Messina for Ed.'

'That's good. I don't like Da Vincis. They're so hard to dust.'

I watch as Tiffany waltzes in. She smiles. She could be a friend! My first ever *real* friend. I smile back. *Wait, hold on . . .* I'm not going to let something stupid like *friendship* get in the way of my plan.

I take a step back and gawk at the house. It looks even bigger close up, like Buckingham Palace or the Kremlin. My knickers are wet. Of course, I'm doing this for *Nino*, but I want that house. That car. I want Ed Forbes' billions and Tiffany's A-list lifestyle. The money is just a by-product for doing the right thing. And, to be honest, I deserve it.

There's a pond in the middle of the driveway filled with orange fish. I lean over the clear green water. One of the fish swims up. He floats there just beneath the surface giving me the evil eye.

'What are you looking at?' I ask.

The fish doesn't reply. I wish I had my sushi knife. This fish is playing with fire. The carp opens its ugly mouth then shuts it again. It's like it's trying to say something. *What? What's your problem, fish-face? Huh? Come on, spit it out. No, I didn't think so.*

At the edge of the pond – staring back at me – is a large ceramic frog. It's glossy and green with big bug eyes. It looks Chinese. Expensive.

What are you gonna do, Kermit?

I glare at the frog.

I take a deep breath and walk into the house, ignoring the hostile animals.

Tall oak double doors lead into a triple-height entrance hall. A sweeping staircase leads away from a multi-level atrium. The hall is filled with natural light. The floors are pink and marbled. They have even got a *lift*.

'Wow,' I say. 'Oh wow.'

My mouth hangs open like the fish. My eyeballs pop out of their sockets. I swallow. Hard.

'Oh? Do you like it?' asks Tiff. 'We had it built last year. Ed and I bought the plot and knocked down the old house that was here.'

I follow Tiffany.

There's a palm tree in a pot. I reach out and stroke it. The bark feels rough against my skin.

'That,' says Tiff, 'is a very rare plant. Ed had it flown in from Giza.'

It's a fucking *tree*.

'If you want to wait in the living room, I'll go and deal with that nanny. I shouldn't be a minute,' says Tiff. 'Then you can meet the baby.'

I trail Tiffany down the hall. We pass an enormous tank. Inside is what appears to be a shark floating in water.

Tiffany sees my face. 'Oh, I know, tell me about it. It's a hammerhead shark. It's preserved in alcohol, or is it formaldehyde?'

'But why?' I say, peering in through the glass. Its beady black eyes stare back. That thing looks vicious. I shiver. It's lethal but *dead*.

'It's one of Edwin's art installations,' Tiff says, rolling her eyes. 'I suppose I ought to be grateful. At first he wanted a *great white*; they're over six metres long . . . Please, take a seat,' she says with a smile.

I sink into a suede armchair with a recline button. As soon as Tiffany leaves the room, I slide the knob to recline it, then I sit it up again. Up. Down. Up. Down. This is so much fun! I could lie here forever and ride it. It has a *massage* function.

I scan the double-volume room that spans the entire rear facade. I gasp at the style and elegance, at the beautiful hand-crafted finish, at the luxurious textures: sumptuous satin, smooth silk, Italian leather. The colour palette is browns and mochas, creams with accents of silver. The carpet is a rich champagne. There's an art deco bar with stunning ivory panels. French doors lead to formal gardens and beyond are fabulous of views of what must be Highgate Golf Club.

I sit and wait and bite my nails. I can hear that nanny sobbing. There's the sound of the front door slamming. *Why am I so nervous?* I am feeling out of place like a frog in a French restaurant or a fish in a great white's tank. It's good I don't have any smokes. Tiffany might not like it if I sparked up in her house. I need to keep her happy until I figure out my plan. Nino would have smoked, but Nino isn't here, not now. And I am more *strategic*.

I glance at the clock. Shit, look at the time. I've missed the start of my shift at the Savoy. I am probably fired. But it's OK. It's fine. I don't need that job any more. Not now I've found the Forbes. It's a shame I won't get to perve on Jack, but I must prioritize.

A woman strides in through the door and marches up to me. Whoa. *Who's that?* Where did *she* come from? I shrink back in my seat. She's wearing a slick black suit with black-patent stilettoes. She's carrying an iPad in one hand and an iPhone in the other. Her nails are long, more like *talons* than nails, and painted a deep, dark red. She presses the 'up' button on my chair while maintaining eye contact. I feel her hot breath on my face. She smells of Listerine mouthwash.

'Er, *hi*,' I say. 'Who are *you*?'

'Who am *I*?' she says. 'Who are *you*? And where did you come from?'

'I'm . . . I'm . . . I'm . . .' Ah, shit. What the hell is my name again? She's staring at me like I'm a piece of dirt that Tiff dragged in on the sole of her Louboutin.

'Siobhán!' I say. I take a deep breath. 'My name is *Siobhán*.'

'What are you doing here?'

OK, so now I get it. *She's* the *guard dog*.

> *Do not fuck with me,*
> *Lady. The body count will*
> *Rise to THREE. #Promise*

Thankfully Tiffany reappears and sashays in through the living-room door.

I beam at her as she sits down beside me. She beams back.

'I see that you have met *Jacinda*, my PA,' she says.

'*Executive assistant*,' Jacinda corrects with a tight smile.

'Jacinda, this is *Siobhán*,' says Tiff. 'We met at Christie's yesterday.'

'Hello, *Jemima*,' I say.

Jacinda glares at me as though I had just killed her kitten in a slow and painful way. *Aww, did I get your name wrong?*

'Mrs Forbes,' she says, 'you have that photo shoot at *one*.'

'Cancel it.'

'But it's for –'

'Clear my diary for today.' Jacinda kind of *whimpers*. 'I have a *baby* emergency. Siobhán is helping me.'

Jacinda looks at Tiff and then glares at me. Again. She opens her mouth as if to say something, but then she hesitates. She spins round and leaves the room, tripping up in her stilettoes.

'She seems *lovely*,' I say. 'You have a *very* beautiful home. It's just like in *Through the Keyhole*.'

'Oh, I don't really like this place. It isn't very *homely*.'

Tiff looks away out of the window and says, 'I grew up on a council estate.'

'I thought you were born in Chelsea?'

She smiles. 'I was. A council estate in Chelsea. Siobhán, are you *stalking* me?'

'*As if*.'

My heart starts to beat a bit faster. A look of sheer panic floods my face. I try to smile. Do I look like a maniac?

She laughs. 'I know. I'm joking. Sorry. But I get some crazy fans, you know, who know *everything* about me.'

'Fucking *psychopaths*. What's that picture over there?' I gesture to a painting. It's a Seurat of some people standing by a lake. I know it's a Seurat. It's easy. I can tell from the dots. All his pictures are dotty. 'It is a *Seurat*, isn't it?'

She nods. 'Ed is obsessed with art,' she says. 'Look at this. It's so funny. If I get bored of pointillism, I can press this button over here and – ta-da – now it's a Dalí!'

Tiff gets up and presses a button underneath the painting. I hear a quiet whirring noise and the picture spins 180 degrees. A surrealist landscape takes its place: a desert with rocks and strange figures.

'Ah, yes, that's better,' I say. 'It was making my eyes go funny.'

She giggles. 'Look at this Lucian Freud.' She presses another button: a whir. 'On the back there's a Lichtenstein.'

'I don't like that one either.'

I study a bronze on the coffee table. It's a statue of a

ballerina. She is wearing a tutu and standing in fourth position at rest.

'What about *that*?'

'It's by Degas.'

'What does *that* turn into?'

'Nothing,' says Tiff. She sits down again next to me on the sofa.

'So, it's not, like, a Transformer? I thought it might change into some kind of killer robot.'

'Now that would be cool,' she says. 'I'll suggest it to Ed.'

The housekeeper knocks and enters the room. She's wearing a stylish black uniform. She is holding a pug in her arms.

'I cleaned him up for you, Mrs Forbes. I gave him a bath. He was muddy. There were *leaves* stuck in his hair. It was horrible, really.'

'Thank you, Fifi,' says Tiffany. 'Poor baby had a shock.'

I study the dog. It has crooked teeth and furry rolls of fat. It glares at me with bulging eyes and I glare back. The dog growls a deep low growl and I'm about to growl back when Tiffany says, 'Siobhán, Meet Baby.'

Huh. The baby is the *dog*.

Fifi brings the dog to me. At least it's not the pit bull from that scary 'BEWARE' sign. I'd like to keep my fingers.

'A pug! Oh God, I just *love* pugs! The pug is my spirit animal!'

'Really? Wow. How do you know?' Tiffany asks, amazed.

'The Archangel Gabriel came to give me that message.'

'No, he didn't!' Tiffany giggles.

'Yes. He did. It was extremely spiritual. He had a magnificent voice. He sounded like Idris Elba.'

'What did he say?'

'He said, "Siobhán, I have a message from God: *the pug is your spirit animal*."'

'What? That's it? And then he left?'

'And then he left.'

She grins. 'Siobhán, you are *hilarious*.' She pushes me playfully.

I laugh too. I'm not sure she believes me. 'It's true. He really did!'

I turn my attention to the dog. '*That* is a *lovely* baby,' I say, speaking slowly as though to a child. 'He's the cutest little puggle-wuggle that I've ever seen.'

'Yes, he is. Thank you,' says Tiff, tickling the puppy.

I'm going to play along. What have I got to lose?

Fifi gives me a knowing look of solidarity. Then she bows out of the room.

'Thank you, Fifi,' says Tiff.

I reach out a hand to pet him. The hair on his head is soft. I'm guessing he uses the best conditioner to have such silky locks. Kérastase. Moroccan oil. Or perhaps a Brazilian blow-dry. And – WTF? – are those *highlights*? His fur is gun-metal grey but streaks of silver are woven through to give it a sun-kissed look. Is that ombré or balayage? His hair's nicer than Jessica Alba's. I wish I had hair like that. Mine is still bright orange.

'How old is your baby?' I ask, feigning interest.

I want that nanny job.

'He's only four months old,' says Tiff, stroking the puppy's tummy.

He licks her hand and chews her fingers. Slobber everywhere.

'Siobhán, I know you have other clients and I'm sure you're *very* busy, but is there any chance that you could babysit for a couple of days? It's just till we can sort out a nanny. You're welcome to stay in our guest house? What do you think?'

I pause for effect. This couldn't have gone any better. I bite my lip to stop myself from grinning like an axe murderer. I bite my nails. I look out of the window and study a willow tree . . .

'I don't think I can,' I say. 'I have to go to Harvey Nick's . . .'

'Baby could come. You can take the Rolls?'

'I'm not sure. It's difficult. I'll have to make a couple of calls.'

'You'd be doing Ed and me a *massive* favour,' Tiffany says. 'I'm volunteering at a homeless shelter and they said *no dogs* . . .'

'Will you excuse me for a moment?' I take my phone from my bag and pretend to make an important call. '*Ciao, ciao*, Maurizio,' I say. '*Sì. Ciao.*'

I walk out of the room and into the hall. '*Pizza, pasta, cappuccino.*' I pretend to have a conversation with an Italian count.

Two minutes later, I stroll back into the living room. 'OK. Yeah, fine. I can do it. I quit my job. I'm all yours.'

'Oh, thank you. Thank you,' she says, jumping up and hugging me.

I pause, then lean my cheek against her shoulder. I breathe her honeyed scent. Wow, she smells *amazing*. It's not perfume; it's just *her*. I stroke her hair. It's silky. Smooth, like the tiny dog's. It's a very spiritual moment between us. I know I only just met her, but Tiff feels like the sister I never had. I know I had a sister, but Tiff is so much nicer than Beth; she really doesn't count.

'I feel so lucky to have met you,' she whispers in my ear.

'It was serendipity.'

'You're an angel,' she says.

First Stasimon

My life might have been very different if Mum had got her way back in 1998. It might have changed *everything*. I wouldn't have murdered anyone. I wouldn't have killed my sister, her husband, my boyfriend, that nun in Rome last year, etc. You get the picture. Perhaps I would have been a 'nice person'. Maybe I would have been 'normal', whatever the hell 'normal' means. It sounds *boring AF*. I'd never have discovered my passion for killing. My superhero power . . .

EIGHTEEN YEARS AGO

'Right. That's it. I've had enough. Get in the car,' says Mum.

'What? Why? Where are we going?'

'You'll see,' she says. 'Now shut up.'

My mum grabs her handbag and opens the door. 'Come on, *out*,' she says.

I roll my eyes and haul myself up from the sagging sofa.

'See you later,' Beth says.

'I hope not.' I glare at her. 'Why doesn't *she* have to come?'

My mum doesn't reply.

I follow my mother out of the house and we get in the car. She floors the gas. We swerve on to the road.

'Where are we going?'

'*Church.*'

It's a Roman Catholic church called the Sacred Heart of Our Lady. The brakes screech as we come to a stop on the kerb outside. I trail my mother down the path with my feet dragging.

'Stop dawdling, Alvina.'

I walk even slower.

We step into the church and our footsteps echo in the cavernous interior. The flames of tiny candles flicker. It smells of incense and dust. We make our way down the aisle to the altar at the back of the church. I start sneezing (because of the dust).

'Wait here,' says my mother.

I flop down on a wooden pew.

'Father?' calls my mother, heading 'backstage' through velvet curtains to the VIP area.

My eyes trail round the ancient church. Why are we here? It's not a religious holiday. No one's getting married. There isn't even a baptism . . . I study the marble cherubs: tiny wings and rolls of fat. They haven't thought through the aerodynamics; there's no way they'd fly.

Eventually a priest comes out through a rusty creaking door. He wipes his mouth with his hand and brushes cake crumbs from his front.

'Yes, madam. May I help you?'

'This is my daughter, Alvina, and I need you to perform an *urgent* exorcism.'

I jump up. 'Mum, you're not *serious*?'

'I'm *deadly* serious,' she says.

I stand and blink.

Mum turns to the priest. 'She is *tormented*,' she says.

'No, I'm not!'

'Well, *I* am,' she says. 'I am tormented by *you*. Do you know what she did?' she turns to the priest. 'She set fire to the headmaster's car and now she's been *expelled*.'

I open up my mouth to speak, but no words come out.

Mum turns to me with blazing eyes. 'And she killed the neighbour's cat.'

'I did *not*. It was *old*. It just *died*.'

I curl up into a ball and – I can't help it – I sob. The tears fall freely, hot and wet. Snot pours from my nose. *This is so unfair.* 'I *hate* you!'

How could she do this to me? Why was she always so mean? She wasn't mean to Beth at all, but she was a witch to *me*. Ever since I could remember, I was the 'naughty one', but I just wanted to be *loved*. Doesn't everyone?

'Madam,' says the priest, interrupting us in a calm priest's voice. He walks over to my mum and rests a hand on her shoulder. 'Please, I understand you're distressed –'

'*Distressed?* I'm on the verge. I called last week to get her aborted –'

'*Aborted?*' the priest exclaims.

'No. Not aborted. *Adopted*, I mean. They said *no* anyway.'

I look up and gawk at my mum, my vision cloudy with tears.

'Don't worry,' she says. 'They wouldn't have you. So I'm stuck with you. And I am having you *exorcised* if it's the last thing I do.'

'No, please.' I find my voice but it is barely audible.

'Yes. About that,' says the priest. 'I'm not sure you understand . . .'

'Oh, I understand *perfectly*. I've seen *The Exorcist*. Expel the devil from her, Father. Rid her of diabolic possession.'

The priest and I exchange worried glances. My heart is pounding now.

'I can't exorcise her,' he says.

'And in God's name *why not*? Do you have something more important to do? Her soul is in danger, Father.'

'How do we know she requires exorcism?'

I shake my head. 'I'm *fine*.'

'She's not right, Father. Never has been. Cast out the devil and his demons, I beg you. Save her before it's too late. She has a double dose of original sin.'

I look at the priest; my eyes are wide. I *really* don't want to be exorcised. It sounds painful. Terrifying.

'There is a *procedure* to follow,' he says. 'For a start we need to check if there are any other ways to describe her behaviour other than *possession*. The Catholic church requires a medical examination to check for mental illnesses or physical disorders. Only after consulting with a psychiatrist qualified to evaluate the potentially possessed can we ascertain the need to perform the rite.'

'Yes, yes. I've done all that. She has the devil inside her.'

He sits down and shifts in his seat. 'All right, I suppose I could perform a *simple* exorcism . . .'

'No!' I scream.

They stare at me.

'And what is *that*?' asks my mother.

'It's just a blessing to rid the subject of evil influence. It only takes a minute.'

My body stiffens. I feel sick. I think I'm going to throw up.

'That won't do at all,' says my mother. 'I need the real deal: her head spinning, her body in convulsions, the voice of a demon spewing curses as you battle to save her soul.'

I hang my head and stare at the floor. It's suddenly cold. And quiet. I wrap my arms round myself. What if my mother's right? Maybe I *do* need an exorcism? I'm *trouble*; she's always said so. She said I was *born* evil and I'm not like Beth, who is perfect.

'Has she been demonstrating signs of demonic possession?' asks the priest gently. 'Speaking or understanding languages that she's never learnt?'

'*No*,' I say.

'Not that,' says Mum. 'What else is there?'

He frowns. 'Knowing things she has no earthly way of knowing?'

'*No*,' I say.

'Not that,' she says.

'How about physical strength beyond her natural physical make-up?'

'*No*,' I say again.

My mum scowls and shakes her head. 'No. Not *yet*.'

'Does she have a violent aversion to God or the Virgin Mary? To the cross or any other symbols of the Catholic faith?'

My mother beams. '*Oh yes*.'

The priest frowns. 'Is that true?'

'I mean, I'm not that into *God*.'

My mother is triumphant. 'She never watches *Songs of Praise*!'

The priest sighs. 'Even if, and that is a very big IF, she

does require an exorcism, I can't do it *now*. Casting out the devil is not a part of a priest's daily duties. I've never performed an exorcism. It isn't a specialized area of study in seminary school.'

'Couldn't you just have a go? Father, I am *desperate*.'

The priest shrugs. 'I'm not up to date with the new rite the Vatican issued this year. They revised the exorcism rite in the *Rituale Romanum*. The previous rite is out of date. They wrote it in 1614.'

'Just do the *old* rite,' my mother says. 'Who cares?'

'Even if I did,' he says, 'I don't have the right clothes. The priest must dress in his surplice and his purple stole. My stole is at the dry cleaner's. I'm picking it up on Saturday.'

'Just do it in *that*. You look *great*,' says my mother, gesturing to his clothes.

The priest is wearing jeans with an old black T-shirt tucked into the waist band. His white dog collar sits on top. Cake crumbs cling to the fabric.

'I'm out of holy water,' he says. 'I just did six baptisms back to back. I've been run off my feet.' My mother looks blank. 'I need to sprinkle holy water over everyone in the room. And I need a *relic*,' he says. 'Oh yes. That is *very* important.'

'A relic?' says Mum. 'Forget about that. Most of them are fake.'

'I need a *genuine* Catholic relic, something associated with a saint. I'd have to order it in especially from the Vatican.'

No one speaks. I want to go home. *I don't want to be exorcised*. But is that the *devil* talking? Or is it me? How would I know? Do demons live inside me?

'How much?' says Mum after a while.

'I beg your pardon?'

'How much do you need?'

'Madam,' he says, 'I am not a *harlot*. You cannot *buy* my services.'

'Three hundred pounds?' she says, removing her purse from her bag. 'Come on. Don't you need a new roof or something? Do you take Mastercard?'

My mother and the priest lock eyes. I hold my breath. It's *tense*.

He hesitates. '*Five* hundred pounds. And I need to ask the bishop.'

I never did get exorcised. The local bishop said no and Mum gave up on the idea. I never forgot it, though.

Second Episode

'Come on, let me show you to your room. Well, I say *room*, but it's more of a detached guest cottage.'

I follow Tiffany through the house and out to the beautiful gardens. We cross the lawn and make our way to the Forbes' 'guest cottage'. More *chalet* than *cottage*.

'Wow. I love it. Is this for *me*?'

Tiffany nods. 'It's modelled on Ed's childhood ski lodge in Val d'Isère.'

I gawk at the house. I feel like I'm in the Alps or something. All it needs is a snow-covered roof and a killer view of Mont Blanc. Everything is made of wood (fire hazard). There are slatted shutters on the windows and geraniums the colour of fresh blood in window boxes. We step inside. There's a fireplace. A deer head hangs on the wall with shiny glass eyes that are glossy and wide, as black as diesel oil.

'If there's anything you need,' says Tiff, 'anything at all, just press the star on the house phone here and give Fifi a call.'

'Don't worry, I will,' I say. 'I'm *desperate* for a Reese's chocolate and peanut butter milkshake, so I'll order one of those.'

Tiff laughs. 'Thanks again,' she says. 'You're *really* saving me.' She lets herself out through the door.

'You're welcome,' I shout through the wood.

A wide smile spreads on my face. I do a silent fist pump. *Oh my God*. Look at this place! I can't believe my luck. It must be that leprechaun. I've never been so lucky. See that, Nino? *Unbelievable*. I dance around the room.

As soon as Tiffany's footsteps fade, I wander around my chalet, checking out all the rooms. There are *a lot* of them. There's a sauna, some bottles of Jägermeister (*no, Alvina, leave it*), a framed map of Switzerland and a pink pair of skis. Two bedrooms, a bathroom, a Poggenpohl kitchen, a living room/diner. I think of Roxy and Bob at the hostel. They would *love* this place. I've got a fab new nanny job! Somewhere pimp to live! I'm one step closer to my goal . . . I am *nailing* this.

Monday, 8 August, 9 a.m.
Fierce Grace Hot Yoga, Crouch End, London

'You can't tie your dog up there,' says the girl at reception.

'What am I supposed to do with him then?'

She shrugs. 'I dunno.'

'Can he come to the class with us?' I ask.

'Inside the studio?'

'Yeah. Why not?' I say. 'In LA they do yoga with *goats*.'

She shakes her head. 'Uh-uh. No way. This is *Crouch End*, babe.'

I frown. She frowns. I grab the dog. I yank Baby's lead and drag him out of the reception and out on to the road.

95

I spot a fire-exit door propped open with a brick. We'll sneak in there. I'll hide the dog. He's only little.

I wait five minutes till I'm sure the naked yoga has started, then I sneak in with the dog and creep into the changing room. I'll have to leave him in a locker. He'll be fine; he'll have plenty of room. He can have a nap. We'll only be an hour. I pick him up and shove him in. I click the lock on the door. *One, two, three, four.* I'd better remember the combination or things could get awkward.

Tiff and everyone else have gone. They're already in the studio. I take off my clothes and shove them in my bag. I wrap myself in a towel. It's good we're here, actually; I need to get in shape. If Siobhán is going to be successful in her murder quest, she needs to haul her ass down to HIIT class or Pilates or something. She'll have to be physically fit to pull off this double hit. There are always walls to climb and drainpipes to scale, etc.

I push through the door to the studio and the dry heat hits me like a slap in the face. My eyes flick around the crowded room. Nobody else is *naked.*

Shit, I knew it. I *knew* it. Goddamn it. Why aren't I wearing clothes? It's not like a sauna. It's more like aerobics. How was I to know? Tiff said it was like doing yoga in a sauna. *No.* Saunas are Swedish and Swedes are naked. What was she talking about?

It's not too late. Nobody has seen me. I still have time to . . .

Oh.

The heavily pregnant yoga instructor at the front of the class looks up and sees me. The whole class turns to gawk. I spot a guy in the back row with abs to make the angels weep and the face of a Michelangelo. Tiffany stares at me with wide eyes. Then she starts to giggle. Urgh. Whatever. I'm going in. I refuse to be a victim.

'Whoa! You're *really* pregnant,' I say, stepping into the room. I grab a rolled-up mat from the shelf. 'How far along are you?'

'Er.' The yoga instructor woman cradles her baby bump. 'I'm eight months pregnant, actually. But the first ones are usually late.'

'Well, you look like you're about to *pop*. Are you knocked up with *twins*?'

I squeeze between the people and mats to a space by Tiff at the front.

'*No. I'm not.*'

She glares at me.

I try to ignore the eyes on me like I'm on *X Factor Live*.

The towel is more of a *hand* towel than *beach* towel. It barely covers my bum. I roll out the mat and stand at the top, ready for a downward dog, and time slows down to a trickle as the towel . . .

falls . . .

off . . .

The whole class gasps. Tiffany snorts a laugh, but pretends it's a cough and covers her mouth with her hands.

I wait for preggers to get on with the class, but she just stands there, staring.

'*What?*'

'You need to get dressed . . .' she begins.

'I am *fine* like this. Look, a towel!' I grab the towel and hold it up in the air.

'That is not a towel; it's a *flannel*.'

'What are you? A towel racist?'

'Towels don't have a race,' she says.

'A sizeist? A towel sizeist?'

Nobody speaks.

I glare at her. She glares at me. You could hear a pin drop. I glance at Tiffany. She is laughing so damn hard I think she might actually pee.

'JESUS. I'm not going to sweat in my brand-new Lulu-lemons. Those things are really expensive.'

I sweat. This heated studio's *scorching*. Must be why they call it 'hot' yoga. Oh well, I suppose it's good for you. There's no point in being *fit*, if you're not *flexible*. I spot my reflection in the mirror. My Brazilian's overgrown and I'd forgotten I'd dyed it ginger. Ha. It looks like a hamster.

The other people in the studio cast their eyes to the floor.

'You're *amazing*,' Tiffany says under her breath to me.

'Get dressed or *get out*,' says the yoga instructor.

We lock eyes. I hold her gaze. She holds mine, but then I blink (because sweat drips into my eye).

'OK. *Fine*,' I say.

She's won *this* round, but I don't care: this is a war, not a *battle*.

'Stand at the back of the class,' she says.

'See you,' I whisper to Tiff.

I pick up my bag and my mat and huff and puff through the bodies until I spot the one that looks like a hippy Chris Hemsworth.

'Hi,' I say, 'I'm Siobhán.'

He grins. 'Jason,' says the hippy Chris Hemsworth.

I pull on my brand-new Lycra, yanking off the store tags.

It takes a while as the fabric sticks to my (now sticky) skin. I pawned a Prada Saffiano bag, and with the money I bought a metallic silver top and matching shiny leggings. I stand behind Jason and his butt. He turns to look at me. I wave and smile. I *think* he smiles, but it's hard to tell because *beard*.

I follow the sun salutation. A downward dog. A tree. We hold a shoulder stand for what feels like twenty minutes. We plank. We stretch. This shit is *hard*. How the hell is she doing this *pregnant*? We do the pigeon. A triangle. Jason's drop-dead gorgeous. Phewph. Is it me or is it getting *hotter*? Sexy tattoos. Long hair. Piercings. I wipe the sweat with my towel. Jason has a silver earring in his left ear. He also has a flower tattoo. It's a pretty pink one.

'Jason,' I say. 'JASON? JASON!'

He turns round. 'Yeah?'

'I like your tattoo,' I say, glugging water.

'Thanks.'

'I also have a tattoo.'

'Yeah,' he says. 'I saw. DIE NEMO. Very cool.'

I beam at him.

The instructor tells us to do the chair pose. That one's really tricky. It involves crossing your arms and legs and balancing on your toes.

'Find a "drishti",' says the instructor. 'You need a focal spot. It helps you keep your balance if you have something solid to look at.'

I use Jason's butt as a drishti. Buns as tight as marbles.

'Your ass is *magnificent*,' I say.

Jason turns. 'Sorry, what?'

Ah shit. I'm wobbling. My focal point has gone. I fall on to Jason, *hard*, and my elbow strikes his face.

10 a.m.
Juice Bar, Crouch End, London

'Siobhán, he was *gay*,' says Tiff.

'Are you sure?'

'Yes, I know his boyfriend,' she says.

Argh. Such a waste. Why does this always happen to me? He was really fit. First Tom Daley and now *this*.

'I can't believe you walked in *naked*,' Tiffany says. 'I love you. Oh my God, you're hilarious. Baby is going to like you.'

Tiffany, Baby and I push through the door to the juice bar. The stench of raw ginger in the air makes my eyeballs water. A young man's standing by the bar scratching his balls and frowning. He wears an apron stained with blood or possibly beetroot juice.

'All right?' he says.

'I'm great, thank you,' says Tiffany.

I climb on to a stool at the bar and rest my face on the counter.

'I've had better days,' I say. 'We've just been to yoga.'

'Any good?' he asks. 'I've not tried it.'

'I don't recommend it.'

I study his name badge: 'Nathan'. Nathans don't do yoga.

Tiff said yoga is good for stress. She said it helps you relax, but I feel like I want to end the next guy who walks in. My hair is damp and matted. Gross. I am hot and sticky. I look like I've been dragged backwards through the Amazon rainforest. (Tiff took a shower while Jason and I put ice packs on our bruises and now she looks like she's just stepped out of *Vidal Sassoon*. Jason has a black eye. Then there was all the stress with the dog. I couldn't remember the code to get the mutt out of the locker. It took me *fifteen* goes.)

There's the hum of the refrigerator. I study the rainbow display of fruit and veg and herbs and shit.

> *Carrots, lemons and*
> *Blueberries, spinach and, er . . .*
> *What the hell is THAT?*

There's a fruit with bright pink skin and lime-green-coloured leaves and bright white flesh with black polka dots.

'What is *that*?'

Nathan looks where I'm pointing. 'That's a dragon fruit.'

'Or pitaya to give it its native name,' Tiffany says, joining in. 'It's the fruit of a cactus plant indigenous to the Americas.'

I study the dragon fruit, squinting. 'Did it *grow* like that? Have you *painted* it?'

'No, we haven't . . . *painted* it.'

'Is it *poisonous*?'

'No . . . it isn't . . . poisonous.'

I frown. I still don't trust it. 'I don't want anything with *that* in. Got it?'

Nathan says, 'Understood.'

Tiff takes a photo of the fruit and uploads it to Instagram: #Healthy #Vegan #Beautiful.

He's waiting for us to place an order. I check out the blackboard. Grimace. The names of drinks are scrawled in chalk. I scan the list. Make a face. 'Green Machine' or 'Green and Lean' or 'Best Youthful Green Goddess'? None of the smoothies sound appealing. I'd rather drink milk from a goat. The only green stuff I used to consume was lime in G and T and I used to pick that out every time and flick it at strangers' feet. I wasn't keen on the mint in mojitos or the single olive they'd put in my extra-dirty martinis. I like *meat*.

Tiffany beams at me. 'What are you going to have, Siobhán?'

'One of the ones with the kale and the, what is it . . . pondweed? Seaweed? Whatever.'

If I'm going to do it, I'll do it *properly*. No fannying about. You are what you eat and I need to become a *biological weapon*. You need to be as fit as a top athlete to pull off a hit like this. Venus or Serena Williams or Jessica Ennis.

Nathan looks at me like he doubts my ability to drink something that gross.

'It's OK. I can handle it. I've swallowed worse-tasting things. I want it extra-*extra* green. Do you have any . . . algae?' I ask.

'We don't have algae,' he says.

'Mangroves?'

'We don't have any . . . *mangroves*.'

'How about wheatgrass?' I ask. Tiff is always drinking that. I've seen her down endless shots of wheatgrass on her vlog. 'It's really good for you, isn't it?'

'What? Don't tell me you don't have wheatgrass?'

He shrugs. 'We're fresh out.'

I glare at Nathan. 'Right! I'll go and get some myself,' I say. 'There's a square over the road. You can blend *that* with the kale.'

Nathan looks blank.

Tiff says, 'What?'

I give Baby's lead to Tiffany and storm out of the juice bar. I stride out into oncoming traffic. A lorry beeps and swerves. I run across the road to the square and kneel down on the yellow grass beside the war memorial. It hasn't rained for *months*. It's dry. I rip up brittle handfuls of stems and when my pockets are full I shove the grass into my bag.

A guy on a ride-on mower approaches. I jump up and flag him down. I wave my hands in the air and shout. 'HEY, YOU. STOP.'

The lawn mower is deafening. The blades whir round and round. He stops the mower, slams on the brakes and removes his ear protectors.

'Yes? Can I help you?'

'I want some grass.'

He frowns. 'You want some *what*?'

'Can I have some grass?' I say.

'I'm a *gardener*. I don't sell *drugs*.'

'Huh? I don't want to *smoke* it,' I say. 'I want to make a shake.' I point to the mower where the grass is piling up. 'Can I have some of *that*?'

I grab a handful of chopped-up stems.

'Well, I don't want it, do I?'

I grab a fistful and shove it in my bag. Then some more.

And some more. When the bag is full, I run back across the road to the juice bar. Now I'm *really* thirsty. And hot. I lean on the juice bar, panting.

'Got my kale?' I ask.

Nathan nods.

I'm feeling dehydrated. Tiffany sips a beetroot shot; her lips are stained purple. I shove my grass on the counter. I have a big pile now. I pull out my Samsung phone and take a picture for Insta. I choose a filter called 'Woodland glow' that makes the grass look greener.

'Humans can't actually digest –' Nathan begins.

I interrupt.

'Blend that up with lots of ice. And kale. Remember the *kale*. And it had better be *organic*.'

I'm feeling light-headed.

Nathan looks at the blades of grass and blinks. He looks at me. 'Er, are you sure?'

'Do I *look sure*?' I lean into him, breathing.

I watch him drop the grass into the industrial blender, along with a cupful of neon-green powder, some ice and a ton of kale. The blender's whir is deafening. It sounds just like that lawnmower. He pours the mixture into a cup and hands it to me with a straw. (A *paper* straw; he doesn't want to kill the baby turtles.) The surface of the drink froths and bubbles like primordial slime or some kind of radioactive waste.

'That will be six pounds ninety-five.'

'How much? Fuck.'

I nearly pass out, but manage to steady myself on Tiffany. I give him a tenner.

'Cheers,' says Tiff.

'Cheers!' I say.

I take a sip, then spit it out.

6 p.m.
Hampstead Heath, London

'So, let me get this straight,' I say. 'You want me to follow you and pick up all the dog shit?'

'Yes, that's right. You don't mind, do you? Feeding the baby, bathing the baby, faeces management . . . It's all in the temporary contract I gave you.'

I didn't read the small print.

I tuck the plastic gloves in my pocket. At least I have some *gloves*.

'No, it's fine, really,' I say. 'I don't mind at all.'

Faeces management has always been an aspiration of mine. Ever since I was a child, I've dreamed of shovelling shit. It's a real step up from my last job at the Savoy.

'Great,' she says. 'I can't do it myself because I am allergic.'

'You're allergic to *shit*?'

'Yes. Oh, and shellfish,' she says. 'And I'm a coeliac.'

'What a shame. That's a real bitch.'

I'll remember that thing about *shellfish* . . .

Tiffany begins to jog. I follow her with the pug.

We jog along a winding path that leads across the heath. I keep my eyes glued to the pug. His little legs stick out from his tiny Ralph Lauren jacket. He has impeccable taste.

Do not poop. Do not fucking poop, plays on a loop in my head.

We climb a slope up Parliament Hill. There's a great view of London. I could push her off the edge of this hill? But she might not *die*. She'd probably just twist her ankle. Get her clothes all muddy. I hear heavy footsteps thud. A jogger races past. Then I spot a woman pushing a pram. It's a Filipino nanny with a small blond boy. I give her a solemn nod of solidarity. We nannies must stick together. She makes a face like *what do you want?* Whatever. I'm through being *nice*.

When we get to the top of the hill, Tiff turns to me and says, 'I'm going to do a spot of qigong. Would you like to join me?'

I have no idea what she's on about, but I say, 'Of course.'

I tie the puppy to a bench and watch as Tiffany flaps her arms up and down, up and down, like a flightless bird.

'Wow,' I say, as she stands very still with one leg bent at ninety degrees. 'You look like a sexy flamingo.'

'Come over here and I'll teach you.' She smiles. Her eyes are sparkling.

It's way too busy to kill her here: joggers, babies, nannies . . . It's broad daylight for a start too.

I join her on the grassy knoll and look out at the view. You can see the whole city from here: the Gherkin, the dome of St Paul's. I'm so close I can almost taste her. Tiff's skin smells like cream soda. I let her position my arms and legs. We stand side by side like flamingos.

'This is Crane Spreading Its Wings and *you* are a *natural*,' she says.

What is she on about?

'Can you feel it?' asks Tiffany.

'Feel *what*?' I ask.

'The energy?'

'Oh *yes*! Definitely. It's . . . really tingly.'

'Push the chi to and fro. Inhale. Exhale,' she says.

I feel like an idiot. It's like swimming through treacle.

She puts her hands over my hands and moves them for me.

She laughs. 'Shall we film this for my vlog?'

I swallow. Social media? A guest appearance on Tiffany's vlog is just asking for trouble . . .

'I'd love to, but I can't,' I say.

'Come on, why not? You'd be great.'

'No, no, I'm sorry. I can't.'

No one must know I am here . . .

'OK, I won't post it,' she says. 'The video's just for me. Just for fun. Come on,' she says, grinning.

'Fine. How does my hair look?'

8 p.m.
The Bishops Avenue, Hampstead, London

Tiffany, Baby and I chill out and watch a movie. The pug watches *Lassie* on his iPad and growls at the collie. Tiff picks *Romy and Michele's High School Reunion*. It's the one where best friends Romy and Michele return to their high school after ten years and pretend to be successful. It's the ultimate feel-good chick flick with Lisa Kudrow and Mira Sorvino. Justin Theroux plays a hot young cowboy (eleven out of ten). We watch it in the Forbes' private cinema: with massage chairs, Dolby surround sound, papaya face packs, detox tea and sugar-free caramel popcorn. I enjoy the eighties soundtrack and Tiffany likes the nineties clothes.

We laugh. We cry. We braid our hair and paint each other's toenails.

When the movie is over, Tiff suggests that we all get in the hot tub. There's a Jacuzzi at the bottom of the Forbes's garden. Tiff disappears to fetch some drinks, so I take off all my clothes and jump into the hot tub with the tiny dog. The sun is setting. I look out at the view. The water is warm and the bubbles soothe all my aching muscles. I'm still stiff from yoga. And CrossFit nearly ruined me. And whatever that shit was today in the park. Chinese martial arts? The puppy paddles around in the tub like a pygmy hippopotamus.

'Hey,' says Tiff, coming out of the house. 'I got you a swimming costume.'

'Oh,' I say, looking up at Tiff. She's wearing a bikini. 'Ah. I thought . . .'

I look down at my boobs bobbing around in the water.

She laughs when she sees. 'Siobhán, are you naked *again*?'

'It's just that . . . aren't we *skinny-dipping*?'

I used to go skinny-dipping with Nino. That was really fun.

She shrugs. 'We are! Of course we are,' Tiffany says with a giggle. She peels off her swimming costume and sinks into the tub.

'Tell me a bit about yourself,' she asks.

I swallow. Hard. Why does she even care? 'Er. What do you want to know exactly?'

'I don't know. The usual,' she says, splashing me with water.

I wipe my face with my hand and blink. Then I splash her back.

'Where did you grow up? You know . . . Do you have any brothers or sisters?'

'I grew up in Ireland, in *Cork*,' I say. 'I had a twin but she died.'

'Oh my God, I'm so sorry,' she says.

'It's fine. She was a cow.'

'Really? Was she *awful* to you?'

'She was perfect in every way.'

My voice shakes. I'm feeling . . . *odd*. Huh. It must be the bubbles. Those air jets are *powerful* and I am sitting on one.

'You really miss her, don't you?' says Tiff, stroking the hair on my head. I let her caress my cheek. It's a bit weird but whatever.

'Yeah. Like flowers miss the rain.' I *don't*, but that sounded good. 'What about you?' I ask, trying to change the subject.

She shrugs. 'I'm an only child. How about your parents?'

My shoulders tense. 'What about them?'

'Do you see them much?' she asks. 'My mum is my best friend.'

'How nice. My mother is a *bitch*. She used to lock me in the attic.'

'Oh, Siobhán. You poor thing.'

She puts an arm round my shoulder.

'It's fine. That was *ages* ago and I'm definitely over it.'

'That is terrible. How about your dad?' she asks. 'My dad died when I was seven. Car accident. I was in the car, but somehow I survived. I really miss him.'

'I miss him too.' I frown. 'I mean . . . I miss *my* dad. Not *yours*. Of course.'

'So your dad isn't around any more either? Is he a star in the sky?'

'Huh?' What is this? *The Lion King*? I shake my head. 'Turns out my mum killed my dad when I was a baby. She murdered him and hid his corpse in the shed at the bottom of our garden. I only found out about it last year. She's due to go on trial for it any day now.'

'Seriously?'

'Seriously.'

'Oh my God, that's *awful*.' Tiff looks deep into my eyes, her blue eyes brimming with tears.

'It's *fine*. I hardly knew him,' I say.

'But you still miss him,' she says.

'I do, I guess. Huh, I never told anyone that.'

Tiffany nods her head, encouraging me to go on.

'For years I tried to find him,' I say. 'My mother said that he'd left. I thought he'd run away from us.'

I stare up at the sky. It's night now. There are so many stars. Is one of them really Alvin?

Tiffany gasps. 'You need a hug.'

The next thing I know my head is enveloped by Tiffany's arms and my cheek is squashed into her breasts. *What's going on?*

'Shh,' she says. 'You've been through so much.'

The hug goes on and on and on . . .

For some reason, I get that song *'I Got You Babe'* in my head.

Eventually the bubbles stop and I pull away.

'Come on,' says Tiff. 'It's getting late. I'll walk you back to the cottage. It's way past Baby's bedtime now.'

'Oh, OK,' I reply.

We climb out of the tub and I wrap the pug up in a fluffy towel.

'I've never met anyone like *you* before,' she says as we walk through the garden.

I panic. 'Huh? What do you mean?'

'You're so *strong*.'

I swallow. 'Yeah, I guess.'

I look down and realize *we're holding hands*. WTF? I study our fingers; they're intertwined. You can't tell whose are whose.

We reach the cottage and stop by the door. My shoulders drop. I exhale. I feel a bit better after that hug. I'd been keeping a lot of tension in my neck and now I'm relaxed.

'Goodnight,' she says.

She gives me a squeeze.

'Goodnight,' I say, hugging back. I bury my nose in her hair.

'Let me know if you need anything. Anything at all.' She pauses, then gives me a peck on the cheek. 'Love you,' she calls.

I stand and stare as she takes the dog and wanders across the lawn. I touch my cheek where she kissed me. Huh? Did she just say she *loves* me? *Again?* She said it before in the juice bar, but I thought it was one of those things people say, like 'You're the best', and don't actually mean. She probably tells everyone she *loves* them: the binman, the window cleaner, the woman who comes to do her nails . . . *Don't take it personally.* I rack my brains and try to remember the last time someone said that . . . I come up blank. No one's ever said it. Not ever. Not even Nino. *Wow.*

OH MY GOD. SHE LOVES ME. SHE LOVES ME. SOMEBODY FINALLY LOVES ME!

You know, I could get used to this: a rich best friend, a cushy job, a hot tub in my garden and a sweet new pad. I stretch out on the sofa and snuggle into a cushion. The cushion is embroidered with the face of a pug. I kick my shoes on to the floor and hum a little song: 'You Belong With Me' by Taylor, one of my all-time faves. I feel like a weight has been lifted after our soak in the tub. A problem shared is a problem halved, isn't that what they say? I just told Tiffany things I've *never* told anyone. I mean, she doesn't know my *name*, but now she knows *my soul*. Do I really need to kill her? Couldn't I just kill Ed? *He* was the one that Nino was pissed at. But what about the *cash*?

Hmm. I'm not sure what to do. I fancy a sauna, so I get naked and turn the heating up to max.

I am lying fully nude on a wooden bench at the top. I've been flicking through Tiffany's *Vogue*. Tiff is really growing on me. She gave me a kiss. A *hug*. And I'm not ready to kill her yet. My plan is *bullet points*. And I'm not fit enough. Not yet. CrossFit nearly *killed* me. I'm not going to do it all on my own. It's insane. It's a madcap plot.

'What about our plan?'

I look up. That was Nino's voice.

And then there he is – he materializes through the wooden door. I jump up on the bench and gawk. I stare at him wide-eyed. Where the hell did *he* come from? Is he dead or alive? I am used to seeing Nino in my mind's eye, in fantasies, in daydreams, but this – *what the fuck is this*? I blink around the sauna, expecting to see some kind of portal to the underworld.

'A deal's a *deal*,' Nino says. 'And you're not on your own, are you? I'm always here.'

'Are you?'

'Yes.' He nods.

Nino stands by the sauna door. He doesn't speak or move; he just kind of floats a couple of feet from the floor. He looks the same apart from the round black hole in the middle of his forehead: I study the bullet wound. It was a *perfect* shot. You'd think as a *ghost* he would be *pale*. But *no*. He looks healthy. And *hot*.

'I've changed my mind. I don't want to kill them,' I say, sitting up on the towel. I pour some water on to the coals. They sizzle as steam rises.

'Really?'

'*Really.*'

Nino's ghost voice is a cross between the sound of a hydraulic hammer that you use for smashing up roads and somebody gurgling mouthwash.

'I mean . . . they're *nice*. I like them,' I say. 'Tiff gave me a job, a place to live . . .'

'I thought you were a *professional*.'

'I am. It's just that . . .'

'*What?*'

I pause. 'It's just that I never *liked* them. You know, when I killed the others. That's why it was so *easy*.'

He pounds his fists against the wall.

'Except for *you*, of course.'

113

Oops. Not cool. I forgot about *him* . . .

'Thanks.'

'My bad,' I say.

Nino floats to sit down next to me on the wooden bench. He leans his head on my shoulder and I put my arm round him.

Nino looks into my eyes; his eyes are smouldering like the coals in the sauna. 'What about the *money*?' he asks. 'You need to kill *her*. The *wife*.'

I sigh. 'Her name is *Tiffany*.'

Nino shakes his head. 'This was our last hit,' he says. 'You're doing it for *me*.'

'I know,' I say.

Oh God. He's so fit.

Nino takes my hand. '*I* can't do it. It's up to *you*. All those billions of pounds . . . Imagine what we could do.'

I lean in towards him and somehow we kiss. Nino's tongue's inside my mouth. I can't believe he's *here*. His hands on my body are pulling me close, like we could merge into one. I feel his hand on my naked thigh, sliding slowly upwards . . .

'OK,' I say, pulling away. 'Say I kill Tiff. Then what?'

He stares at me. 'It's obvious. We've been through this. You seduce Ed. You *marry* him . . .'

I take sip of – now warm – water. Man, it's hotter than hell. It was already warm outside in the heatwave, but in here it's a *furnace*.

'Nino,' I say, 'I'm *flattered*. Really. I know that was the plan, but how do I get Ed to *marry* me? It's *impossible*.'

He pulls me up so I'm standing before him, his body pressed against mine. 'Alvie,' he says. 'Alvie, baby. Don't you understand? You're the most beautiful woman I ever saw. You're a fucking *goddess*.'

And I *melt*. Oh God. He's *so* romantic, especially now he's *dead* . . . I needed this pep talk, actually. I was having a confidence crisis.

I look into Nino's eyes. He knows how to be persuasive (he probably learnt that in Sicily when he was in the mafia). He pushes me back on to the bench; the wooden slats are scorching. I'm sitting on the magazine, so I toss it out of the way. He shoves his head between my legs. I gasp. Hot air scalds my throat. I feel his rough hands on my thighs, spreading my legs wide open. Nino's lips are on my lips. His tongue is on my clit.

'Oh God. That feels *amazing*.'

I dig my nails into the bench. I let my head fall backwards. Lamplight casts an orange glow and everything is golden.

I can't take it any more. I pull his head towards me. My fingers grip and tear at his hair. His hat falls on the floor. His fingers are inside me now. I moan. My head is spinning. I'm dizzy. He licks me harder, faster. His fingers hit my G-spot. My skin is hot and slippery and sweat drips down my face. I arch my back and something flashes.

'I'm coming,' I say. 'I'll do it for you, baby. They're *dead*. So dead. Dead, dead, dead, dead.'

And I'm so hot that I catch fire. Lights are blinding now. My head explodes as I come and come.

I float up higher . . . higher . . . then I crash down on the bench.

And the whole world's shaking.

Wow. What's *that*? Is this *afterglow*? I open my eyes and blink.

Everything is *red*. That's weird.

Nino wipes his mouth.

I look up and shout, *'Holy fuck!'*

Flames are licking the ceiling.

'Shit! The *Vogue*.' The magazine has fallen on the coals and now it's set the sauna alight. Everything is burning.

'FIRE!' I yell.

I watch the blaze burn bone-dry wood. I tear my eyes away and look around for Nino; he's gone. Even his hat has disappeared. I jump up and run outside, choking on the fumes and cough-cough-coughing my guts up.

Suddenly the sprinklers start and I gasp at the cold. The fire alarm goes off. It's loud. I stand here, naked, alone again, watching the sauna burn down.

Tuesday, 9 August, 9 a.m.
The Bishops Avenue, Hampstead, London

'Oh, I've got a good one,' says Tiff.

'OK then, let's hear it.'

Tiff sits up tall and clears her throat. I lean back in the massage chair.

'I'm so fucking *spiritual* that when I'm with the Hopi tribe of North America they mistake me for the Messiah.'

'Ha!'

'They think I'm the "True White Brother". Their prophecies speak of him and he is due back any time.'

'I hope you tell them you're *not*?'

'I do! But it doesn't work. All their elders say that

only the true Messiah would claim that they were not the Messiah.'

'Well, *I'm* so fucking *spiritual* that I'm shagging Deepak Chopra and cheating on him with Gandhi's ghost.'

'What a love triangle!'

'Sometimes,' I say, 'David Copperfield comes.'

'Have you had David Blaine?' she asks.

I nod. 'I did him last year. It was mind-blowing.'

We explode into giggles.

'I'm so fucking *spiritual*,' I say, 'that every Hallowe'en I get the signs of the stigmata on my hands and feet.'

'At Hallowe'en? Why Hallowe'en?'

'God works in mysterious ways.'

'Wouldn't it make more sense at Easter?'

'I get them at Easter as well. Ooh, I've got another one. I'm so fucking *spiritual* that I don't see *dead* people. I see people who are *still alive*. They are *everywhere*.'

'You do?' Tiff asks.

'They're walking down the street or in a shopping mall. I see them in a restaurant, a café, a nail salon . . .'

'Can they see you too?' she asks.

'Of course. What a fucking ridiculous question.'

Tiff wipes her eyes. She's crying with laughter. Baby licks her face. He probably likes the salt in her tears. Animals like salt.

I flick the switch on the massage chair and the buzzing stops. I press the button and the seat whirs as it sits back up.

'I'm sorry,' I say, 'about last night.'

'It's fine,' she says. 'These things happen.'

'It was an *accident*,' I say.

That sex was really on fire.

'Don't worry,' she says. 'I understand.'

Why is she being so *nice*?

I frown. Arson is one of my hobbies, but this time it wasn't planned. I find that a little disconcerting, like I am losing my knack.

'At least you weren't hurt,' says Tiffany. 'I'd never be able to forgive myself if anything happened to you.'

Tiffany rests her hand on mine. Aww, I think she *means* it.

I cough. 'I think I have black lung.'

'From the smoke inhalation?'

'Yeah,' I say, pulling away. *Come on, Alvie. Snap out of it.* I can't afford to get attached, all gooey and sentimental. I need to fillet her like a fish, pretend she's a hunk of salmon. 'I guess the electrics in the sauna were faulty. It's lucky the firemen came so fast or that cottage would be history.'

At roughly 1 a.m. last night, a truckload of firemen arrived at the mansion on the Bishops Avenue to put out the blaze. They ran around in their uniforms with their powerful hoses and sprayed the fire until all that was left was a soggy mountain of ashes. Normally I'd have been all over *that* like a paedo at Scout camp. But I wasn't in the mood after Nino. Those firemen really missed out.

Tiffany seems to be convinced that I'm a safe pair of hands. *Hilar.* So I take Baby out for a walk around the magnificent grounds. There is still no sign of Ed. I'm getting impatient now. I've been looking out for him. He can't still be *sleeping*. The mutt and I step through the French doors and out into the garden. The sun shines down between the leaves and the air is filled with birdsong. The pug is on a smart blue lead and Tiff told me to watch out for his collar. Apparently it's called 'Amour Amour' and cost several thousand dollars. (Tiff seemed almost *embarrassed* about it. It was a gift from Ed. I almost wish *I* was their dog to wear that kind of bling . . .) Baby's jewellery is better than Beth's was. It crosses my mind to steal it, but Tiffany is sure to notice if I'm wearing it . . .

Stop it, Alvie. You're a magpie. Leave the collar alone. You're never going to win Ed's heart by being materialistic. I need to try to be like Tiff. She is zen as fuck. She doesn't even *want* to be rich. If she weren't in love with Ed, she'd renounce her worldly goods and live in a cave in the Himalayas with some yaks and shit.

Baby barks as if to say *I don't trust you, nanny.*

I take in the mansion's grounds. They're dazzling green in the sun. There's a formal statue garden with sculptures in marble and bronze. I study a striking figure of a mother holding a child. It's voluptuous pale green. I check the plaque. It reads: 'Henry Moore, 1975'. I think of Beth with her little boy. Of Tiffany and Baby. I feel a twinge of something. Am I *broody*? Weird.

I walk further down a path that leads to a tennis court. Beyond the court is a neoclassical colonnaded pool house. I peer in through an open window. There are *three* swimming pools, including the one outside in the garden. Surely that's excessive? A sign on the wall says 'Solarium'. Another says 'Turkish Bath'. There's no question: the place is pimp. It's like the Burj Al Arab.

I follow the path at the side of the house till I'm back at the front by the driveway. The dog stops walking then squats down right in the middle of the drive.

'No. No, you can't do that *here*.'

I tug on his lead, but he won't budge.

'Shit. Shit.' I don't have the gloves. This is bad. I am going to get fired.

A few seconds later and Baby stands up, his little tail wagging with pride. How did a pug that fucking small produce something that size? I study the poop. Oh God. Why me? It looks like an elephant did it.

I bend down and growl at the dog. 'I'm going to turn you into a *hat*. I am Cruella De Vil.'

I hear the sound of the front door open and Ed's booming voice spills out.

'I'm *fine*, Tiff; it was just the jet lag. I'll see you tonight for your birthday.'

Birthday? Yes, of course! I remember the date from Wikipedia. Tiff was born on 9 August 1985. I know, I'll get her a gift! Something really special. But what? I'm running out of cash and designer bags to pawn.

I glance at my Birkin on my shoulder. No way, the poo's not going in *there*. I stoop down and pick up the poop and chuck it in the fish pond. I stand up just in time. Ed's approaching. I stare – I can't believe I just did that – and Tiff and Ed stare back.

'Ed, darling, remember I told you Baby has a new nanny? Siobhán, this is my husband, Ed. Ed meet Siobhán.'

Our eyes meet, but I look away.

'So, you're the latest one, are you?'

I squirm. I look down at the floor.

He offers his hand and I shake it. Urgh. I can't help but grimace.

'Whoa,' says Ed, withdrawing his hand. 'You are very . . . *moist*.'

'Thank you,' I say, looking up at last. 'Just admiring your fish.'

We stare at each other. I shift on my feet. I bite the inside of my lip.

Ed narrows his eyes. 'You look . . . *familiar*. Have we met before?'

He frowns at his hand and wipes his palm on his trouser leg. I look at my shoes and shuffle my feet on the gravel drive. He *was* drunk the other night. His memory must be hazy.

'Er, no. I don't think so,' I say. 'I'd remember *you* and I only met your wife recently. Happy birthday, by the way.' I turn and smile at Tiffany. She beams back at me. 'I was working abroad before that, so I can't have met you.'

'I see,' says Ed. 'I must be mixing you up with someone else.'

'People often say I look like Angelina Jolie, so you're probably thinking of *her*. I could be her double.' I feel my cheeks burning up as Ed studies my face. 'A *ginger* Angelina, though . . . obviously.'

He *kind of* recognizes me, but not enough to place me as the girl from the bar at the Savoy. I look into his eyes and blush. Out here in the daylight he looks even hotter. *Damn it, Alvie. Control yourself.*

'Bejeebus. To be sure,' I say, just to be *extra* Irish.

'Well,' he says, 'I'm very sorry if I forget your name. We have so many members of staff it's hard to keep up,' he says.

I smile. 'Of course. No problem, Mr Forbes.'

But I think that's unlikely. Something tells me that Ed Forbes will *never* forget about me.

I just spent *all* my money on a Tibetan singing bowl. I have spared *no* expense on Tiffany's birthday present. The bowl makes a low humming sound when you rub a stick round the edge. I bought the bowl in Hampstead Village at a gorgeous (overpriced) shop that was *very* spiritual. Tiffany would have *loved* it. It had lots of things like dreamcatchers and sandalwood incense. She's going to adore it. I know she will. She'd better; it's non-returnable.

I run up the stairs with the puppy darting in between my legs. I nearly trip over him, fall and break my neck.

'Tiff? Tiff? Where are you?' I say, panting. 'I got you a present.'

We run up to the sixth floor. Should have taken the lift.

'Oh, hey, Siobhán. How are you?' she says, giving me a peck. 'I was just picking out an outfit for my party tonight. Want to help?'

'Er. Yeah, sure,' I mutter. 'I er . . . got you a birthday present.'

Tiffany opens up her closet. Oh. This won't take long. I was expecting the sales floor of Harrods, but there aren't many clothes. She gives most of her stuff to charity. She could be a *monk*.

'It's a toss-up between this silk kimono I was given in Japan and these upcycled ripped-up jeans?'

'Hmm,' I say. I study the jeans. They are basically just *thread*. 'What would you wear on top?'

'Well, I've got this pretty bra I borrowed from Zoe Kravitz.'

She holds up a golden bra. I think it's *real* gold. It's shiny and yellow and beautiful. I don't want to know how much it cost. I want it. I really want it.

'Show me the kimono on?'

Tiffany tries on the dress. It's every colour of the rainbow and ethical as fuck.

'Definitely the kimono,' I say. 'You look *hot*.'

She smiles. 'Thank you. I *love* this dress. It was from the Japanese ambassador for my work on sustainable fishing.'

'I got you a present,' I say again a little bit louder this time.

'Oh!' she says. 'You shouldn't have.'

I look up then see a singing bowl on the shelf behind her. It's *exactly* the same as the Tibetan one that I just bought for her.

Tiff looks at the gift in my hands. It's wrapped in shiny paper and tied up with a curly ribbon in a pretty bow. There's a tag and on it I have written *For Tiffany, Happy Birthday, Love Siobhán XXXXXXXX*.

'Is that the gift?' she asks, reaching out to take the present.

'Er, no. Not this. That's not it.' I hide it behind my back.

'Oh? What is it?'

'It's for the bin.'

I should have bought the dreamcatcher. Why the hell didn't I buy the fucking dreamcatcher? I can't even take this back. *No returns.* 'I'll give you your present later tonight. What time are we leaving?'

She pouts. 'Oh, Siobhán . . . I'm so sorry,' she says. 'We're going to Sushi Samba. Ed has hired the thirty-ninth floor of the Heron Tower. I am *really* sorry but they have a strict no-dogs policy. I need you to stay at home and look after the baby. OK?'

'It's fine,' I say to the floor. 'I hate sushi.'

I LOVE SUSHI SO MUCH.

'I'm so sorry,' she says. Again.

'Tis only a step-mother would blame you,' I say and head back downstairs to the kitchen.

'I'll bring you back some sushi.'

'Don't worry about it,' I yell upstairs. It's probably *vegan* sushi.

'I'll bring some sashimi for the dog in a doggy bag.'

'Yeah, sure, whatever,' I say, stomping down the steps.

I chuck the stupid bowl in the bin. I mean, I could try to *sell* it, but nobody's going to want it, are they? I mean, what the hell is it? I'll get her something else. But what? I'm skint. I lean my forehead against the wall. This really sucks. Then I get an idea . . .

3 p.m.
Holloway Road, London

What do you get the girl who has everything? Tiff can buy whatever she wants. Anything her heart desires: cocaine, diamonds, Gucci, yachts . . . But don't they say *it's the thought that counts*? It doesn't really matter. I guess she'll like whatever I choose. Still, I'm feeling the pressure . . .

I turn off the Holloway Road with Baby on his lead. I open up my purse and sigh. No notes, only coppers and silvers. The coins add up to *fifty pence*. Fifty pence *exactly*. I stop outside Poundland. It's worth a try. I bet Tiff's never had a present from *Poundland* before. How unique. And, in a way, how very spiritual.

I step inside the crowded store and eye the rows of shelves. They're lined with bottles of Fairy Liquid, 1,015ml. I turn down another aisle with make-up and accessories: eyelash curlers, brushes, files and stick-on nail extensions. There's an extensive dental section with Listerine spearmint mouthwash. I pick up a purple packet of *Colgate* toothbrushes. They'd be handy for when she travels. Tiff is always jetting off to international auctions. I'll get these. They're *perfect*.

I march to the till and wave the pack at the cashier. She's sitting eating Wotsits; her chin and lips are stained bright orange. Baby barks at her.

'How much is this?' I ask.

She licks her fingers and studies the packet. 'I need to scan the barcode.' She holds up a handheld scanner. The scanner beeps.

'A pound.'

I roll my eyes and turn on my heels and head to a different aisle. A toothbrush is a *stupid idea*. She's probably already got one. I'm going to have to do better than *that* or she'll think I made zero effort.

There's a section with vaping paraphernalia. I pick up a bottle of something called '88Vape E-liquid menthol', 11mg, but I'm not sure if Tiffany vapes. No, she probably doesn't. Still, she could start? It's never too late. But it's not very spiritual. I chuck it back on the shelf. What else? I scan the rows.

There's a sign saying 'Home and Garden'. Ace. I'll find something down there. I spot a mini screwdriver set and some pliers, a nice silver pair. But I don't think Tiff does DIY. She'll have a handyman to change light bulbs and stuff like that. I want a *handyman*.

Oh, look: the confectionary aisle, which is chock-a-block with retro sweets: flying saucers, Push Pops, Nerds. They look good enough to eat. Yes, that's more like a *birthday present*. I feel like I'm back in Woollies. Baby sniffs the candy wrappers. My mouth waters. I can almost taste them: the nutty crunch of a Mr Tom, the sour thrill of a sherbet. I grab a shiny red box of Maltesers and tube of chocolate mint thins and push past the customers back to the checkout.

I spot the cashier and grin. 'How much is this?' I slam down the Maltesers.

She scans them. 'That's a pound.'

'And this?' I give her the chocolate mint thins.

Beep.

'A pound as well.'

I grit my teeth. 'It doesn't matter. It's probably too much sugar. Tiffany's body is a temple.' I frown. 'Do you have a discount section? You know, like special offer?'

'We don't. It's *all* a pound.'

'Everything?'

'*Everything.*' She scowls. 'The shop is called *Poundland*.'

Sarky bitch.

This is getting ridiculous. I can see that I'm wasting my time. Ha. So much for *customer service*. I am outta here.

I storm back along the aisles. I'll never find anything. I push past a bunch of spotty school kids laughing at condoms.

'Get the ribbed ones,' I say.

I grab a pack from the shelf and throw it at a lanky youth. He looks like he might pass out.

'Trust me,' I say.

5 p.m.
The Bishops Avenue, Hampstead, London

I turn on to the Forbes' street and march down the road with the dog on his lead, stamping my feet and kicking up the stones. I can't turn up empty-handed. I promised her a gift. This is so embarrassing. I open the gate.

My feet crunch on to gravel. Hang on. Hold up. *Wait a minute . . .*

I glance at the house but there's nobody watching. The CCTV faces the street. I bend down to scoop up a stone. Not a stone, a *pebble*. It's small and smooth and round. Yes, yes, this will do very nicely. I shove the pebble into my pocket.

'Don't say a word,' I say to the dog.

Baby cocks his head.

'Yo, Tiff,' I say, walking into the living room. 'Happy birthday, babe.'

She's sitting on the sofa, legs crossed, with her eyes closed.

'Tiff?' I say again. She can't hear me. What is she listening to? She's wearing AirPods. 'Hello?' I say, prodding her on the shoulder.

'Oh! Hey, Siobhán. Hello, Baby. I didn't see you there. I'm just listening to this,' she says, gesturing to her iPhone.

'Yeah? What is it?' I ask, taking the AirPod that she offers me and sticking it in my ear. I frown.

'Have a listen,' she says. She grins as she presses the phone screen. I sit down next to her on the sofa and listen to . . . *What the actual fuck?* I have no idea.

It sounds like someone hitting a stick with another stick every five seconds. Again and again. It is *banging*. Repeatedly. It goes on and on and on. I suppose it could be really, *really* boring minimalist techno?

'What is *that*?' I say eventually, taking out the AirPod.

'Don't you just *love* it?'

I look at Tiff. 'I love it. What the hell is it?'

'It's *shamanic drumming*.'

'Of course it is.' I should have guessed.

'I usually listen to it with Baby. Baby likes it, don't you, Baby? Come here, boy.'

She picks him up and cuddles him, then makes him listen to drumming. He whimpers and jumps off the sofa then jumps up next to me. Poor mutt. The dog and I have better taste in music than Tiffany.

'Happy birthday,' I say. 'By the way, how old are you?'

She laughs. 'I'm not telling you. That's a well-kept secret.'

It's *not*. It's on her Wikipedia. She is thirty-one.

'If you told me, you'd have to kill me?'

'No. I'm thirty-one.'

I laugh. 'You didn't have to tell me. I never tell anyone. When people ask my age, I say, "*Thirteen point eight billion years: the same age as the universe.*"'

'You identify with the creator?'

'With *the whole of creation*.'

Tiff nods like she understands. 'Because you're made of stardust.'

'Look. I got you this,' I say.

'Siobhán, aww, you shouldn't have.'

I take the bit of grit from my pocket and give it to Tiffany. 'Happy birthday,' I say again.

'Oh, thank you!' She frowns. 'What is it?'

'You don't know what it is?'

'It looks like . . . um . . . is it some gravel? Is it a *gratitude pebble*?'

'No.' I shake my head. '*That* is an ancient fragment of a precious meteorite that originated in the ring of Saturn.'

'What? No way.'

'It absolutely is,' I say with my straightest face.

She picks it up and studies it, holding up the pebble to her face and squinting at it.

Baby barks. Tiff doesn't speak.

'You *hate* it,' I say. I jump up and storm out of the room.

'No, wait, Siobhán,' says Tiff, jumping up and following me. 'Come back, please. I'm sorry. I don't know what to say. It's too much.'

I stop and turn round. I walk back into the room and sit down next to her on the sofa.

'You're welcome,' I say. 'Just promise that you'll keep it safe and love it with all your heart.'

'I'll have it made into a necklace.'

'For Christ's sake, don't do *that*. Keep it locked inside a safe and never take it out. This is not a *scented candle*.' I say. 'Do you know how hard it was to find? Do you have any idea? Do *not* regift it.'

'I love it,' she says. 'It's my favourite present.'

Tiffany tucks the pebble away in her purse. She takes

my hand. 'I am going to treasure it. It's spiritual, like *you*.'

I smile. 'Just out of interest,' I ask, 'why *are* you so spiritual? I mean . . . what started it all off?'

'Oh my goodness,' she says, her eyes wide. She grips my hand even tighter. 'Really? I didn't tell you?'

I shake my head.

'I can't believe you don't know,' she continues. 'I had an NDE, a near-death experience as a little girl. Do you remember I told you about the car accident? The one that killed my father?'

'Yes,' I say.

'Well, I actually *died* for a couple of minutes. It can't have been for very long, but I remember floating above my body. I saw myself in the hospital bed. I felt my awareness expand and fill the whole of the building. I could see *everything* that was going on, even my mother down the corridor talking to a doctor. I floated higher until I could see the whole of the planet. I felt myself moving along some kind of tunnel until I reached bright light. I can't describe the feeling. It was the most incredible unconditional love that you could ever imagine. I heard God's voice inside my mind. He said, "Child, it's not your time." Then I woke up in the hospital bed . . .'

'That's so fucking cool.'

(It is actually very cool. I really did mean that.)

'What about you?' Tiffany asks. 'Why are *you* so spiritual?'

I don't know what to say. I'll make something up.

'I died too.'

'You did?'

'Uh-huh.'

'How?'

'I got struck by lightning!' I say. 'There's a scar on my head. Do you want to feel it?'

'Oh, yes please.'

I let her touch the scar on my head from a scooter accident that I had when I was a kid.

'Wow,' she says. I can tell she's impressed. 'I can't believe that you survived. You know being struck by lightning is a shamanic initiation? Do you ever see ghosts or spirits?'

'Er, yeah, I guess.'

'I knew it!' she says. 'I bet you're a shaman.'

'I probably am.'

'I knew there was *something* about you,' she says, gazing at me as though for the first time. 'Ever since we met . . . I couldn't quite put my finger on it. What happened when you died?'

'Er . . .' I scratch my head by the scar. What am I going to say? *'Exactly* the same thing that happened to you. Every last detail.'

'No way.'

'*Way*. I swear to God.'

'We have so much in common.'

9 p.m.

I spend the night with Baby eating Tiffany's dairy-free ice cream and Insta-stalking Tiffany's live feed from the Heron Tower. It looks like they're having a *grand old time*. Tiff's having fun without me. The food looks *great* with edible flowers and real gold leaf and shit.

I finish off the 'ice cream'. Salted caramel, my ass. I

131

read the label: no sugar, no cream. What the hell is it made of? Dust? I dump the tub in the bin then peer out to the corridor. It's quiet. This is my chance to explore. There's nobody here except me. The mutt is asleep in his four-poster basket. I can hear him snore. To be fair, he's too small to make into a *hat*. Perhaps a pair of *earmuffs*? I'm sure I saw something similar on the runway at Dior.

I tiptoe out of the dog's suite and into the spacious hall. I am going to search the whole house. I want to see *it all*, but especially Ed and Tiffany's room. There is something I need from there: Ed's sleeping pills.

I creep out to the corridor and look both ways down the hall. I hear my phone ring in my pocket.

'Shit.' It'll wake the dog! I run into a room to answer it. Softly I close the door.

'Hello?' says my mother's voice.

Mavis. Why did I answer?

'Hi,' I say through gritted teeth. 'How nice of you to call.'

I'm in some kind of utility room: washing machines, tumble dryers. I sit on top of the washing machine. It's warm. It smells nice, like fresh flowers.

'Where are you?' she asks.

'Nowhere you know.'

The washing machine rocks and shudders. It makes a pleasant humming sound.

'The trial has been postponed. But I'm not worried about it,' she says. 'I'm pretty sure they'll let me off. The evidence is shaky and I have the best defence lawyer. It's really just a formality.'

I glance at the tumble dryer. That one's shaking even more. I hop off the washing machine and jump on that instead. It bang-bang-bangs against the wall. It is quite distracting.

'How did I know that you weren't calling just to see how I am?'

'My lawyer represented Oscar Pistorius,' she says, 'when he got off.'

'What the hell are you talking about? He went down for murder.'

'Did he? Damn. I need a new lawyer.'

The dryer shakes and wobbles.

'How can you afford him anyway?'

'He's doing pro bono work.'

The vibrations are getting stronger. My pussy is wet.

'I'm fine. By the way. I've never been better. Thank you for a-a-a-*asking*.'

Oh my God. This thing vibrates better than a Power Plate. I grip on to the sides and hold the phone under my chin.

'OH, OH, OH, OH.'

'Alvina? What's going on?'

'N–n-nothing.' I catch my breath. 'Just doing a spot of laundry.'

'There's a first time for everything.'

I push on to the wall to stop myself from falling off.

BANG, BANG, BANG.

'AY CARAMBA!'

I come on top of the tumble dryer and bang on the wall with my fist. 'I've got a new job,' I say, panting.

'Oh, you do?' she says.

Wow. This thing is a revelation. Nino's ghost is out of a job.

'And what new job is this?'

I can tell that she doesn't believe me. I am highly employable, damn it.

'I work for *Ed Forbes*,' I say, showing off. 'I am in his house right now. It is very nice. I've got my own Swiss chalet and everything.'

Ugh. Why did I tell her *that*? I'm not thinking straight after that fabulous orgasm. I wanted to prove that I'm wanted. Not only do I have a *job*, but I work for a *billionaire*, a world-famous art collector, a super-sexy banking tycoon.

I've said too much.

'*Edwin*?' my mother says. 'You're working for *him*?'

'I am. You've *heard of him* then?'

My mother laughs. 'Have I *heard of him*?'

'What's that, Ed?' I say. I cover the mouthpiece and pretend to speak to someone else. 'I've got to go. Ed needs my help with a spreadsheet or something.'

'Wish me luck with the trial,' she says. 'They've postponed it *several* times. I don't know what the delay is. I wish they'd hurry up. I've lost my reputation!'

'Break a leg,' is all I can manage. I'm about to hang up when my mother starts quoting *Othello*.

'*Oh, I have lost my reputation, Iago . . .*' she begins.

So dramatic.

I jump down from the dryer. *Phewph*. My knickers are wet. I rub my cheeks with both my hands. Slap myself round the face. Now, what was I doing? Oh yes. The house.

My murder quest. I click into Basecamp on my phone and edit my list:

- Become Siobhán.
- Find Ed.
- Drug Ed.
- Kill Tiff.
- Seduce Ed.
- Marry Ed.
- Kill Ed and spend all his money on clothes and hide from the police.
- Bribe a corrupt judge to put my mother away for life.

I shove my phone back in my pocket and wander around the house, my head still spinning. My mum always has that effect on me, a bit like doing bongs. I open a door to an underground car park with what looks like a motor museum: a Ferrari in bright yellow, a Veneno Roadster, a sexy little vintage McLaren and an Aston Martin Valkyrie. I spot the car from *Chitty Chitty Bang Bang*. Weird. What's *that* doing there? I stroke the bonnet of the Ferrari. It reminds me of my old Lambo, the one that Nino and I stole from Beth's husband, Ambrogio. The paint is smooth and glossy. I try the door. *Yeah, baby.* It opens and I push inside and sit down in the driver's seat. I grip the steering wheel tight. I'd love to take this for a ride. I remember driving through Italy with Nino by my side . . . Soon, soon, this ride will be mine. Only two bodies to go! I've just got to keep my cool and do what I was born to do . . .

I ride a lift up to the Forbes' suite on the sixth floor. I want to find those sleeping pills. I have a great idea. I step out to a corridor lined with four closed doors. I try one: it's Tiff's dressing room. Another door leads to Ed's. Another to an airing cupboard. It must be *that* door then. I creep along the corridor towards what must be the Forbes' suite. I try the handle. It's not locked. I step into the room: bouquets of roses, polished floorboards, a super-king-size bed covered with throws and *more* pug cushions.

'YES. YES. YES.' I spread my arms out and fly around like an aeroplane.

I freeze. I stop and stare. What's *that*? What is *that* doing here? Above the bed, attached to the wall, is a beautiful Samurai sword.

Is this a dagger which I see before me, the handle toward my hand?

Perhaps it's only ornamental? A gift from a business trip? The sword's almost a metre long and shining polished silver. The blade looks sharp. I like it. I *love* it. I miss my sushi knife.

I cross the room towards the en suite, the floorboards creaking underfoot. I pass the glitzy Badminton Cabinet that Tiffany told me about. It's nice with all the rubies and shit, but I'm more interested in another cabinet . . . I'm on bullet point number three: *Drug Ed.* I need to get on with it. *Hurry up, Alvie. Move it.* I'm running out of time. What if a member of staff comes in? How do I explain my presence? I'll say I have a migraine and am looking for some aspirin.

In the en-suite bathroom there's a roll-top bath with shining taps, a rain shower, a pair of his and hers basins and a medicine cabinet. I open the door to the cabinet, using my sleeve to cover my hand, and find a little packet of pills with 'Edwin Forbes' written on the prescription label. I read the box: Temazepam. I've found the sleeping pills! I press four capsules out through the foil and slip them into my pocket.

Wednesday, 10 August, 11 a.m.
Oxfam, Highgate village, London

'Aren't you even going to keep the Chloé bag? It's *gorgeous*.'

I stroke the leather bag on the counter: it's pink with a golden 'C'. The leather is as soft as peaches. The bronze clasp shines like liquid. I'd give my right arm for that bag. My left one too, to be honest. (But then how would I carry the bag? I haven't thought this through.)

'I don't need it. I have a bag.'

'You have *one* bag?' I say.

'One bag is enough. I can't wear *two* . . . No, Baby! *Stop it*.' Tiff yanks hard on Baby's lead. The puppy is chewing a boot. 'Sorry,' she says to the man at the desk. 'We're still training him.'

I glance at the shaman's pouch Tiff's carrying. Yeah, it's cool and spiritual, but I prefer the Chloé bag. It's much more whimsical.

'Do They Know it's Christmas?' by Band Aid blares from speakers, an interesting choice for summer. Perhaps they're *very* religious? I glance around the charity shop. It's my first time here. I thought it would smell of mothballs and damp, but it doesn't. It smells quite pleasant. It's the scent of laundry detergent. Ocean Escape or something. The clothes on all the rails look nice. I'd assumed it would be pyjamas

137

and dressing gowns old people had died in, but no. It's quality stuff. There are posters on the wall of kids in Africa. I get it. I do. But what about *me*? I'm *poor* as well.

Tiff pulls out a few more items from the cardboard box.

'These are just some gifts I received, but I don't need *more* possessions. Here we have the Louis Vuitton stuff from *Nicolas*.'

'*Nicolas Ghesquière*?'

Tiff nods.

'Was he at your party last night?'

She frowns. 'Of course he was. He's a friend and *very* generous.'

She empties the bag on the desk. There's perfume, chocolates, a velvet hair accessory and a beautiful silk scarf.

The man at the desk takes the scarf and sniffs. 'Has this been *washed*?' he asks.

'It's never been worn,' Tiffany says.

'Is it dry clean only?'

'Yes.'

He frowns.

'Is that a problem?'

'Perhaps.'

I reach out to touch the scarf – smooth silk like double cream.

'Let go, Siobhán,' Tiff says, '*Let go*.'

I don't let go. I *can't*.

The shop man whisks the scarf away.

Tiff holds up a bag. 'This one is from Stella.'

'McCartney?' I ask. 'The daughter of Sir Paul?'

'Yes,' says Tiff. 'That's the one.'

I gasp. I want it. I *need* it.

Tiff pulls out a crystal necklace, a purse and pretty belt. There's also a hat.

'Ooh, pretty,' I say.

'A Balenciaga beanie in oatmeal.'

I grab the cashmere hat from her hands – it's as soft as angels' wings. I rub the wool on my face.

The shop man glares at me. 'Please stop.' He grabs the hat. I grip it hard. It stretches.

'Be careful with that,' I say. 'Do you know how many goats died to make it? Or silk worms?'

'Neither,' he says. He gives me a look.

I watch him fold the beanie and leave it on the pile of clothes. It's such a waste. Such a shame.

Tiff rummages around inside the box. 'I think that's it . . . Oh no. I forgot all about these from Bulgari.'

She pulls out another bag. Inside are some sunglasses; they're black with gold flowers on the sides and dark brown ombré lenses.

I whimper.

Tiff hands them to the man. The gold flowers shimmer and sparkle in the light from the neon light blinking overhead.

'That's it!' she says. 'Thank you again. See you same time next week.'

'Yeah, cheers,' says the man, glaring at me.

Baby barks.

That's at least five grand's worth of stuff. It has to be.

Tiff picks up the dog. 'Let's go, Siobhán,' she says. 'Come on.'

I try to drag my eyes away from the sunglasses, but they won't budge.

The puppy barks again.

'Siobhán?' says Tiffany, walking over to the door. 'Siobhán? Siobhán? Siobhán?' She stands and holds the door open.

I turn to her and shout, 'Just a minute!'

I lean in towards the man and whisper in his ear. 'Put all this stuff on hold for me. *All* of it. Do you hear? I'll come back when I've been paid. You sell it: you're *dead*.'

I do wide eyes so he knows I'm not joking, then I back out of the shop, maintaining eye contact with him till I'm out on the street with the dog.

Tiff climbs into the waiting Bentley. I pick up the dog and join her.

'You do that *every* week?'

'Yes, I do,' she sighs. 'People keep on giving me clothes to wear on social media because I am an "influencer". And last night at my party I was really spoilt. I don't need any of it.'

'I could go to Oxfam for you? You know, with the dog . . . as a field trip?'

She laughs. 'It's fine. I don't mind doing it. I get a warm fuzzy feeling. I just love to *give*. Don't you?'

'I do . . . because I'm so spiritual.' We look out of the car window. I think about the stunning crystals on that necklace. 'Oh, I know, I've got one,' I say.

'OK, go for it.'

'I'm so fucking spiritual that I have a crystal that when you keep it in your pocket you can communicate with cats.'

She laughs. 'With *cats*? What do they say?'

'Not much. It's mostly about food. "Have you got any food? Give me some Go Cat." That kind of thing. It's boring. I've got another crystal that's better.'

'What does that one do?'

'If you leave it in your window in the light of the full moon, it makes you slightly less of a bitch when you have PMS.'

'Oh, I have one too,' says Tiff, joining in now. 'I have a crystal that when you wear it as an earring you can hear the sound of nuns.'

'*Nuns?*'

'They're yodelling psalms.'

I laugh. Tiff laughs. 'I love crystals,' she says, getting serious now. 'I love the fact that their beauty comes from their imperfections. If they were *perfect*, they'd have no colour. Crystals are like *people*.'

I nod and do a solemn face. 'That is very meaningful.'

Thursday, 11 August, 9 a.m.
Waitrose, Hampstead

Tiff gave me some petty cash to pop to the local Waitrose. I'm supposed to buy some fillet steaks. Baby doesn't eat *dog food*. The puppy sniffs and pulls on his lead. He barks at the sausages.

'*Earmuff! NO.*'

The butcher spots the dog and says, 'Sorry, miss, no dogs allowed.'

I should have hidden him under my top. *Damn.* I think on my feet.

'But you DO allow disability dogs and I am *blind*.'

'THAT is a *guide dog*?'

'Yes, it is.'

We stare each other out.

'Aren't they usually Labradors?'

'This is a Labrador, isn't it?'

The butcher looks at the tiny pug and sighs. He shakes his head.

'He is an EXCELLENT guide dog. I don't even need a cane!'

The butcher nods. I try not to laugh.

I pick Earmuff up and carry on with my shopping. He growls back at me. I sniff and the scent of fresh blood wafts and fills my nostrils. Oh God, I love the smell of a butcher's. I order a couple of grass-fed steaks from a man with a mullet. I watch as he slices up the meat and admire his stainless-steel cleaver. I head for the shelves with the pet food on and find some pouches of *Pedigree Chum*: 'Real meals in gravy'. It actually looks quite nice. There's a picture of juicy meat with bits of peas and carrot. That will do. I'll feed *this* to the puppy. These grass-fed steaks are for *me*. A dog that doesn't eat *dog food* – I've never heard anything so ridiculous in my whole damn life.

I pop next door to Snappy Snaps. I stick my phone's memory card into one of the photo machines. Huh, I could have used Bluetooth. I print out the pictures of Ed with the Savoy hookers to seven by five inches. That should be big enough. Ha! It doesn't look good for Ed. These pictures are dodgy as hell.

9.45 a.m.
The Bishops Avenue, Hampstead, London

I let myself into the Forbes' kitchen. There's nobody here. The chef has gone for his weekly shop to the food hall at

Fortnum and Mason. I leave the plastic bag on the work-top and snap the dog off his lead. He barks and barks and barks at the worktop. He must be hungry, like me. I look around the designer kitchen to find something to eat with my steak. Inside the fridge I spot a jar of Italian white Alba truffle, some Yubari King melons and a tin of Almas caviar. None of those things are right for my steak, so I go and look for a pantry.

I notice a door in the corner of the room. I wonder where that leads. I open the door on to stairs. The door swings shut behind me. It's suddenly pitch-black, like I'm blinded. I push on the door but it's stuck. Oh man. This is bad. You shouldn't go looking in people's cellars; you might live to regret it. A sinking feeling spreads through my stomach. I picture bodies, a monster or captives. I remember that movie, *Room. Damn it, Alvie, your curiosity is going to get you killed.*

I find a switch on the wall and flick it. The lights come on and hurt my eyes. *Get a grip, Alvina.* Row upon row of wine bottles stretch out down beyond the stairs. There are hundreds and hundreds of bottles of red. A few hundred whites. A few hundred champagnes. I must have died and gone to heaven. Heaven is a wine cave.

As I reach the bottom step, there's a shelf with a decanter, two crystal glasses and a 1945 jeroboam of Château Mouton Rothschild. The glasses sparkle in the light. My mouth is watering. I'd kill for a drink. Or a just a sip. I really want to taste it. I know. I know I'm sober now, but this is too good to miss. I would never forgive myself if I passed on a chance like this. There are *thousands* of bottles in here. The Forbes won't notice if I take *one*.

My fingers reach out to stroke the bottle and feel the

cool, smooth glass. I won't take *this* one; they might spot it's missing. I'll take one from right at the back. I like new strategic Alvie. I tuck a bottle under my arm then sprint back up the steps again. The door's not *stuck*. There's a knob and I twist. *Relax, Alvie. You're killing it.*

7 p.m.

Baby licks the silver bowl. He liked the Pedigree Chum. The steak is *delicious*. I cooked it bloody rare. I think the French call that '*bleu*', but it wasn't *blue* – it was *red*. I pop the last morsel into my mouth and chew. I study the label on the bottle I took from the wine cellar: 'Château Lafite, 1787'. Huh, that date must be wrong. I take a sip of the burgundy liquid then spit it out again. Urgh, that's *gross*. Is it *corked*? It tastes sour, bitter. I sniff it: damp basement or mouldy dog. I can't drink it, that's for sure. It's disgusting. *So* disappointing. It's a sign from the universe; I really shouldn't drink.

The pug waddles to his basket and lies down heavily on one side. His round fat belly is sticking out as though he's eaten a football. I hear a sound like faraway thunder: Baby's stomach rumbles.

'Siobhán?' comes a woman's voice.

Oh shit, that's Tiffany. Quick, hide the Pedigree Chum. I throw an empty dog food packet into the pedal bin.

'Ah, Siobhán, there you are,' she says as she walks in. She gives me a peck on the cheek.

'*Ciao.* What's up?' I say.

'I'm just checking on my love . . .'

Ed's not here. She means the dog, I think. Or me? No, no, the dog . . . definitely.

She bends down to pet the pug. She spots the bottle of red wine open on the kitchen worktop.

Tiffany emits a shriek just like a frightened parrot.

'Oh my God, what is it?' I ask.

'That wine . . . that wine . . . that wine,' she says, 'was owned by Jefferson.'

'Jefferson? Who's Jefferson?'

'The president, *Thomas Jefferson*.'

'He won't care. He's dead,' I say. That explains the date then.

'It was Ed's. A Christmas present. It cost a hundred and fifty thousand dollars. I bought it at auction in New York.'

'To be fair, I didn't know that.'

Tiffany picks up the bottle and cradles it in her arms. 'Look, his initials are carved on the glass.'

I shrug. 'That could be *anyone*. It wasn't very nice.'

'Of course it wasn't *nice*. It's a hundred-and-fifty-year-old claret. Clarets only last fifty years. I didn't buy it to *drink* it.'

I roll my eyes. *Be nice, Alvina. Remember why you're here . . .* I need to keep her on my side. I'll have to *apologize*.

'I'm *very* sorry, Tiffany,' I say with a straight face. 'I promise not to drink any more wine once owned by presidents.' I laugh, then cover my mouth with my hand. 'I really am sorry,' I say. 'Look, we can pour the wine back in and shove in the cork. Good as new. No one would notice.'

'Yes, Siobhán, *they would*.'

But Tiff laughs too as she watches me try to force the cork in the bottle. It doesn't fit and some wine spills out in a little puddle.

'It's fine,' she said, 'you didn't know and I overreacted. I forgive you. It's no big deal.'

Why is she being so *nice*?

'*You're the best*,' I say, and I mean it. No one's ever been this sweet to me. No one's given me so many chances . . . and for a moment I'm speechless. I look at the puddle on the counter and suddenly feel emotional. *Snap out of it, Alvie. Jeez.* I grab some kitchen roll and mop up all the dark red liquid.

'I'm sorry,' I say. 'It won't happen again.'

'Siobhán, relax. I'm over it.'

Baby whimpers in his basket. His stomach rumbles *again*. Tiff frowns at me and scoops up the dog. He whimpers louder this time.

'What's the matter, darling?' she says, rocking him in her arms like an infant.

Shit. Now what? Have I poisoned the dog? He doesn't look so well . . .

Baby flops in Tiffany's arms, his tongue lolling out dramatically.

'What did you feed him?' Tiffany asks. 'He's never behaved like this before.'

'Fillet steak, just like you said,' I say but glance at the pedal bin.

Tiffany looks where I am looking. A corner of the empty packet of Pedigree Chum sticks out of the lid. She looks at me.

I freeze. *Not good.* I don't speak. I don't move. I look down again at the empty packet.

Tiffany bends to grab it.

'No!' I say, but it's too late.

She holds up the packet and sniffs it. She wrinkles up her nose and gags.

'You are *fired*,' she says.

'Please. This isn't what it looks like . . .'

'And what does it look like?'

I rack my brains for an excuse, but I can't think of one.

'I'm taking him to the vet,' she says. 'Pack your things and leave.'

'Tiffany, no. I thought we were friends.'

'First the sauna, then the wine and now the baby,' she says.

'*Dog*.' I correct her. 'It's a *dog*.'

Tiffany gasps.

Oh my God. She's just like *Beth*, I convince myself. Spoilt. Manipulative . . . I grit my teeth. I tense my jaw. I wouldn't be her friend if you *paid* me, no matter how spiritual she is.

'OK, fine, whatever,' I say. 'You can't *fire* me because you never hired me. I was doing you a favour, remember? And you can't fire me because I quit. I don't want to work here anyway.'

I feel the heat rise to my cheeks and my voice is shaking. How dare she fire me! The cheek! And how am I going to do my hit if I'm not working here? This really fucks up my plans.

Jolene appears at the door with an iPad in one hand. 'Mrs Forbes, there you are,' she says. 'Is everything all right?'

Tiff doesn't speak. She hugs the dog.

Jessabelle continues, 'I wanted to confirm the schedule for the auction in Venice tomorrow?'

Venice? What? The tiny cogs in my brain begin to whir. I wasn't planning to kill her *tonight*, but it might be my only chance. (I'm not so bothered about killing her now. Tiff has broken my heart.)

The PA gives me a dirty look. I smile sweetly at her.

'I'll be with you soon, Jacinda. Wait for me in the lounge,' says Tiff.

'Of course, Mrs Forbes,' says Joanna, glaring at me as she leaves.

Tiffany turns to me and sighs. 'I'm *very* disappointed, but I wish you all the best. Please give Fifi the keys for the cottage on your way out,' she says.

No. No. She can't go. She can't *leave*. I need to do something. But what? Then I remember the card up my sleeve. Luckily it's an *ace*.

'Wait, Tiff. Before you go, there's something you need to see. I didn't want to show you, but . . .'

Tiffany frowns. 'What is it?'

I reach for my Birkin. I knew these would come in useful.

'They were posted *anonymously*. I don't know who took them, but as you can see . . . it doesn't look good. I'm really, *really* sorry.'

I hand her the shots of her husband with the hookers at the Savoy. I watch as she studies the photos of Ed and her face turns pale.

'It's like Hugh Grant all over again getting nicked off Sunset Boulevard. Why would he go out for *burgers* when he has *steak* at home?'

I pace the driveway up and down. I wish I had a Marlboro. Tiff and Ed are fighting upstairs. Tiff's voice is getting louder. A window is open on the top floor and their words spill out. Ed says, 'That is *not* my bottom.' Tiffany says, '*Please!*' I check the time: it's half past nine. They've been yelling for nearly an hour. Something smashes – a glass? A vase? Their voices are getting shriller. A high-pitched shriek escapes from the window. A bird cries. Is it a raven? It's loud. It's chaos. Probably the whole road can hear them. They can hear them in *Archway*. This is perfect, actually. The louder the better. But hopefully no one calls the cops. That would be problematic. Tiffany flipped when she saw the pics. Everything's going to plan. This is it. It's *happening*. I am SO excited. Everyone will think that Tiff and Ed had a big row, then Tiff will mysteriously 'disappear', and suspicion will rest on the husband.

> *I am Hela, the*
> *Goddess of death. I am*
> *Diana, the hunter.*

How am I going to do it then? What would Jason Bourne do? I need some kind of weapon, obvs. Something *innocuous*. I glance at the fish pond. Six koi carp are floating at the surface. Huh. What's up with all the fish? They're motionless, their bellies up. The water looks kind of *murky*. That's strange. They seemed just fine before. I prod one with a finger and it floats across the water.

I spot the ornamental frog sitting by the fish pond.

It's the size of a cantaloupe: bug eyes and glazed green skin. The thing is hideous, grotesque, but I bet it cost a fortune. Tiffany probably picked it up at one of her fancy auctions.

'Kermit, you ugly motherfucker, come to momma,' I say.

I grab the ceramic frog and weigh it in my hands. Heavy. Yes, yes, this will do very nicely. Ideally I'd use a gun, but needs must, I suppose.

Excitement bubbles up inside me as I approach the house.

I press the button to call the lift that leads up to the Forbes' suite. Time is of the essence now. I must expedite my plan. If Tiffany has thrown me out, then I can't lurk around the house waiting for the perfect moment to strike. I must act NOW.

The doors ping open. I step inside the lift and poke my head out. I look both ways in case someone should see, the maid or the chef or the butler, but there is nobody. I press the button for the top floor and up to the Forbes' suite. The doors swish shut and it's suddenly quiet. A shiver runs down my spine.

I study myself in the mirror. Wow. The lighting's *incredibly* flattering. I have my mother's high cheekbones and tonight I look *exquisite*. There's something about the ginger hair . . . It brings out the green in my eyes. Being Siobhán is really growing on me.

The lift pings and I creep out. I can hear voices again.

Tiffany says, 'How could you, Ed?'

Ed says, 'But I *didn't*.'

I tiptoe down the corridor till I find the airing

cupboard. It's in the hall a few feet down from the Forbes' suite. The wooden door has narrow slats. I open it and squeeze inside. I pull the door shut. Man, it's cramped. I hope this won't take long. I feel the sleeping pills in my pocket. I count them: one, two, three, four. Now all I need is for James, Ed's butler, to come up with Ed's nightcap.

I find the plastic gloves for the dog poo in my jacket pocket. They are stretchy too-tight latex. They make a snapping sound as I put them on. I don't want bloody fingerprints all over the Forbes' suite. It's stupid shit like that that gets you caught and I intend to walk free. I've stuffed a see-through pakamac inside the other pocket. It's the kind you buy at festivals to keep the weather off. I found it hanging in the dog's suite with his leads and squeaky toys. I pull it on just in case. I can easily take it off again if I hear the lift and James coming up. But I have to be *prepared*.

I sigh and close my eyes. Oh man, I wish Nino were here.

But I screw my courage to the sticking place.

I wait. And wait. And wait.

I check the time on my Samsung phone. It's nine forty-nine. I have eleven minutes until James comes up with Ed's nightcap.

Hurry up, hurry up, hurry up.

All is quiet. The voices have stopped. I strain my ears to hear. A handle clicks and footsteps pad. A door creaks as it opens. Somebody walks down the hall. Who is it? Tiff or Ed? Or is it James, the butler? Damn, I can't tell from in here. The spaces in between the slats darken as a figure passes. I open the cupboard door – a crack – and see the back of Tiff's head. Shit. She's leaving. It's now or never. But what about my plan? Ed's still awake, but I have to act. I gawk at Tiffany's head. Her blonde hair swishes and sways like a pony's. She looks like Beth from this angle. I close my eyes. *You can do it, Alvie. Nino's right here with you.*

But all I can think of is my *friend*. It's *Tiffany*. She *hugged* me. She said she *loved me* for God's sake.

I open my eyes. *Come on.*

I push through the door and lurch down the corridor, raising the frog above my head. Tiffany turns and we lock eyes; my stomach churns and flips.

'Siobhán?'

I pause. I open my mouth, but no words come out. *I'm sorry*, I want to say. *I'm not perfect. I'm a crystal.* Something deep like that. Instead I bring the frog down hard. I act without thinking. My muscles have a memory of all the times I've done this.

CRACK.

Kermit smashes into her skull and blood splatters my arm. Tiff falls back and I catch her, dropping the frog on my big toe.

'Ow. OW.' That *really* hurt. I bite my lip to stop myself screaming. Have I broken my foot? *Bad, bad frog.*

Tiffany sinks into my arms. It's lucky I'm wearing the mac.

What have I done? 'Tiff? Are you all right?'

Her body slumps against my chest. She doesn't reply. I stagger backwards under her weight.

My best friend! My soul sister!

A streak of blood snakes through her blonde hair, so

red it looks like ketchup. Her eyes roll back into their sockets.

I shake her. 'Tiff!' I hiss.

I think I'm having an asthma attack and I don't even have asthma.

'NO. NO. I didn't mean it. Tiffany? Talk to me.'

I slap her once across the face. Her head lolls to one side.

Oh God. Oh Shit. What time is it? Should I take her to hospital? Surely it is not too late? I bet Ed's got a helicopter. We could whisk her to A and E. We could patch her up and given her some Lemsip and act as if nothing has happened.

I open her eyelid and study the pupil. It is as wide as a saucer. *It's too late, Alvie. Tiff is* dead. *Finish the fucking job.*

I drag her backwards into the cupboard and try to bundle her inside, but she flops against the shelves. I was angry because she *fired* me. She shouldn't have fucking *fired* me. Oh God. *We could still be friends.* I was seeing *red.* God damn it. Sometimes I get so cross. Tiff's legs buckle and I drop her. She sprawls across the hall; her limbs splay out in every direction.

Hurry up, Alvie. Move it.

Warm blood trickles to the floor. I'll have to clean that up.

The lift pings somewhere downstairs. The mechanics begin to whir. I take a sharp breath. I have less than a minute. Things are getting tense.

I kneel down and roll her in. I chuck the frog in after her.

'Stay in there and shut up, Kermit.' The frog lands with a clunk.

I crouch down and wipe up the blood with a fluffy

towel. I scrub at the floor until it's all gone. My heart bu-bump, bu-bumps.

The lift's getting louder. Someone's coming up.

I pull off the mac and shove it in the cupboard. I check my clothes for signs of blood. The doors to the lift open just as I close the door. I wipe my mouth on the back of my hand. Shit, I'm still wearing the gloves! I whip them off and shove them in my pocket, and look up and see the butler. Tiff was right: James always brings Ed's nightcap up at 10 p.m. on the dot. Look at that: he's right on time. I flash him a smile. He's wearing a smart white suit with a white tie and waistcoat. Whoa, that is *a lot* of white. Better keep him away from the blood. He steps out of the lift to the hall with what looks like a glass of whisky balanced on a silver tray. *Awesome.* That Scotch is just what I need for my new and improved plan.

I look down and spot Tiff's fingers sticking out from the cupboard door. I freeze. Four fingers are poking out under the wood. It takes me a moment to react. I jump – electrocuted – then take a step back to stand over her hand with my body between Tiff and James. Don't look down. Do *not* look down. If he sees *that*, I'm screwed. There's no way I could explain a *corpse* in the laundry cupboard . . .

'Hi,' I say, as he approaches. My heart pounds in my throat. I'm sweating like I'm at a rave and on five grams of coke. 'We haven't met. I'm, er . . . *Siobhán.*'

'Are you all right?' he asks.

Why? What's wrong? Do I look strange? I manage a nod.

'James,' he says, as we shake hands. He frowns at my

sweaty palm. I wipe my hand on my thigh. 'Jacinda told me about you.'

Breathe, Alvina. Breathe. Breathe. I look up into his face with my eyes as wide as the frog's. James is *cute*: an eight out of ten. Dark hair and light blue eyes. He reminds me of Harry Styles. I get a whiff of something seductive: Christian Dior's Sauvage? His outfit gleams like he's just washed it in a vat of Daz.

'Well, I know who *you* are,' I say, trying not to sound creepy. 'I've heard all about you from Tiff and Ed.'

'Oh?'

'All *good*,' I say. 'I think you're their favourite.'

He laughs. 'Of course I am. And you are Tiffany's latest then?'

'Huh?'

'You're the dog's new "nanny"?' He winks.

'I am.' I lean in and whisper, 'It's not a *dog*; it's a *baby*.'

'Of course. How could I forget?'

I glance at the tray and my eyes linger on the glass of whisky. Better late than never, I guess. *The best-laid plans of mice and men* . . .

'I can take that drink for you. I'm just going in anyway.' I beam at James.

He doesn't flinch. '*I* always give it to Ed.'

I widen my smile and grit my teeth.

'We don't *both* need to disturb him. It sounded like they were busy in there.' *Come on.* I hold my breath. I clench my fists. I'm sure that he is going to refuse. 'They've been fighting like cats and dogs. Things were getting *nasty*. Let me take it in.'

James looks at his feet. Shit. Fuck. *Do not look down.* He'll see the fingers! I shuffle around so my feet are positioned right over her hand.

He changes the subject. 'Hey,' he says, ' Did you see what happened to the fish?'

I shake my head.

'It's so weird. All of them are *dead.*'

I panic. How can I persuade him? I don't care about the fish. We stand there for a moment in silence, then I get an idea.

'Jacinda doesn't like me, does she?' I say in my most wounded voice.

James frowns. 'It's just that, well, she was Tiffany's favourite, you know, before you came along. She's jealous, that's all.'

I look into his eyes and bite my lip. I let my eyes fill with tears. (I imagine I'm chopping an onion with fumes like mustard gas.)

'I don't know what I've done wrong. I really wish she liked me.'

'Don't worry. She'll come round. She just . . . *really* likes Tiff.'

I sigh and look at the drink on the tray and let my eyes do the talking. The tension builds while I wait . . . and wait.

'OK. Cheers, Siobhán,' says James, handing me the drink on the tray. 'Catch you later then.'

Yes! It worked. I can breathe again.

'Catch you later, James.'

I watch him get back in the lift. He gives me a funny look, but then he waves as the doors swish shut and I give him a cheery wave back. The lift's mechanics begin to whir as the lift descends. My heart is going batshit now. That was intense. But the last thing I need right now is a cardiac arrest.

I look down at Tiffany's fingers sticking out under the door like the wicked witch's feet from that house in *The Wizard of Oz*. Tiff wasn't a *bad* witch, though. She was a really *good* witch. She was Glinda and I'm the fucking tin man with no heart. I kick her hand back into the cupboard and close the door. *Phew*. I reach into my jacket pocket to find the sleeping pills. I need Ed *fast* asleep for this bit. I don't want him waking up and busting me with a *corpse*. I crack the capsules and shake the powder into the glass. Not too much, but just enough. I don't want to *poison* him. Ha ha. Not yet. That's bullet point number *seven*.

Round about the cauldron go, in the poison'd entrails throw.

I stir the mixture with my finger. All I need is a broomstick and hat.

10 p.m.

I knock on the door.

'Come in,' says Ed.

I enter the room. I wince. My foot is *killing* from the frog. I try not to limp like a muppet. Ow. It really fucking hurts. I probably need an X-ray. But there's not a lot you can do with a toe. Just strap it up. Paracetamol.

Ed is sitting on the bed in his boxer shorts. He jumps up when he sees me coming.

'Siobhán? I'm so sorry,' he says. He grabs a pillow to cover himself. 'I thought you were *James*.'

'Oh no, *I'm* so sorry,' I say. 'I was looking for Tiff, but I can see that she's not here.'

I try to tear my eyes away from his naked torso, but his abs are too damn fine and I like his shoulders also. My mind fills with fantasies of the maid and master. I'd love to find a frilly little black-and-white French number. Ordinarily, of course, I would hop right on. I'd ride that pony until sunrise. We wouldn't stop until dawn. But these aren't ordinary times. I'm a woman on a mission. There are more important things than *sex*. (See how focused I am?) Also, as I'm sure you'll recall, we're still on bullet point number four. The whole *seducing and marrying Ed* thing will have to come later on.

'James asked me to bring this in. I wanted to ask Tiff if it was OK for me to book the dog in for a manicure.'

'Thanks,' he says, taking the glass. I watch him as he sips it.

My eyes flick down to the floor and I blush and – I don't know why – I *curtsy*.

'I'm ever so sorry again, Mr Forbes.' Our eyes meet. I bite my lip.

'Please, just call me Ed.'

I curtsy again and limp out.

I close the door and do a silent fist pump. Yes! He drank it! He didn't notice anything strange about his Scotch at all. I hobble to the airing cupboard. My toe's probably broken. Or fractured. I bet it's gone *purple*. Gross.

I open the cupboard door and Tiff falls out, so I pick her up and bundle her back in again. There's not much room for the two of us, Kermit and the towels. Tiff's head flops against my shoulder. Her blood runs down my arm.

Damn, it's getting all over the towels. I'll have to take them and burn them.

I stroke Tiff's hair and softly sing a verse of the Irish lullaby 'Too-Ra-Loo-Ra-Loo-Ral'.

'I'm sorry, Tiff,' I whisper. 'I wish things could have been different between us, but, you know: Nino, the cash . . . and you did go and *fire* me, which wasn't very nice.'

I check the time on the phone in my pocket. I'll give it half an hour. Ed should be sound asleep by then. Then I'll crack on with my plan.

10.45 p.m.

I pull on the pakamac and gloves and tiptoe out of the cupboard. It's *way* too hot for this plastic coat, but I'm not taking any chances. I tap-tap-tap on Ed's bedroom door, then lean in close to hear. Hopefully he's fast asleep, but what if he opens the door? How do I explain my *look*? I haven't thought this through. I'll have to declare my lust for him and pretend I couldn't sleep. Yes, that should do the trick. 'You're *irresistible*.' Flattery always works. The pakamac and gloves could pass as (very niche) fetish gear.

My mouth is dry. I wait. And wait. I consider running back and hiding in the airing cupboard, but I pause. I wait. I press my ear against the door. All is quiet inside. I tap again just to be sure, then open up the door and stick my head through the gap. It's dark, but I can see Ed's figure sleeping beneath the blanket. Soft snores float up from the super-king-size bed. He is out of it.

I run back down the corridor and open up the cupboard door. I grab Tiff underneath her arms and pull her out again. I wrap a bloody towel round her head in a makeshift turban to stop the blood making a mess, then I drag her down the hall. I limp backwards through Ed's door, pushing it open with my bum. I drag the body along behind me. Man, this is hard work. Dead folk are surprisingly heavy and my foot is fucked. Even though Tiff's a size six, it feels like she's obese, like one of those people who can't fit through doors and have to be airlifted out. My muscles strain. I huff and puff. I *wish* I could airlift her. But I don't stop. I keep on going. All that crap with dead lifts and weights has finally paid off.

I check the tumbler on the table – it's empty; he drank it all! Great, that should give me a couple of hours. I don't want surprises. I heave the corpse across the room and past the Badminton Cabinet. I drag it into the en suite, close the door and lock it.

I stand and pant with my back to the door. I flick on the light. My eyes adjust. I squint at the corpse. Urgh, I'm really sweating. This plastic pakamac is like wearing a greenhouse. The night feels hot and stuffy. Moist. I grab Tiffany by the ankles and pull her legs into the tub. I take the body by the wrists, bend down and haul it in. The corpse lands with a clunk and a thud inside the oval bathtub. I stand with my hands on my hips and admire my handiwork. I'm torn: I feel bad about killing Tiff, but proud I've got this far. And there's something very satisfying about crossing items off a to-do list.

The story is, Ed and Tiff had a fight, then Ed got drunk and did *this*. He flipped. The French call it a *crime passionnel* or something. His mind will be blank. He won't remember bashing his wife in her pretty little head.

But what about the murder weapon? There's no way he would use that frog. My eyes trail round the en suite. What could he have used? There's a loo brush by the loo, a glass on the shelf by the sink, a ceramic soap dish on the bath in the shape of a scalloped shell. Yes, it's perfect. I'll use that . . . I grab the soap dish and leave it on the floor in Tiffany's blood so it looks like a weapon. I unwind the red-stained towel I wrapped round Tiffany's head.

I hear a sound. Did Tiff make a noise? No. No way. She's *dead*.

At that moment Tiff starts to move; she's trying to sit up. 'Argh,' I scream. '*What the fuck?*'

I stagger backwards from the tub; my feet slip in the blood.

'Help!' she says.

'I thought you were *dead*?'

Oh God. Oh God. Oh God.

I clutch my hands to my chest; she nearly gave me a heart attack. Why the hell is she still alive? This wasn't the plan. Did she have another NDE? What is *wrong* with her?

Tiff starts sobbing silent tears. Her mouth hangs open; her eyes are wide.

She grabs the edge of the bath and tries to get out. Her fingers leave red streaks on the tub. She's making a big mess.

'Wait there,' I say. This is bad. Very Bad. 'I'll go and get some help.'

Damn, I need to finish her off. I haven't killed her properly.

I'm about to leave the room, when Nino materializes.

The Samurai sword, he says in my head. (We communicate telepathically.)

'Oh yeah! I forgot about that. Great idea,' I say.

I was going to fetch the *frog*, but on second thoughts the Samurai sword would be more effective as a murder weapon.

I push past him and open the door a crack then creep out quietly. The light from the bathroom spills out in an orange glow on the floor. I hear a noise. Ed stirs in his sleep and rolls on to his side. Tiffany's scream has roused him, but he carries on snoring. Thank fuck for that. I'll have to be quiet.

I tiptoe through the bedroom to the sword on the wall. Nino is a *genius*. I climb on to the bedside table and reach up to grab it. It's cold and smooth. I test the blade; it's sharp, almost as sharp as my sushi knife. Then I hear a noise from the en suite. Tiff's climbing out of the tub!

I jump down from the bedside table and the floorboards creak, but Tiff's still sitting in the bath. She screams when she sees me coming with the massive sword in my hands. I have no time to think or question what I need to do. I'm on autopilot now and have hysterical strength. I grip the handle with both hands and slash her once across the throat. The blood spills out like Niagara Falls; a crimson fountain splashes the walls. It splatters all over the tub and the floor, as shiny as fresh paint.

I close my eyes and breathe in deep.

I hear her voice in my head . . .

'*I'm so fucking spiritual that I have an NDE every time I close my eyes.*'

'*What's an NDE?*'

'*A near-death experience.*'

'*Don't you need to die?*'

'*Every time I blink, I die.*'

'*That is very spiritual.*'

'*I have to be careful not to wink. That can get confusing. You know, a bit like Schrödinger's cat?*'

'*Schrödinger has a cat?*'

'*Alive and dead at the same time.*'

'*Yeah, that is confusing.*'

12 p.m.

I study the his and hers sinks, but which one is which? Hmm. The one with the razor must be Ed's. I'll use that one. I run the cold tap in Ed's sink and scrub the blood from my gloves. I wash my arms, my face and neck. I clean my pakamac. I make sure that I get it all off. This stuff is *incriminating*.

I shove the mac into my pocket. It folds up really nicely. The material's super thin. It would be practical for Glastonbury. I grab the bloody towel and pull on the gloves again. I pick up the Samurai sword from the floor. I wish I could keep it. My eyes trail the blood-soaked room; it looks like an abattoir. I feel a twinge of something. *No.* I don't have time for this. No regrets. No fucking soppy sentimentalism. I can't think about what I've done. I've just got to get on with it.

Right, now hurry up, Alvie. I've got to run. Got to hide. And I've got to lose the frog. Got to burn these towels to ashes.

The blood is pumping through my veins. I feel so alive.

My heart skips a beat as I tiptoe through the door out to the Forbes' suite. I grip the Samurai sword and leave a trail of blood on the floorboards, so it's obvious something's up. Ha. I make a big old mess. It's all part of my plan. I stand over the bed. Ed is lying there, dreaming. I wipe some of the blood from the sword on to Ed's open hands. A little blood on his face, perhaps? A few drops on his arms. I hold up the Samurai sword and drip some blood on his cheek. Ooh, it's like a Jackson Pollock, all I need is some blue and some black and I'll have a masterpiece.

I lay the sword down on the quilt within Ed's fingers' grasp. I wrap his fingers round the hilt, slowly, carefully.

Don't wake up. Do not wake up.

Not yet anyway. (I need him to wake up eventually, so we can go on a date.)

What else? I need him to think *he* did it. Yes. It's brilliant. I go back into the en suite and pull some strands of hair from Tiff's head. She always had such lovely hair. It seems a shame to break it. I grab six or seven strands. They lie like spun gold in my fingers. Yes, that should be enough. I tiptoe back to the bedroom and scatter the hairs on to Ed's hands, winding the strands through his fingers. I step back and study the scene. Wow. We could be in *Hollywood*. If *I* woke up like that, I'd be *sure* that I had done the deed, but then I am a *serial killer.* I wouldn't need much persuading.

I grin. There's *no way* Ed will call the cops after *this*

spectacle. Even if he's not convinced that he killed Tiff himself, he'll know he looks as guilty as hell. It's incriminating as fuck.

I sneak out of the room and grab the frog. I remember to fold up the towels so that none of the blood is showing. I call the lift. It pings. I step inside and press the button for the ground floor. I lean on the mirror, breathing hard. I'm *so* good at this.

I creep out into the hall. It's late. There's no one around. I run out through the front door and on to the gravel drive.

It's dark. It's almost midnight now. There's the sound of footsteps passing on the street outside. I freeze. Who is it now? I hear the clickety-click of heels. A woman passes the house. Oh help. Is it Jemima? Or Venus? Security lights flick on. I'm blinded. I remember the CCTV. But the cameras look out at the road and not at *me*. I stand very, *very* still until I'm sure the woman passes. I wait till the lights flick off. That was close. That was *lucky*.

I rinse the frog in the murky pond and pop it back in its place on the ledge above the pond. No one will know it was missing. The creature's glazed ceramic eyes stare back at me, unblinking. Wherever I go, it's watching me, like the *Mona Lisa*.

'What the fuck are you looking at, Kermit?'

I stand and glare and dare the thing to move or blink, but it doesn't. *Relax, Alvina, it's a frog. Frogs can't talk.*

Second Stasimon

Perhaps I was destined to be a killer? Murder runs in our family. It's a genetic thing like sickle-cell anaemia. My mother's a killer; my gran was too. I remember a story she told me. It made a real impression on me. Yes, it was a corker. She saved it for her deathbed. I always remember her fondly. She wasn't just a little old lady, sweet and endearing with soft grey hair and a penchant for sherry; she was a fucking *badass*.

SIXTEEN YEARS AGO

'Beth,' she said – she meant *Alvina* – 'come here, I want to tell you something.'

It pissed me off that she called me Beth. She did it all the time. Sometimes she even called me Mavis or Philip (my uncle's name).

'Yes, Gran?' I said, sitting down next to her on a rocking chair.

'During the war,' her story began, as so many of them seemed to do, 'something *terrible* happened.'

'No shit, Sherlock,' I replied. 'Wasn't that the point? Isn't war supposed to be *terrible*? Otherwise, why bother?' I watched Gran sip her milky tea and dunk in her custard cream. 'Just to be clear, which war was this? The first, second or Crimean?'

'The Crimean? Bloody hell. How old do you think I am?'

'I don't know. A *hundred and one*?'

'I'm seventy-four. The Crimean War ended in February 1856. I mean the Second World War.'

'So, what happened?' I stifled a yawn.

'As you know, I grew up in Jersey, which was occupied by the Nazis during the Second World War.'

'Was it? I didn't know that. But you guys kicked them out again, right?'

'What are they teaching you at school?'

'Don't know. I got expelled.'

'Anyway, as you can imagine, things were *very* difficult. I was only a child at the time, but I remember it well.'

'How old were you when they invaded?'

'I had just turned ten. The Germans bombed St Helier harbour and I lost my best friend. We were walking down the street and we were laughing and joking. She was telling me about a boy she liked and they had even kissed! She stopped to tie up her shoelace and I walked a few feet ahead. I heard the shell before I felt it. That day nine people died. But that is not the terrible thing.'

'It isn't?'

'There's something else.'

I glanced at my watch. It was five to three. Gran's stories could be lengthy and I didn't want to miss *Round the Twist*.

'How long is this going to take?'

'My father had joined the army, so I lived with my mum

and my brother, but because we had a big house we had to take in some Nazis.'

'What, you let them stay *with you*?'

'We didn't have much choice. Six young men in battle-dress showed up one day at the house. My mother was baking in the kitchen. I was playing in the orchard with Fred. The soldiers moved into the bedrooms upstairs and we slept downstairs in the kitchen. My mother suddenly had six more mouths to feed. Six grown men can get through food like you wouldn't believe. She used to make incredible cakes, fruit tarts and real plum puddings. My brother and I used to gather the fruit from our allotment garden.'

'I can't believe you *baked* for them when they'd just killed your friend.'

'Ever since I could remember, my mother used to say, "When you eat the apricots, you must throw the stones away." Apricot kernels contain something called amygdalin. If you ingest it, the body turns amygdalin into cyanide.'

'Cyanide? That's *awesome*.'

Gran nodded and smiled. Fine lines spread in crows feet from the corners of her eyes. 'Ingesting just *one* apricot kernel can be lethal for a child. Now, I'd been eating apricots sitting under that gnarled old tree for ten years, give or take. There was a big pile of stones in the grass beneath the tree. That's a lot of amygdalin. One night, while everyone else was asleep, I snuck out to collect them. I sat for hours at the bottom of the garden cracking open the kernels with a rusty hammer that belonged to my father. I scraped out the flesh inside the stones and stored it in a jam jar. I must have cracked hundreds of stones. My fingers were red-raw.

'The next day, I persuaded my mother to bake her famous apricot tart. I remember the smell of it baking in the oven like it was yesterday. The scent of shortcrust pastry wafted into the garden where I was playing with little Fred. We were playing cowboys and Indians.

'Once the pastry shell was crisp, it was time to add the filling. You don't add the filling before you've baked the base. Are you listening, Elizabeth? There is *nothing* worse than a soggy bottom.'

'Nothing worse,' I agreed.

'I added the jar of amygdalin when my mother wasn't looking. I gave it a good old stir with the sugar and apricots.'

'I think I can guess what's coming,' I say.

My gran sighed and closed her eyes. Her head sank into the pillow. The effort of telling her tale was exhausting.

Come on, get to the good bit.

'The tart was ready just before the soldiers came back home. I told my mother and my brother, *Do not eat the tart.*

'"Why not?" my mother asked. "I spent all afternoon making it. I deserve a slice at least."

'"I can't tell you why," I said, "but this apricot tart is just for the *soldiers*. Please, it's *very* important."

'Eventually she agreed.'

I shifted my rocking chair a little closer to the bed. Gran's voice was growing fainter and I wanted to hear the rest.

'That night, for dessert after a dinner of chicken and potatoes, the Nazis tucked into the tart with a dollop of cream. I watched the men swallow it down and help themselves to seconds. My mother, my brother and I sat and watched them chewing. I was sick with nerves. By the time that they were done, there was only one slice left. We didn't have a fridge back then, so my mother covered it up with a clean tea towel and left it on the sideboard.'

'Grandma, you're a *legend*,' I said. 'Please tell me they died?'

My grandma chuckled and smoothed the blanket on her eiderdown.

'Within a few minutes I could hear the men were breathing faster. Their faces turned waxy. Their eyes were glassy. A few of them fainted. They were the lucky ones.'

'Oh, Grandma, this is *epic*.'

Gran paused. She took a sip of tea. The cup clinked on the saucer.

'I glanced at the sideboard expecting to see the apricot tart still there covered by the tea towel, but the tart and the tea towel were gone. Fred was staring back at me like a little ghost.'

'Oh my God. Fred ate the tart. He ate it, didn't he?'

'I froze to the spot. I couldn't move. I felt sick to my stomach. Fred had finished the tart. It was the worst thing that could have happened. My mother flew out of the house, but it took her over an hour to fetch the doctor. I sat on the kitchen floor and sobbed, watching the soldiers die, one by one. I held on to my brother's hand. I remember his skin was clammy.

'By the time my mother and the doctor arrived, I was sitting on the kitchen floor surrounded by seven dead bodies.'

'Holy shit, what happened next? What did the doctor say?'

'He knew straight away it was poisoning, but couldn't say from what. He never suspected me or my mother because my brother had died. To this day everyone thinks a British soldier did it. No one knew *who*, but whoever it was he was deemed a *hero*.'

'You killed *seven* people in one night and didn't get any credit? You must have been so pissed off. I mean . . . it's a shame about Fred.'

Gran shook her head. 'I never told anyone that story. I was too ashamed. I never forgave myself for Fred's death. My mum kept quiet till her grave. I'm telling you now because I thought you should know who I really am before it is too late.'

I slapped my gran on the back. 'You are a *war hero*, Gran! You're a fucking *boss*.'

That night my gran died in her sleep. I was with her at the time (my mum and Beth were on a cruise in Mallorca or something). I held her hand all night long, but I didn't *kill her*.

Third Episode

Friday, 12 August, 1 a.m.
The Bishops Avenue, Hampstead, London

I push through the door to my cottage and flick on the light. I stand with my back pressed to the door and listen: everything's quiet.

'Nino?' I whisper.

There's no reply.

He isn't here. There's no one.

I make my way to the fireplace and dump the towels in the grate. I chuck the plastic gloves in too. The pakamac. Then I draw the curtains in case a member of staff is being nosy.

I rummage around in my Birkin and find my Zippo lighter, then crouch down low and light the corner of a fluffy towel. I know it's strange to light a fire in a heatwave in August, but I don't really have a choice. And at this time no one will notice. They're all asleep over there in the house. But if anyone asks about it, I'll say I was *freezing* and caught a summer cold. Yes, that should do it.

The flames are spreading easily. I sit back and watch. I hug my knees into my chest and lose myself in the blaze. I love the crackling sound it makes. I gaze at the dancing colours.

Yellow, orange, red . . .
It reminds me of fires I
Started as a child.

The forest fire last year in Rome. The villa I torched in Taormina. I sigh. The blaze looks *beautiful*. It makes me want to be *in* it, like Joan of Arc or the Knights Templar.

The fire goes wild (it's lucky I took the batteries out of the fire alarm). The flames jump high when they reach the plastic raincoat. The air is filled with the acrid stench of burning chemicals. I cough as fumes fill the living room. Thick black smoke tastes like petrol. It doesn't take long for the fire to consume the towels and everything else. I sit and watch till the flames die down and then there are just ashes. That was fun. I stretch and yawn. Bedtime. I have a big day tomorrow.

5 a.m.

'*I'm so fucking spiritual that I sleep with a Tarot pack under my pillow every night.*'

'*That's a great idea.*'

'*Every morning I shuffle the cards and I will not get up if I pick the Ten of Swords. I just stay in bed. I try again the next morning. And the next. And the next. Once I kept on picking that card, so I stayed in bed for a week. It was ace. I got Deliveroo and watched a ton of Netflix.*'

'*The Ten of Swords? What does that mean?*'

'*I have no idea, but the picture is of a man with ten swords stuck in his back.*'

'*Ooh, that's nasty. Much safer in bed.*'

'*It's why I'm still alive.*'

173

I keep having conversations with Tiff inside my head. It's weird. Remembering old conversations we had. Imagining new ones. I hear her voice as I stare at the ceiling. This time she's on about Tarot. I can't sleep. I toss and turn. I'm worrying that Tiffany told Ed or Jasmine or someone else about me being fired. I need everyone to think that we were on good terms. I need to keep my nanny job. The only way I can work on Ed is if I'm in his house. I bite my nails. I'm pretty sure she wouldn't have had time to mention anything to Ed about me being fired. I think she left the dog's suite and went straight upstairs to Ed. So Juliet won't know a thing. I think I'm safe. I *think*. And now that Tiff is definitely dead (she *definitely* is this time) I'm on bullet number five of my plan: *Seduce Ed.*

Eventually I fall asleep, but then I wish I hadn't. I have The Nightmare, the one I've had on repeat since I was a child . . .

'Get in the attic.'

'No, I don't want to.'

Mum pushes me up the ladder that leads into the roof of our house.

'No, Mum, not *again*.'

'You're not coming down until you've finished the Rubik's cube.'

'I can't, Mum. It's *dark* up there.'

I stumble into the pitch-black attic as Mum slams the door shut behind me. All I can see is a thin square of light framing the trapdoor. I trip over a wooden beam and land with a thump on the floor.

'Mum? Mum? Mum? Mum?'

She doesn't reply.

I bang, bang, bang on the trapdoor. I try to pull the handle. I yank at the thing until my hands are bruised and my nails are broken. But the door is locked from the outside and there's no other way out. I feel the panic rise in my chest.

I'm going to die in here.

I sit in the dark and hug my knees, the Rubik's cube in my hand. All I did was say it's not fair that Beth gets pocket money. I don't get a single thing: no money, no clothes, no sweets. Hot tears well and slide down my cheeks. I wipe them away again.

It's cold up here. A freezing draught blows through a hole in the roof. I can hear the howling wind and rain that beats like a drum. It tastes of dust and rotting wood. It smells of damp. There's the *drip, drip, drip, drip* of a leak somewhere far away.

'Argh!' What's that? A spider? A rat? Something runs over my foot. I throw the Rubik's cube at it. *Did I hit it? Did I miss?*

I grope around on the ground in the dark. I can't find the Rubik's cube. Now there's no way I can do it. Not that I ever could. Even if I peeled off the stickers, I can't see past the end of my nose, so how would I put them in the right places? I'll be stuck here forever.

I feel the tears coming again.

No, Alvina, stop it. What doesn't kill you makes you stronger. Pull yourself together.

I flop down on the wooden floor and curl up like a foetus. I need to get some thicker skin. I need to grow a backbone. I don't know how long I lie here. I'm too scared to sleep. The house makes creepy groaning sounds, as though it were in pain. The pipes moan. The floorboards creak . . . I curl up even smaller.

Mum is such a cow. I hate her. This is so unfair.

I could be here for a week or a month. Nobody would care.

I sniff and shiver in the darkness. One day I'll run away. Mum and Beth won't see me again. I'll be happy. *Free.*

Eventually, when I'm about to pass out with exhaustion, I hear footsteps downstairs.

I jump up and bang on the door.

'LET ME OUT. LET ME OUT. LET ME OUT.'

'Alvie? Is that you?' It's Beth. That's my sister's voice: breezy and carefree.

'BETH! LET ME OUT,' I shout.

The bolt slides in the lock. There's a blinding flash of light as the trapdoor opens.

'What are you doing up there, silly? Come down here,' she says. 'Look, do you like my new dress? I got it in Topshop.'

She spins around in a bright pink thing with ruffles like a bird. I don't reply. I won't. Or can't. I shield my eyes from the light. I blink, blink, blink around the attic. Oh my God, what's *that*? A brown mouse lies by the Rubik's cube. It's dead. Its spine is broken. I pick it up by its thin pink tail and peer into its lifeless eyes. It *was* alive, but I killed it. It's *my* fault it died . . .

I climb down the ladder with the mouse.

I show my twin. She screams.

I suddenly feel powerful, like I am a supervillain.

At 5.30 a.m. the alarm goes off on my mobile phone. The jingle is loud and too high-pitched, like nails scraping a blackboard. I sit up and turn it off. Man, I hate that sound. I didn't sleep a wink anyway. Who could on a night like this? You'd have to be a freak, insane or one of those sociopaths, someone with no empathy: Ted Bundy perhaps. I feel bad for Tiff. I do. It's a shame she had to die. I liked her (up until the point that I got *fired*). I sit up and yawn. I rub my eyes. The cottage still smells of smoke from the burning towels.

Tiff gave me a Tarot pack. I slept with it under my pillow. It's a bit lumpy, to be honest, but I'm getting used to it. I pull out a card at random: The Fool. Is that good or bad? Whatever. I'd better get on with my plan and I'm not sure I believe in it. I don't want Ed to find the corpse *without* me. It is crucial that I'm the one to wake him up. I need to be a witness.

I jump out of bed and try to get dressed, but I'm all fingers and thumbs, putting on my top backwards and sliding my feet into the wrong shoes. I let myself out of the cottage and creep through the grass to the house. Shining drops of dew cling to the tiny blades of grass. The sun is just beginning to rise over Highgate Golf Club. There's a chill in the air and I shiver. This next bit is *critical*. I need Ed to think that *he* killed her. He is going to be shocked, confused as hell and probably groggy after those sleeping pills. I'll have to channel Charlize Theron and do some serious acting.

I open the sliding door to the house and step into the living room. I tiptoe through the lounge – no maid, no James and no Joanna – and sneak into the dog's private suite. Baby's still asleep, but his ears prick up when he hears me come in. Aw, bless, he was dreaming about rabbits.

'Hello, how are you today?' I ask. 'Is your tummy better?'

I grab him by the scruff of his neck and carry him into the kitchen. I check, but there's no chef. It's too early. No one else is awake yet. The puppy's big bug eyes pop out of his head like his brain might explode.

'Listen, Earmuff,' I say to the dog. 'You stay here and be quiet. I'll come and get you in a couple of hours and then you can do what you like.'

I open the door to the wine cellar. The pug begins to whimper.

'Shh, you'll be fine. Just go back to sleep. This is all part of the plan.'

I throw him in and close the door. The dog begins to bark, but his barking is muffled like it was in that locker. It's fine. There's no one around. Nobody will notice him and he has plenty of room.

I head back out to the hall and step into the lift. I stretch it out and yawn and my reflection yawns back at me. I'm as pale as a ghost – I'm sleep-deprived and I need some sun – there are bags under my eyes from my late and sleepless night. You see that, Nino? *Professional.* I am nothing if not *committed.* I could have slept in until *ten,* but look at me: I'm smashing it. The early bird catches the worm.

I close my eyes and see the body in the bathtub. *Bleeding.* As the doors of the lift slide open, I expect to see a tsunami of blood crashing over me. But it's quiet. There's nothing.

I take a deep breath and stand up tall and make my way across the hall. I *tap tap tap* on Ed's bedroom door. I hope he's still asleep. There's no answer. I knock again, a little bit louder this time.

'Hello?' I call. 'Hello? Hello?'

My heart is pounding now. What if he already got up, freaked out and left the house? I press my ear against the door. I hear the groaning of springs in a creaky bed. That must be Ed waking up.

'Argh!' comes a voice.

He must have just discovered the Samurai sword!

'Hello? Is everything all right?'

I swing open the door and rush into the bedroom. 'Mr Forbes, I'm *so* sorry to wake you –'

Ed is sitting up in bed transfixed by the Samurai sword. He studies his bloodstained hands. I have literally caught him red-handed. I clock his sculpted abs and pecs. A platinum chain glints at his neck. I take him in and bite my lip, devouring him like prey. There is something *very* sexy about a man covered with blood with a sword between his legs.

'Oh my God. What happened?' I say, closing the door behind me. 'I came to say I can't find the dog. Is that . . . Whose *blood* is that?'

I flick on the lights. The room is suddenly bright and dazzling. Ed looks up at me and blinks, then looks at his hands again. He gawks at the sword lying in his lap.

'It must have fallen down.'

He looks up at the space on the wall where the Samurai sword once hung. Then he jumps out of the bed and joins me over by the door. He stands and stares at the sword and steadies himself against the door frame.

'What's *that*?' I say.

I point to the trail of blood leading from the bed to the en suite.

Ed turns to me. His face is pale. His eyes are wide with shock.

Slowly, slowly, *very* slowly, he starts to follow the trail across the room until he's standing by the bathroom door. I follow him – the excitement is mounting and butterflies dance in my stomach – then reach in through the bathroom door to turn on the light.

Ed makes a noise like an animal.

Tiff's still there in the tub, which is a big relief, to be honest. I thought she might have fucked off. Anything might have happened since I left her here last night. I study her face, her long blonde hair . . . Part of me wishes she'd survived the blow to the head with the frog and the slash across the neck. Part of me is glad she is dead. Oh man, I'm confused. *I'm torn.*

'Oh my God. You killed her,' I say. 'You killed Tiff. You *monster.*'

I start to shake. I shrink back from Ed with my back flat to the wall. I dial up the acting style to Mexican telenovela. I pant. My fists are clenched, knuckles white. I consider *screaming,* but I don't want to wake the whole house. We still have lots of work to do and I don't want that butler prying.

Ed doesn't speak. He doesn't move. He doesn't make a sound. He just stands there, frozen, like Elsa has turned him to ice. Seriously what is wrong with him? Did I pop Ed's corpse-cherry? But what about Nino's dad? He was also dead. I watch Ed's ass as he enters the room very, very slowly. He drags his feet and staggers as though in a hypnotic trance. He is still zonked from those pills. He probably thinks he is dreaming. Sorry, babe. This is *real.* It is not a nightmare.

Ed approaches the mess in the tub and kneels down next to it. He takes one of Tiffany's hands and clutches it to his lips.

'Who did this?' he says under his breath. 'Who could do such a thing?'

He sinks down to the floor and slumps against the wall. His head flops down into his hands like this is a *massive* head-fuck.

'It's pretty obvious who did it,' I say, leaning on the door frame.

Ed looks at me and shakes his head. '*I* didn't do it. I swear.' His eyes are like two snooker balls. 'I swear. I swear. I didn't.' He tries to stand up again but slips; he's weak with shock. He spreads open his red-stained hands. 'I-I-I-I was *sleeping*.'

'Uh-huh. Do you have an *alibi*? Someone that isn't *dead*?'

'I couldn't have done it *in my sleep*, could I?'

I fix him with a hard stare.

I watch as he considers this. His expression changes. He is thinking about their fight, the Scotch, his sword, the blood . . . so much blood. There's blood on his hands and blood on his *face*. He hasn't spotted that yet.

He staggers up and sits down on the loo (with the loo seat down). He spins the wedding ring on his finger. This is almost too easy.

I study Ed sitting there. I feel like a lioness hunting a gazelle, but a crap gazelle with broken legs and type two diabetes.

'The whole street heard your fight last night,' I say. 'You are clearly a *madman*. Give me one good reason why I shouldn't call the cops?'

His eyes flick up at this. *Of course.*

'What? Don't do that. Please. Please.'

I turn my back to leave. I pretend to go and find a phone to call the police.

'Siobhán, no. Please, no.' He leaps up and follows me. 'Stop. Where are you going? Help. I'll do anything.'

BINGO.

I turn round to face him. *Guilty.*

'This . . . this is a set-up,' he says, gripping on to my forearm.

'Hey!' I look down to where his fingers dig into my arm.

'Sorry,' he says, letting go.

'OK, listen, calm down.'

I take him by the elbow and sit him down on the bed. He stares at the sword. His shoulders slump. *Oh, Eddie, Ed my boy* . . . I sit down right next to him, so close that our thighs touch. I can even smell his breath: last night's whisky smells smoky, peaty.

I lower my voice. 'Mr Forbes, can you tell me what happened?'

'I . . . I can't. I don't remember.'

I rest my hand on his leg. 'Temporary amnesia is normal for these kinds of things.'

'*No.* It's not like that at all.' He turns to me; he looks *ill.*

'They're called "crimes of passion",' I say, getting into my stride now. 'The amnesia is a dissociative symptom. Trust me, I know these things . . . I read a lot of crime fiction and watch Netflix documentaries. You could plead *insanity,* but you probably wouldn't get off. And even if you *did,* it's a lifetime of *One Flew Over the Cuckoo's Nest* and you're Jack Nicholson.'

He shakes his head. I'm freaking him out. I've got him

right where I want him. He'll do what it takes to save his skin. He's putty in my hands.

Ed sits up a little taller, clears his throat and says. 'How much, Siobhán? Just give me a figure. How much do you need to keep quiet?'

I give him a pitying look. *Oh, Ed, I want it all . . .*

I take his hand and give it a squeeze, and slowly shake my head.

'Mr Forbes,' I say, feigning shock, 'you clearly don't know me. I am *not* that kind of girl.'

'I'm sorry,' he says. 'I'm so sorry.'

I try a reassuring smile. He shrinks back from me. 'I *am* going to help you,' I say, 'but only because I *like* you.'

Ed starts sobbing quietly.

'Mr Forbes, *look at me*. Your life isn't over. I promise. OK? I'm going to make it all right. Trust me, I am *good* at this. I'm like a spin doctor.'

'I thought you were the dog's new nanny?' Ed looks up, confused.

'Yes, but I can multitask. I am a *woman*.'

He nods.

Disposing of corpses is child's play. I've done this many times before. I am going to be *ace*. Just watch. This is going to be fun. I look into Ed's pale blue eyes and rest my hand on his shoulder. I soften my voice and sweetly say, 'I'm going to need a *chainsaw*.'

7 a.m.

'I'm so fucking spiritual that I've already donated all my internal organs.'

'You have a donor card?'

'I had the doctor take them out and give them to terminally ill children. All I've got left is my appendix and, of course, my heart.'

'No way. That isn't possible. How are you still alive?'

'Cocaine. And beans. My God, I'd be dead if it wasn't for beans.'

'Baked beans?'

'No, the magic beans they used to replace my organs. Bean technology is the future. The plant kingdom is our friend. Instead of a liver I have beans. Instead of intestines, beans. Instead of a spleen I have more beans. I am legume-powered.'

'Do you have kidney beans instead of kidneys?'

'No, don't be ridiculous.'

Ed makes a strange noise as I use the saw to slice up Tiffany.

'Who *are* you?' says Ed.

I pause. 'I'm Siobhán, the dog's new nanny?'

I thought we'd been over this? Ed is clearly getting forgetful in his old age. A spot of Alzheimer's perhaps? Now is not the time to start forgetting basic stuff. I need him on my side.

'No, I mean, *who are you*?' says Ed. 'Where did you learn to do *that*?'

'When I was young, I did work experience with a lumberjack.'

That's not true, but I think it's best if I don't mention the *mafia*. The mafia tend to freak people out. Don't know why.

We're blasting opera from the stereo to drown out the noise of the chainsaw. Ed is playing Classic FM; it's *Madame Butterfly*. It's hot work, so I've stripped down to just my bra and pants. I didn't want to mess up my clothes, but I burnt my mac last night.

I saw off Tiffany's fingertips to destroy her prints. Then I remove Tiffany's rings. *Those rocks*! I salivate. There's an *enormous* engagement ring with a diamond the size of an orange. Her wedding band is an infinity set with dazzling jewels. I give the rings a rinse in cold water then shove them in my pocket. Oh my God, they're beautiful and worth *millions* of dollars.

Ed sits on the edge of the bed, wringing and wringing his hands. Urgh. He's being *useless*. Not much help at all. He's working his way through a bottle of Johnny Walker Blue Label. The fumes alone are making me float. I can taste it from here.

'Can you bring me a couple of suitcases?' I ask. 'I'm going to need *two*.'

Ed hauls himself up from the bed and staggers out of the room.

He brings me a couple of Louis Vuitton cases from Tiff's closet. I like the shiny locks and retro monogram design.

He flops back down on the bed again and grabs the bottle of whisky. I roll my eyes. Fucking useless. Why do I have to do everything? If only Nino were *really* here. I mean *physically*. It's at times like these that I miss him. We had a great time in Sicily. Shooting mobsters. Killing priests. It was cool in Rome when we blew up all those cops with that hand grenade. But, no, I'll do it *all on my own*. *Ed owes me*. But I guess that's the point, after all. Ed's going to owe me *big time*. He'll be forever in my debt when I save his ass.

I tie a knot in one of the sacks. I'm good at tying knots from my time with the Girl Guides. I learnt about knots and starting fires. Always *be prepared*.

'What was Tiff going to do today? What was her plan?'
I ask.

I know she was supposed to go to Venice, but I don't want Ed to know that I know . . . if you catch my drift.

'I have no idea,' says Ed. 'My mind's a total blank.'

He rubs his eyes. He's tired. And stressed. But I need him to *focus*. Now is not the time to nap or have a nervous breakdown.

'Mr Forbes, *snap out of it.*' I grab him by the shoulders. I slap him once across the face. 'Work with me here. *Jesus.*'

Ed clutches his throbbing cheek.

'Go and check her diary. We need to go on as if nothing has happened. That is *paramount.*'

'How the hell are we going to do that?' Ed asks, his voice raised.

'Relax, I have a plan,' I say. 'To be honest, it's *genius.*'

He nods. That seems to have woken him up. I cradle my aching hand.

He grabs his phone and clicks the screen. 'She was supposed to be flying to Venice. She had an auction to attend.'

'Yes. Venice. Good . . . *I'll* go instead of Tiffany. I'll pretend to be *her*. We need to make it look as though she wasn't murdered *here*. If we can get the body out and make it look like Tiff disappeared in Italy, then you are in the clear!' I beam at him. '*You're welcome.* You'll have watertight alibis right here in London. And you'll be able to distance yourself from her "disappearance".'

'Yes,' says Ed. 'That's right. Of course.'

'*But* – and this bit's tricky – at passport control, they're going to want to see Tiff's *face,* aren't they?'

'No,' says Ed. 'Don't worry about that. We always take

Percy to Venice. They know us there. They wave us through at Marco Polo.'

'*Huh?* Who is *Percy?*'

'My private jet.'

I laugh. 'Of course. And what the hell is *Marco Polo?*'

'Venice airport.'

'Right. Will you stop speaking in *fucking code?* We're on a deadline here.'

'Sorry,' says Ed.

I roll my eyes. 'When you say they *wave you through* . . . ?'

'They never check our passports,' he says. 'They know us there. Know the plane.'

'Great!'

That *is* a stroke of luck. It's true about the Irish. It's like the stars are aligning for me in my murder quest. Who was it that said 'Fortune favours the brave'? *Brave* is my middle name.

'When was she supposed to leave?'

Ed checks his Patek. 'In about an hour,' he says. 'But what about all *that?*' He gestures to the cases standing on the bedroom floor.

'That is coming with *me*,' I say. 'You are staying *here*. Wait right here till I get back. *Do not leave the house.*'

9 a.m.

I step out of the shower in a cloud of steam and hop on to the bath mat. I've rinsed the bath and washed my hair and even shaved my muff. I stand, naked, in front of the mirror and blow-dry my hair with Tiffany's brush. I apply her perfume liberally (too much. It makes me sneeze.) Ed paces the bedroom, drinking. I catch him watching me. When I'm done and my hair is *gorgeous*, falling in soft waves by my face, I have a look through the Badminton Cabinet and find a pair of knickers in lace. I find a matching bra to go with them, but it's not my size: Tiffany was a D cup (bitch), but I am just a B. Shit, that could be my undoing. What if they notice my tits on the plane? The pilot is sure to spot Tiff's sudden breast-reduction surgery. I grab a couple of slouchy socks, roll them up and shove them in my bra. That's better: an instant boob job. Huh. They look pretty natural.

I apply some of Tiffany's make-up: Benefit lip gloss in palest pink, a slick of turquoise eyeliner, a flush of blush in rosy peach, a couple of strokes of brown mascara. I smile at the girl in the mirror and move in for the close-up. Wow. I look like Julianne Moore. Totally fucking gorgeous. If it wasn't for the ginger hair, I could be *Tiffany*. Oh, and apart from the *face*, of course. I don't look like her.

Next, I raid Tiffany's closet – there's not very much in here. It is pretty disappointing; she gave most of her clothes away. The Dog's Trust, Water Aid, Barnardo's . . . *What am I going to wear?* I find a fabulous flat-brimmed hat. I need that to cover my hair. The hat is palest ivory and inside on a label is written: *For Tiff from Philip Treacy xoxox.* I find a silk scarf by Hermès and wrap it round my hair, then hide it all inside Tiff's hat. I make sure that no locks spill out. Not a strand of carrot! That would be a dead giveaway. Then I pull on a pair of sky-high Manolo Blahniks. Ow. OW. They're *two sizes* too small and my toe still hurts from that dumbass frog. I try to walk and *wince*. Oh God. But one must suffer for fashion. *Man up, Alvie. No pain, no gain. Nino wouldn't* notice.

I grab a simple Gucci dress in cream with stripes of black. As soon as I see it, I know it won't fit, but I won't give up like *that*. I wriggle and writhe, but it's a *size four*. Motherfucker. *Come on*.

'Ed? A little help with the zip? You're a darling,' I say.

He downs the rest of the whisky and stands up from the double bed. Wow, he necked that *quick*. He stands behind me in the mirror and tugs and tugs at the zip. I breathe out so my lungs are flat. I don't want it to rip.

'It won't do up. It's stuck,' he says.

I gasp and gasp for breath.

'It *will*. I've got big bones,' I say. 'You've just got to *force* it. Trust me, we are both the same size. If anything, I'm *thinner*.'

Eventually the zip slides up.

I turn round. 'Ta-da!'

Ed looks like he's seen a ghost. I know, I look *fantastic*. I take off my engagement ring, the one from the hand grenade, and shove it into Ed's hand.

'Guard this with your *life*,' I say.

I take Tiff's rings from my jacket and slide them on to my fingers. The wedding ring sticks, so I shove my finger into my mouth and suck it. My saliva lubricates the skin like KY Jelly, and the wedding band slips on eventually. Ed looks at the rings and his face crumples up. Will he *cry*? I roll my eyes.

'What do you think?' I ask, twirling around. I really do look the part. I am rather pleased with myself. I try not to grin.

'I never noticed it before, but you do look a *bit* like my wife.'

'Wait until I try on *these*.'

I grab a pair of Chanel sunglasses in tortoiseshell. They complete the look to perfection. I look totally A-list.

'It's just that . . .'

'What?'

'I mean . . . well, er . . . what can we do about your *face*?'

My shoulders slump. I turn to the mirror. God damn it, he's right.

'You're right. If I'm going to pass for Tiff, I'll need a better disguise. Listen, do you have bandages?'

Ed nods, then he goes off to fetch a bandage.

I grab Tiff's shaman pouch. I take some more plastic gloves from my jacket and shove them inside. The shaman's pouch! At last. It's mine. Oh wow. It's *gorgeous*. I stroke the dead fox fur. It's soft, like stroking the pug. I check inside: Tiff's purse, her phone and her burgundy passport. I shove Siobhán's passport in too. I'll need that later. I open up her purse. There is at least a *thousand* pounds in here in fifty-pound notes and a thousand euros as well.

Ed returns with a thick roll of fabric. I wrap the bandage round my face, round and round, like an Egyptian mummy. You can see ten per cent of my face. It's a good look, actually. Now I see why Muslim ladies wear those burka things. *Kinky*.

I pull open a gap in the bandage so I can speak to Ed.

'The story is that Tiff had a facelift and lost her voice,' I say.

Ed nods. 'I hope it works.' He looks worried.

'Of course it will. *Trust me*.'

Ed picks up the house phone. 'James,' he says. His voice

is shaking. 'We're going to need the Rolls. Tiff is taking Percy. Come up here and fetch her bags . . .' He hesitates, his voice faltering. *Shit*. What will he say? 'There's a good chap,' he says then hangs up.

I thought he was going to *break*.

I wrap my arms round Ed's neck. 'Now remember, I'm *Tiffany*. I'll see you soon. I'll dump the stiff and be back in a couple of days. Don't you worry about a thing.'

I squish his button nose, then give him a quick peck on the lips through the bandages. He blinks.

'It's called *role play*, Ed. You have to act as though *I'm your wife.*'

'Er, yes, well, about that . . .'

'But when I come back, I'll be *me*.'

'Me? You mean you'll come back as Siobhán?'

'Of course I'll be Siobhán.' That was *close*. I was going to say *Alvie*.

1 p.m.
Elstree Aerodrome, London

On the plane I gaze out of the window sipping sparkling water. There's a cloud in the sky in the shape of a pug and one in the shape of a cock. On no, the dog! I completely forgot. He's still locked in the cellar. I can't ask Ed to set him free or he'll know I knew where he was. That was my cover for coming into the bedroom in the first place. I could ask *James*, but I don't trust him not to blab.

I'm stuck. But it's *fine*. The dog will be all right for a couple of days. I won't worry about him. You can live three days without water. I'm sure I heard that on Bear

Grylls. I munch the salted roasted nuts and flick through Tiffany's *Tatler*.

I sink into the cream-leather seat and study the plane's interior. I've never been on a plane like this. It's nicer than Ryanair. It is an eight-seater craft with a wide-screen TV and lounge area. The seats are all recliner beds. The carpet is icy silver. There are purple orchids on the tables and silk-wool throws on the chairs.

I reach into Tiffany's shaman's pouch to extract my phone, but I don't have *my* phone; I have *Tiff's*. I freeze. *No phone?* Oh my God. I don't have *my phone?* Oh help. I have nomophobia: the irrational fear of not having one's phone. Irrational, *my ass*. I grab Tiffany's phone instead because *her* phone is better than *no* phone. The phone is locked. It asks for a code. Oh no. Not another passcode. Come on. Oh God, what is it? What? I rack my brains. What is it? What number would Tiffany use? Suddenly I get it. I remember a *Breakfast with Tiffany* episode in which Tiff discusses the ancient science of angel numbers. Could it be 1111? My finger shakes as I type the numbers. I only get three goes. 1111, I recall, is a sign from the angels that anything you wish for will be manifested.

Ping.

It works! Of course it does. I *know* her. I can read her mind. We have an undying connection from beyond the grave.

I click into Tiff's gallery and scroll through her recent photos. There are sixty almost identical pictures of the tiny dog. I stop when I get to the video of Tiff and me on Hampstead Heath. I press play. I want to watch it. I want to see her face. There we are doing a spot of qigong. Ah.

Don't we look *happy*? My hair looks *great*. And I look hot. Tiffany's eyes are sparkling. It would have made a *great* vlog post. Damn it, she was right. She was right about most things, I guess. She was very wise.

My finger hovers over the picture of a bin. Should I keep it? No, I should *definitely* delete it. That's the sensible thing. I don't want to risk having evidence of my close relationship with Tiff. It's one thing being the dog's new nanny; it's another being BFFs. If the cops suspected we were *close,* I might become a suspect. It's always somebody you know that does you in in the end.

But then I pause. I reconsider. There's something else I could do. Something daring, risky, ballsy. It's what I need to do. There is Wi-Fi on this plane and I *am* supposed to be Tiffany. She's supposed to be alive. And what is she always doing? Posting videos and photographs on Instagram etc. If I post this video now, it would prove that Tiff was alive on the plane on the way to Venice. It's a great idea! The cops would definitely check the time of her last video post. And I'd get to fulfil my lifelong dream (OK, well, not *life*long) of being on *Breakfast with Tiffany.*

My finger hovers over the share sign. Fuck it, I'm going to do it. If any one of her ten million followers asks *who's your hot friend?* – I was *just* a member of staff and had absolutely *nothing* to do with Tiffany's brutal murder. It works with my cover as the dog's new nanny. We were walking the mutt on Hampstead Heath and Tiff got me to join in.

I upload the video on to Tiffany's vlog and hold my breath as the buffer spins round and round and round. It finally loads.

I stare at the screen. Immediately *eight* people like it. Someone writes, *Great post, Tiff! I <3 qigong.*

There isn't any mention of *me*. Not yet anyway. Although I'm clearly the star of the show and upstage Tiffany.

I scroll through the rest of Tiff's phone. There's an app called Momento. Huh, what's that? Is it like Basecamp? I click into it. Momento is some kind of a diary. Awesome. I open it and read Tiff's latest entry. It is dated 9 August.

> *My thirty-first birthday. Happy birthday, me! Siobhán gave me a bit of gravel as a birthday present . . .*

I sit up taller in my seat and grip the phone a bit tighter. It's fine to read her diary if it's all about *me*.

> *Siobhán's so funny. She pretended it was a meteorite, but it was just a bit of gravel from the drive. Bless her. She wanted to give me a present, but I don't think she has much cash. We'll have to give her a pay rise soon. Siobhán has a heart of gold.*

What?

That's it. That's the last thing she wrote. I read it again to be sure: *Siobhán has a heart of gold.*

A *heart!* A *heart!*

Tiffany thinks I have *a* heart of *gold*? Really? But my heart is in the wrong place and it always has been. It's on the right and not the left. It's weird. (It's my sister's fault.) My mum always said that I was cold-hearted. And sometimes she even said I was *heartless*, which contradicts the previous statements. I blink at the phone. I can't believe it. That's what she wrote on her *birthday*? She didn't mention

194

the super-yacht that Ed bought for her (500 feet in length and moored in St Tropez. Where else?) She didn't write about the slap-up meal at Sushi Samba. She wrote about *me*. Little old me. No one's ever said anything nice about my heart before. Not even Nino. Ha. As if. He preferred my vagina. Something slowly starts to sink into my brain. Tiffany hugged me. Nino only hugged if it was foreplay. Tiffany said she *loved* me. *Twice*. I furrow my brow. Did she mean it? Nino never said 'I love you,' though he did *propose* . . .

Oh man, I'm confused.

Eileen, the air hostess, comes to fill my drink and replenish my plate of peanuts.

'Everything all right, Mrs Forbes? We'll be landing in ten minutes.'

I tilt my hat and hide behind my Dior sunglasses. Eileen studies my hand. *What? What are you looking at?* I've been using my *right* hand instead of my *left*, just like Tiff, but I should have put on gloves. *Leather* gloves, not plastic. Eileen frowns at my hands and I freeze. I'm wearing Tiffany's diamonds, but these are clearly *not* her hands. It's like we're a different species. Tiff had the hands of a piano player. Her fingers were long and elegant. She could have been a hand model like David Duchovny in *Zoolander*. I, *on the other hand* (shit pun), have stumpy little fingers and hands like a hobbit's. I haven't done my nails. They're short, all bitten down and bleeding around the edges. I glance up. Will she suspect? I breathe in and choke on a peanut. I cough. It's gone down the wrong way.

Eileen whacks my back. 'Mrs Forbes, are you OK?'

I cough and cough and cough.

The nut comes sailing out of my mouth and hits the back

of the chair in front. I'm blue beneath the bandages. I actually nearly *died*. I nod – *I'm fine* – and take a sip of my drink. I'm sweating *buckets*. I wish I could take off my hat, but it's not safe. Not yet. I need to keep it on till we land. It will be the fucking *peanuts*. That is what will give me away. I'll bet Tiff never touched the snacks. She was too spiritual.

My heart is beating double time. There's only so much luck a girl can have and then you blow it. And I don't have my leprechaun! How am I going to pull this off without my lucky charm? I know Ed said they'd wave me through, but what if he is wrong? Why did I have to push it? Why? I was doing *fine*. I'd managed to lay low for twelve months. Nobody had found me. That cop was looking for a *squirrel*. Why didn't I stay in the hostel?

I rest my face on the table. Why did I have to kill Tiffany? Her smiling face. Her sparkling *eyes*. I replay the video in my mind. She said I had a *heart of gold*. She hugged me *several* times . . . It hurts. It hurts. It hurts.

'Mrs Forbes, please fasten your seat belt. We are about to land.'

The brakes screech and the engine screams as the plane shudders on to the runway. I look out of my oval window; the sky is far too blue. I squint, despite my sunglasses, blinded by the sun.

5 p.m.
Marco Polo Airport, Venice, Italy

I spot *three* cops on the tarmac as I climb down the stairs from the plane. I grip on to the banister and nearly trip on the steps. Those cops are here for me. For sure. It's too soon to be searching for *Tiffany*, but last time I was in Italy I did a lot of murdering. Somehow they have tracked me down. Of course they're here for *me* . . .

I finally make it to the bottom of the stairs and step on to the runway. I glance at the cops. They're smoking by the double doors to the airport.

A porter takes my cases. He loads Tiff on to a trolley.

I want to say, 'Be careful with her!' but I can't. I'm powerless.

The airport manager himself comes out to the tarmac to greet me.

'*Benvenuto*, Signora Forbes,' he says with a broad smile. He frowns when he sees the bandages, but has the tact to ignore them. He envelops me in a bear hug. He's a large man, like Pavarotti. 'No Signor Forbes today?'

I shake my head.

'What a shame.'

I watch the cops stub out their fags then push back through the door.

'Mrs Forbes has lost her voice,' Eileen says, gesturing to her throat. 'Signora Forbes *non parla*.'

'Ah,' he says. '*La povera*. Please, come this way.'

I couldn't speak if I wanted to. The adrenaline is pumping. Where are the cops? Have they gone inside to get military reinforcements?

The airport manager takes my arm. Now where are we going? Is he taking me to passport control? We head for the airport building.

'I hope you will enjoy your stay in La Serenissima.'

The last thing I'm feeling is serene. I want to run. I want to scream.

'Your water taxi awaits, *signora*,' says the airport manager.

I drag my feet as I follow him across the busy runway. What is he on about, *water taxi*? Where are all the cops? My knees are weak and it's all I can do to stop myself from fainting, but instead of heading inside we walk towards the lagoon and a row of boats lined up outside the airport.

No one even *mentions* a passport. Ed was right about that. Money opens doors, I guess. And international borders.

I can't believe what's happening. I could cry with joy. I feel like a cat – I have been given yet another life.

Carlo and Eileen wave goodbye and head back to the plane ready for their return flight.

This *is* going well.

The porter loads the cases and I board a glossy wooden boat.

'Hotel Danieli,' says the manager.

The captain nods. *'Andiamo.'*

I wave at the airport manager and he waves back at me. I have to say that even though Jezebel is *annoying* she seems to have arranged Tiff's trip pretty flawlessly.

I sit down on a bench on the boat and look out at the view as Venice begins to emerge from the water like a beautiful ghost. I think of Tiff. It would have been fun to come to Venice with her on a girly weekend: me, Tiff and the dog. I mean, I know that Tiff *is* here, but it's not the same. We would have had a blast. We would have taken in the sights on a bobbing gondola, sipping decaf soya lattes, nibbling gluten-free *biscotti* . . . The glorious Renaissance churches, the gothic architecture, Tiff and I would have seen all the art and listened to all the opera.

I gawk, open-mouthed, at the views from the boat. The Grand Canal is a deep sea-green in the afternoon sun. Palazzi reflect on the water's surface, shimmering reds and yellows. It's like an open-air museum. It's all very Canaletto. A marble church appears like a phantom. It looks like it's made of lace. How do they make *metamorphic rock* into those intricate patterns? I look up as we pass beneath a bridge over the canal. Is that the Rialto or Bridge of Sighs? This place is *incredible*.

If Tiff were here with me (and the dog), she'd have whisked us around St Mark's Basilica saying things like, 'Wow, Siobhán, can you feel the energy?' And I would have pretended to like it, while being bored out of my brain, but secretly really loving it. I study the basilica. It's stunning. Everything is *gold*. The gilded roof glints in the sun. I can see why Siobhán is a Catholic. Catholics do good bling.

Water splishes and splashes against the sides of the boat. We sail up to some gondolas and the captain moors the boat. A bellboy appears and offers his hand to help me disembark. He looks a bit like Robert De Niro in *Goodfellas*. He is wearing linen gloves. They're starched and white and perfect. I study them enviously. I wish I had gloves like *that*.

'*Buongiorno*,' the bellboy says, beaming at me.

I'm about to reply, when I give him a nod. Oh yeah. No Voice. Facelift. *Bandages*.

The captain of the boat says something in hurried Italian: 'Blah blah blah.' I catch the end: 'Signora Forbes.'

The porter takes the cases. I flinch as I watch him struggle to lift them.

'*Piacere*. Please, follow me,' he says, regaining composure.

I remember I'm supposed to be Tiff and reach into Tiffany's purse to extract some fifty-euro notes to give to the captain.

'*Grazie, signora*,' he says with a grin, as I tip him a couple of hundred.

In case he is asked I want him to remember he ferried me. And by me, of course, I mean the famous Signora Tiffany Forbes.

I trail the bellboy across a pavement bustling with tourists. We cross the Riva degli Schiavoni and approach the hotel. I look up. The Hotel Danieli consists of *three* palaces of various architectural styles joined together to create one luxurious whole. It sits, pride of place, at the water's edge sparkling in the summer sun: three storeys of terracotta, peach and gleaming white. *Alvie, be cool. You're* Tiffany. *You've been here loads of times before.* But I feel like Annie, that orphan girl – it's not for the likes of me.

I follow the bellboy through a gorgeous art deco door and emerge into a cavernous courtyard inside the hotel. I follow him to the reception. He's panting from the weight of the bags. He wipes his forehead with a gloved hand and speaks to the receptionist at a wood-panelled desk.

'Signora Forbes,' he says. 'Blah, blah, blah.'

I give him fifty euros.

'*Grazie, signora*,' he says with a bow, taking the note and folding it and tucking it in his pocket. 'I bring your bags up *presto*.'

I watch him haul the suitcases towards an ancient lift. I grit my teeth. I don't want to let Tiff out of my sight for a minute. I'm feeling rather protective of her. It's actually quite sweet. I'd prefer to take her up myself, but that might draw attention. I guess it would look very strange if I insisted on carrying my luggage to the room myself. Tiff would *never* do that.

'Good evening, Signora Forbes,' says the receptionist. She's a pretty girl with long hair tied in a ponytail. 'How are you today?'

'Fine,' I say. Ah, balls. My voice. How well does she know Tiffany? Am I OK to talk? I'll lose the Irish accent at least. Tiff is not from *Cork*.

'We have your usual room ready, the Lagoon View Suite. Will that be to your satisfaction?'

'Hmm,' I say, 'Let's see. Is that the *best* room in the house?'

She smiles then hesitates. The girl checks her computer screen. 'That would be the Doge Suite. It's in Palazzo Dandolo. It has a king-size bed, two bathrooms, a living room and a dining room, a walk-in-wardrobe, a balcony and a lagoon view.'

'Put me in that one, would you?'

The balcony might be useful and I think it's time for an upgrade. I might as well *enjoy myself* now that I'm *Signora Forbes* and came all the way here to *Venice*.

6 p.m.

I pull on the plastic gloves. I can't touch *anything*. If the police find my prints in this suite, it could be the end of me. The cops might have my prints on file from last time I was in Italy. And Siobhán/Alvie/whoever the fuck isn't supposed to be here.

I pace the hotel room. I've been waiting for *fifteen minutes*, but there's no sign of Robert De Niro or my suitcases.

How long does it take to ride a lift? I'm going to kill somebody.

I throw open the double doors and step out to the balcony. I need some air. I'm restless. Tense.

Wow. This view is *insane*.

I lean over the metal railing of the balcony. It's the best view I've ever seen, but I'm too cross to appreciate it. I won't even take a picture for Insta. I don't care about *the view*. I am too distracted. Stressed. And my mind is racing. Those cases are *vintage*. They looked really old. Perhaps a zip has exploded? What if one of the seams has split? Shit. Shit. Shit.

I run back into the room and grab the hotel phone. My hands are shaking, my fingers fumbling.

Eventually I manage to hit the 'o' and the phone rings.

'*Buonasera*,' comes a woman's voice.

'This is Tiffany Forbes,' I say, trying to keep calm and stop my voice betraying my nerves. 'I am in the Doge Suite, but I'm still waiting for my bags.'

'Apologies, Signora Forbes. I will ask Luigi where he has taken your things. We'll have them sent up in an instant.'

I hang up the phone and lean my head against the wall. The room's spinning. I suddenly feel so alone. I head back out to the balcony.

'Nino?' I whisper.

I wish he was here with me. Man, I really miss him.

I feel a breeze caress the skin on my neck. I turn round to see Nino materialize, stark bollock naked. He's floating a couple of feet above the floor of the balcony. I sigh a sigh of deep relief.

'*Ciao*, baby,' I say.

He always shows when I need him most. I take him in

202

in all his glory. A pink scar runs down one of his cheeks. There's a bullet wound on his forehead. His dick swings down between his legs; it's definitely *Nino*.

'When I told you to *lose* her,' he says. 'I meant *lose* as in *kill*.'

I grit my teeth. 'I *did* kill her,' I say.

'But now you've *lost* her,' he says.

There's a sharp knock at the door.

'You stay *here*,' I say.

'Where am I gonna go? That had better be the stiff.'

I really hope so too.

I draw the curtains across the door that leads to the balcony. I don't want anyone to spot him standing there butt-naked.

I take off my gloves and hide them in my pocket. I open the door. My hands are trembling as I clock Luigi there with the cases. He's sweating even more than before. I glare at him through the bandages.

'*Mi dispiace*,' he says. 'I'm so sorry. I go to the wrong room.'

I look both ways down the corridor. 'Quick, hurry up, get them in here.'

Luigi lugs them across the floor and dumps them in the living room on an antique Persian rug the colour of Prosecco.

Out of the corner of my eye I see something *oozing* from the bottom of one of the bags. He brought them in just in time. They're starting to leak. I knew it. I *knew* I should have *triple-bagged* them. But it's only a *bit* of blood. I can clean that up. Hopefully.

Luigi wipes his brow in a very, *very* theatrical manner. He gives me a look as if to say, *lady, you really owe me.*

I give Luigi another fifty euros. Then another fifty euros just in case. Those cases are heavy.

'No, *signora*. Is too much. I cannot. You already pay.'

'Just take it, you lunatic. Take it and go away.'

I wave the money in his face. Luigi shrugs and grabs it. Then he bows out of the room, walking away backwards.

Nino turns to face the view and stands with his back to me. His butt looks like it is sculpted from marble and belongs to Zeus or Apollo or one of those other Greek gods, whichever one is hotter.

'Why are you naked on my balcony?'

He turns to look at me. I take in his chiselled abs and thirteen-inch penis.

'Why do you think?' He wraps his arms round my waist. 'I missed you.'

I smile. 'I missed you too,' I say.

Wow, he is *warm* for a ghost. And surprisingly substantial. I kiss him on the neck (through the gap in the bandages). I breathe the scent of Nino's skin and it feels like home: salty sweat and pheromones. My hands slide to his crotch. I love the feel of his hot smooth skin and that's one serious six-pack. He must have been working out (in hell? They'll have a CrossFit for sure.) I reach down and grip his cock. I gasp. His erection is *throbbing*. It's even bigger than I remember, like a baby holding an orange.

He looks into my eyes.

'Alvie, baby. You and me, we would have been *great* together.'

And I *melt*. It's what I wanted to hear. *Exactly* what I wanted. It's like Nino can read my mind. Huh, perhaps it's a ghost thing. I lean in and kiss him. Hard. Our tongues meet, intertwine. I pull him close and kiss him deeper. Oh my God, *I've missed this*.

I moan. My eyes roll back in my head. I bite his bottom lip, taking it further into my mouth, like I want to eat him. He pulls away and we stand panting, holding each other's gaze, breathing in each other's breath. My pussy is *aching*. Nino runs his hands up and down my curves in Tiffany's dress. My skin is electric where he touched me. My nipples are erect.

He spins me round and tears the zip all the way down my back. The dress falls in a heap at my feet. I kick off my shoes. He starts to remove my latex gloves.

'No, not the *gloves*. Keep them on,' I say.

He touches me through the lace of my knickers.

Fuck, it feels amazing.

I jump up and sit on top of the wrought-iron balcony. The metal feels cold on my thighs. I grab on to the railing. I look down. Shit, *bad idea*, I shouldn't have done that. It's a long way down to the street. I try to grip on harder, but my palms slide and I slip. I don't want to *die*.

Nino pulls my knickers down. He kneels between my legs. I lean back and see the sky. He pushes his mouth into me. I push myself back into him. I arch my back. *I love it*. I feel like I'm about to erupt and I'll *die* if I can't have him.

He licks me harder, faster, up and down and round and round and round, until I can't take any more. I jump down from the balcony into Nino's arms. He bends me over the metal rail and I come as soon as he enters me, my body shaking, jerking.

'*Alvie.*'

I feel like I'm floating . . .

out over the pale lagoon . . .

past an ancient church . . .

all lit up with golden lights.

The church bells are ringing.

Everything is magical . . .

And my mind is calm.

Wow. Is this what heaven feels like?

I land on the balcony.

The curtains billow through the doors that lead into the suite.

I catch a glimpse of myself in the mirror inside the hotel room. I'm still wearing all my clothes. My hand is down my pants. I look around for Nino, but he's gone. There's nobody here. I'm alone.

I wander back into the suite. I still feel like I'm floating. It takes me a while to come back to earth. I sit down on the carpet next to Tiff, and I put my arm round her and stroke her suitcase tenderly, glad to have her back.

8 p.m.
Venice

I pay for the packet of bubblegum and lift up the bandages to shove a piece into my mouth. They don't have Hubba Bubba. It's an Italian brand, something unpronounceable. The bubblegum is strawberry flavour. That is my joint favourite (strawberry and cherry are tied, *bubble-gum* flavour is second).

I stroll out of the newsagent's and glance at the news-papers. I pause, then pick one up from the stand. I flick through some of the pages. I check the *Corriere della Sera* and *La Repubblica*, but there aren't any photos of me or Tiff. It's too soon. I'm just being paranoid.

I chew the gum and blow a bubble. I see how big I can blow it. Huh, that's pretty big, actually. But then I suddenly pop it. *What am I doing walking down the street and blowing bubbles?* Aren't I supposed to be Tiffany? Tiff Forbes does *not* blow bubbles. That's an *Alvina* thing. *Come on, Alvie, think.* It's stupid shit like that that gets you caught. I glare at the hordes of tourists.

I take the corner that leads to the street with the Hotel Danieli. The Riva degli Schiavoni. There are lots of little stalls selling souvenirs. I wish I could shop till I drop, but not right now, maybe later. There are some stunning oil paintings in the style of Canaletto, gondolier T-shirts and colourful ashtrays made of Murano glass. But that's not what I'm looking for. I'm looking for something else . . . I scan the walls. Right there! Yes, I *knew* it. There's a CCTV camera. The lens is aimed at the hotel. It's pointing right at my suite. Ha. I can forget about a blind spot. That camera will have to go. But how? Not now in broad daylight. Not with all these people around with their nosy iPhones and their fucking selfie sticks. I'll have to do it later on when it gets quiet and dark.

Hang on a minute, if that camera's pointing at my balcony, does that mean that they filmed the whole thing with Nino's ghost earlier? LOL.

I waltz back into the Danieli. The hotel staff nod and smile. I sashay along the red carpet like I'm a celebrity. I ride the lift humming Taylor Swift and study the bandages in the mirror: it really could be anyone under there. I step out to the corridor and pull on my plastic gloves. I open up the door to my suite; it smells like rotting eyeballs. Urgh. The air conditioning's on max. There's nothing I can do. Those suitcases are two stink bombs. I gag as I enter the room. It's a shame that Tiff wasn't spiritual enough for her body not to rot, to be *incorruptible*, you know, like saints and stuff. Paramahansa Yogananda didn't rot at all for something like three whole weeks. Now *that* is impressive.

I find Tiff's phone and blink at the screen: twelve missed calls and six messages all from that hostile PA, Jolinda or whatever. I hit reply to one of her texts. How can I say this nicely in a Tiffany kind of way? I need to let her down gently.

'YOU'RE FIRED FOR BEING ANNOYING.' Send.

So long, Jackie.

I dial Ed's number. It only rings once and he picks up. Aww, bless him, he must have been sitting by the phone waiting for me to call. I bet he really misses me. He's eating his heart out. Yes, we definitely have a bond. It will be easy to seduce him once I'm back in town.

'Hello?' he says.

I clear my throat. 'It's me. *Tiffany*.'

'At last,' says Ed. 'Thank God. I was beginning to worry.'

I can hear the relief in his voice from hundreds of miles away.

'I have arrived safely in Venice. I'm at the Hotel Danieli.'

'That is *wonderful* news,' he says. 'Did your flight go well?'

'Everything went smoothly,' I say. I glance at the suitcases. '*Shit.*' From this angle I can see a pool of Tiffany's blood. There's a deep-red stain on the carpet about the size of a pug.

'What? What is it? What's happened?'

'Er, nothing,' I say, my voice unnaturally high-pitched. 'Everything's under control.'

'Darling, what's wrong?' says Ed.

'It's nothing. Nothing. *Oh God . . .*'

I get down on my hands and knees and inspect the leak. Even if I scrub the blood, the mark will still be seen. I glance around the room in a panic. What could I use to hide it? I could move the table? The sofa? That cupboard. But no. It won't work. Housekeeping would move it back and there's no rug to cover it up because the stain is *on* a rug. The bloody stain is so big and red that a bottle of Vanish wouldn't help me.

'Oh no. We're screwed. This is bad,' I say. 'Ed? Imma call you back.'

I hang up just as Ed is protesting. I'm not in the mood to *chat*. What the hell did I think I was doing getting freaky on the balcony while the fucking corpse was *leaking*? That was a schoolgirl error. I'm going to have to *concentrate* to pull off this complex plan . . . No more quickies with phantoms, OK? Nino isn't Patrick Swayze. This isn't fucking *Ghost*.

Tiff's phone rings – it's The Black Eyed Peas' 'I Gotta Feeling'. The screen flashes with 'Ed'. I put it on silent. Urgh. That song is *so* annoying. The phone vibrates in my hand. Ed is still calling. I hit reject.

Shut up, Ed, I need to think. This wasn't part of the plan.

My finger hovers over the settings icon on the phone. It would only take a second to change the stupid dumbass ringtone. I could change it to 'Bad Blood' by Taylor Swift or something. Sure, that would make my life better but would it be a giveaway? I'll just leave it on vibrate. It isn't worth the risk.

I turn my attention to the bloodstain. It's getting bigger by the second. I probably ought to move the cases and leave them in the bathtub. I'm about to grab a handle, but then I pause. *Hang on.* Actually, this is *perfect*. It's an awesome red herring. If the cops were to see this blood, they'll think *this* is where Tiff was murdered. Ed (and I) would be in the clear. We wouldn't be suspects at all. Not if we are back in London, which of course is where we are – Ed and Siobhán are in the mansion on Bishops Avenue. They will think that Tiff was murdered in this very room. Yes. I'm a genius. Now all I have to do is make the corpse disappear. I am thinking *canal*. There'll be *loads* of corpses in there. And then – in a puff of smoke – I will vanish too.

Now then how am I going to do that? If I take a commercial flight as Siobhán Faelan, then there would be a record of Siobhán here in Italy. That will look dodgy as fuck. The cops might check on the whereabouts of Tiffany's friends and family, her staff, all the people close to her . . . I'll stick out like a sore thumb. I'll have to take the train or a coach or hitch-hike across the border into France or Switzerland. I'll cross that bridge when I come to it. Where there's a will there's always a way. I'll figure it out as I go along. Fly by the seat of my pants.

I check the time. It's ten to nine. I'll have to wait a bit

longer. I'll do it in the middle of the night at three or four in the morning. But what am I going to do until then?

I stifle a yawn. I'll need some caffeine to stay awake for that long. Ideally I'd do some coke, but I wouldn't even know where to score. (I could probably ask the concierge. They ought to have dealers on speed dial.) I miss you, Big C, you miracle worker, your perfect pearly powder . . . It's true, I've made some sacrifices for this murder quest. I killed my best friend, that's number one obviously. That *sucks*. But losing the snow, the candy, the blow? That comes a *very* close second.

> *Oh cocaine! Let me*
> *Count the ways I love thee: Thou*
> *Art the best of drugs.*

Nino had better appreciate all the effort I'm going to.

I grab the phone and dial '1'.

'*Pronto*,' comes a man's voice.

'*Ciao*. Is that room service?'

'*Sì*, madam. How may I help you?'

'I want *six* espressos,' I say. 'Bring them up to the Doge Suite. And bring some air freshener as well. This room *really* stinks.'

9 p.m.

There's a knock at the door. A waiter is standing in the corridor with a retro wheelie trolley with espressos on. I don't want him to come inside. The Doge Suite reeks of offal, so I pick up the tray with the cups and carry it into the room. My hands are shaking and the coffee spills, dripping down to the carpet. I'm making a real *mess*. It would be so much easier if they made hotel carpets red or black or brown. But *cream*? What were they thinking? I shove what remains of the coffees on to a coffee table, then head back over to the door. The waiter is still there. He hands me a bottle of air freshener. I study the bottle. The writing is in Italian, but there's a picture of some bed sheets drying in the breeze.

'Please sign the check?' asks the waiter, producing a hotel-branded pen and a paper slip.

I glance at the hotel-branded paper. My heart skips a beat.

'I'll give you some cash. I don't need to sign this.'

'Everything is charged to the room.'

I panic. I hadn't thought this through. I don't know Tiffany's signature.

'Don't you know who I am?' I say. 'I don't have time for *this*.'

'*Mi dispiace*. I'm sorry,' he says. 'My boss say everyone sign.'

I take a deep breath and compose myself. *Alvie, you can do this.*

'This is *most* inconvenient.' I give him a hard stare.

Keep it cool. Keep it casual. Remember: you're *Tiffany*.

'Just a minute,' I say, rolling my eyes.

I walk over to the coffee table and search in the shaman's pouch. I grab Tiffany's burgundy passport. I check the last page where Tiff has scrawled her signature. There's a curly capital 'T' and a scribbled 'Forbes'. It doesn't look that hard, actually. I reckon I could copy it.

'I thought I heard my phone,' I say, returning to the waiter. 'Give me the bill and I'll sign it, of course.'

'*Grazie, signora.*'

The waiter hands me the pen and the bill. I hold it in my *right* hand. My fingers are trembling. My palm is sweaty; I lose my grip on the pen. He watches me sign on the dotted line. I try to remember the autograph and reproduce Tiffany's name as best I can, but the pen is running out and the words look kind of scratchy. When I'm done, I examine the signature. It looks really strange. You can hardly read it at all; the ink is so faint it looks ghostly. But if anyone ever checked it to see if Tiff was really here, they'd never be able to tell from *this*. Fortune is smiling on me.

Saturday, 13 August, 3.50 a.m.
Hotel Danieli, Venice, Italy

'*I'm so fucking spiritual that when I wake up in the morning my pillow looks like the Shroud of Turin.*'

'*Does it wash out?*'

'*No, it doesn't. There's this outline of my head and face kind of seared on the cotton. You can even see my eyelashes.*'

'*Wow. How does that happen?*'

'*I think what it is, is because I'm so spiritual in my sleep I achieve a state of perfection akin to Christ's.*'

'*Do you ascend?*'

'*I think so. I basically turn into a goddess and my flesh transforms into light. The flash of light is so powerful that a photographic negative is burnt on to the pillowcase.*'

'*Nice! I'd love to see it.*'

'*You can't. You'd go blind.*'

'*But you always come back in the morning?*'

'*Yes, I'm halfway through* Game of Thrones *and I don't want to miss it.*'

I prop myself up on the pillows on the king-size bed, chatting to Tiffany in my head and downing all six espressos. The inky coffee tastes bittersweet. I shovelled in twelve sugars to give myself some energy for the night ahead. I spend five hours watching incomprehensible Italian TV. I sit there, grinding my teeth and understanding sweet FA. I try to watch the news, but I have no idea what's going on. At least there are no 'breaking news' newsflashes with Tiff's face on.

I check the clock . . .

And check the clock . . .

I want to get out of here.

I'm primed. I'm ready. This is the moment we've been waiting for.

At 4 a.m. on the dot I leap off the bed: my eyes wide, my jaw clenched, my body lit from all the sweet strong coffee.

I stand and stare at the suitcases. They need to disappear.

I remove the scarf from my hair and my carrot locks spill out. I unwrap the bandages to reveal my face. I smile at myself in the full-length mirror and blow myself an air kiss. Badass *and* beautiful. I feel like Black Widow – she's ginger. I chuck the bandages on the floor. I don't need *those*. I'm Siobhán. Or, hang on a minute, do I? Hmm, should I keep them on? I don't want to be recognized as *me*. If anyone should spot me, you know, disposing of a *corpse*, it's better to remain anonymous. On the other hand, the staff at the hotel and all the people from the airport etc., have all seen Tiffany wrapped up in *these*. She's very recognizable. It is a distinctive look. And if 'Tiff' is spotted running around Venice at four o'clock in the morning, at a time when she's supposed to be *dead* . . . No, no more bandages. They were getting stuffy anyway.

I creep down the corridor and into the lift. I nod at the man standing at reception.

'Good evening,' he says.

'Top o' the evening to you,' I say in flawless 'Cork'.

His expression is blank. He doesn't recognize me as Tiff, of course. And he didn't say 'Good evening, Signora Forbes,' which is *ace*.

I take the back door out of the hotel. Outside on the pavement it's quiet. I chew my bubblegum and creep round the building down a dark and narrow path. There's nobody around. I step out to the promenade. All the bars and cafés are closed. Yes, I picked the right time. But soon the world will start to wake up. Delivery boys. Fishermen. German tourists leaving towels by hotel swimming pools. I don't have long to pull this off, so, *Alvie, don't fuck up*.

St Mark's Square is to my right. To my left, there's a pretty bridge. I strain my eyes to see in the dark. I cross the promenade. There are a few street lights shining, otherwise it's black. I head for the CCTV camera, approaching it from behind with my back pressed flat against the wall, inching my way along. I grab a nearby bin and jump up, agile as a fox. *This* is why I killed myself at CrossFit with those box jumps. But the stupid thing wobbles and crashes down. There's the smash of trash and glass bottles. Rubbish spills and rolls about.

'*Shhh*,' I say. '*Be quiet*.'

The sound echoes.

I look around, but there's nobody, just a startled cat running out from the shadows across the Riva degli Schiavoni. No one saw, but did anyone hear? I look up and check the windows, but I see no curtains twitching or faces peering out. I pick up the bin and climb on it again. This time I stay up. I reach up high towards the camera, keeping my face out of the frame. I spit the chewed-up bubblegum out and stick the gum on the lens, using the knuckle of my finger to press it into the glass. There, now, that should do it. They won't see a thing. I jump down then wipe the plastic bin with the hem of my skirt, so there won't be any fingerprints. *This* is why I'm so good . . .

I head back to the hotel. The man at reception looks up and frowns, like, *huh? You're back already*? I make a sign like I'm smoking a fag. He nods and then looks down again. He continues with his game of Sudoku/watching silent porn.

I ride the lift back to my room. It's going smoothly so far. I push through the door and glance around the Doge Suite. I need to make it look as if Tiff was murdered *here*. I need to make a big old mess. A sign that there was a ruckus. I kick off her shoes and leave them on the floor. That's better. My toe was *killing* me, and I haven't even been whining about it. *Hardcore.* And *you're welcome.* I tip over the tables and chairs and throw ornaments on to the carpet. By the time I'm finished the rooms looks *trashed*. It looks like Tiffany struggled a bit before they did her in. Yes, she fought them tooth and nail and smashed some porcelain shit.

Tiff's shaman's pouch is on the bed with her sunglasses.

I grab the bag and look inside. I leave her passport and phone, but grab her purse and pull out the remaining fistful of notes. I yank out the slouch socks – forgot about those – and shove the notes into my bra. I leave the socks in Tiffany's bag. Tiffany's *lovely* bag . . . I sigh. I don't want to leave it here, but I have no choice. I guess it's crucial evidence. I'll find myself another one when all this is over. *Keep your eyes on the prize, Alvina. There are other shaman pouches.*

I find Siobhán's passport and shove that down my bra as well. I glance at the bloodstain on the floor: it's the size of a St Bernard. *How much blood was in the girl?* Definitely more than average. I head for the door and rub the handle with the skirt of my dress to remove the fingerprints. That's it, isn't it? I didn't touch anything else without the plastic gloves on. Apart from all the cups.

I jog back over to the tray of tiny espresso cups and give them all a wipe as well. Phew, I almost forgot. I had to touch the suitcase handles before, when I was travelling, but I couldn't exactly walk around in plastic dog poo gloves. That would have looked incredibly odd. Not very 'Tiff'. And I can't wear the gloves, not now. If anybody spotted me, they'd be a dead giveaway of criminal shenanigans. I wipe down the sunglasses, the handles on the pouch, the Manolo Blahniks, Tiffany's phone. What else? That's it.

I strip the bed and tie the bed sheets together to form a makeshift rope. I'd guesstimate that it's five metres. It should be long enough. I *hope*. I open the door and lug the cases out to the balcony. I check for Nino, but he's gone back to the underworld. My bare feet slam on to cold tiles. A shiver runs down my spine. I stick my head out over the wrought-iron railings and look down. I search the street by the canal. That cat is still hanging around, but that's the only sign of life. I am good to go. I tie the rope to one of the suitcase handles and lift the bag on to the rails. Oh man, the suitcase weighs a *ton* and it's only *half* of her.

I lean back and grip the rope with one foot up on the railing. I lower the case down to the street. I try to let it down slowly, but it's heavy and the rope slips through my fingers and I drop it. It doesn't help that I'm doing this in a size 4 Gucci dress!

'*Bollocks.*'

The suitcase lands with a thump. Oh no. Did I *break* it? I drop the rope and crouch down low and peer through the railings. The suitcase is still intact. It's lying on its side. This is more stressful than I thought. My poor nerves are shot. (I'll have to book in for a massage at that spa where Tiff takes the dog.) I wait to see if someone comes out. I strain my eyes to see. But it's fine – the coast is clear. OK. *Go*. It's now or never. I climb over the railing and grab on to the drainpipe. The metal creaks under my weight. That sounds bad. Is it going to crack? Oh God, it's high. I hate *heights*. I can manage a *tree*, but not a four-storey building. I shimmy down as fast as I can, my feet slipping and sliding. My fingernails scrabble against the metal for a firmer grip. Ha. I'm like that guy in *Free Solo* – not even a rope. I finally reach the street and jump down, my head spinning.

I untie the makeshift rope from the suitcase handle, then haul the case against the wall, where it's camouflaged by shadows. It should be OK for a minute. If anybody sees, they'll assume that a tourist forgot it. That or they'll think it's a bomb.

I loop the 'rope' round my neck and climb back up the drainpipe. It's ten times harder going *up*, even with *these* biceps. Sweat is dripping down my back. Each second feels like an hour. This stuff always looks so easy when they do it in movies. My feet press against the wall as I scramble up the drainpipe, wishing I had suction cups in my hands like some kind of lizard. Eventually I reach my room then leap over the railing.

Then I lower the second case down to the street. This time I *don't* drop it. I chuck the bed sheet over the rail and climb back down the drainpipe, remembering not to look *down* and cursing the thing as it wobbles.

Suddenly I hear voices. People are approaching. I snap my head in the direction they are coming from. It's a man and a woman speaking Italian. I freeze, clinging on to the drainpipe like Incy Wincy fucking Spider having an enema. *Not now. Please. Not now. Go away.* The couple are nearing the entrance of the Hotel Danieli. Hurry up, goddamn it. I can't hold on for much longer. My hands are sliding. I lose my balance and my foot slips. *Come on, girl. You've got this.* I grip on to the drainpipe like my life depends on it.

The woman giggles. It sounds like they're drunk. At this time of night they probably are. I watch as the couple stop on the street outside the front door. The suitcases are by the wall less than five metres away. Hopefully they're too pissed to notice. Or if they do, they don't care. They lean into one another and kiss. For God's sake *get a room*. Don't leave me hanging here, literally hanging. I close my eyes and think of the kiss with Nino . . .

I lose my grip and fall the last two metres to the street below, twisting my ankle.

'OW. *Buongiorno*,' I say way too loudly. I manage a cheery wave.

The couple look up and blink. I pick up the bed sheets and cases then leg it as fast as I can (which isn't very fast at all, these cases weigh a ton) round the corner into the alley. I drop the cases. *Ow.* I'm panting, sweating. Everything hurts. My ankle is throbbing. My toe. I can feel it swelling up. I don't even have any painkillers.

I count to ten then poke my head round the wall, holding my breath. Are they still there? Are they following me? But no. They're not interested. The horny couple continue to snog pressed up against the wall. Oh, please, do take your time. Don't worry about *me*.

I watch his hand creep up her skirt. GET A FUCK-ING ROOM. They're standing outside a *hotel*. There are *loads* of rooms. Eventually the couple part. The man carries on walking and the woman pushes through the door into the hotel. What? That's it? He's just going to leave her? How un-chivalrous. He could at least have finished her off. I watch as he wanders away.

5 a.m.
Venice

I shove the bed sheets in a bin. I know it's not ideal, but I don't really have a choice. It was the bin or the alley. I guess I've got to pray that if the cops find the bed sheets, then there's no kind of evidence linking them to *me*.

Thirty-something gondolas line up at the water's edge. They are covered with tarpaulin and tied to red-and-white posts. I grab hold of one of the cases. I glance left and right down the street, then lug the suitcase after me. I pick a gondola at random. I hear a door close in the distance. There's the sound of footsteps. A dog barks. *I need to act fast* – more haste, less speed. I try to rip off the tarpaulin but the stupid thing is stuck. I jump in the boat and unhook the plastic. I chuck it into the canal. There's the sound of water lapping against the hull as it bobs. I smell the scent of damp, the musty stench of rotting wood. With a super-human strength I dump a case in the boat. The gondola rocks and tilts in the water. I think it's going to tip up as the water splashes and crashes around it.

Shh. Stop that. Shut up.

I see a light flick on upstairs in one of the hotel windows. I freeze, half expecting a head to poke out or a voice to shout 'Stop!' But it's probably just that woman arriving in her hotel room and looking for her dildo.

I limp back across the street to fetch the other case. I haul it over to the boats, letting it drag on the pavement. It doesn't matter about the *blood* leaking all over the tiles. In fact, it's good. It's more evidence that Tiff was slaughtered *here*. It helps with the verisimilitude. It supports my story. I hear a vaporetto engine chugging somewhere. I glance around and strain my eyes to see in the dark. The water is glossy, oil-black. There's no sign of the boat. But try telling that to my pulse, which is racing like Usain Bolt.

I pick up the suitcase and throw it at the gondola, but – somehow, I don't know how – the suitcase misses the boat and crashes down into the water. Oh God. Not *here*. Not *now*. There's a splash as the case disappears somewhere deep between the wall and the gondola. It sinks down, down, down into the inky water.

'Tiff!' I call out. I can't help it. 'No! Come back. COME BACK.'

I feel like Rose clinging on to the raft in *Titanic* as Jack sinks away.

I almost jump in after her, but it's too late. She's gone. Poor Tiff. I wanted to dump her body further out in the lagoon away from the hotels. And what about my fingerprints on the suitcase handle? I was going to wipe them off. I didn't rub it down! They won't just *wash off* in the water. This is bad. It's *terrible*. It won't be long till the case pops up and floats along on the surface. Methane gas, hydrogen sulphide and carbon dioxide will fill that case like a hot-air balloon. It will puff up like a Zeppelin.

I take a deep breath. *Chillax, Alvie. All is not lost. Be cool.* It wasn't *just* my prints on those handles: the bellboy at the hotel, Ed, James and Eileen all touched that case as well . . . but mine will be the most recent. They will be intact.

I try to untie the gondola from its mooring post, but my fingers are jelly and I am all thumbs. At least there is no padlock. I graze my skin on the rough cord. Finally the rope comes loose and I chuck it in the water. I grab the oar and push the boat out from the little jetty. The gondola rocks as I stand up. I've got to get out of here.

I punt as hard and as fast as I can, but the stupid thing only moves at about a mile an hour. It's fucking *leisurely*. You'd think that after *centuries* the gondoliers would've got sick of this and installed petrol engines. This is *so inefficient*. Soon the sun will start to rise and I'll be caught in Tiff's clothes with a corpse on a stolen boat. (OK, so it's only *half* a corpse, but if anything, that's *worse*.) I scan the street, the promenade, but it looks like a ghost town. I can't work out what to do with the oar. It's hard to move in a straight line. I jab the water with the oar over and over and over, stabbing at the surface like the oar is a Samurai sword.

I punt until I think my arms are about to fall off. How the hell do gondoliers do this all day every day? I bet they've got big bulging biceps. Yes, they must be ripped. I picture topless gondoliers in hats and tight black trousers.

The oar gets stuck and I lose my balance. I fall on my swollen ankle. I yank the oar, but it's stuck in a hole or a crack or the mud at the bottom. I pull the oar as hard as I can. It suddenly gives and I fall, lurching backwards the other way. I cry out in shock and smack my head on the side of the boat.

There's a gash across my face and hot blood pours down. I touch my head and my fingers feel wet. The blood looks black in the moonlight. I look out over the water to where my oar is floating. It is too far out to reach. I watch as it floats off. I look down at my hands. My whole head throbs. My palms are covered in blood.

> *This place is trying*
> *To beat me up. I feel like*
> *I've been in a war.*

The gondola glides along on the water. I look around and I shiver. Now what am I going to do? I can't move or steer. I'm two hundred metres away from the fucking shore. I wish Nino were here. Two people shorten the road. That's a popular Irish phrase.

'Nino?' I call.

The night is cold. My forehead pounds. It is worse than a migraine. I'm all alone on the water. I sigh and flop down on the bench.

I drift . . .

and drift . . .

and drift.

My eyes lock on to the suitcase. Eventually I haul myself up and limp over towards it. I summon all my remaining strength, grab the suitcase handle and rub it with the skirt of Tiff's dress. *No fingerprints this time*. I haul it over the edge of the boat. I let it fall. The boat sways and ice-cold water splashes up into my face. I watch as the suitcase sinks. Bubbles rise to the surface. The water is black and dead. It's a very spiritual moment. I want to say something like *Good-bye, Tiff,* but the words catch in my throat. I blink back tears. I don't know why I'm suddenly emotional. I'm usually so professional when it comes to losing cadavers. Cool as a cucumber. Calm and collected.

But I know what I have to do (I really, *really* don't want to, but I can't be caught with Tiffany's things. That would be unfortunate). I slide off Tiffany's diamond rings and study them – it hurts! A stabbing pain like love in my chest. I chuck them in the water. Oh man, it's such a waste! They're *gone.* I really wish I could keep them. Or, you know, sell them on eBay. I would make a *killing.* I peel off her Gucci dress and fling that overboard. It doesn't sink. I reach over the edge and push it down with my fingers. The last thing I want is to run around Venice *naked,* but I don't have a choice. I can't be seen in anything belonging to Tiffany.

I collapse in the gondola in my underwear and lean my head against the wood. The caffeine has worn off now. I'm cold. So cold I'm shivering. I wrap my arms round myself and my eyes close by themselves. I have a dream about me and Tiff learning Sanskrit in an ashram.

7 a.m.
Lido, Venice, Italy

I wake up as the sun is rising and the sunlight shines too bright. I sit up and rub my eyes. Blink into the morning light. Where am I? I look around. I'm still in the goddamn boat, but I'm far from the city now. I must have drifted through the night. How long was I sleeping for? The sun is low in the sky, so it's early morning still. My hands are numb. I'm *freezing*. Tiff's skimpy underwear is hardly keeping me warm.

I can see what looks like a beach. Huh. Are there *beaches* in Venice? I thought it was all canals? I jump up and the gondola wobbles. I need to get out of here. I have to lose this boat. There isn't a moment to lose. Damn, I shouldn't have *slept*. But I was knackered from the travelling. And the killing. And the sex . . . I peer out over the water. It's definitely *not* a canal. It must be the Adriatic. It's a good thing I woke up. I might have drifted too far out and ended up in Croatia.

I shield my eyes from the blinding sun and gaze towards the shore. The golden sands are quiet. Deserted. I reckon I could swim back. The beach doesn't look too far off, a hundred metres or so. Two hundred metres at a push. Three hundred at most. I check inside my bra: I've still got the euros and counterfeit passport. They'll get wet, but what can I do? At least the bra is a push-up bra, so it's tight and pretty secure. I can't stay here in this boat and *freeze*. I'm a sitting duck. I swing my legs up and over the edge, take a deep breath to steel myself then jump into the water.

Plop.

It's colder than I'd imagined. I gasp as my skin hits the sea. I gulp and swallow salty brine. A wave crashes over me. I sink down, my arms flailing, thrashing. I kick my legs and swim up. You have to float when it's icy like this, stay still and float or you'll drown. I take a deep breath and reach for the boat, but my fingers slide off it. My whole life flashes before my eyes. I'm under water again. What the hell do I think I'm doing? Why do I always fuck up? Now I'm going to drown right here in the sea. My whole body shakes. I try for the boat again. This time my fingers curl round the edge and I cling on, breathing hard. I look down: I can't see the bottom. The sea is opaque, dark. I don't want to think about the creatures swimming around inside. Jellyfish or stinging rays. Eels. Killer whales. The shore seems further now: at least five hundred metres. Maybe even a kilometre. I'm not sure I'll make it. I never had swimming lessons. Mum got those for Beth, but not me. I wasn't worth the investment. She didn't care if I was eaten by piranhas or shredded by giant crabs.

What's that? Over there on the horizon? A little black dot the size of a pea? I'll bet my bottom dollar that's a fishing boat heading my way. Right, that's it. It's now or never. I've done too much and come too far just to be busted by some dickhead catching sardines.

I lean back into the water, feel the currents rushing past my head, my bare neck and shoulders, and I start to swim for my life. My arms slice the water like scalpels. I front-crawl towards the shore. I sing T-Swizz songs in my head. Ride the waves like a wild horse. I thrash my arms like a propeller. Kick my legs and feet. Eventually my foot hits the sand.

Oh, thank God, I'm safe.

I lie prostrate on the beach. My muscles ache, burning. My heart is pounding in my chest like it's trying to break free. The shore was further than I thought. I came *this* close to drowning. My head throbs from where I bashed it. I reach up and find dry blood . . .

My breathing slowly returns to normal. Salt crystals dry on my skin. Oh my God. I did it. I did it! I'm here. The relief is intense. I have lost the corpse *and* the boat. Survived a shark-infested sea. That's it. I am no longer *Tiff*. Now I can be me. (At least I can be *Siobhán*, but you know what I mean.) Now all I have to do is get my ass back to London and finish off my Basecamp plan. I'm on bullet point number five.

I stand and brush damp sand from my ass, my knees, my calves and thighs. I like the way the rough sand feels against my naked skin. I wander along the beach where the water laps at the shore with the breeze in my hair and a smile on my face. I sing some more Taylor Swift. I stretch my arms up overhead in a delicious stretch. I find a pretty shell and chuck it out into the sea.

I look out along the beach. There's a young man practising backflips while smoking a roll-up. He's wearing a Hawaiian shirt with ripped denim cut-offs. His dark blond hair blows in his eyes. It looks wet from the sea. Perhaps he has just been for an early-morning swim, like me? I spot a small cut on his cheek. He looks like an *angel*. Fuck me, where did *he* come from all of a sudden? Perhaps there is a god? Wow, he's *really* good at backflips. I stand on the sand and watch.

He sits down on a rock on the beach and lights another roll-up.

'Well, hello there,' I say, striding up to him.

He looks up and spots me and I watch his eyes go wide. I smile. He smiles. He has blue eyes and blond hair, unusual for an Italian. He reminds me of Leo DiCaprio on the beach in *Romeo + Juliet*.

'*Buongiorno*,' he says, sparking his smoke.

Up close like this he looks younger, even younger than I'd imagined. Twenty or maybe twenty-one? His body is lean and taut. Mmm, I would like a taste. And unless I am mistaken, it is breakfast time.

I study the beach. It's empty apart from me and now *this* guy. I notice him checking out my booty in the lingerie. I don't blame him. I look hot, if a little dishevelled. But most of the blood has washed off now. (My ankle is purple and swollen.)

'I am *Juliet*,' I say, extending a hand.

'Silvio. *Piacere*,' he says with a cheeky grin.

I take his hand. 'Do you mind . . . Is it cool if I join you?' I ask.

'Please,' he says, moving up along the rock and gesturing for me to sit down.

I smile and sit down next to him. He looks up. We make eye contact. *Hello, Silvio*. I wonder if he knows what

I'm thinking? I mean, we've only just met and it's eight o'clock in the morning . . . Will he be up for this?

'You're very beautiful, Silvio,' I say, reaching out and stroking his tousled hair. I look into his eyes.

'You are . . . *bella*.'

I flutter my eyelashes and look down at his crotch.

'Now, Silvio, I don't usually do this, but I've just had some good news and I am feeling, *you know* . . .' I bite my bottom lip.

His eyes light up. 'What is the good news?'

'I am totally buzzing . . .' *From the kill and my success in disposing of the corpse.*

I grab his hand and jump up. 'Shall we? Shall we just pop down *there*?'

Silvio stands. I pull him along behind me and we climb on to the rocks and down to a 'private' area of rock pools and surf. The water crashes against the rocks, sending salt spray splashing. Seaweed, shells, hermit crabs, that kind of thing.

'Where are we going?' Silvio asks.

'Shhh, Silvio, it's OK. Follow me,' I say. I turn round and wink at him. 'Come on, it will be *fun*.'

We step down on to the sand. It smells of brine. A crab scuttles across my toes and leaps into a rock pool. Our footprints leave wet marks in the sand. There's a pleasant breeze. The air is cool and sticky with humidity from the sea. I sit down on the beach and reach up for Silvio to join me. He sits down on the sand next to me and I lean in to kiss him. At first he's shocked and he pulls away, but then I say, 'I want you,' in a Russian accent. I don't know why; it just comes out that way.

He shakes his head. 'I don't have *money*.'

'It's fine. My treat,' I say.

'You English girls are *crazy*.'

'Yes, we are.'

I take off my bra and fold it up with the passport and money. I tuck it underneath a rock. Silvio stares at me.

'*Merda*,' he says.

His eyes rest on my tits. I caress my nipples. This time, Silvio kisses *me*. He tastes of tobacco and something salty like capers or olives. Mmm, he tastes *delicious*. I explore his mouth with my tongue and reach down for the buttons on his shirt. I unfasten them one by one.

'Juliet . . .' says Silvio.

'Shhh, don't talk,' I say.

I like his Italian accent and all, but I don't want *distractions*. I want the taste of salt on his skin, the feel of his hands on my body and the sweet release of animal sex, wild and meaningless. I reach down and grab his cock through his denim cut-offs. Silvio groans. He reaches down to feel me through Tiffany's knickers. I push up into him. Oh yeah, that's *good*. I want him. I unzip his jeans and pull down his shorts to his knees. He isn't wearing boxer shorts. I wasn't expecting *that*. I see black pubic hair and – then – I gasp. The shock of his cock sends a thrill through my cunt. It is fucking *gorgeous*. Silvio rips off my knickers and throws them on the sand. I push him on to his back. We're both naked now. I like it better like that. I climb on top of him. Silvio reaches for his shorts, grabs his wallet and pulls out a condom. I watch him rip the pack with his teeth and roll the rubber on. The clear pink latex stretches out over his perfect dick. Oh my God, I want it. I *need* it. I *earnt* it definitely. I reach down for Silvio's hands then sink on to his cock.

His erection is hot and throbbing. I lean back. Sink deeper. Silvio watches me as I ride him. Up and down. Man, I love to fuck outside. On a beach like this it's *hot*. Seagulls cry out overhead. Silvio groans. I'm panting, I'm short of breath, my skin burning up. The cool breeze washes over me. I move my hands along his chest. My fingers slide round his neck and my hands begin to choke him. I close my eyes and waves of pleasure build and build and build. I squeeze his neck. I feel the heat rise from my cunt to my brain.

I shudder and shake and Tiffany's face appears in my mind's eye.

'Oh my God. OH MY GOD.'

I come in crashing waves, again and again and again and again.

'HELL YEAH,' I say.

Silvio struggles and writhes beneath me. I grip his neck even *tighter*, digging my nails into the flesh. I look down. He's gone *red*. He throws me off and I fall on a rock, smashing up my shoulder.

'Hey!'

He leaps up, gasping for breath. '*MA SEI MATTA?*' he says. '*MI HAI QUASI UCCISO!*'

'*What*? I don't speak Italian.'

He rubs his throat and glares at me.

'What? What did I do?'

He grabs his clothes from the sand then scrambles off over the rocks.

'Silvio? Where are you going?' I say. I watch him run

down the beach. 'It was nice to meet you too,' I say. I'll never see him again.

That's better. I needed that. It had been too long. All that stuff with Nino's ghost is nice and everything, but it's *nothing* compared to the real thing. Now, where are my knickers? I find my bra and put it on, stuffing the passport in one cup and the notes into the other. Whatever. I'll let him run off. It's not like we're going to be *pen pals*.

I stagger up and off the beach and scan the road ahead. I get some funny looks from the locals. I'll need to get dressed if I'm going to lay low. I need to fly under the radar. Where can I find myself some clothes? There don't seem to be any shops open. Where is Gucci when you need it? I sigh. Not even a Primark.

I hop across the sand. I can't put any weight on my ankle. I rub my shoulder where the skin scraped off against that rock. There's a café on the beach. It's tiny: one table, some chairs. It's more of a shack than a café really. Less of a shack, more a shed. An old woman is opening up with a fag in her mouth and pink rollers in her hair. A couple of grizzly fishermen sit outside drinking shots. The women and the men stop and stare at me as I approach them. What can I say? I'm smokin' hot. And this two-piece is miniscule. Smaller than my sister's bikinis or her under-wear. Tiff's lingerie is by La Perla: see-through lace and scalloped straps. I look like a bust-up Bond girl: Halle Berry emerging from the sea in *Die Another Day*. I limp my way across the beach. I'm a British Sophia Loren.

The woman is wearing an ugly floral nylon overcoat. It's a light housekeeping jacket to protect her other clothes. It's way too big, food-stained and shapeless, a retro sixties flower design. I pull a soggy hundred-euro note out of my bra.

'Take this for your coat. I want to buy it.'

I shove the money into her hand.

She looks me up and down and frowns. 'No, no.' She shakes her head.

I stand and shiver. I'm cold, so cold now that my teeth are chattering. 'Please.' I tug on her sleeve. I rub my arms up and down and offer the money again.

'*No, guarda, questa e sporco.*' She points at a stain that could be chocolate or, more likely, coffee.

'I don't care. I'm freezing,' I say.

Goose pimples cover my skin. The fine hairs are raised on my arms and my thighs. I cough. There's blood under my fingernails.

The woman peers into my eyes, a look of pity on her face. '*Va bene, aspetta,*' she says. She turns her back and walks inside.

'No, where are you going?' I say. 'OK. Two hundred? Two hundred?' I scrabble around inside my bra and find another note.

The fishermen watch where my fingers go. Do they want my tits or my cash? I follow the woman towards the shack.

She comes out with a package, then she unwraps an identical jacket: another floral housekeeping coat. She tears off the cellophane and unfolds the overcoat.

'*E nuovo. E meglio.*'

'OK. Whatever.'

I try to hand her the money, but she refuses to accept it, shaking her head and her hands. She helps me to put on the coat, then smooths it down and fastens the buttons.

It's not very warm, but it will do. It's not like I have much choice.

'*Siediti*,' she says, looking stern. She gestures to a chair.

I glance at the chair. It's cracked and old. Its white plastic legs sink in the sand. The chair is at the table with the wrinkly fishermen. I plop down into the seat and wait as the woman fetches a glass.

She pours out a shot of grappa.

I look at the glass.

'*Bevi questo*,' she says with a smile.

But I am three weeks sober . . . the last drink I had was that Malibu before my AA meeting. But it's tempting and I'm *celebrating*. You've got to celebrate success. Otherwise what's the fucking point? OK, let's do it!

'*Slàinte!*' I say, knocking it back. That is 'cheers' in Irish.

The fishermen knock back their drinks. They eye me suspiciously. They both have salt-and-pepper beards that are more grey than black, deep brown tans from years at sea and skin resembling scrotums.

'*Vai. Vai. Un altro*,' she says. She fills my glass with grappa again and I down it in one.

It warms me up. I can feel the fiery liquid swimming around inside my gut. Oh God, that's good. I needed it. I grin at the woman. I can feel the alcohol swimming up into my brain and making me all giddy.

'Do you have a toilet?' I say to the woman.

She looks blank.

'A toilet?' I stand up and point inside, then mime crossing my legs and writhing.

'Ah! *Sì. Un gabinetto.*' She ushers me inside.

I go to the loo and then look in the mirror. My hair is a

big salty mess. I'm having a bad hair day. It's less Bond girl and more *bomb victim.* I look like I've been run over. There's a bruise on the side of my face from when I fell in the gondola. I study the shiner on my temple. There's blood on my cheek and on my lip. I look at my hands. My nails are destroyed and my left ankle is easily twice the size of the other one. It's all puffy and bluish. *I'm a bleedin' state to be sure.* I can't help it – I laugh. I look so bad it's *funny.* But I'm free! And finally corpseless! And at least that grappa is numbing the pain. No wonder that woman took pity on me. She probably thought I was running away from some wife-beating asshole. That's why she wouldn't take any money. That's why she plied me with alcohol . . . I giggle, giddy from the grappa. I scrub off all the blood.

I push through the door and back out to the café. I look a bit more presentable. Huh. I wonder what else I can get?

The woman looks up and smiles.

'Ow,' I say, limping towards her. 'Have you got any *shoes*? Flip-flops will do. Just . . . anything?' I gesture to my toes.

'*Vuoi delle scarpe?*' she says. She points at my feet. 'Shoes?'

I nod my head. 'Yes. Shoes. Shoes.'

'*Sì, un momento,*' she says.

I hiccough and help myself to another shot of the lovely grappa. Then another. And another. The fishermen gawk at me.

She hobbles off towards a door that leads out of the back of the shop. I stand and eye the fishermen. They stare back. *What?* They're getting through that grappa too and it's only 8 a.m. Their eyes look wasted, soulless and they smell like peppered mackerel. They remind me a bit of Nino, apart from the mackerel.

The woman returns with a pair of bright pink plastic flip-flops. I try them on. They're not my size, but they'll do for now. It's better than nothing, I guess. I wish I hadn't dumped Tiff's shoes. They were Manolo Blahniks. But it was the right thing to do. They were two sizes too small and *very* incriminating.

'All right then,' I say. '*I'm off.*'

All three pairs of eyes are on me as I sashay down the street, working it like I'm Gigi Hadid. The alcohol is making me floaty. This housekeeping coat is *hilar.* I look like Mrs Brown from *Mrs Brown's Boys*, but at least I'm not naked or wearing the clothes of my last murder victim.

I break into a skip as I turn down a street called the Lungomare Gabriele D'Annunzio. I pull the money from my bra and I'm about to go and look for a cab, when someone grabs me from behind and drags me into an alley.

10 a.m.
Lido vaporetto terminal, Venice, Italy

'Help! Help! I've been robbed,' I say, as I stagger out of the alleyway and on to the main road. *Fucking fishermen.* 'Help. Help. I've been mugged.'

I look both ways down the road. There is a couple pushing a baby in a pram. I run up to them.

They look alarmed and swerve the other way when they see me coming. They cross the street just to avoid me. What am I going to do? Those fishermen took all my cash. I was too exhausted to fight them. How am I going to get home? I check the other cup of my bra for Siobhán's passport. It's still there. Thank God for that. That's all I've got: a passport and a floral housecoat. This is beyond a joke.

I pace up and down by the lagoon, scowling and muttering. I won't give up. I will *not* give up. I'm getting out of here. I've been through too much to just *stop* and break down *here*. But where *is* here? I'm not paying attention. I've walked all the way to the port. I look up and study the roof of the ferry terminal; it looks like the wings of a bird raised up on tall white pillars as though it were about to take off. There's the *chug-chug-chug* of a ferry approaching, the splashing and crashing of water, the honk of a horn as the ferry pulls up and bumps against the moorings. I can't even afford a ticket for the fucking boat. I'm destined to spend the rest of my days here on this *nowhere* island. I gaze out over the lagoon at the stunning view of Venice, at terracotta palaces and elegant church spires. I can see pink buildings and the pale green tiled roof of the campanile. It is fucking *beautiful*. There are worse places to live on the street as a hot foreign tramp. It's warm and mild enough to sleep rough. The food that people *throw away* is tastier than the stuff I used to cook at the hostel. Not that I ever *cooked*. (Does adding boiling water to a packet of chow mein instant noodles count as cooking?) There are plenty of tourists to rob: shuffling around with their bumbags stuffed with hundred-euro bills, Rolexes and gold earrings and bulging Prada totes. They are fucking *everywhere*. It's true – I could make a *killing*. But that is not a long-term plan. We'll call it *plan B*. I can't risk getting arrested for pick-pocketing right now.

If I can just get back to Ed's, there's a whole world of opportunity. Ed's forever in my debt. I *must* find my way back to London. But *how* without any money? I can't exactly hitch-hike from Venice all the way to London. That could take weeks or more. I need another plan. I'm sure Ed could wire me some cash, but I don't want a trail from him to me. Siobhán Faelan was *never* in Italy. I am *not* supposed to be here. And Ed can't have any links to Venice. There's got to be another way . . .

I'm not looking where I'm going and walk into a tree. I look up and rub my head. Where did *that* come from? It's like the *only* tree in Venice. It's not very green around here.

'*Idiot.*'

I look up. A kid is laughing at me. It's a tourist; he looks about fourteen years old. He's wearing cut-off shorts and a Man United T-shirt.

'What are you looking at? Am I the fucking *entertainment*?' He runs away. 'You'd better *run*. Yeah, go back home to Mummy.'

That's not a bad idea, actually. I *could* be the entertainment. People are staring anyway. I am eye-catching as fuck in this neon floral thing. Maybe I could busk? But what could I do? *Dance*? But to what? There is no music. I know, I could sing! I know all the words to all Taylor's songs. I wouldn't need a microphone; I could just sing really loudly. Yes, that's it. I'm a genius. I'll sing for my supper. But what will I use to collect all the money? I need some kind of *receptacle* . . .

I head for a bin overflowing with rubbish and extract a used coffee cup.

I go and stand under an olive tree (the one that I walked into). It's right next to the vaporetto stop where it gets busy. I put the coffee cup on the floor by my feet and clear my throat. Which one should I start with? 'Love Story', 'Blank Space', or 'Shake It Off'? They are all so good, I can't choose. I settle on one of my favourites: 'Bad Blood'. It's a classic. I take a deep breath and sing my heart out.

I sing and sing at the top of my lungs. I'm good. I'm better than *good*. I'm *great*. I'm a whole tribute band. I could be on *The Voice*. I even do the rappy bits that Kendrick Lamar does. (I must still be pissed . . .) People on the pavement stop and stare. They smile, approach and gather round me nodding their heads in time to the beat. I start to dance. I can't help it. My feet begin to move by themselves. I'm overcome by the rhythm. The lyrics. The pure adrenaline. And, before I know it, I'm doing a whole routine with cancan kicks and twerking and shaking my ass like it's a Polaroid picture. If only Tiff were here to see me. She'd be into this. I'm sure Tiff loved Taylor too. Everybody does.

A crowd of tourists shuffles off the boat. There's the hubbub of voices from lots of different continents: the guttural grunt of German, the staccato sound of Japanese and the nasal twang of New York. A large group of Chinese tourists stops and stares at me. I bet they think I'm the *real* Taylor. I'm not going to deny it. They'll have a great story when they get back to Beijing and tell all their friends that they saw Taylor Swift perform for free in Venice. (Plus they might cough up more cash if they think I'm legit.)

I move on to 'Shake It Off'. This one's *vigorous*. I do some Irish dancing and I lose myself in the song. I'm high on the rush. The adoration. I dance like my life depends on it, which in a way it does. A Chinese man drops a green note into my coffee cup. It's a whole five euros. Ace. An American matches that. That's *ten*. It keeps on coming and coming. I'm singing 'Blank Space' now. This one's proving popular. There's a crowd of thirty or forty people and they're clapping and cheering along.

I eye my cup: it's overflowing with euro notes and shiny coins. But I need *more*. I have to pay for a boat, a coach and several train tickets. I spot a man at the front with a Ralph Lauren polo, a gold chain and a golden watch. He's short and fat and bald. I pick up my cup and dance over to him. I sing like it's just for him. I start vogueing like Madonna. I do the Harlem Shake. He smiles and reaches for his wallet. He pops a fifty in my cup. I shake the cup so it rattles. He laughs and drops in another note and I dance off again.

The man pulls out his mobile phone and starts to film. *Oh shit.*

'*NO FILMING,*' I say, running over. I grab his phone and delete it. I can't have this routine going viral. Everyone would know I was here. No, no, no, that would be a disaster. That is the *last* thing I need.

I finally get to the end of the song and collapse in a sweaty heap on the floor.

'Show's over. You've been *great,*' I say to the crowd.

'Encore,' calls the man, but his wife appears in a fanny pack and Crocs. She drags him away along the street. The people disperse. I go and sit down underneath the tree and start to count the money. There are *hundreds* of euros here. I knocked it out of the park. OK, so it's not enough to pay for train tickets across half of Europe, but it will get me out of the city and I can always hitch-hike . . .

Monday, 15 August, 3 p.m.
The Bishops Avenue, Hampstead, London

I ring the bell and the butler answers.

'Where have *you* been?' he says.

'I went on a training course . . . in *Basingstoke*,' I say. I give him a smile. He's glazing over. He doesn't really want to know. 'It was all about *dog grooming*: how to groom your dog, you know. How to perm your puppy's hair, how to plait its tail –'

'OK. Whatever. Get in,' says James, stepping aside.

I'm in!

'So, did I miss anything?'

'No,' he says, 'It's been dull. Tiff is off at an auction in Venice and Ed isn't feeling well. He's just been moping around in bed.'

'Awesome,' I say. 'I mean, *aww*.' James looks up and frowns. 'Er, yeah, *poor Ed*. What do you think is wrong with him?'

'Probably just a hangover, but he's claiming it's the flu.'

I nod then cross the floor to the lift. James watches through narrowed eyes.

'In *Basingstoke*?' he calls.

I nod.

'Huh. Where is that then?'

'Um, I don't know.' The lift pings and I hurry inside. 'About an hour away, I guess? I told the Über to take me there, and it did.'

'Unbelievable.'

The doors close in James's face and I flip him the bird.

I study myself in the mirror . . .

Right, now, Alvie, this bit's *key*. I know you're all upset about Tiff, and it is very tragic, but Ed needs to know that you've got this, OK? He needs to know he can trust you. He doesn't know you two were *best friends*. He thinks you're the dog's nanny. So keep it cool. Keep it casual. *He* can grieve. You be *breezy*.

The doors ping open and I skip out towards the Forbes' suite.

'What's the story, horse?' I say, letting myself through the door. It's a popular Irish phrase. I don't know what it means.

The door slams shut behind me. Bang. It's dark. All the curtains are drawn and Ed is fast asleep in bed. I check the time on the grandfather clock – just after 3 p.m.

'Ed?' I say, sitting down on the bed. 'It's *fine*. Please *don't get up*. It's only *me*. I just risked my *life* to save your ass. Hello? Hello? Ed? ED! I just travelled to *Europe* and back.'

'Tiffany?' says Ed, rolling over under the pug-soft cash-mere blanket. He peers at me and rubs his eyes, then sits up on the pillows. He yelps. He looks like he's just seen a ghost. 'Siobhán?' he says *at last*.

'That's right. You remember me?'

'Of course I do,' he says.

'Oh good.' He really fucking owes me. 'I'm pleased you remembered my name.'

That line would have had more impact if I weren't los-ing my voice. I'm croaking like a frog. And my throat is sore. It's all that singing and seawater swimming. I prob-ably have polyps on my vocal cords (like Adele) and now I'll need surgery.

I flick the light on the bedside table. Ed shields his eyes like he's blinded.

'Urgh. What happened to *you*?' I ask, although it's obvious.

An empty bottle of Johnny Walker lies on its side on the table. He clearly hasn't shaved since I left and stubble spreads across his face like a dirty rash. There are purple bags under his eyes. For the first time he looks his age.

Ed frowns.

'*What?*' I ask.

'I haven't heard from you for *days*. I've been worried sick,' he says. 'I didn't know what was happening.' He gives me a wounded look.

'Yeah, well, I was *busy*,' I say. 'I had to do *that job*. And I couldn't take the plane. I had to get a *coach*.'

'*Shh*,' says Ed with a glance at the door.

That isn't *strictly* true. I mean, it's true about the *coach*. And that was simply *awful* now that I'm used to private jets. But I decided to take some time off. A little holiday. After I'd disposed of Tiff and worked out how to earn some cash, I did a bit of sightseeing and stuffed my face with gelato. By 'sightseeing', of course, I mean I saw some Italian men. After Silvio (10/10) there was Giancarlo (in a park, 7/10); Gianfranco (in a Fiat, 8/10) and Gianni Bello (under a bridge, 9/10). So what if I took a day off? A girl needs a break sometimes. And I've been working *really* hard. This is a tough hit to pull off. I think it was the *grief* as well. I had to comfort-eat. And mourning always makes me horny. It's just human nature.

I grab the remote control and point it at the stereo. I want to turn some music on so we can talk openly. I don't want any members of staff to hear what I'm about to say. Fifi or that pain-in-the-ass *butt*-ler James. I click the buttons and 'Dancing Queen' by ABBA comes on way too loud.

'What the *hell* have you been listening to?'

Ed shrugs. '*Classic ABBA.*'

I click next and 'Gimme! Gimme! Gimme!' blares at full volume.

'I was trying to cheer myself up.'

I roll my eyes. Click next.

It's 'The Winner Takes it All'. ABBA? Interesting.

But then I remember item five on my Basecamp list: seduce Ed. *Come on, Alvie. Think.* I've got to be Tiffany 2.0 to stand a chance to win Ed's heart. I've got to be *smoking hot.* And I have got to be *spiritual.*

But first I need a drink.

'Ed, can you call down and have someone bring me a herbal tea or something?' I ask. 'Please, *darling,*' I add.

Ed sighs and picks up the house phone. 'Fifi? A herbal tea in my suite.' He hangs up. 'So . . . did you *do it*?' he asks, biting his nails.

I roll my eyes and sit up straight, pulling my shoulders back.

'What about "Hello, Siobhán, you look great. Thank you SO much for busting your gut to go all the way to Venice and carry my dead wife around . . ."'

He opens his mouth, shocked. 'I'm sorry,' he says. 'Of course you look *great.*'

'I know. I caught the sun in Italy. It's brought my freckles out.'

'Your top . . .' he says. 'Is it new?'

'It is!' I say. 'Cute, right? Do you like it? I got it in Venice.' I look down and smooth out the fabric. I'm wearing a cotton ITALIA shirt: blue with the Italian flag. 'I got a matching one for you,' I say, reaching into a plastic bag and grabbing the *tricolore* T-shirt wrapped in cellophane. 'I got a *medium*?'

Ed just looks at it. He doesn't say *Thanks* or *I love it* or *No, I would have preferred a large.*

I chuck it on the bedside table. *So ungrateful.* Next time I won't bother, but I thought it would be sweet to bring him a little souvenir.

'I got these as well,' I say.

I grab two Venetian masks with fabulous pink feathers and tiny diamanté jewels stuck all over them. I try one on and tie the ribbon in a bow at the back of my head. But Ed doesn't even react. How could he not *love* them?

I tie Ed's mask on for him. 'There! You look fabulous, darling.'

I take a photo with his phone. '*Smile.*'

Click.

I show him. He looks like a bird of paradise crossed with David Bowie.

'So . . . did you do it?' he asks again, as 'Waterloo' comes on.

He takes off the mask and hands it to me. He looks like he might cry. He bites his bottom lip, a worried expression on his face.

I feel a pang somewhere in my heart. *Don't let him get to you, Alvie. Don't start getting emotional. You are strong, like an ox.*

'I did it. Don't worry, Ed. It all went *swimmingly*. Tiff's at the bottom of a canal. We need to move on,' I say. I reach out and squeeze his hand. 'It's hard for me too,' I say.

Oh man. This is getting so morbid.

I rifle around in my plastic bag and pull out a miniature figurine. It's a little gondola complete with a gondolier in a red-and-white stripy shirt. 'I suppose you don't want this either? It was this or a snow globe.'

Ed doesn't reply.

I study the tiny man. He looks a bit like Giancarlo or was it Gianfranco? Whatever. I chuck it on the bedside table with the T-shirt and the masks.

I look at Ed. He looks down at his hands and spins his wedding band round and round on his finger. I suddenly feel flat. This was supposed to be my big moment. My jubilant return. A moment of celebration. But Ed doesn't seem as pleased to see me as I thought he would be. And I am feeling empty, not psyched to get on with my plan . . .

'Ed, where's my ring?' I say suddenly. He'd better not have lost it.

Ed reaches into the drawer on his bedside table and hands it to me.

Phew. I slide it on. *That's better.* I felt naked without Nino's ring. I wiggle my finger. To be fair, I preferred Tiff's diamond rings . . .

I lean in towards him and sniff. Has he even *showered*?

'I've hardly left the bed,' he says, reading my mind. 'I've been so worried. Jacinda has been badgering me non-stop, asking about Tiffany. And my investors keep on calling. I can't take their calls. I've barely slept.'

You shouldn't have killed your wife.

'But you were sleeping when I came in?' He's had more

sleep than *I have*, running around Italy, scaling drainpipes and nearly drowning in the fucking *sea*. 'What have you been doing then?'

'Watching movies, drinking . . .'

He smells like several different people's sweat combined. It's gross.

I jump off the bed and cross the room to open up the curtains. He really needs to snap out of it. He's going to make me depressed. I open the window as wide as I can to let in the fresh air.

I take a deep breath. *That's better.*

Ed gets out of bed fully nude.

'Whoa,' I say.

I mean . . . I wasn't expecting *that*. He's caught me off guard. I study his ample crotch. Ed's penis is slightly longer than average, veering almost imperceptibly to the left. One of his balls is hanging down a centimetre lower than the other. Fully erect, I'd guesstimate seven and three quarter inches.

'What movie did you watch? Jason Bourne?'

'*Brokeback Mountain, Philadelphia*.'

'I haven't seen either of those. Did they cheer you up?'

'No.'

'Are you just going to stand there, naked?'

'I was going to take a shower.'

'No, not *now*, you aren't. Come here.'

I grab his hands and sit him back down on the bed. He complies. His skin feels soft like he's never done a hard day's work in his life.

Ed is looking very concerned like I might be about to jump him.

'First you're going to call the Danieli and ask to speak to your wife. And when they say that she's not there, you're going to call the police. You're going to be out of your mind with worry and say your wife has disappeared. The last time you saw her was the night before she flew to Venice.'

There's a knock at the door.

'The cops?' says Ed. Blood drains from his face.

'That will be my *tea*.'

'Oh, right.'

I go and answer it.

'Hi, Siobhán,' says Fifi, smiling. She has my tea on a silver tray.

'Hey, Fifi,' I say. 'How are you?'

'I found the dog in the cellar,' she says in a hushed, low voice in my ear.

Shit. I forgot all about the dog. He's lucky to be alive.

'I heard him scratching and barking,' she says, 'so I let him out.'

'You *what*?' I fix her with a stare. 'I wish you hadn't done that. Where is he now?'

'He's in his suite. I'm so sorry,' she says. 'I thought he might be hungry or thirsty or . . . or . . . or . . . or . . .'

I shake my head. I think on my feet. I need a good excuse. I'm his *nanny* after all. 'The *cellar* was a crucial part of his training, and now we'll have to start again.'

'I'm so sorry,' she says.

I roll my eyes. 'I'll come and get him when I'm done. I hope I can still train him. It is *very* difficult to teach an old dog new tricks.'

'But I thought he was a *puppy*?' she says.

I give her a hard stare. I take a noisy sip of tea, maintaining eye contact.

It's hot and burns my mouth. I glance at the label. It's *turmeric*. The kind of shit that Tiff used to drink. It tastes fucking nasty. Yuck. I spit it out and slam the cup back on to the saucer, almost cracking the Wedgwood. I shove the saucer on to the tray, close the door and step back in the room.

'Go on then, *call*,' I say to Ed, sitting back down on the bed.

'Can't you do it?' Ed says. 'Please. I'm in pieces. I'll say something wrong.'

Oh, for fuck's sake. Seriously? Why do I have to do *everything*? I'm the only one doing any work around here. He's lazy, that's his problem. And he has a weak mentality. He's falling apart just because (he thinks) he murdered his wife.

I grab Ed's phone and google the number for the Hotel Danieli. I hear it ring and a woman picks up.

'Hotel Danieli, *pronto*.'

'Just do it,' I hiss and shove the phone into Ed's hands.

'H-h-hello?' he says. 'Can I speak to Tiffany Forbes? This is her husband, Ed.'

I'd better go and get the dog. I'm supposed to be his *nanny*. And now that Tiffany isn't here I'm his primary carer.

I enter the dog's suite. Baby's asleep in his basket. *Bless.* He wakes up when he hears me come in. He jumps up and barks. I bend down to pet him and he licks my feet, my face.

'All right. Calm down. Come here,' I say, laughing.

What's going on? Did he *miss* me?

The little dog runs round in a circle, chasing his own tail. He barks and barks, then sprints back to me and licks my hands. My arms. My knees. He's *really* happy to see me.

'Aww, hello, Baby,' I say, stroking the hair on his tiny head. I wipe the slobber from my hands, then tickle his furry tummy.

I don't think anyone, human or otherwise, has ever been this pleased to see me.

I scoop up Baby. He smells of dog.

'Walkies?' I say.

Tuesday, 16 August, 8 a.m.

'Ed, they're here, the cops,' I say, shoving a piece of bubble-gum into my mouth and chewing it like my life depended on it.

'Shit,' says Ed, pacing the bedroom.

I watch through the window as a patrol car approaches the gate to the drive.

The pug jumps off the bed and runs round in a circle, barking.

I guess the dog doesn't like cops. It's not just me then.

I hide behind the Venetian blind and glower at the patrol car. *I don't like cops.* And they don't like *me*. This is going to be *painful*.

Ed called the cops to say Tiff was missing. (I made him do it.) We had no choice. We had to do it. That was the logical thing. Now they're here to ask Ed some questions. But even though we expected them, I can't help but panic. I'm feeling tense. I need to stay in control.

'It's OK. Be cool,' I say, blowing an enormous bubble

then popping it. 'I got this, Ed. Follow my lead. You're going to be *great*.'

Ed is standing at the bar on the far side of the room downing what looks like a triple shot of Johnny Walker Blue Label. He wipes his mouth with the back of his hand and joins me at the window. Ed and I peer out through his and Tiffany's bedroom window. James buzzes the cops through the gate and the cop car crawls on to gravel. It purrs along the drive and comes to a stop by the marble fountain. Two policemen step out . . . Hang on. Whoa. Who's *that*? Even from the top of the house, from the sixth floor, I can tell that policeman is *ripped*. My top five uniforms for men are: policeman, fireman, soldier, pilot and matador (very niche).

I gawp as hot cop approaches the pond. I can see Kermit from here, but will *he* notice the murder weapon? I have no idea. I should have smashed it or buried it or thrown it in the sea. But *no*. It's a *ceramic frog*. No one would ever suspect that it was involved in the bloodiest hit this town has ever witnessed. It would have attracted *more* attention if the frog had vanished, but sitting there in the very same place that it has always been it just looks like a stupid ornament, which it is.

I heard that, Kermit says in my head. *Stupid yourself.*
Shut up.

I hear the sound of footsteps in the hall outside the door. Then there's a knock and Ed looks at me.

I run my fingers through my hair and open the door.

I let the cops into the room. Hot cop is wearing a drop-dead-gorgeous tan, mirror aviators, a criminally tight pair of kecks and a smile that says he's about to ruin my fucking day.

'Hello, officer,' I say, swishing my hair like a model in an ad for something fancy by L'Oréal. I look into his mirror shades; my eyes reflect back. Argh. I look really frightening, like Regan in *The Exorcist*. Man, I really need some *sleep*. I need to go to a day spa and get some kind of rejuvenating facial or very expensive mud mask.

He pushes his mirror shades back into his hair to reveal dark eyes, the kind of eyes that could melt a glacier faster than global warming. I sigh and picture him naked . . . *Nice*. He's *fit,* but then I remember: shit, I just killed somebody and her corpse is floating in the lagoon or possibly the Grand Canal, depending on the currents.

'Good afternoon, Mr Forbes,' says hot cop, extending his hand. 'My name is PC Marks.'

I watch as he and Ed shake hands.

'Ahem,' I say. What about *me*? I want an introduction. To be fair, I want more than *that* . . . anything involving lubricant.

'And I am PC Turner,' says the average-looking cop. He shakes hands with Ed as well.

I gaze at PC Marks.

Ed clears his throat. 'Hello,' he says. 'Er . . . this is our dog's nanny, Siobhán. She is a friend of Tiff's.'

'*Ciao,*' I say and blow a bubble in my strawberry gum as I stare at PC Marks. I blow until the bubble is the size of my actual head, then it pops and I gobble it up in a seductive manner. *Jesus. Stop flirting, Alvie. Pay attention. Be professional. This is a really critical moment. Keep your muff under control.*

I shake hands with the cops, but when I shake hot cop's hand I squeeze it really, *really* tight and watch his eyes go wide.

'Mr Forbes, would you sit down, please?'

'Why? What's wrong? What's happened?'

Hot cop glances at average cop.

I give Ed a thumbs up.

'Just sit down, please, Mr Forbes.'

Ed sits on the bed.

'I'm sorry, but we have some rather distressing news for you.'

'No,' says Ed. 'No, no.'

He's doing very well.

'We regret to inform you that . . . *half* of a body we believe to be your wife's has been found in Venice,' says hot cop, looking sad but hot.

'Jesus Christ,' says Ed. 'You mean . . . *Tiffany is dead*?'

'Subject to identification, we think she is, yes, sir. I am sorry. My deepest condolences.'

Ed rests his head in his hands.

I chew my gum and look sad.

The dog jumps down from my arms and starts to lick his balls on the floor.

I spot the tiny gondola lying on Ed's bedside table. I *squeak* then sprint over to grab it and shove it in a drawer. *Shit*. That was close. That is *incriminating*. It's lucky I'm so *smart. And quick* . . .

'The case is being treated as homicide.'

'Oh God,' says Ed, 'poor Tiff.'

'There were signs of a struggle in her hotel room and we hope to be able to identify her by her dental records. Her dentist has been contacted and forensics are doing analysis.'

'Shit,' I say. 'I mean . . . *how sad.*'

Tiffany had lovely teeth.

'Mr Forbes,' says hot cop, 'would you please be so kind as to identify a suitcase that we believe belonged to your wife.'

'Yes, of course,' says Ed in a daze.

Hot cop produces a photograph and shows it to Ed. The photo is of a Louis Vuitton case in light brown leather. The soggy case rests on a metal table at what I assume is the police station in Venice.

'Yes, that's right,' says Ed. 'She always travelled with those cases. They are her favourites. *Were* . . .' Ed speaks slowly. His voice is shaking. 'At least it looks like hers.'

Hot cop nods. 'We have fingerprints from the suitcase handles.'

I choke on my gum and cough, and the gum flies out of my mouth to the floor. It lands on the carpet. I look at it. Oops. Did anyone notice?

'What do you mean *fingerprints*?' I ask PC Marks.

Of course they found the one with the prints. Talk about bad luck. But I didn't have my leprechaun, so go figure.

Hot cop glances at PC Turner before addressing me.

'Do you know what fingerprints are?' He is speaking slowly as though attempting to explain quantum physics to a child.

Ordinarily I'd call him out on the mansplaining, but instead I say, 'I'm not familiar with . . . the ways of the police.' I shift on my feet and look at the floor. I study the bubblegum. It looks a bit like the intestines of a tiny man. The dog walks over to it, sniffs and gobbles it up.

'The Italian police have collected a set of fingerprints. We believe they either belong to Mrs Forbes or the perpetrator.'

I glance at Ed. 'Oh right. I see. *Those* kind of finger-prints . . .'

I should have wiped the fucking case. I can't believe I dropped it before destroying the evidence. That was a schoolgirl error.

'If it's OK with you, Mr Forbes, we would like to see one or two of Mrs Forbes' personal items to collect her prints. We would have taken prints from the body, but . . . unfortunately the skin on her fingers had been damaged.'

I know, genius, that was *me*. Always two steps ahead. I unwrap another piece of gum and shove it in my mouth.

Ed doesn't reply, so I give him a kick in the shins. 'Ed? The policeman asked you a question.'

'Of course, be my guest,' he says.

PC Turner pulls on plastic gloves and then walks over to Tiffany's dressing table. He picks up her hairbrush. 'Was this hers?'

'Yes,' says Ed. 'It was.'

'And this?' he asks, picking up a bottle of Tiffany's perfume: Marc Jacob's Decadence.

'Well, it wasn't *mine*! *Jesus Christ*,' says Ed, leaping up from the bed and banging his fist on the bedside table. We all stare at him. 'I'm sorry,' he says. 'It's just . . . a shock.'

I grin at Ed from across the room. '*Very good*,' I mouth. '*More* like that.' I feel like a director. Sofia Coppola or someone.

'We'll need to see a breakdown of Mrs Forbes' activities: where she's been and who she met with over the past two weeks.'

Ed gulps. 'Yes, I'll ask her PA to email the details,' he says.

'Er, Ed, I think Tiff fired her,' I say.

'What? Who? Jacinda?'

'*Jemima.*'

'Jacinda?'

'What was her name? That woman who used to hang around here?'

'Tiffany's PA?'

'Yeah, *her.* I'm pretty sure she got fired . . . for being too annoying.'

'I'll send it myself,' says Ed to hot cop.

Ed fiddles with his iPhone. I turn my attention to PC Marks as the other cop collects prints, sprinkling the hairbrush and perfume bottle with some fine black powder.

'So,' I say, taking a strand of hair and twizzling it round my finger like a horny cheerleader on prom night.

'Wait a minute,' says hot cop, turning to me. He studies my face. I expect him to say something like you're *very beautiful* . . . but instead he says, 'I recognize you. PC Turner, come here a minute, would you?'

I swallow. Hard. I expect him to say, 'We just watched a video of a Taylor Swift impersonator *killing it* in Venice,' but instead he says, 'We just watched Mrs Forbes' latest vlog post to see if there might be any clues to the circumstances surrounding her disappearance.'

'Oh,' I say. 'You did?'

'We did. And unless I'm much mistaken, the woman in the video with Mrs Forbes is *you* . . .'

I'm about to deny it but there's no point. He clearly remembered my face; he fell in love with me at first sight. It must be my fabulous bone structure.

'Yes, yes, it is,' I say. 'She wanted me in the video. I'm very good at qigong, you see.'

Hot cop and PC Turner exchange glances.

'What did you say your name was?'

Balls. Don't write it down . . .

'Siobhán Faelan,' I say in my best Irish accent.

Hot cop writes it down. 'S-I-O-B-H-A-N?'

'Yes, that's right.' I think.

'And you're spelling "Faelan" how?'

Ah shit. I can't remember. I need to look at the pass-port. I'm just going to have to guess. If it comes up, I'll say he wrote it down wrong. Whatever.

'F-E-E-E-L-A-E-A-N,' I say.

Hot cop frowns.

'Thank you, Mr Forbes,' says PC Turner. 'We have everything we need. We can show ourselves out.'

'Right,' says Ed. 'Thank you . . . for everything.'

Hot cop reaches into his wallet and pulls out a business card. He gives it to me. I read the print: *PC Anthony Marks.*

'Call me,' he says.

I stare at the card. Does he mean for a date?

He hands Ed another card.

'If you have any leads or evidence that will help with the case.'

Ed says, 'Yes, of course. We will.'

The two policemen stroll out through the door to the corridor. Hot cop catches my eye. I shake my head and look at the floor. I glance up as he swaggers off and admire his iron glutes. Man, the sacrifices I have to make!

I grit my teeth and glare at Ed. 'You were acting *guilty*.'

'Well, what about you?' Ed says, his voice raised. 'You were *flirting*.'

'Ed,' I say, '*darling*, that was all part of my plan.' Nice save. *Good cover, Alvie.* 'The flirting was . . . a *distraction* to throw him off the scent. I had to do *something.* You couldn't *talk.* You looked like a murderer. I'm only telling you this as a *friend*, but it was highly suspect.'

Ed paces the room again. 'I'm going to have to lawyer up. I'm going to need some hot PR to spin this thing. Oh God. And what about the fingerprints on the suitcase handle? Were they *yours*?'

My blood goes cold. I freeze. I gaze into the middle distance.

'Siobhán? Are you all right?' Ed asks. 'You're looking a bit pale.'

'I'm fine. I'm on my period,' I say. 'I've lost a lot of blood.'

Urgh. The fucking *fingerprints.* I'd hoped they wouldn't come up. But clearly they have and this is *shit.* They could be my undoing.

'Ed. Ed.'

'Mr Forbes.'

I hear voices from outside. I run to the window and look out over the drive. There are a ton of cars parked up on the road outside and five or six reporters with cameras are shouting through the gate.

Ed's phone rings. He picks it up. The dog growls at the phone.

'Hello?' he says. He swallows. Hard. He covers the mouthpiece with his hand and whispers. 'It's the *Sun.*'

I roll my eyes. 'Just say *no comment*, then hang up.'

Ed sighs. 'Yes, I just found out. Bad news travels fast. Naturally I am distraught. I'll draft a statement for the press as soon as I can.'

ONE MONTH LATER

I stick on some false eyelashes, then run out of the house. We're about to leave for Tiff's funeral. It took *ages* to arrange, what with the investigation slowing everything down . . . They still haven't found the other case. We only have *half* of her, but it is the half with the head and apparently that's enough to pronounce her legally *dead*. They *finally* released the body after several weeks. The autopsy and the inquest all took place in Venice. Ed flew out for that, of course. I stayed at home with the dog. They asked for Ed's permission to examine all Tiff's organs. Ed said *yes*. I suggested he refuse to let them do a post mortem for undefined spiritual reasons, but he said that was a bad idea. He said that he'd look guilty if he didn't cooperate and that would draw attention. The coroner's inquest came back with some big surprises. It said the cause of death was a blow to the head, which was *wrong*. The slit across the jugular was what finished her off in the end, but I guess with all the sawing, it was difficult to tell. Luckily they had a little trouble ascertaining the exact time of death (lucky for *Ed*, at least). They guess to within a couple of hours. They can't be very accurate. They take a number of different factors into consideration: rigor mortis, livor mortis, degree of putrefaction, stomach contents, insect activity and corneal cloudiness . . . But still, they got it *way, way* off. These people are amateurs.

259

They guessed the time of death to be early in the evening of 12 August, but that's when I arrived at the hotel and she'd been dead for *hours*.

'You're not wearing *that*?' says Ed as Baby and I join him in the back of the Rolls.

'Why not? What's wrong with it?' I ask, looking down at my outfit.

I bought a gorgeous vintage Versace number with my pay check from the Forbes. It's every colour of the rainbow, a low-cut backless mini dress with peephole cut-out panels. Ed is wearing a black suit with a black bow tie and white handkerchief.

'Everyone else will be wearing *black*.'

'Uh-huh,' I say. 'Tiff would *hate* it.'

He shakes his head. 'Chelsea Old Church,' he says to the chauffeur.

'You ought to celebrate her *life*, not mourn her *death*,' I mutter.

'I know, but it looks *disrespectful*.'

I scoff. 'It's *very* respectful. Tiffany was a *fashionista* and this looks *great* on me.'

He gives me a look.

'What?' I say. 'Tell me I don't look *fabulous*.'

'OK. Fine. You look *fabulous*. And it goes really well with those shoes.'

I have paired the Versace number with a pair of suede trainers with shimmering crystal details. Ed's right. They do look *ace*.

I relax on the back seat and sink into the leather. I *love* riding in the Rolls. It makes me feel like I've made it. Which I have. *Almost*. There are a few more things to do.

Some 't's to cross and 'i's to dot. It won't take long now. The next thing on my Basecamp list is to seduce *this man*. As soon as we have buried Tiff, I need to drive him wild. I'll reel him in like a fish on a line. We'll be married in no time. I've done it a *million* times.

I smile at Ed. He looks at me but doesn't return the smile. Oh yes, that money's practically *mine*. I can almost *taste* it. Now all I have to do is figure out how I want to spend it. I'm one body down with one to go. This is my shot, like in *Hamilton*, and I'm not going to waste it.

I glance at Ed. He looks the other way out of the window. I suddenly have a twinge of doubt. What if he doesn't want me? What if I don't want him? I mean, sure, he's rich and attractive, but I'm not sure I *fancy* him. *Come on, Alvie. Snap out of it.* Perhaps it's weird to sleep with your best friend's husband.

Perhaps I'll retire to Val d'Isère? Get a little place in the mountains? I'm *loving* my Swiss chalet and I've always wanted to learn how to ski. Beth had skiing lessons, of course. She was sent to Switzerland for private tuition every season, but not me. Not *Alvie*. There weren't any snowy slopes in rural Gloucestershire. We had a *dry* slope, but if you fell, it chafed like buggery.

We drive through Hampstead into town. Ed stares out of the window. We are nearly in Chelsea when my stomach begins to growl. Oh no. Not *now*. But I need to eat. I glance at Ed. He won't mind, will he? It will only take a sec.

'Ed, can we pull over? I'm famished. I'll grab a snack in that corner shop.' The driver slams on the brakes and Baby and I jump out of the car.

Ed frowns. 'Really? *Now?* We'll be late for the funeral.'

'If I don't eat, I get hangry, you know? Hungry and angry?'

I slam the door and blow an air kiss through the window at Ed. What shall I get? I need to eat. I am feeling faint.

I push into the corner shop and eye the rows of shelves. Wotsits? Pringles? Kettle chips? I settle on a giant bag of toffee-flavoured popcorn. I pay the girl and jump back in the car, opening the packet.

'Want some?'

Ed shakes his head and gawks at the family-sized packet of Butterkist popcorn that I'm munching. He looks glum and we drive the rest of the way in silence towards Chelsea Old Church.

Urgh, is he going to sulk all day? He shouldn't have murdered Tiffany.

I crunch the corn and brush some crumbs off my dress and pick out the bits stuck up in between my teeth. I wish I had a toothpick. The driver stops the car by the main entrance to the church. The hearse is already there with the undertaker in his top hat. Every inch of the pavements outside are covered with cards and flowers: lilies, roses, chrysanthemums, gladioli, carnations. Placards with 'WE LOVE YOU, TIFF' and 'TIFFANY RIP'. There are balloons in the shapes of hearts, angels and unicorns. Crowds of wailing fans line the road. They must have seen it on Twitter. I get all my news from Twitter. If it's not *trending*, it's not happening. #TIFFISDEAD is trending now (at number 5), so is #DEADTIFF (number 9). Elton John has written a song. There's a dozen paparazzi hustling for a better view as we step out of the Rolls. Lights are flashing. Cameras clicking . . .

'Ed? Ed?' the reporters call. 'Did you kill your wife?'

I laugh. 'Of course he didn't,' I say.

Ed turns white.

'Isn't it always the *husband*?' shouts a woman with a placard.

'No,' I say. 'Look at *Gone Girl*. Did you people learn *nothing*?'

There was a front-page article in the *Sun* that was a little provocative. What did it say? 'BILLIONAIRE ED FORBES SUSPECTED OF KILLING WIFE TIFFANY'. Something like that. I forget the exact words, but that's the gist.

Baby growls at the hacks and the fans.

'Come on, Ed,' I say, putting my arm round him as we push our way inside.

Ed sighs.

'You're cool. I got you.' I squeeze his hand. It's a very tender moment between us.

Someone from the BBC shoves a microphone in Ed's face. The reporter leans in. And the cameraman.

'FUCK OFF,' I say. 'GET THE FUCK OUT OF HIS FACE. DO YOU HEAR ME?'

'No swearing, please. We're live on air.'

I flip the bird to the camera.

I shove Ed inside the church and close the doors behind me. The press aren't allowed inside the church and there aren't any cops. That's good, I can be myself. I can *relax*. I check the time: it's ten past two. Uh-oh, we're *late*. The church is already packed with hundreds of pale-faced guests. Ed was right. They're all wearing *black*. Urgh, so boring.

I have no idea what to expect. This is my first funeral. (I don't count the hole in the ground in the woods where we buried my twin. And when my mother killed my dad she hid his corpse in the shed. No one knew he had actually *died*. We all thought he'd fucked off. He never had a funeral or any kind of wake. No one invited me to my grandma's funeral unfortunately. There was some confusion about how she died and for some reason I was a suspect.)

Inside there are thousands of stunning white lilies arranged in vases. The air smells sweet; it reminds me of Tiffany's perfume. The man on the organ starts to play Michael Jackson's 'Gone Too Soon'. The music makes me feel kind of strange in my stomach. Or is it period pains?

I follow Ed down the aisle and we sit at the front on a wooden pew. Baby jumps up next to me and rests his head on his paws. James is already here. He gives Ed a hug as he sits down beside him. He brushes some imaginary dust off Ed's suit shoulder, so I brush some imaginary dust off the other one.

'Hi, Siobhán,' says James. 'You all right?'

'My heart is breaking,' I say.

Tiffany said she liked my heart. I have a heart of 'gold'. I suddenly feel a weight on my chest, like my heart is made of lead.

'What the hell are you wearing?' he asks. 'You look like a drag queen.'

'Fuck you,' I say. 'This is vintage Versace. *That* looks like a catalogue suit two sizes too small.'

'Fuck you too,' James mouths at me then turns to face the back.

Oh my God, he's such a *bitch*. What is his problem?

I look too. There are six soldiers dressed in smart red coats and black trousers with red stripes. They're carrying a coffin loaded with lilies down the aisle. It's a very long aisle. It takes them ages to reach the end. I spot the vicar wearing a long white dress with a long black waistcoat. A silver chain with a crucifix hangs round his neck. He looks cool. It's a strong look. I bet he got that necklace from Dolce & Gabbana; they do rosaries and stuff. They tramp up to the front of the church and stop by a tall gold candle.

I hear someone sniff and blow their nose. I look over at Ed. He dabs his eyes with his handkerchief then pops it in his pocket.

I shiver. It's cold in here. There's a draught blowing through the church. And it doesn't help that the dress I'm wearing is the size of a cocktail napkin.

'Ed,' I say, 'it's *freezing* in here. Can I borrow your jacket?'

'No,' he says. 'Seriously? You should have worn some clothes.'

'But I'm *cold*,' I say, sneezing theatrically. 'I caught a cold in *Venice* splashing around in the Grand Canal. I nearly *drowned* in there . . .'

'Stop, Siobhán, please,' he hisses. 'You can't talk about that *here*.'

I wink at him. 'Right. Mum's the word.'

I think I'm making him nervous. His eyes look like they might pop out of their eye sockets. All the blood has drained from his face. He takes off his jacket and hands it to me.

The vicar tells us all to stand and we open up our hymn books at Page 121. It's something called 'Guide Me O Thou Great Redeemer'. I don't know it, but I'm not going to let that stop me. I make up for a lack of knowledge of the melody with volume and enthusiasm. I sing at the top of my lungs like I'm Taylor. I'm really going for it now. I let the words sing out, reaching the top notes like a pro. Halfway through the song Ed grabs my hymn book and slams it shut and shoves it on the bench.

'Oh. OK then.'

I sit down again. Whatever.

The vicar is banging on about heaven when I hear him say Ed's name.

'Oh, look. You're on,' I say.

Ed stands and approaches the microphone. He clears his throat. 'Romans 8.38–9.'

I lick sticky toffee from my fingers as he reads.

I reach over for his hand as he sits down again.

'You killed it,' I say. 'That was *epic*.'

'Thanks.'

'I think . . . I feel like I should . . . I'll just say a few words.'

It's the right thing to do. It's a nice thing to do. It is very spiritual. And as Tiff's friend and employee, I feel it is appropriate . . .

I pick up the dog and jump up and grab the microphone from the vicar. At first he resists. He won't let go, but I am stronger than he is and manage to yank the microphone from his hands.

'Hey, everyone,' I say, looking out at the mourners. Row upon row of faces stare back. They gawk at my clothes. I

266

pull at the hem of my skirt. It is quite short, actually. I pull the jacket over my cleavage. I look *great*. It's *fine*.

'My name is Siobhán and, er . . . I, er, I just want to say a few words. Not many people know me but . . . I was Tiff's best friend.'

There's a yelp from somewhere. I look up and see Josephina glaring at me. *Yeah, you wish, bitch*. As if *she* was Tiff's best friend.

'*New* best friend,' I continue. 'We only met a few weeks ago, but we got on like a sauna on fire.' I smile. No one smiles back. They don't know I burnt down the sauna, so that joke didn't work.

James is frowning at me from the front. I know what he's thinking: *you're just the dog's new nanny. What are you talking about?*

'Even though our friendship has been tragically cut short, the memory of our time together will never leave me. *Never.* I learnt so much from Tiffany: about how to be spiritual, how to be a better person, how to . . . Oh no. That's it, actually. Tiff once said that I reminded her of *her,* that I was like a younger, skinnier version. And that was the biggest thrill I've ever had because she was just so *awesome.*'

I'm surprised to see that my voice is shaking. I've squeezed out a tear and it is sliding down my cheek cinematically. I lean on the lectern for balance. I wish I had some tissues. One of my false eyelashes starts to come off.

There's a woman sitting in the front row. She looks a bit like Tiff but twenty-odd years older. Either that is Tiffany's mum or she had a secret twin who was addicted to sunbeds and it's really damaged her skin?

I pause. *Oh God.* Tiff was my *friend.* My best friend in the whole world. And I killed her!

'She said . . . she said she *loved* me,' I whisper in a hushed low voice.

I blink through tears. The church blurs. I summon all my strength.

I wipe away the tears and the false eyelash falls right off in my hand. I sniff and blink at the congregation. They're staring back at me like I just did a naked pole dance to 'Stupid Hoe' by Nicki Minaj.

'I'd like to end by reciting a haiku that I wrote especially for the occasion. It's called: 'Thank you, God, for Tiff-Any'.

> *Thank you, God, for Tiff-*
> *Any. If only there were*
> *Someone else like her.*

I sit down again. It's silent. You could hear an ant breathe. Ed lets me hold his hand and I stroke his thumb with my thumb. I *caress* it. I think he liked my moving tribute. It was more emotional than I'd planned. I think I need a hug. I remember my hug with Tiffany. She was great at hugging. I was *really* excited to attend my very first funeral, but this is such a *downer.* Now I feel kind of terrible.

Eventually the funeral ends and people begin to file out. I spot Josephina out of the corner of my eye. She looks *cross.* She storms along the aisle up to me and grabs me by the arm.

'Ow.'

'*You*,' she says.

'What?'

She grips my arm even harder. I struggle to pull away.

'I don't trust you. Everything was fine until *you* appeared.'

I finally manage to wriggle free. '*That* is going to bruise. I bruise very easily. It's a genetic condition.' I rub my arm.

'I'm going to find out what happened to Tiff.'

'Sure. Good luck with that. Let me know what you discover. I'll tell Ed.'

'Everything all right?' asks Ed, taking in Jemima's flushed face.

I smile at him. 'Everything is *fine*. Janine here was just asking if the cops had got any more leads in their search for who killed Tiffany?'

'Er, no, not yet,' he says, frowning at me.

'Because she has a motive, don't you, sweetie? She was fired on the day that Tiff went missing. Isn't that a *coincidence*? Have you been to Venice recently?'

She looks at me, then Ed, then me, and her mouth hangs open. She turns on her heel and legs it back down the aisle and out of the church.

I doubt that we'll see *her* again. I try not to look smug.

The woman who looks a bit like Tiff comes up to me. I tense. What does she want? She's heading for me with a determined look.

'Hello, Siobhán. I'm Cher,' she says.

For a moment I don't reply.

'Cher?' I say. 'You're *Cher*? Oh my God. I'm a *massive* fan.'

Of course *Cher* would be at Tiffany's funeral. How could she *not* come?

I'm about to kneel and kiss her feet, but then I pause,

hesitate. I look up at her face again. She's had a *lot* of work done.

'I loved "If I Could Turn Back Time" and "I Got You Babe",' I say.

I take in Cher's light blonde hair and aquamarine eyes.

'No, I'm not *Cher*. I mean . . . I'm not Cher the singer,' she says. 'I'm Tiffany's mum. I'm Cher Cawdor.'

'Oh,' I say, withdrawing my hand. I feel silly now. 'I bet you get that all the time.'

'Actually . . . *no*.'

We look into each other's eyes. I look down at my shoes.

Cher moves in for a bear hug. I flinch. I think she's going to hit me, but she wraps her arms round me. *Ah*. She smells nice, like Tiffany.

'Thank you,' she whispers into my ear. 'That was a lovely speech. Tiffany was very lucky to have a friend like you.'

She pulls away. I stand and stare. They're a very *huggy* family. Not like mine. I don't remember getting a hug from my mum. The only kind of physical contact I got were slaps and punches and her hands on my butt when she was pushing me up the stairs to the attic . . . Cher gives me a warm smile. My stomach is in knots. I *really* should have eaten lunch. 170g of popcorn was not a good idea on an empty stomach.

'Any friend of Tiffany's is a friend of mine,' she says. 'Let me know if you need anything. Anything at all.'

She turns and walks away. I frown. Why is she being so *nice*? And what does she mean by *anything*? A new flat? A Prius? I watch as she walks off. But there's a little voice in my head telling me to stop her. The voice in my head – who?

Nino? Tiff? Beth? – is telling me to *confess*. It wants me to tell Tiffany's mother that I killed Tiff. *I'm sorry, I did it. It wasn't Ed or a mental fan.* But that's a ridiculous idea. That is just *insane*.

I sit down next to Ed on the bench, making a mental note to *not* listen to that voice in my head with the *shit* ideas. We wait until everyone – two hundred people, give or take – have trailed out of the church.

'Ed, are you coming?' James asks, appearing and glaring at me.

'Just give me a minute,' Ed says. Then he stands up and heads for the coffin.

I stand up too and follow him.

'You don't need to come,' he says.

'We're a team. We're partners in crime. And I want to say goodbye. I loved her too,' I say.

Ed places a hand on top of the coffin. It's not an open casket. That's strange. I thought they always did open coffins at these kind of things.

'Goodbye, Tiffany,' says Ed.

My go . . . I hesitate.

'*I can't.* Oh, Tiff. Oh, Tiffany!'

Something *snaps*. I throw myself on to the coffin and try to *hug* the thing, crushing all the lilies and sobbing.

'Tiff was so kind to me. She was like . . . a *sister*. A twin!'

I wipe my snotty nose and look up into Ed's kind eyes. He puts his arm round me.

'I know,' he says. 'She was always so loving. Do you need a minute?' he asks. 'I'll wait.'

'No. I'm cool. Let's go.' I sniff and wipe my tears with my knuckle.

Urgh, great. My mascara is running.

I put my arm round Ed's shoulder as we walk the three hundred metres down the aisle towards the back of the church and the main exit.

'I feel lost to be honest. We were married for *seven years*.'

'I know, me too. Completely lost.' I stare into the middle distance.

Ed's phone rings.

I glare at him. My phone is on airplane mode.

'Hang on,' he says. 'I'd better take it.'

'*Now?*'

How disrespectful.

'It could be work. Could be the police,' he says. I roll my eyes. 'Hello? Oh yes, PC Marks . . .'

My ears prick up. That's *hot cop*.

'Ah yes, the fingerprints. Of course, I see. Any news?'

I feel the blood drain from my face.

I shift on my feet and watch Ed closely for clues of what hot cop is saying.

'Indeed?' says Ed. 'Well, do let me know if there are other leads. Goodbye and thank you for all you are doing. I really appreciate it.' He hangs up.

'What did he say? About the prints?' I ask.

He frowns. 'He said the prints they took from Tiffany's hairbrush and perfume match the prints on the suitcase handle, so whoever killed her must have worn gloves and the prints must be Tiffany's.'

BINGO, BABY. BACK OF THE NET. I AM OFF THE HOOK.

'Awesome,' I say.

'Shhh,' says Ed. He glances around the church, but it's OK. The church is empty. 'It must have been *your* prints on the perfume bottle and the hairbrush.'

'Yes,' I say. 'I did use those. Ha. The luck of the Irish.'

I say a couple of silent Hail Marys under my breath as we continue down the aisle. I reach out and take Ed's hand as we walk side by side.

Ed and I walk out of the church and into a sea of reporters. I know I'm supposed to do a sad face, but I can't help looking *ecstatic*.

SEVERAL MONTHS LATER

Sunday, 1 January, 4 p.m.
Hampstead Heath, London

Ed and I are walking the dog on the heath. It's freezing. It's snowing. Our footprints leave deep wells in the snow. All I can see is *white*. Baby's in his Canada Goose down jacket and deerstalker hat. I huddle into Ed for warmth. Ed is looking glum. I don't know why he's so miserable. All the heat over Tiff has died down. He is no longer a suspect. The tabloids have stopped printing nasty headlines and the cops in Italy are trying to pin the murder case on the Mafia.

'I gave Baby a Thai massage this morning; he *loved* it,' I say.

'That's nice,' Ed says, sounding distracted.

'It was a New Year's Day treat.'

'Uh-huh.'

273

He isn't listening. It's probably *work*. He's been working too hard, even over Christmas. He hardly took any time off to play with me and the pug.

He clicks the tiny keys on his BlackBerry, squinting through the snowstorm. He is so retro. I mean, who has a BlackBerry these days?

'Then I took the baby to Harrods for some beluga caviar. That's his favourite,' I continue. 'He licked out the dish and everything, and then he wanted more.'

Ed sighs and shoves his phone in his pocket.

'What's up?' I shout through the wind. 'Come on, Ed. Everyone makes mistakes. Don't beat yourself up about killing your wife. She wouldn't want you moping around because of one bad decision. Would she? Huh?'

He doesn't reply.

'Would she? Would she?'

'*No.*'

I smile and pat him on the back, but my smile is empty. I need to take my own advice. It's been hard these past months without her . . . living in her house. Surrounded by her things. Her dog. Her stuff still smells of her. *Come on, Alvie. Stiff upper lip. You're doing really well with my plan. You're doing it for Nino.*

I think of Nino. His handsome face. I haven't seen him for a while. Not since Venice, actually. He hasn't been around. I've missed our chats, the sex, etc. I think he must be pleased because I'm working on our hit. He's leaving it to me. He knows I'm a pro. I'm on top of things.

'I lost another client,' says Ed. 'My biggest investor in Moscow just moved his cash to a rival firm. It doesn't look

274

good. Other investors might lose confidence in my fund and follow him.'

I nod. 'The thing with Tiffany . . . was bad for business, I guess?'

'It isn't just that,' he says. He looks into my eyes. I can see that he's wrestling with something. He seems to have aged a decade; it must be all the stress. 'The newspapers are cooling off. It's fine. Listen, Siobhán,' he says, 'I've got an idea. I think it will help. It's . . . well . . . you might be surprised. But what do you think about us getting married?'

I blink at him through the falling snow. 'Where did *that* come from?'

'I know it's big. It's soon . . . and we don't know each other that well, but we could? Maybe? Couldn't we? We're already partners in crime. So why not in life too? I enjoy your company – I don't like being alone. And you are *great* with the dog. Baby *loves* you. So what do you think? Happy new year.' He shrugs.

I lose the power of speech.

My brain cogs whir at a hundred miles an hour. I process it. Why is billionaire Ed Forbes asking me to *marry him*? I mean . . . I've been working on my plan to become more like Tiffany. And if Ed liked *Tiff* enough to propose, then I guess it follows that he would like me. I've become much more spiritual recently. I have taken up spinning. And I have read more self-help books than Oprah fucking Winfrey. I've even started eating tofu. (It's utterly bland and tasteless.) I didn't think it would work so soon, but apparently I've *nailed* it. And in just a matter of months! Nino was right all along.

But *get married*? Seriously? There must be more to it . . .

Is he scared that I'll *blackmail* him? Ha. I mean, that's *preposterous*. As if I would do such a thing. But he knows I know too much. I have all the dirt on him. I know where the skeletons are in his closet. *Literally*. Yes, it must be that. It's possible he's in love with me, but more probably he wants to keep his friends close and his enemies closer.

I study Ed through the falling snow.

'*You* really want to marry *me*?' Am I tripping on psychedelics? Surely I'm *hallucinating*.

'Sure, why not? Is it really such a bad idea?'

I stand and stare at Ed. Oh wow. He might actually be in love with me . . .

'Are you coming?' he calls.

He's a few metres off now. I can just about make out his figure in the white-out.

I feel *high*. Is this happening? Am I in a music video? Are we filming something with DJ Khaled? I stand in the snow with snowflakes swirling all around my face.

'Siobhán?'

I don't move. My mouth hangs open. I'm frozen. I stand in the middle of the heath with the icy wind blowing right through me. I didn't expect him to propose and now he has it's thrown me.

'Siobhán, it's OK. We can talk about it. We don't need to rush into things. Let's go home before we freeze. It's really tipping it down.'

'Ed. ED. *Listen to me*,' I shout, running towards him. 'This is a *big deal*. You don't just marry *total strangers*. You can't just go and get engaged to your dog's fucking *nanny*.'

'You're not a *stranger*,' Ed shouts through the howling wind. 'You've lived with us for a while now and you were friends with Tiffany. She was a *great* judge of character. And you do yourself a disservice. You're not *just* the dog's nanny. You're also a talented sushi chef. The sashimi you made the other night was *out of this world.*'

It was.

'I guess, that's true,' I say, coming round.

'I'm very grateful for all you've done,' Ed says. 'And I need a wife. I am useless without one.'

> *Oh my God. Oh my*
> *God. Oh my God. I'm Getting*
> *Fucking MARRIED. WHAT!?!?*

Third Stasimon

I've been dreaming of my wedding ever since I was *twelve*. I was planning my big white wedding with a boy called Jacob Welch. I *loved* him. We were going to get married. Then *Beth* screwed it up.

FOURTEEN YEARS AGO

'Beth, can I borrow your shoulder pads?'

'No, get your own,' says Beth.

'But I think they'd really transform my look.'

My sister rolls her eyes.

Beth and I are getting ready for our first school disco. I'm wearing my platform flip-flops, a Day-Glo yellow shell suit and stick-on earrings in the shape of fruit (there's a different pair for each day of the month and today's pair are *cherries*). I'm trying to style my hair in the mirror, but my haircut looks like a hairdresser's worst nightmare and the stench of burning rises up from my sister's crimpers. I've stolen some of my mother's red lipstick and kohl eyeliner and I've streaked the black along my lids like I am Cleopatra. I've never done my make-up before, but tonight is a *special occasion*. I think I look *great* like I could be on *Top of the Pops*. Beth is wearing a little black dress. It's *so boring*. Unoriginal. She looks like a blonde Wednesday Addams. She looks like she's going to a funeral.

Usually, on a Thursday night, I'd be killing Tamagotchis, losing at *Super Mario Bros.*, *Tetris* or *Pac-Man*, or spending hours on WordArt making 'GET LOST' signs for my door. But not tonight. Tonight is different. Tonight I'm getting excited because of *Jacob Welch* . . .

I apply the finishing touches to my epic look. I spritz my hair, my face and arms with silver glitter hairspray, stand back and admire myself in the mirror. *Perfect.* I could be in Aqua. Yep, or I could be Gwen Stefani. Jacob will take one look and he'll be mine forever. I can hear those wedding bells . . .

'Wow,' says Beth, when she sees me. 'That's . . . you look . . . really . . . *wow.*'

'I'm going to dance with *Jacob* tonight. I bet we *kiss*,' I say.

'Gross,' says Beth, making a face.

'With tongues and *everything.*'

'I bet he kisses like a washing machine.'

'I bet he doesn't.'

'Well, *I* wouldn't kiss him.'

I practise kissing myself in the mirror (with tongue) and leave snail trails and lipstick on the glass. Yuck. It tastes of Mr Muscle: chemically bitter. I wonder what Jacob Welch will taste like? I've never kissed a boy. I've seen him eating burgers at lunch, so he'll probably taste of those.

'Alvina!' my mother calls from downstairs. 'Come down here this instant.'

I sigh. What is it now? I was really getting into that. In my head kissing Jacob Welch is like kissing Leo DiCaprio in the car on the *Titanic*: steamy, sweaty, naked. I wipe the glass with the sleeve of my jacket. Saliva blurs and smears. I run my fingers down the glass and leave a sticky handprint.

'I'm coming,' I say, running downstairs and tripping up in my flip-flops. I tumble down the last few steps and land on my ass on the floor.

My mother stands in the living room, scowling, hands on hips. Lips pursed.

'You're not going *anywhere* until you've untangled *that*.'

She points at my sister's slinky lying on the pouffe, like a roadkill rainbow serpent.

'But why do *I* have to do it? I didn't mess it up.'

'Urgh, you're just like your father,' she says. 'Irresponsible. Making a mess and then leaving it for someone else to clean up. I don't want an argument, young lady.'

Huh. She called me a *lady*.

'And I use the word "lady",' she says, 'in the loosest possible way.'

I grab the slinky and start to unwind it. I feel like Cinderella. I can't unwind it. The stupid thing's stuck.

'This is *impossible*.'

I hate her. My mother's a monster. I see where Beth gets it from . . .

I hear the sound of footsteps thumping down the stairs. It's Beth.

'You look lovely, darling,' says mum, as my sister waltzes in. 'You'll be fighting off those boys.'

I frown. My sister looks *dead*. Her pale face looks even paler against the black of her dress. She's not wearing make-up and her hair remains *uncrimped*. She's hardly made an effort at all. She might as well not go. It's like she doesn't know that this is The Social Event of the Century.

'I'll just take a photo,' says Mum. 'Beth, you stand there and smile. That's it. Say *cheese*. Work it, baby. Make love to the camera.'

Jeez.

Mum picks up her Polaroid camera and *clicks*.

'What about me?' I say. 'I untangled the slinky.'

I've *finally* managed to pull the spring apart and it hangs limply from my hands.

'Oh no, I've run out film.' My mother shakes the picture. 'There, look at that. Cindy Crawford.'

'But, *Mum* . . .'

'Alvina, your sister's Rubik's cube still needs completing.'

'But, *Muuuum.*'

'That's enough. I don't want to hear it!'

I skulk across the room and grab Beth's Rubik's cube from the shelf. I start to peel the stickers off and stick them in the right places.

Beth laughs. 'Can we borrow your phone?'

There's *no way* mum will let her. I shuffle the squares around. The *mobile phone*? Are you kidding? That's the Holy Grail. It has *never* been loaned before on any other occasion.

'Of course,' says Mum, 'then you can call when it's time to pick you up.'

I look up. My mouth hangs open. *The phone?* I don't believe it.

My mother reaches for her handbag and rummages around in all the crap inside.

'Here it is,' she says at last, handing the phone to Beth.

My sister smirks. 'Right, in the car.' I stand up to leave. 'Not *you*,' says Mum. 'Stay here and finish the Rubik's cube.'

Oh my God. Not this again. Last time there was a party, I had to sneak out of the upstairs window and run all the way in the dark. 'Look, I'm nearly finished,' I say.

This is so unfair. I follow my mum and my sister out through the front door, peeling off the green and red and blue and yellow stickers. My mum gets into the driver's seat. Beth gets in the back and slams the door right in my face. I see her lock it. *Cow.*

'Wait,' I say, banging on the car roof. 'It's finished, look. Let me in.'

I wave the Rubik's cube at my mum. She scowls through the windscreen. She starts the ignition and for a split second I think she'll run me over.

'OK. Get in,' she says, revving.

My sister unlocks the door. I open the back door and squeeze on to the seat next to Beth.

'You can carry it,' says Beth, dropping the phone on to my lap. 'That thing's *really* heavy.'

I cradle the ugly Nokia like it's a bar of gold.

'If you lose it . . .' Mum says, turning round and leaning over the driver's seat towards me. 'Don't bother coming back.'

Beth and I arrive at school at 7 p.m. sharp. The speakers are blaring and 'Saturday Night' by Whigfield booms at full volume. I follow my sister into the hall. Coloured lights are flashing. One of the teachers has hung a disco ball on to a rafter. I study the crowd. *Where's Jacob Welch?* I can't see him yet. He's fashionably late, of course. He's a cool guy, obvs. I go and sit on the edge of the stage and drink a Capri-Sun. I let my legs swing in and out and kick against the wood. I watch the girls and boys swaying to the music with butterflies swirling around in my stomach. It smells of Lynx and body odour and teen spirit. A few of the kids spot me and laugh. There are nudges in ribs, pointing, giggling.

'Nice outfit,' some kid says, laughing.

'Yeah, I know it is.'

It's *way* better than school uniform. It's cooler than what *they're* wearing. All their outfits are boring. I'm the best dressed here. The boys are wearing jeans and T-shirts in blue, white or black and the girls are wearing dresses so short that you can see their bum cracks.

I sit up tall and watch the door.

'Vicky has vodka,' shouts one of the kids over the pounding bassline of Will Smith's 'Men in Black'. I glance at the teacher standing guard. Mrs Hunt hasn't noticed. Mr Clarke, the football coach, is on the decks. He's crap.

Vodka sounds ace. I bet it tastes *delicious*. I'm going to go and find Vicky Jones and see if she'll let me try it.

I jump down from the stage and push through the crowds, scanning the girls. She's not here, so she must be outside. I head out through the doors to the corridor. Vicky and a couple of girls are by the fire exit, huddled round what I assume is the alcohol.

'All right, Vicky?' I say, strolling over. Vicky is popular and ordinarily I wouldn't dream of approaching her. But curiosity killed the cat and I want to try that vodka. The alcohol might calm my nerves. I've never tried it before. It's worth a shot anyway. I'm as jumpy as hell about Jacob.

'What have *you* come as?' asks Vicky, eyeing my Day-Glo ensemble. 'I didn't know it was *fancy dress*.'

'Whatever. I'm Sporty Spice.' I gesture to the bottle of Smirnoff sticking out from under her top. 'I'll give you my multicolour pen if you let me have some of *that*.'

My biro is my greatest treasure. It has four different colours: red, green, blue *and* black. I know she wants it. *Who wouldn't?*

Vicky laughs. Then the other girls laugh. 'No way. Get lost, Alvina.'

They turn their backs on me and swig the liquid, giggling.

I stomp back along the corridor. They can get lost. Stupid cows. I push through the doors to the dining hall. Jacob is here now. I can see his curly blond hair sticking up above the crowd. He's taller than the other boys and as skinny as a lamp post. He smiles his cheeky smile. His grin spreads to his ears and I melt. He's hotter than Leo DiCaprio or anyone in *Boyzone. Oh my God.* Jacob is lush. I could kiss him now . . . We are going to get married. I know it. We're meant to be.

Beth runs up to him, high on sugar, sucking lemonade through a straw. She glances at me; her eyes are flashing. What's she doing now? The music's loud. The chorus of 'Living on a Prayer' plays at full volume. Jacob starts to dance with *my twin*. I blink. I can't believe it. But Beth and Jacob are dancing. That's her for sure in that stupid dress. I stand and gawp. Bon Jovi screams. My sister turns and grins. I stare at her. I feel sick. What is happening? My whole world is crashing down. All my dreams are shattered. Vicky pushes past me. She's still got that bottle of vodka hidden up her top. I grab the vodka and race across the hall and into the ladies'.

'Hey! Come back,' Vicky shouts.

I don't care. I lock the toilet door and slump down on the toilet seat and down the stupid vodka. The alcohol burns my throat and I gag.

'Urgh,' I say, spitting it out against the cubicle door. This stuff is *disgusting*. It tastes worse than Mr Muscle. But I don't care. I'll drink it. There's over half a bottle left and I will finish it. No one's going to stop me. Not Vicky. Not Beth. Not even my mum. Not Mrs Hunt. Not anyone.

I swig the clear alcohol, my eyes weeping, my nose running. I swallow it down, choking back tears and coughing up the liquid. When I'm finished, I throw the bottle on the floor and it spins.

I rub my eyes. My black eyeliner comes off on my hands.

There's a banging sound. Someone is thumping on the door. It's Vicky. I can see her feet under the gap.

'Alvie! Alvie! Give me my drink back.'

I kick the bottle and it rolls under the door.

'What? You *finished it*? There was nearly *a litre* in there. You owe me six quid.'

I hear the sound of glass clinking as Vicky grabs the bottle. Then footsteps pad across the floor. There's the sound of the toilet door slamming. I rest my head against the cool of the cubicle wall. I can't believe my sister danced with him. How could she do that to me? Beth knows I've had a crush on him for *months*. Since '96. She didn't even like him. I slip down on the toilet seat. The cubicle spins round and I am seeing double. Oh God, what is going on?

Fourth Episode

Monday, 2 January, 4 p.m.
Hatton Garden, London

Ed takes me engagement ring shopping in a posh part of town. We walk down the street arm in arm with the dog, past windows shining with jewels.

'Here,' says Ed.

We walk into a store and the sales man greets us.

'Mr Forbes, what a pleasure,' he says.

I eye the rows of diamonds.

Ed's phone rings. 'I'd better take this. I'm sorry,' he says with a shrug. 'It's a new investor from Russia.'

'That's fine, baby,' I say. Baby barks. 'Not *you*.'

'*Zdravstvuyte*, Dimitri,' says Ed. 'I'm fine, thank you. How are you?'

I study the rings in the display case. Some of the diamonds are *massive*.

'No, no, it's fine,' says Ed. 'Everything's under control.'

'How about this one?' I mouth, pointing to an engagement ring with a beautiful heart-shaped diamond.

Ed nods. *Awesome.* I don't bother checking the price tag. It is bigger than Tiffany's rock that I chucked in the Grand Canal.

'No,' he continues. 'Please, don't worry. Your money is safe with me.'

'Can I try that one?' I say to the shop assistant.

'Certainly, madam.'

I pull off the ring from the hand grenade, the one that Nino gave me, and shove it in my Birkin. I try on the new ring. It sparkles in rainbow colours on my finger. 'This one! I *love* it,' I say.

'Yes. Yes,' says Ed. 'In fact, I am engaged to be remarried! Yes, to a *woman.*' He laughs.

I wiggle my ring finger at him. I wish I could show Tiff.

Wednesday, 4 January, 10 a.m.
Pronovias, New Bond Street, London

There's the deafening din of a pneumatic drill as we approach some roadworks. The Bentley turns off Oxford Street and on to New Bond Street. I peer out through the tinted windows. We pass Miu Miu. I glance both ways down the busy street: this is shopping heaven. It's a fashionista's wet dream of designer boutiques: Ralph Lauren, Mulberry, Celine. Down there is Victoria's Secret. Ooh, I'll pop in there a bit later to buy some bits for the honeymoon. Something hot to get Ed going. I might have to go into Soho. We haven't had sex yet, which is *weird*. We're saving it for our wedding night. He probably wants it to be special, with scented candles and shit. He probably thinks I'm a virgin (bless) what with the Irish thing and being a very strict Roman Catholic. Well, I haven't denied it. If he says anything about a hymen, I'll just mention *tampons*.

Men can't talk about tampons. The more I think about sex with Ed, the more confused I get. We've barely had any physical contact. Not even a kiss. I get it. He's traditional. He's older, after all. But what about me? I look at Ed, and I'm drawn to him. He's a very attractive man, but if I'm honest with myself, do I want to *shag* him?

Whatever. Does it matter if I don't? I can't help feeling *I've made it*. This is the fucking life. I've got my man's AmEx in my wallet with no spending limit and by next week my name will be *Mrs Edwin Forbes*. Ha! There is no stopping me. A smile creeps to the edge of my lips. A high-pitched giggle escapes. This is beyond my wildest dreams: the cash, this car, the house . . . And now I'm going *wedding dress shopping*?! I am winning at life. Of course, I still feel bad about Tiff. But I won't let it bring me down.

I yell at the driver to stop on New Bond Street at Pronovias. I climb out of the Bentley with the pug on his red leash. We fight our way past tourists.

'Move it,' I say. 'Watch the dog.' The puppy barks and growls. I bend down to scoop him up and Baby licks my face. 'Urgh. Mind my make-up,' I say. 'So gross.' I wipe off the drool.

I barge through the brass and glass doors into Pronovias. I look around and angels sing. It's not a *shop*; it's *paradise*. This place is bling. It's a tourist-free zone. The air is vanilla-scented and they're playing classical music, something with violins. The shop is a vision in white and pink, gold, silver and cream. I gasp – the dresses are all so pretty I'm almost too awed to approach them. I glance at my hands to check if they're clean and study my fingernails. I take a deep breath and stand up tall, then Baby and I cross polished tiles towards the girl at the desk.

A Jo Malone candle flickers in the breeze from the air conditioning. I catch a glimpse of myself in the mirror. Ha! Who am I kidding? *Me?* A *bride*? Maybe the bride in the *Kill Bill* trilogy. Will *this* end in a massacre or a fairy-tale wedding? My twin sister was always the one who was the 'wife' material. I was the one in the high-school yearbook: 'Most likely to die of something venereal'.

'Hello, can I help you?' she says with a smile. Her teeth are as white as the dresses.

'I am engaged,' I say to the woman, 'and I am going to get married.'

'Congratulations,' she says, like she means it. 'I'm guessing you're here for a dress?'

'I am,' I say. She can read minds. She's *wasted* here if she's a psychic.

'I'm sorry,' she says, frowning at Baby, 'but no dogs allowed. It will have to wait outside.'

I gasp. '*The baby* is staying with *me*.'

She opens her mouth to say something else.

'Do you like my ring?' I ask. I flash the diamond on my finger. She eyes my engagement ring. The rock is the size of a small country – Wales or possibly Liech-tenstein. I can tell that she's impressed. I wiggle my finger a bit.

'I'm Gabriella,' she says with a smile, extending a mani-cured paw. 'What is your name, mademoiselle?'

'Siobhán,' I say. 'And this is Baby.'

Gabby pets the dog. 'Do you have a reservation?' she asks. Baby licks her hand.

'No, is that a problem? He only proposed recently, but I wanted to try on some dresses.'

'Well, you're in the right place,' she says. 'The Pronovias dresses are *gorgeous*, and there are lots of different styles. We can choose some to try on.'

She leads me over to an area with low chaise longues and armchairs.

'Will your bridesmaids be joining us? Any sisters or friends?'

I glare at her. 'No, not today.' Then I blurt out (I can't help it), 'My friend, Tiff, is *indisposed*, but she'll be here next time.'

Gabby nods.

'She will. She promised. She couldn't come today. She wanted to. She really did, but she's having major surgery.'

Gabby does a sad face. 'Oh dear, I'm so sorry to hear that.'

'Yeah, me too,' I say. 'I only hope that she recovers in time for the wedding. She's my maid of honour. I couldn't get married without her.'

'Of course,' she says. 'I hope it's nothing serious?'

'A . . . vasectomy,' I say.

'She's having a *vasectomy*?'

'She is. They're very painful.' *Damn*. That's the dick thing, isn't it? 'Tiffany is transgender, not that it's any of *your* business.'

She gives me a pitying look. 'Don't worry. I'll help you decide. That's what I'm here for after all!

'The *dog* will help me choose,' I say. 'He has excellent taste.'

'Please, take a seat,' she says, smiling and gesturing to a sofa laden with inviting cushions.

'Oh yes. That's *good*,' I say. I sink down into the armchair and pop my feet on the coffee table. There's a cake stand laden with pastel-coloured macarons and miniature wedding cakes complete with tiny brides and grooms. I gawk at the food. It's too pretty to eat, but my stomach rumbles.

'Would you care for a glass of champagne?'

'Better not,' I say. 'I'm a recovering alcoholic.'

Gabby nods and smiles. 'What style of dress are you looking for?' she asks.

'Something *really* special. Something that makes you cry for no reason. You know, like royal weddings?' I hear the sound of ripping. 'Shit? What's that? The dog?' I look around. The pug has run off and has got one of the dresses stuck in his teeth and is tearing the taffeta. 'I'm not paying for *that*.'

'It's fine,' Gabby says with a grimace.

I grab the dog and sit down again with the pug in my lap.

'He's hungry. Eat,' I say. I give Baby a cake and a macaron. He gulps them down greedily, licking his nose with a wet pink tongue.

'Let's start with the silhouette. What kind of line do you like? We have Princess, Mermaid or Short?'

'Mermaid, *obviously*.'

Oh my God, how cool is that? Mermaids are freaky-sexy.

'Actually, I've changed my mind. I want Princess instead.'

'Princess. Great,' she says.

'I know, I want a fuck-off train. Longer than Princess Diana's was. How long was her train again?'

'I believe it was twenty-five feet.'

'Uh-huh,' I say. 'That is *quite* long. I want twenty-six feet.'

'Twenty-six feet.' She writes it down on a pad. 'How about the neckline? We have Strapless, Bateau, Sweetheart, Crew, V-neck, Tattoo . . .'

'Tattoo?'

'Yes.'

'You tattoo the dress?'

'It's not –' she pauses and looks at me sideways – '*an actual tattoo*; it's tattoo *effect*.'

'So, it's not, like, an actual dress tattooed on to you?'

'The dress is like your second skin. It has an illusion design. Floral appliqués in thread blend into the neckline. Do you remember Kate Middleton's dress?' It's also reminiscent of Grace Kelly's dress when she married Prince Rainier of Monaco.'

'Whatever. Show me some dresses. I want you to blow my mind.'

Gabby goes to fetch some options. I feed macarons to the dog. When she returns, she is wheeling a rail with six dresses on.

'What do you think of this one?' She holds up a floor-length gown. It's a flouncy Victorian thing with sleeves and a tiny waistline.

'Too long,' I say. '*Way* too long. Have you got anything shorter?'

She puts the dress back on the rail and holds up another one.

'Shorter,' I say.

She pulls out another.

'Shorter. Shorter. Shorter.'

She shows me the last dress on the rail.

'No, no. Even shorter. Something that shows off your thighs. I've been working on my thigh gap.' I don't actually have one yet, but it's just a matter of time.

Gabriella takes a bottle of Dom Pérignon from the fridge. She pours herself a glass and takes a long hard sip. Then she rolls the rail thing off to fetch some other dresses.

She comes back with another selection and holds up a knee-length gown.

'This is from our "Romantic" collection. I love the lace and embroidery. It has a beautiful flowing fabric, soft tulle and hand-stitched beading . . .'

'Urgh. You've got to be kidding me. It looks like my gran's net curtains.'

'Right.' She shoves the dress on the rail.

'Have you got anything *sexy*?'

She grabs another dress from the rack. 'This one is –'

'No, no, no.' I roll my eyes. 'I want him to take *one* look and jizz in his pants. You feel me?'

Sometimes I worry that Ed doesn't fancy me. I know it's *ridiculous*. I mean, he wouldn't *marry* me if he didn't want to *shag* me. We've been living together for *six months* (well, I'm still in the guest cottage . . .) and not so much as a *fingering*. No, not even a *knob job*. Nothing. It's disconcerting. But if I'm really honest, it's not like I'm keen to mount him either. What is going on? Perhaps my libido has taken a hit since those guys in Italy? Nino hasn't been around. (Perhaps he's annoyed about Silvio?)

Gabs pours herself another glass of Dom Pérignon and then she downs it all in one without taking a breath. She closes her eyes and breathes for a moment then fixes me with a stare and grabs another dress from the rail.

'How about this one? This is from our "Sexy" collection. It has a plunging neckline and a fit and flare silhouette that highlights the female figure. Sheer, almost transparent fabric for the décolletage. It's short at the front and long at the back . . .'

'That's about as sexy as *frogs*.'

'I'm sorry . . . *frogs*?'

'Uh-huh.'

I guess I'm still thinking about Kermit. That's weird. I thought I'd be over it. Tiff's face appears in my head.

'How about a bikini?' I say. 'But not, like, a *normal* bikini. A wedding bikini made of lace?'

Gabriella doesn't reply. She just purses her lips.

'OK. Fine. No swimsuits. I get it. Show me the most expensive dress in the whole shop.'

Gabby scurries off again. I feed Baby champagne. My dress will cost more than my sister's did, no doubt about it.

She comes back with a poofy thing that takes three people to carry.

'And how much is this? Not that money's an object. I'm just curious.'

'It's three hundred thousand pounds.'

I gulp. 'It is *perfect*.'

I pull the heavy curtain back and step out into the store.

Gabby gasps, her hands to her lips, her eyes brimming

with tears. A single tear slides down her cheek. She bites her bottom lip.

'I see that you can fake cry too. It's useful,' I say, 'isn't it?'

'I'm not *fake crying*. You look beautiful. I'm sorry, I get emotional.'

I take a look at myself in the mirror. You can see my face, but that's it. The rest of my body is wrapped inside an avalanche of lace. I look like I'm on my way to a party and the theme is *cake*, and I have chosen to attend as an Alaska (baked). The skirt is as poofy as *fuck* and sticks out at a right angle from the bodice, which is low-cut and covered in glittering crystals.

'You're right. I *do* look beautiful.' I hear my phone ring in my bag. 'Urgh, hang on a minute.' Just when I wanted to wallow in the second coming of Princess Grace . . . I tear myself away from the mirror.

I study the phone: 'Unidentified caller'.

I answer.

'Hello,' comes a woman's voice. 'This is Louise at [inaudible].'

'Er . . . yeah . . . hi?' I say. I don't know anyone called *Louise.*

'We have details about the accident you were involved with in the past three years.'

I swallow hard. 'Who is this?' Shit. How the hell does she know about that? 'Yes, in Sicily. It *was* an accident,' I say.

'And it wasn't your fault.'

I think they're talking about Beth. They know my sister died.

'No, it wasn't my fault,' I say. 'Is this . . . is this the *police*?'

Or is Louise in the Mafia? Is she going to blackmail me?

'We can help you to claim compensation.'

I hang up. She sounds like a robot but, even so, I said too much. I nearly gave myself away. I shove the phone in my bag and step out to the lounge again. *Fucking automated cold calls.* Those people are Satan.

'Would you like me to take a picture to send to your mother?' asks Gabs.

'No. I don't *send things* to my mother.' Maybe *letter bombs.* 'My mother won't be attending the wedding,' I say.

'I'm so sorry. Would you like to see a selection of veils to complement your dress?'

'No, I don't want a veil,' I say. 'It might get stuck to my lip gloss. Perhaps a crown?'

The dog looks at me and barks. He likes the dress!

EIGHT MONTHS LATER

Saturday, 2 September, 3 p.m.
The Chapel, Blenheim Palace, Oxfordshire

The sun comes out from behind a cloud. It's a nice day for a white wedding.

'OK. NOW. GO,' I say.

The man releases the doves. They rush out from the baskets and fly up high into the chapel. The white birds swoop up to the roof, cooing: a flurry of feathers. A few of them perch on the crucifix, but most of them flap overhead. *Thirty* doves. Was that enough? I should have ordered more. But then there's the danger of *excrement.*

(I should have said not to feed them . . .) A bird lands on a candelabra. Shit. *Is it going to catch fire?* Like when the Koreans incinerated the peace doves at the Olympics? I hold my breath as the candles flicker. But it's OK. It's not burnt.

'ACTION,' I say to the sixteen-piece kettledrum band at the church entrance.

The musicians begin to play the traditional Bridal March. The sound of the kettledrums rings out like a thousand tubular bells. I sit and wait for the bass to kick in.

'OK, that's enough. Now *my* song.'

Taylor Swift begins to sing 'Look What You Made Me Do'. She's ace. So much better than Wagner. He's boring. All the tiny hairs on the back of my neck stand up. I've got goosebumps. Taylor is worth every penny Ed paid to fly her in from Los Angeles. Taylor's hitting the high notes now. I'm really getting my groove on. Graffiti artists spray fake rainbows. The people from Chanel spritz the nave with twenty bottles of Coco Mademoiselle.

I hired some ugly 'character' models to carry my train and be bridesmaids. There's a fat girl, a girl with a big nose and one with weird crossed eyes. (I wasn't going to take the risk of being upstaged by someone with Pippa Middleton's perfect ass.) I've dressed them up in unflattering jumpsuits in a queasy shade of green. They're making me look *fantastic.*

'Have you got my train? Don't drop it.'

The cross-eyed girl nods.

The man opens the wooden doors. I climb up on the horse, grip the reigns and dig my heels down into the stirrups.

'GIDDY UP, MURPHY. *LET'S GO.*'

The white horse whinnies. He throws back his head and his pink mane flows out in the summer breeze. Murphy is wearing a harness with six-feet-long Pegasus wings attached. A unicorn horn protrudes from his forehead. We trot down the aisle and the congregation gawks. They watch me riding my white horse with my train flowing out like a river behind me: pearls and lace and tulle. All twenty-six feet of it. I feel like a queen.

The pug sits on my lap with his tongue lolling out. Baby has the rings attached to his head with a handsome ribbon. Baby is going to give me away. It's unconventional, but we have an open-minded vicar. It's that or Ed has bribed him. We had to do a lot of bribing to arrange this wedding so quickly. I wanted to marry in Westminster Abbey, but Ed wanted to keep it intimate, what with the press hounding him and the ongoing investigation . . .

Blenheim is a nice plan B. I look around the chapel. I can't help but notice that no one is sitting on my side of the church. But that's all right. Ed has enough friends and family for us both. The groom's section is fit to burst with people standing up. It's not like I wanted to ask my *mum*. My sister and my father are *dead* . . . Tiff was my only friend. I guess my mum will be in Lower Slaughter now with Ernie. It would have been nice to have *him* here. He's the only person that I would have liked to invite. He'd look cute in a bow tie.

I didn't tell Mum I'm tying the knot. Of course I would have *loved* to reveal that I'm marrying a *billionaire* who absolutely adores me. Beth only married a *millionaire*, so that makes me the winner. But it wasn't safe to invite her.

She'd reveal my true identity and ruin the whole damn thing. I haven't spoken to her for a while. She hasn't called me and I haven't called *her*. I have no idea what is going on with the trial . . . if she's locked up or free.

I spot Ed standing at the altar in his smart white suit. I've not been stood up. That's a relief. I almost feel like I *love* him. I hope I don't get *too* attached, then I won't be able to kill him.

I beam at Ed as he turns round to watch. He has a strange expression. I try to read his face, but I can't. Indigestion? For a moment I panic. Has Ed worked out that *I* murdered his wife? Or were the unicorn wings *too much*? Perhaps Ed's odd look is a deep desire for me now that he's seen me in my dress? I *do* look sexy.

James, the butler, is Ed's best man. That's weird. Why him? He's just *staff*. He smiles and nods. I don't smile back. As soon as Ed and I are married, that guy has got to go.

Ed reaches up to help me down from the saddle. I grab on to him and jump off the horse.

'Hello. You look nice,' I say.

Ed smiles. 'You look nice too.'

I land in a flurry of tulle and lace and look into Ed's eyes. And I suddenly know it was worth all the effort. Everything led to *this*. All the killings. The suffering. I wish Tiff were here. She could be my maid of honour. But you can't make an omelette without breaking eggs . . . and I *really* like omelettes.

'Welcome,' says the vicar, and I jump.

Ed's mum is sitting in the front row in a lovely lilac number. She must be nearly ninety years old. She beams at me. I beam back.

'Ladies and gentlemen,' says the vicar.

This is where I drop off. I can't listen to vicars without falling asleep. I stifle a yawn. I blink. I turn and study the chapel. It's pretty, smaller than Westminster Abbey, but they've done a decent job with the interior design. A few too many pictures of Jesus. A few too many statues. My God, it's like they're *obsessed* with this guy. It's like a cult or something.

The vicar says, 'If any person present knows of any lawful impediment to this marriage, he or she should declare it now.'

I snort a laugh. This is the moment in Hollywood films when you would start to get nervous. But not *me*. I'm chill—

'I do,' comes a woman's voice.

I look up and see Jolene standing at the front of the church, on Ed's side, obviously.

'*You* again? Give me a break. Who invited *you*?'

'Jacinda?' says Ed.

'Oh, Ed, you can't marry *her*,' she says. 'What about *Tiffany*?'

Ed looks over at James and widens his eyes and nods at Jessica.

'Come on,' says James, taking her by the hand and leading her away. He walks her back to her seat.

'Sorry about that,' says Ed. 'She's taken it all really hard.'

'Anyone else?' says the vicar.

Why is he asking *again*?

'I do,' comes another woman's voice.

This time my blood runs cold. I'd know that voice anywhere. Oh my God. It can't be . . . can it? But it is.

'*Mum?*' I whisper.

I spin round to see Mavis standing in the door of the church. She's very small and far away, but it's *definitely* her. Sunlight frames her silhouette: pink suit, big hat, high heels, posh bag. She begins to walk down the aisle. The congregation stares.

I freeze. What the hell is *she* doing here?

The vicar frowns.

There's a small boy at her side. Shit. It's *Ernie*. I haven't seen him for *two years*. He was only a *baby*. The last time I saw him was in Taormina. He's grown. He's a *toddler* now! I can't believe it's him! My heart melts. I want to *hug* him. I want to feel his tiny body and hold him tight between my arms and never let him go.

'I thought it was odd you were working for Ed, but now *this*,' says my mum.

I stand and gawp. I'm speechless. My heart begins to pound. Shit. This is bad. This is Very Bad. I suddenly feel nauseous. The earth quakes beneath my feet. I hold on to Ed for balance. There's a tight feeling in my chest as though someone's wrapped my lungs up with duct tape. I'm light-headed. Seeing stars. I think I'm about to pass out. My face is plastered all over the gossip pages of the *Sun* and all the other newspapers. Of course she was bound to find out.

My mother strolls along the aisle. She doesn't hurry or anything. It's like she's walking in super slow motion or on the moon or something. Ernie follows just behind. Ed just looks confused.

She eventually comes to a stop at the altar. I glare at her. She looks *amazing*. My mother's suit fits *perfectly*. I bet it's made to measure. Her shoes are patent Louboutins with six-inch heels. She's a *grandmother*. She's draped in three long strings of pearls. Her hat is perched at an angle that says 'I know, I'm older than *sin*, but you know *you still would*.' (She is basically Joan Collins circa 2001.)

I study my nephew. He's totally *gorgeous*. His curly hair is blond and he has big blue eyes, the colour of the sea. Oh my God, I've *missed* him. I could eat him up. I bend down to Ernie's level.

'Do you remember me?'

He smiles, then hides behind Mum's legs.

I stand up again.

'*You* can't marry *him*,' says my mother, cooling herself with a fan.

'*Why?*' I stand and look at Ed, who is looking pale.

'Hello, Edwin,' says my mother.

'Hello, Mavis,' he says. 'What are *you* doing here? I mean . . . of course it's lovely to see you.'

I look at Ed and then my mother.

'Wait, what? You two *know* each other?'

My mother laughs. '*Biblically*.'

She steps in a little closer and leans in towards me. She whispers in my ear loud enough for Ed and the vicar to hear. 'We had an affair in the late eighties and *you* were the by-product.'

I gawp at Ed and then gawk at my mother.

My mother says, 'Shall I spell it out for you? Edwin is your *father*.'

The congregation gasps.

'OF COURSE HE'S NOT MY DAD!' I scream. 'Are you, Ed? *ED?*'

Ed is gazing at my mother. 'It's been a long time, Mavis.'

'Thirty years, give or take,' my mother says with a smirk. 'I never forgot about you, Edwin.'

'You haven't changed a bit,' says Ed.

I suddenly feel sick. 'I'm sorry, is this *Mamma Mia*? Are you going to start singing ABBA songs? How did you two even *meet*?'

My mother smiles a dreamy smile. 'Ed and I met in Taormina.'

'Taormina? What were you doing *there*?'

'I was on holiday. Edwin had a little place and we met one night in a bar. The rest, as they say, is history. You and Beth were the result. That's why I was so pleased when Beth met that dreamboat Ambrogio and moved out to Sicily. I *adore* Taormina.'

I blink. Oh my God. I knew she was *nuts*, but my mother is totally *batshit*. Nothing she said makes any sense, except perhaps it does . . .

I rip off my train and chuck it on the floor. I look at Ed, I mean, *Dad*, and then my mother. 'Couldn't you just have *texted*?'

'I wanted to see Blenheim Palace. There's a cheese festival on in the grounds. I might pop in a bit later on and buy myself some Brie.'

'Argh. Why are you such a *slut*?' My dress gets caught on one of the rose bushes lining the aisle.

'Like mother, like daughter.'

'So *I'm* a slut?'

'Yes, and also *my* mother.'

I gasp. 'What? Grandma!'

'Well, it's true,' she says. 'I have *no idea* who my father is. Neither did my mum.'

I shake my head. My blood boils. I am seeing red. Nothing makes any sense any more. 'See you later, Ernie,' I say.

He gives me a wave.

'We can do a paternity test,' says Ed.

I say, 'Don't waste your time.'

'I thought you looked *familiar*,' he says. 'You have your mother's eyes.'

At that point Ed's octogenarian mother collapses.

'Someone call 999,' Ed shouts, running to scoop her up. Her glasses have smashed on the tiles.

I storm out of the church.

The wind from the helicopter makes my hair whip around my eyes. It's loud. The blades spin round and round. The ground shakes beneath my feet. The helicopter is bright white with 'Just Married' painted on it and gold and silver fireworks exploding from the tail. It looks *ridiculous*.

I gather up my dress and clamber up into the chopper, slamming the door behind me.

'Take me to Archway,' I say.

6 p.m.
Archway, London

It turns out we couldn't land in Archway on the roof of the hostel, so we had to get special clearance to land on Highgate Golf Club. The golfers don't even stop and stare as I carry the dog across the course in the pouring rain. This must happen all the time. I guess this is normal around here. A dozen paparazzi on mopeds and beat-up cars come skidding by. They slam on the brakes and come to a halt on the road beside the golf course. I'm too tired and heartbroken to tell them to fuck off. I cover my face with the tiny dog. I use him as my shield as I trudge across the field in my wedding dress. The hem of my dress is muddy and my shoes get stuck in the grass. I lose the hacks somewhere in Highgate. They head back to their cars. They couldn't get any decent pics of me with my pug disguise.

I stomp down Highgate High Street and along the Archway Road. By the time I get to the hostel, I'm drenched. Beyond bedraggled. My dress is soaking wet and I can hardly climb the stairs. I hide the pug under my skirt and march past a 'No Pets Allowed' sign. Darragh's at reception playing video games as usual. He barely notices me come in. He's a crap receptionist. Somehow I manage to stomp upstairs and push through the door to my room.

Some of the other residents are chatting. They stop talking and stare when I come in. The pug crawls out from under my skirt and starts barking.

'*Ciao*,' I say.

They're staring at me as though I were an unusual-looking alien that teleported into their home and started speaking in Alien.

'Oh. You're back,' says Roxy.

'Yeah.'

'We thought you'd killed yourself,' says Bob.

'What?' I ask. I stare back at them. 'What gave you that idea?'

'Well,' says Bob, 'we weren't sure, were we? We didn't know where you had gone.'

'I had some business to attend to,' I say. 'It is over now.'

'Did you . . . *get married*? Bob asks. 'Is that a *wedding* dress?'

They examine the dirty, soaking meringue that I am modelling.

'No I didn't and yes it is. It's just fancy dress. I wore it to run a marathon.'

That explains the mud.

'Great,' says Roxy. 'We got you some Pringles. Your favourites. You know, just in case you came back . . . They might be stale by now.'

I blink. 'You bought me *Pringles*?'

'Yeah. BBQ flavour,' says Bob.

'Those are the ones you like, aren't they?' Roxy says, reaching into a bag and pulling out a tube of Pringles.

'Yeah. Cheers.' I take them.

I'm *starving*. I open the packet and munch. Why did they buy me my favourite food? Did they miss me or something?

'Cute dog,' Roxy says.

I pick up the puppy. 'This is Baby. He's staying,' I say.

'I knew you'd be back,' says Roxy.

Baby leaps out of my arms and runs over to Roxy.

She pets him. 'Aww, good boy,' she says.

Bob strokes him as well.

My mobile rings: 'Mavis'. *No way.* I don't want to talk to my mum. I hit reject and – a force of habit – stick on one of Tiff's vlogs.

'I'll be on my bunk,' I say, climbing the ladder.

'Er,' says Bob, 'that's not your bunk any more. You moved out a year ago? Someone else has that bunk now.'

'I could give a fuck.'

I lie spreadeagle on *my* bed and stare at my phone. (The other guy comes back and tries to throw me out, but I scowl and shoot him a look so *murderous* that he skulks out of the room.) I click into Basecamp. My plan has gone awry. But at least I never slept with *my dad*. That would have been super gross.

Monday, 4 September, 9 a.m.
The Savoy, London

I storm into the Savoy Grill kitchen. The stench of frying onions makes my eyeballs sting.

'*Ciao*, it's me. Can I have my old job back?'

'*Siobhán?*' Chef raises an eyebrow. 'Where have you been? You disappeared.'

'Sorry . . . er. Yeah. I had a spot of scarlet fever. All better now.'

Chef rolls his eyes. 'It's been a *year*. You need to call in sick.'

'OK. I will next time.'

'Jack's back on the sushi bar.'

'Yeah, but he isn't as good as *me*.'

Jack looks up. 'No, Chef, that's not fair.'

'Jack, get back on the pot wash,' says Chef.

'No, Chef, not again!'

'Welcome back, Siobhán,' says Chef.

Jack gawks at me open-mouthed.

I shrug. 'It's not my fault I'm *awesome*.'

'What about me?' asks a boy, who I assume is the new pot wash.

'We don't need you now, son. You can go,' says Chef.

The boy peels off his Marigolds and storms off in a huff.

I skip over to the chopping board and grab a slimy fish. It's an eel with big bulging eyes and slippery silver skin.

'I thought you weren't coming back,' says Jack.

'Yeah well, you people need me.'

I chop the head off the silver eel and start to slice it up.

'I'm glad you're back. I missed you,' he says. I glare. 'It wasn't the same without you,' he calls as he walks away.

Uh-huh. Yeah right, whatever.

I stab a fish between the eyes with my sharp-ass knife and watch its tiny brains spill out all over the chopping board.

8.30 p.m.
Hampstead, London

Hurry up. How can there be so much traffic? It's nearly 9 p.m. Rush hour ended *hours* ago. This is *ridiculous*. The double-decker crawls along Hampstead Lane towards Kenwood. I sit at the back of the bus and sweat, chewing my bubblegum. I want to chew the *life* out of it. I want the gum to *die*. I'm gnashing my jaws and grinding my teeth like I am totally wired. It's hot, still humid from the day's sun. There's no air conditioning. My T-shirt clings to my damp back. I can't believe how long this is taking. I've been on this bus for *an hour*. I've got shit to do. There's no time for fucking around.

I shift in my seat. The fabric makes the skin itch on my thighs. I'm listening to 'Lose Yourself' by Eminem. He is very insistent. He's telling me I have *one* shot. I have one shot, that's it. If I blow this, it's over. I can forget about my hit. I chew my gum in time to the bass; my eyes are wide, my fists clenched. It doesn't matter if I want to do it. I am a *professional*. Murder runs in my family. I'm doing it for *Nino*. And if I can't marry *Ed*, I mean *Dad*, there's no point in him being alive.

There's the sound of honking horns. It's gridlocked. Totally choked. The ancient bus hisses and groans. I grip my handbag tight. On my lap, inside my bag, is my sushi knife. Yes, I've got my hunting knife, I stole it from the Savoy. I reach inside to test the blade: the prick of the tip. It's *sharp*. Razor sharp. It should be quick. As easy as filleting cod or chopping up tuna tartare.

I breathe in deeply through my nose and close my eyes. I am Artemis, the death-bringing goddess. The goddess of hunting, the moon and chastity, but mostly the goddess of *hunting*. I'm not so bothered about the rest. The moon, I could take or leave, to be honest. And chastity? *No thanks*. I'm on my way to kill my father. This is my fate. My destiny. I was born to slaughter this man. This is premeditated. I am Oedipus, not Electra. #GenderStereotype. I like to do things differently. I like to break the mould. I should be Electra because I am *female*, but I'm sure Freud would agree that I've never been what you'd call 'normal', whatever that means. No, Electra can fuck off. Electra married her father and killed her mother. I'm not doing *that*. I'm going kill my father and . . . *tolerate* my mum. Perhaps. Just like Oedipus. How about that?

Nino hasn't been around much recently, but that doesn't mean I've forgotten about him or my promise. I'll do this hit for him, as we agreed. Tiff won't have died in vain. I'll finish what I started. I click into my (edited) Basecamp app.

1. Become Siobhán
2. Find ~~Ed~~ Dad
3. Drug ~~Ed~~ Dad
4. Kill Tiff
5. Kill ~~Ed~~ Dad

Jesus. What is taking so long? I glare out of the window at bumper-to-bumper cars. I might as well have *walked*. I jump up from my seat and push through the passengers down to the front of the bus.

'What's going on?' I shout at the driver through the safety glass.

'Someone hit a deer,' he says.

I look where he is pointing. '*Ohhh, shit*. It's a big one,' I say. 'Do you think it's *dead*?'

'I drive this route ten times a day, but I've never seen one. I saw the warning signs all right, but I didn't believe them.'

A deer is lying on its side in the middle of the road. A slick black pool of blood spills out from somewhere on its flank. The bus rolls by. Its glassy eyes seem to watch me back. His eyes remind me of Dad's. I shiver. It twitches. Is it still alive? It's a magnificent beast: a stag, an enormous male.

'Poor old bugger,' the driver says. 'Must be a bad omen.'

He crosses himself. He must be superstitious.

'Very fucking foreboding,' I say. 'Yeah, it's prophetic as fuck. That's a harbinger of doom. We'd better not walk under ladders.'

The driver looks at me funny from beneath his driver's cap. I go and sit down again. 'At least it wasn't a *black cat*.'

Once we've passed the scene of the crash, the bus speeds up again. I watch as the deer shrinks out of sight. A 'bad omen'. Yeah, *right*.

I ring the bell to stop the bus and get off by the Spaniards Inn. Then I stomp along the road towards the Bishops Avenue. The sun is setting. The clouds turn pink and red. When I reach Dad's pimp-ass place I press down hard on the buzzer.

'*Ciao*, it's me, Siobhán. I mean, *Alvie*.'

Whatever. It doesn't matter. Everyone knows who I am, but there are no blue lights flashing. I can only assume that this is because nobody knows my last name and/or the message hasn't reached the cops that I am here. Not yet. It's lucky for me that the British police are so underfunded. Plus the murders I am wanted for were committed on the continent. That was *years* ago now. They might have forgotten about them. And the cops are stretched and busy with things like paedophile politicians. They simply don't have the resources to find little old me. So people know I'm *Alvie*. So what? To be honest, it's a relief to not have to speak with an Irish accent all the time. That was getting tiring. Although now I've noticed that when I speak with my English accent, I still have an Irish lilt. I like it though; it's sexy.

Someone inside presses the buzzer to let me in. That's good. For a moment I thought that Ed – I mean *Dad* – might be cross and not let me in . . . But it's fine. He isn't cross. And it's not *my* fault that he's my dad. How was I to know? I wasn't there when he shagged my mum (and I'm *very* pleased about that).

The gate clicks open and I push through. The gravel crunches underfoot as I stride towards the house. I'm just going to *do it*, Nike-style. One strike across the jugular. I almost don't care if I get caught. I have had enough. I want this all to be over with. I'm tired. So tired and numb. I want some closure. For Nino. For Tiff. I set out to kill this man. Who cares if he's my *father*? I won't let sentimental bullshit get in the way of my plan. My heart beats faster in my chest. My breathing is shallow. The adrenaline rushes through my brain like I've just done a line. The front door opens and I tense.

'Alvina,' says my mother.

I freeze. '*You're* here? What the hell? I thought . . .' I take a step back.

'*Surprise*. Me again,' she says. 'Are you coming in? You're letting all the hot air in.'

I gawp at my mother. I expected Dad, or James, or the housekeeper. Urgh. She looks *great*. She's wearing a silk sarong with dangling gold earrings, oversized Gucci sunglasses and bright pink fuchsia lipstick. I don't move. This is weird. This is *wrong*. It's thrown me, to be honest. It's put me off my plan.

'Why did you name me after my step-dad?'

She pauses. 'I liked the name.'

'Alvin? That's a *shit* name.'

'Is it? Would you have preferred *Edwina*?'

'Yes. I would. I would have preferred it.'

'Like *Edwina Currie*? She had an affair with John Major. Urgh. I did you a favour.'

Ernie comes running to the door. He's carrying a pair of scissors. He hides behind my mother's legs then peers round them to look at me. He looks up at me through long eyelashes. His chubby cheeks are just *too much*. I reach out my hand and give one a squeeze.

'Hello, sausage,' I say. Then I take away the scissors. 'Stop acting the maggot. Let's not run with those, OK? You could hurt yourself.'

I pop them in my bag with the knife. The metal clinks.

'You know . . .' my mother continues, with her head cocked to one side. 'Now that the truth is out I can tell you you've always reminded me of Ed. Ever since the day you were born, you had an air about you.'

I tear my eyes away from the kid. 'I'm sorry, I had an *air*?'

'You had an air that was very Ed.'

'*I* had an air, NOT MY SISTER?'

'Beth? Oh no, not *her*.' She laughs. 'She didn't remind me of your father.'

Ernie shrinks back behind my mother's legs and disappears. I think I scared him when I yelled.

'Sorry, kid,' I mutter.

'Beth was nothing like you or Ed. She took after *me*.'

'Is *that* why you didn't hate *her*?' I grit my teeth. Narrow my eyes. I feel the urge to murder her rise inside.

'Are you coming in?' she asks.

I pause and close my eyes.

I know my life is going wrong. It hasn't escaped my attention that things are spiralling out of control despite my best intentions. First I murdered my twin sister. Then I killed my fiancé. I murdered my first and only friend, the saintly Tiffany. Now I'm about to kill my dad. It's like a Greek tragedy and they don't end well for the hero (or the heroine). I clutch the knife inside my bag. Yes, this is a choice point: two parallel worlds are opening up. There's no going back. This is it. I must make a decision. I need to get it right. The magnitude of this moment hits me: monumental, as heavy as marble. Sweat is dripping down my neck. There's a tightness in my chest. I have the chance to kill them both and complete the tragedy! There is something *cathartic* about it. It feels determined. Written. But if I carry on down this route, then there's no happy ending. There's no *happily ever after.* Not for me. Not now. I laugh out loud. There never has been. I see it now, as clear as day. A veil has been lifted. It's like I drank a truth serum. I need to change tactic. But how? I try to think on my feet. Do I spare their lives and finally try to move on with my own?

'For the last time, Alvina, ARE YOU COMING IN?'

I hesitate. Maybe I'm not the mad, bad, dangerous girl I thought I was? I'm very sweet once you get to know me, despite the twenty-plus bodies. Who am I then? WHO THE HELL AM I? Siobhán? Amazon? Alvie? If I don't kill, then what do I do? I have no idea.

'ALVINA,' my mother says, 'I'm going to shut the door.'

My mother starts to close the door, but I push it back and step into the entrance hall. My mother holds the door as I step into the cool of the atrium. The air conditioning's on full blast and it's cold with all the marble. I shiver. Then Dad appears looking like . . . a *dad* in a safari shirt and khaki shorts. The shorts are pulled up over his belly and secured with a too tight belt. Stripy socks reach to mid-calf. He's wearing open-toed sandals. I gasp. Oh God, what's happened to him? Is that a *safari hat*? He didn't look like *that* before. I'm sure he used to be *hot*. Is he going to start playing air guitar and cracking terrible jokes? Drinking craft ale from a mug saying 'No. 1 DAD'? Did he dress like this before and I just didn't notice? Or has he updated his wardrobe now that he's a *father*?

'Hello, *Alvina*,' he says approaching me and giving me a bear hug. 'My *daughter*, hey? Who would have thought?' He ruffles my hair up as though I were the dog. 'And a grandson!' He beams at Ernie. 'Lucky me.'

'Your son is your son today, but your daughter is your daughter for life,' I say.

'Huh?' says Dad.

'It's a popular Irish phrase.'

'But . . . you aren't *Irish*?'

Shit.

'Yeah, I know,' I say.

This is going to take some getting used to.

'Why did you change your name to Siobhán?' he asks.

'Stalker ex-boyfriend. I had to change it by deed poll. That's my actual name now.'

I guess Mum told him *everything*.

'Your mother never told me she was pregnant,' says Dad.

'Oh, Edwin, it was *over*,' my mum says with a laugh. 'It was just *one night* of passion. You do remember, don't you?'

'Barely,' mutters Dad.

'Please. Spare us the details,' I say.

My mother continues. 'We had sex on the beach, Alvina. Your sister and you were conceived doggy style over the back of a rowing boat called *Amore*.'

'Er . . .' says Dad. 'I was drunk at the time. I don't quite recall . . .'

315

'It was a little blue boat with an Italian flag.'

I stand on the welcome mat and stare, first at Dad and then my mother. The strap of my handbag slips through my fingers and the bag falls to the floor.

'You've moved in then?' I ask my mum.

She looks smug, triumphant. She nods. 'I have. At least for a while. Edwin and I have a lot to catch up on. I told him all about Elizabeth and Ernesto, of course.'

'I'm so sorry about your twin,' Dad says, rubbing my shoulder. 'It's such a shame.' He looks into my eyes. Oh man. He looks really cut up.

'Yeah, well, we all die eventually. It's just a matter of time . . .' I glare at my mother. I bet she told him that Beth was her favourite.

'I can't believe I never met her.'

'She looked like me. You didn't miss much.'

'I feel like I have lost a *daughter* and gained a *daughter*. Does that make sense?'

I sigh. 'It does because that's what happened.'

He smiles. 'You understand. Come with me,' says Dad. 'Alvina, I want to show you something.'

My mother nods and smiles. 'Go ahead.'

I trail Dad into the living room.

'Sit,' he says.

I flop down on to one of the massage chairs and turn the setting up to max. Oh yeah, that's good. That's *great*. I needed a back rub, actually. I was feeling *tense* . . . All this confusion about who to murder has really taken its toll. My mother perches on the edge of the cream-leather sofa. I can smell her perfume from here: lashings of Dior Poison.

Ernie runs into the room. He picks up Dad's matches from the coffee table and starts trying to light one up.

I jump up and grab the packet. 'Ernie, *no*. They're dangerous. DO NOT TOUCH. You could burn the house down.'

I chuck the matches back on the table. He looks like he's about to cry. I roll my eyes and give him a hug. Poor kid, he has no chance. I bury my nose into his hair and breathe in deep. He smells *wonderful*. His soft hair brushes against my cheek. Oh God, I could hug him forever. His body feels so warm in my arms. He hugs me back, then looks up at me with eyes as blue and infinite as the fucking sky.

I nearly had a baby once. He would have looked like this. I wonder what my life would be like if I'd had Ambrogio's kid. If I hadn't miscarried, I mean. Would I still be doing all *this*? Or would I be at Rhyme Time singing 'Humpty Dumpty'?

Dad comes back into the room clutching some kind of folder. It looks official, like legal papers or something from the police.

I release the boy and stand up. 'What's that?' I ask, pointing.

'My will,' says Dad, taking out some papers and passing them to me.

I grab the document. 'Your *what*?' I flick through the stapled pages. He has signed them all at the bottom with a swirling 'E' and 'F'.

'I contacted my lawyer when I heard that I had a child.'

My mother snorts. 'A *child*. She's *thirty*.'

'Again? For the love of Christ. I'm *twenty-seven*,' I say.

'*Nearly* thirty.' She gives a wry smile.

'I had him change my will,' says Dad, 'so you'll inherit . . . half.'

I blink. 'You what?'

He laughs. 'It's OK. I know it's overwhelming. I'll leave *half* my money to you,' he says, 'and *half* to my grandson.' He beams at Ernie, who's sitting on the massage chair and fiddling with the buttons just like I was. He's a chip off the old block. 'Ernie's money will rest in a trust fund until he's eighteen, but you will receive your half upon the distribution of my assets.'

'*Me?*'

'Yes.'

My mother beams. Urgh. What's *her* problem? Why is she so happy? She isn't getting anything.

'Do you have, like, a terminal illness that you haven't mentioned?'

'No, no, I don't. I'm fine,' he says, laughing. 'There's life in the old dog yet.'

I frown and study the papers. They do *look* official.

I gawp at him and he grins.

My mother has her arm round him. She's beaming at him like he's just won gold at the Olympics.

'Edwin's leaving you *a billion pounds*,' says Mum. 'Isn't that nice?'

Nice? I feel like *God*. The *Messiah*. I feel like *Jesus Christ*. I wish Tiff were here right now. I could share this moment with her. She'd be happy for me, for sure. Although Tiff didn't care about money . . .

'Until my demise you can have an allowance of fifty thousand pounds per month. I hope that will help to cover your basic expenses?'

I hand the papers back to Dad. 'All right then, cheers,' I say. I stand and blink for a moment, then walk towards the living-room door.

'Where are you going?' asks Dad.

'I'm going home to Archway.'

'You can stay here if you like?'

'Nah, my friends are expecting me. They might think I'm dead again.'

I move as though in a trance.

'But you only just got here?' says Dad. 'Let's open a bottle of Moët.'

'I don't drink.'

Ernie has the matches again. This kid is a liability. I storm back across the lounge and grab the matches from him.

'Matches, matches never touch. They can hurt you very much.'

Ernie laughs.

I let myself out through the front door. There's stunned silence behind me.

'Bye, honey,' Dad says, giving me a cheery wave. 'She'll come round, Mavis. She's in shock.'

'Bye then,' calls my mother.

'Do you want the Bentley?'

'I'll get the bus.' I take three steps and then stop. 'Actually, do you have any cash? I need to buy a ticket.'

My mother looks blank. 'I don't carry . . . what is it? Hand money. Ed?'

'Do they take AmEx?' he asks. 'I've never been on a bus.'

I shake my head and turn my back. 'It doesn't matter. I'll walk.'

I push the buzzer to open the gate and step out to the

Bishops Avenue. Mum and Dad stand in the doorway watching as I go. The obvious thing to do now is *kill him* and make it look like a heart attack. I'd inherit a *billion pounds* and laugh all the way to the bank. But Dad is giving me an allowance and I can definitely live off that. And there is something nice about finally having a *dad*. I sigh. I need to think about it.

TWO WEEKS LATER

Monday, 18 September, 3 p.m.
Number One Top City Hostel, Archway, London

I lie on my bunk and stare at the ceiling. I think it used to be white, but now it's kind of beige and almost dark brown in places. There's a water stain in the middle of the room and a smoke alarm with a shower cap pulled over the top of it so people can still smoke. The pug is sleeping curled up in a ball on my pirate-print duvet. And I can hear Roxy snoring on her bottom bunk. (She works nights and sleeps during the day like some kind of bat.) Bob's gone out somewhere. Don't know where. He's probably begging in Archway playing his old harmonica and drinking White Lightning.

I still can't believe I'm going to inherit half my dad's billions. It's almost too good to be true. I don't think I would believe it if I hadn't seen it myself, seen it with my own eyes. A billion pounds is a lot, isn't it? I wonder what I could buy? I grab my phone and google 'What costs a billion pounds?' I don't really have a benchmark. I have no idea. I mean, it's 250 million packets of Pringles, but I'm not going to buy that. The first hit is a handy list of ten things you can buy with a billion pounds. I scroll through the items: a baseball team called the Miami Marlins, the Hannah Montana franchise or a couple of Airbus commercial planes. Hmm. No thanks. I think I would prefer to buy Necker Island off Richard Branson and build myself a palace filled with naked male models. I'd buy some Bugatti hypercars in seven different colours and drive around my island with the (aforementioned, naked) models. I would buy some sixty-year-old single malt whisky and drink it on the way to space in a rocket with Channing Tatum. I'd also buy some shares in Amazon. That shit's worth a trillion dollars and I want a piece of *that*.

It's a shame that Nino isn't here to share my winnings with me. It was *our* plan after all. We dreamed it up together. Although he'd probably be pissed off that Dad is still alive. And he'd want to spend all the money on coke, which is *outrageous*. (I plan to spend only *half* on coke, the best shit on the planet.)

I roll over and snuggle down into my pirate pillow. The tiny pirates are smiling and laughing, as if it's all a joke. But it's *not* a joke. This is *real life*. As soon as Daddy snuffs it, I will inherit a *fortune*. I won't have to work a day in my life. I can develop a really, *really* expensive cocaine habit. Yes, I'll do it properly this time. I won't have any nose left.

I wonder what the average life expectancy is for a man in the UK. I google it – it's *eighty years*. Fuck me. That's ages. Do I really have to wait that long? Another twenty years? Surely if I have the decency not to *do him in*, then I could get some advance payments? I could negotiate something. I could even live off the interest. I'm sure we can work something out . . .

I close my eyes and see Tiff's face. She smiles her mega-watt smile and blows an air kiss right at me. I sigh and open my eyes. None of this would be happening if it wasn't for Tiff. If I hadn't murdered her, then I would still be skint. I wouldn't have got engaged to Dad. My mum would never have told him that I was his long-lost daughter. I suppose it was all for the best.

Cheers, Tiff. I owe you one.

But I can't help feeling a twinge of something. What is it? *Sadness? Regret?* Or did I put too much Tabasco on my breakfast taco?

'Tiff,' I say. 'Tiff, can you hear me?'

There is no reply. I close my eyes and breathe in through my nose and out through my mouth. What was it Tiff used to say in her vlog about meditation? Apparently the human brain is like a radio transmitter. Our thoughts are radio waves. Our pineal gland can send and receive thought signals, like Eleven in *Stranger Things*. All I have to do is picture her face in my mind's eye and think of what I want to tell her, then release it into the sky. She said it doesn't even matter if the soul is dead or alive. Telepathy works all the same. I'll give it a try.

I picture Tiffany's beautiful face: her deep blue eyes, her blonde hair.

I'm sorry, I think inside my head.

'*I forgive you*,' she replies.

I nearly fall off my bunk bed. I open my eyes. That was her voice. Did I imagine it? Or was she legit communicating from the other side?

I sigh. I guess I'll never know. There's no way to test it. Seriously I miss her, though. I want one of her hugs.

'I'll try to be a better person, Tiff. Be more like *you* . . .'

I pick up my Samsung phone and click into Tiffany's vlog. I scroll through all the posts on *Breakfast with Tiffany*, but I've seen them all before. The pictures blur, the letters merge and my mind begins to wander. I think about Tiff and when we went to CrossFit together. That was *fun*. I can't believe we won the whole competition! And I hardly cheated at all. We were a great team. I remember the time we went to that shop and donated all those clothes. We watched *Romy and Michele's High School Reunion* . . . I shake my head. *No*. I do not want to think about her. I don't want to *think* at all . . . It's too painful. What's going on? I need an aspirin or something. I remember all the conversations we had about spirituality. We would talk for hours and hours like we were kindred spirits . . .

I'm distracted from my daydream when my phone vibrates. It's my mother calling. Reject. She calls again. *No way*. I'm not in the mood to talk to her.

My Samsung pings with an email. Urgh, it's from my mother. I click into it. This had better be *good*.

From: TheEdForbes@EdForbes.com

To: AlvinaKnightly69@hotmail.com

Date: 18 September at 15.58

Subject: The Marriage of Ms Mavis Knightly and Mr Edwin Forbes

Dear Family/friend,

We are delighted to invite you to our wedding on Sunday, 15 October, 5 p.m., in the chapel at Blenheim Palace. Please

see the attached invitation. We would be honoured if you
could attend.

Kind regards,
Mavis and Ed x

I stare at the phone and grit my teeth. I glare at the email.
She's really twisting the knife in the wound. This is too
much. The wedding's less than a *month* away. She's really
rushing that through. And what about my *inheritance*? What
about my money? How will that change if my dad marries
Mum? Will his will be affected if he remarries now? What
about my allowance? There's an attachment called 'Invitation', but I don't open it – instead I throw my phone across
the room. It lands with a crash.

I'm sorry, *what*? Dad and my mother are getting fucking *married*? I fling off the duvet. The pirates look shocked.
I jump down from my bunk. Roxy rolls over and snarls a
noisy snore and I think she'll wake up but then she carries
on snoring. I pace the room, seething, scowling. I can't
believe she has the nerve. I can't believe her chutzpah. It's
the kind of thing *I* would do. And there I was minding
my own business being all spiritual, practically *meditating –
fuck!* – and thanking Tiff. I know I was going to make an
effort to be a nicer person, to be more spiritual than Tiff,
but now I WANT TO KILL SOMEONE.

I punch and punch the tiny pirates on my pillowcase
over and over and over again right in their stupid faces. I
whack at it till tiny feathers fly out from the seams.

I sigh. Tiff would be *happy* for them. Tiff would buy them
a present. *No!* She wouldn't buy them a *present*. She would

donate some money on their behalf to a charity to buy an African village some goats.

I take a deep breath and pull on my shoes. I shove my (now cracked) phone into my Birkin. I'll go and buy myself a hat. I'll be the bigger person. This is messing up my plans, but I'll play along. For now. If *anything* changes with the will, PEOPLE ARE GONNA DIE.

It's not the first time that Mum stole my guy. I still remember that night in Blockbusters in Cheltenham in 2001. It was a Saturday night and Beth and I were choosing a video . . .

FIFTEEN YEARS AGO

'Again?' I say.

'Yes, *again*,' says Beth.

'But we borrowed it last time. And the time before.'

'I know. I like it.'

'I don't. It's *stupid*.'

'It isn't *stupid*.'

'Yes it *is*. A big, dumb dog that hangs out with kids?'

'I like it when he rescues Emily from the swimming pool.'

I roll my eyes. 'It's ridiculous. Dogs don't rescue kids from pools.'

'They do if they're St Bernards.'

I sigh. Why is Beth so annoying? I wish I wasn't a twin. I guess it's too late now; I should have absorbed her in the womb.

I show Beth the video tape I chose. 'Look, *Dirty Dancing*.'

'There's no way Mum will let us have *that*. It's rated *fifteen*.'

I frown. 'She would if *you* asked her.'

My sister shakes her head. 'I want to borrow *Beethoven*.'

'But we've seen it *so many times* I want to *kill myself*.'

I stride down the rows of shelves lined with videos and games. They're listed alphabetically by sections, like 'Horror' and 'Family'. At the end of the row a selection of posters is mounted on the wall. I spot one of Patrick Swayze posing in a tight black top: big blond hair and bulging muscles. *So pretty*.

'Mum, can we borrow this one? Please?' I show her the video tape.

'Is this the one you chose?' she asks Beth, taking the VHS and studying the picture on the cover. 'Patrick Swayze. Nice. I liked him topless in *Ghost*,' she says.

'I've heard it's great,' I say.

'That's not the one we chose, Mummy,' my twin sister whines. 'It's *this* one.'

'*Beethoven*? Again?' asks Mum. 'You've borrowed it thirteen times. Aren't you bored of that?'

'I'm sick to death of it,' I say.

'It's our favourite film,' says Beth.

I clench my fists and dig my nails into the fleshy bits in the palms of my hands.

'I'd rather poke my *eyeballs* out than watch that again.'

'We'll borrow *Beethoven* . . . again. And that's the end of it.'

'Thank you, Mummy,' Beth says with a smile.

'You're welcome, my angel,' says Mum. She pats Beth's golden hair. 'Now run along and choose some treats.'

'Can't we borrow *both*?' I ask.

'I'm not made of money, Alvina. Ever since your father died, I've scrimped and saved to feed you both. You're such a hungry child.'

I follow Beth towards the till, trudging across the carpet. She *always* gets her way. It's not fair. I *never* get what I want. When I grow up, I'm going to make sure that I get *everything*. I'm going to make up for these years of never getting *anything* . . .

There's a wall lined with treats: crisps, buckets of sweets, chocolates wrapped in coloured foil. I spot a shelf with Pringles. I grab a tube of Cheese and Onion.

'Can I have these, Mum?'

'Not tonight.'

I shove them back on to the shelf. I don't know why I bother.

There's a popcorn cart with a big glass box filled with sweet and salty. There's the *pop-pop-pop* of exploding kernels. That greasy, sugary smell. The heat from the pan seeps through the glass. I fancy that as well . . .

'Mummy, can I have some pleeeease?' Beth asks, pointing to the popcorn.

'Of course you can, my cherub,' says Mum.

Unbelievable.

I go and stand by the front door. Cold air blasts through the gap. Dead leaves and fag butts dance in the wind. I hug myself and watch.

Mum queues up to pay at the till and Beth joins me by the exit. She's listening to her new Walkman. New Kids on the Block is blaring over Michael Jackson's 'Bad' that they're playing on the shop speakers. I watch as my sister munches. Crunch. Crunch. Crunch.

'Do you want some?' she asks.

I shake my head. 'Cow,' I say. I glare.

'WHAT? I CAN'T HEAR YOU.'

'COW,' I say again.

She frowns. 'MUUUUUM, ALVIE CALLED ME A COW.'

I lose my shit. I push my twin and then run at the popcorn stand and knock it over. It smashes to the floor, sending shards of glass and popcorn flying. Popcorn rolls all over the carpet. Everybody stares. The electric heater catches fire and flames begin to spread. The stench of burning sugar. Smoke. The sudden heat on my face.

'Alvina! Stop. Are you crazy?' says Mum.

I sprint out of the shop, through the front door and into the car park. Rain is lashing down. It's dark. The freezing wind whips my face. I run into the road. I run and run without stopping or turning round or slowing down. I run until I can't run any more and I don't know where I'm going. I wander through rural Gloucestershire, tired and hungry and cold.

Three or four hours later, my feet are sore from walking along the pitch-black country roads. My face is so cold I can't feel my cheeks. My lips are chapped, my nose is streaming and my hair is dripping wet from the torrential rain. I'm shaking. I just about manage to crawl into a hole in a hedgerow. I pass out and fall asleep, waking up at dawn.

I find my way home in the morning, ring the doorbell

and then I collapse right there on the doorstep. The next thing I know, I'm in bed with my temperature blazing.

I caught the flu that night. Real bad. I nearly fucking died. Of course I got no TLC from my mum. Beth was the one who was *hugged*. I spent two weeks in bed with nothing to watch but *Beethoven*. I hate that movie. And I hate that stupid dog. If I ever hear Symphony No. 5 again, I'll kill someone. I guess it wouldn't have been so bad, lying there coughing my guts up, if I hadn't caught my mother watching *Dirty Dancing*, stuffing her face with popcorn, getting hard for Patrick Swayze with one hand down the front of her pants and sipping a watermelon daiquiri. I saw him first. He should have been *mine*.

Patrick was my first crush; I would have *died* for him.

Sunday, 15 October, 5 p.m.
The Chapel, Blenheim Palace, Oxfordshire

I almost didn't come to the wedding, but I had major FOMO. (That's *fear of missing out* for those of you who don't communicate via acronyms.) Plus I assumed there'd be food. I can't believe I'm back *here* again. Perhaps Dad got a good deal on the second wedding because the first one didn't work out? And I can't believe my mother didn't ask me to be a bridesmaid. She would have asked Beth, no doubt about it. Little Miss Fucking Splendid. Instead my mum has asked three of her friends to do the honours. They all look like Patsy Stone from *Absolutely Fabulous*. Their bleach-blonde hair is styled in beehives. They're wearing too much make-up.

Ernie stands at the front of the church. I can't take my

eyes off him. He's dressed in a miniature suit. He's the most handsome pageboy. He looks up and I give him a wave. He beams and waves back. My heart melts. I pull a funny face and it cracks him up.

I sit at the back of the church and fidget. I fiddle with my new hat. It's itching and I think it's too small. It's either that or my head is too big. The brim makes it look like a flying saucer and the felt is too bright yellow with plastic flowers that keep attracting flying insects. A wasp buzzes too close to my ear.

'Buzz off,' I say, swatting. The wasp, at last, flies off.

Eventually, after what feels like hours of sitting and wriggling on an uncomfortable wooden pew, my mother says, 'I do.'

Dad says 'I do' as well. Oh God, *the idiot*. He doesn't know what he's doing. Still, he looks pleased and in a way I'm happy for them. Kind of. I mean, obviously I feel sick and am having trouble keeping my breakfast down, but other than that I'm happy for them.

My mother beams and I can see actual dollar signs flashing in her eyes. If she thinks she can steal my cash, then she's in for a nasty surprise. It's her *third* wedding, but she's still wearing *white*. Her gown is minimalist silk, the opposite of mine. It's embroidered with delicate flowers. There are crystals in her hair. She looks ecstatic standing there, *virginal* almost. I snort. If *she's* a virgin, then I'm Pope Francis. I roll my eyes at the thought.

'You may kiss the bride,' the vicar says. It's the same guy we had.

They kiss. I avert my gaze and study some woman's hat that looks just like a jellyfish. I wish I had one like that.

The congregation trails out to the reception hall. The band starts playing ABBA songs. It's all a bit much, to be honest. I turn my attention to my bladder. I really need the loo, so I hang back and find the ladies'. There's a long queue. I wait in line. The toilets are at the end of a corridor. It gives me the time and space I need to think about my plan. I mean, right now I'm so confused about who I'm killing, who is my father and who is not, and whether I am loaded that I don't know what's going on. I scroll through my Basecamp list. I cross my legs and wait for a while, but then I get desperate. Screw it. I can't stand queues. Queues are bullshit.

I go and find the disabled.

'Jesus,' I say, when I open the door.

Dad and his butler are standing there with their pants down. They're having sex over the sink. They look up and stare, like two rabbits caught in headlights. Wowzer. I close the door. *What the fuck?* Was that *Dad?* I open the door again. Yup, that's definitely James in there with him, glaring at me, butt-naked. And that's Dad doing *jazz hands*. I close the door again.

'Thought I'd locked it,' comes a voice from inside.

Then there are some other sounds I don't care to describe.

I shake my head and close my eyes, but *I can still see them*. What? *Dad likes cock?!* Who knew? Not me. I knew that my gaydar was *shit*, but apparently my gay-dad-dar is even worse.

I stand and stare at the door. And James? Wow. In hindsight it's obvious. Dad was too well dressed to be straight, like an old Tom Ford. And I have never seen a straight guy listen to ABBA by choice. He doesn't have a foot fetish; he just really likes shoes and appreciates good design. It all makes sense now . . . But what about the prostitutes at the Savoy? I suppose I never saw my father lay a finger on them. They must have been a gift for the Saudi prince. I remember the suite had *two* bedrooms. Dad must have slept in the other one . . .

I turn round as quick as I can and run back to the toilets. There's no queue for the men's so, *fuck it*, I just go in there. I get some funny looks, but for all they know I'm transgender.

I stumble out to the reception, eyes wide, in a daze. My mother's standing at the entrance with Ernie by her side. She is among adoring crowds.

My mother's loving the attention now she's *Mrs Edwin Forbes*.

'Congratulations,' I say to Mum. 'As your wedding present I have arranged to have a dozen goats sent to the mayor of Weybridge.'

'What?'

'Weybridge is a town in Surrey. Mum, I need to tell you something,' I hiss. 'It's kind of urgent.'

'Get me a drink, I'm parched,' she whispers in my ear as we air kiss.

I can smell gin on her breath. She is kind of *swaying*. She must have been drinking before the ceremony. She's going to get wasted, isn't she?

I flag down a waiter with a magnum of Moët and Chandon. He's about to pour out a flute when my mum says,

'Leave the bottle.' She grabs the magnum and a flute. 'You want some?'

'I quit, remember?'

I hold Ernie's hand and take Mum's wrist and drag her after me. We sit down at a table. Ernie sits on my knee.

My mother pours herself a glass and shoos away the waiter. 'What's this?' She gestures to my hat. 'Have you come as some kind of spacecraft?'

I ignore her snide remark. 'Ernesto,' I say, 'would you like to watch cartoons on my phone?'

He nods.

'I thought so.'

I find *Peppa Pig* and give the phone to Ernie. He giggles and I smile. He reminds me of my inner child. I haven't seen her for a while. I wrap my arms round the kid then fix my eyes on my mother.

I have to tell her. I can't sit here and keep this secret from her. It's their *wedding day* for God's sake. It's too good. I can't resist. But she'll be upset . . . She might even *cry*. And it's her special day. Does she need to know *now*? I'm trying to be a *better* person. I promised Tiffany . . . But then I promised Nino I'd kill Dad, and he's still alive . . . (Maybe I should just accept that I'm crap at promises? I mean, I can't be good at *everything*. I'm not fucking *Beth*.)

I lean in and lower my voice. 'I caught Dad having sex with the butler.'

Her expression is hard to read through the Botox.

'Where?'

'In the disabled.'

She wrinkles up her nose. 'Oh, Ed. The *toilets*. How déclassé.'

She takes a very large swig of champagne then re-applies her lipstick.

'Is that all you have to say?'

'Such bad taste . . .' she mutters. 'Honestly, he owns the Savoy, and he has sex in the *toilets*.'

'Wait. What? He owns the Savoy? Of course he does. Doesn't matter.' I shake my head. My bombshell has failed. 'Dad is *gay*, Mum,' I say.

My mum bursts out in hysterical laughter. I'm worried she'll wet herself.

'I know. I've known for *years*. He's as gay as Elton.'

She wipes a tear away from her eye and pours herself another glass. She downs the whole flute in one go and then fills it up again. Whoa. She's going to be totally shit-faced.

'I'm his *beard*,' she says.

'His *what*? What the hell does *that* mean?'

'This *marriage* thing is a cover,' she says, lowering her voice. 'Ed has investors from Russia and places, you know? Brunei? The Ukraine. They're homophobic. Edwin has to be *married* to throw them off the scent. You didn't know?'

'Of course I did.'

So *that's* why he wanted to marry me. But I didn't know the reason we hadn't fucked was *because he liked guys*. That is a shocker. I thought he was being a *gentleman*. I thought maybe, perhaps, we were waiting for our honeymoon. That would have been romantic. At least my mum isn't going to shag him. That's been giving me nightmares.

'You didn't know.' She laughs. 'Oh God, I thought *everyone* knew. Apart from the Russians, of course. Not the Russians. You're not going to tell them, are you?'

'No, I'm not going to tell the Russians.'

'*Incredibly* homophobic,' she mutters into her glass.

'But you . . . had sex . . . in the eighties?'

'Well, you weren't the *Immaculate Conception*.'

'Did you put him off women?'

'No, I did *not*.'

'Did he mistake you for a *man*?'

My mother glares.

Ha! They must have been *hammered*.

'By the way, I've been thinking,' she starts.

This isn't going to end well . . .

'This whole *money* thing with Ed.'

I know exactly where this is going. I can read her like a book. Not a book I'd want to read: *One Day in the Life of Ivan Denisovich* or *Mein Kampf* or something.

'Well,' she says, taking a swig, 'now that I'm Ed's wife –'

'You've been his wife for all of *five minutes*.'

'I know, but I'm still his *wife*.'

'Let me guess,' I scoff. 'When he dies, the billions go to you now?'

She fixes me with a hard stare as she plumps up her hairdo.

'Should I be so *unfortunate* as to become a *widow* and outlive my *darling* husband –'

'Mum, you're not going to *kill* him?'

She pauses. 'No, of course I'm not.'

'*Mum*.' I hold her gaze. 'Because we both know you've killed before. Hang on, come to think of it, why *aren't* you in *jail*?'

'Innocent until proven guilty. They've got *nothing*.'

'What happened with the trial?' I ask. 'You said you were going on trial, but then you went all quiet. I assumed they'd reinstated the death penalty and you'd been fried.'

335

She laughs. 'It never happened! They didn't have enough evidence. It was a big waste of time.'

I shake my head. *Lucky cow.* 'The evidence might be circumstantial, but we both know you did it.'

She leans in towards me and narrows her eyes. 'Are you wearing a wire?'

'No, Mum. I'm not wearing a wire.'

'It was a stroke of genius! Really. It was *inspired*. I battered him round the head with a frozen leg of lamb, then roasted it for Sunday lunch with mint and goose-fat potatoes.'

'You what?'

'We ate the evidence. We ate the murder weapon.'

'*We?*' I gawk at her, open-mouthed. To be fair, though, that is clever.

'Anyway, I'm off the hook. But that was *ages* ago and he wasn't your dad, so who cares?' she says, topping up her glass.

I gawk at her, open-mouthed.

'That is a *terrible* attitude. What chance did I have?' I say. 'Honestly, what kind of an example is that to set for your daughter?'

'Beth?'

'No, me!'

'You? Ha. You're a lost cause. Always have been.'

I shake my head in disbelief. 'Ever since the day I was born?'

'Yes. You came out bad.' She shrugs and downs another glass. 'You were a *bad egg*.'

'We were *monozygotic*.'

My mum looks up through her eyelash extensions. Her eyes are kind of wobbly. She empties the bottle into her glass. I'm feeling drunk just watching.

'Now listen, Alvina,' my mother says with a serious voice, but then she hiccoughs.

Oh God, what now? I'm not sure I can take it.

'I'm going to inherit Ed's money, of course, and I'll leave the money to Ernie. You don't deserve it,' she slurs. 'You take after me: rotten to the core.'

She rests her cheek on the tablecloth and then stops talking.

The table is soaking wet with champagne. She kind of lolls in it. I wait to see if she'll carry on talking, but then I hear her snoring.

'Mum,' I say, prodding her arm. 'Mum? MUM? MUM!'

I feel the rage building inside: an avalanche of wrath.

I slap her. 'WAKE UP.'

I blink. I'm just like *her*? It's true. *In vino veritas*. It's all coming out now. I pick up her hand and it flops back down. Is she *dead*? No. But *I'll* fucking kill her. How dare she steal my billions? But what did I think would happen? It's *my* money. I worked hard for it. Oh God. Where's Dad? Still boning the butler probably. What a mess.

'Come on, Ernie,' I say, picking him up and taking my phone. 'I'm going to need that back I'm afraid.' I shove my phone in my bag. 'Let's go and find one of Grandma's friends,' I say. We cross the room.

'OK,' says Ernie. I give him a kiss on the top of his head. He's sweet.

'Hi,' I say when I reach the table of ageing Barbie dolls. 'Could someone please watch Mavis's grandson for a little while? She is . . . indisposed at the moment and I've got to go.'

'Of course,' says a woman, standing up. 'I was going to

babysit anyway. I'm Ursula. You must be . . . Alvina? Or is it *Siobhán* now?'

'Whatever. Either's fine. It's *Siobhán*.'

'You look just like your mother.'

I grimace and hand the kid to her.

'I'll see you later, little man,' I say. 'High five?'

'High five!' He puts up his hand and I give it a whack.

I gaze into Ernie's big blue eyes and feel a wave of panic rising in the pit of my stomach. I don't want to leave him. What if I never see him again? What if something happens? I've left him too many times before. I lean and hug him.

Not now, Alvie. Be practical. This isn't the moment. Poor boy. But he'll be fine with Ursula the fucking sea witch. I squeeze his tiny shoulder.

'Mama,' he says.

There's a pang somewhere in my heart that I try to ignore.

I head back to the unconscious bride and spot the chauffeur sitting at the next table along.

'A little help,' I say, gesturing to my mother lying on the table.

'Of course, madam,' he says with a smile as he approaches our table.

The chauffeur and I grab my mother under her armpits and lift her from the table. Her chair falls over. Her glass rolls to the floor. Her wedding dress snags on something. But she's not heavy. She's quite light. I'm used to lifting corpses on my own – and they're a *dead weight* – so it makes a nice change to have someone to help me carry a body around. We drag my mum across the room. Some people turn and stare, but mostly they keep on laughing and talking and dancing, unaware.

We pass the six-tiered wedding cake. They haven't even cut it. There are two conjoined tiny figurines on the top. I yank it out of the royal icing and push it down my cleavage. We pass a table loaded with dozens of beautifully wrapped presents. I can't help but notice a turquoise Tiffany's box tied with black ribbon. I glance at the chauffeur. He isn't looking, so I pick that up too. Poor old Tiffany. I wonder if she liked *Tiffany's*? I shove the box in my Birkin bag. Nobody will notice.

We make our way outside to the white Rolls-Royce parked on the driveway. Its number plate still says 'TiFF 1'. I didn't have time to change it. And nor did my mother apparently. 'MAV15'. *Urgh*. I open up the passenger door and bundle my mother inside. I get in too. I'm about to slam the door when she suddenly *vomits*.

My mother falls asleep on my lap. I watch her chest rise and fall. She murmurs something in her sleep. Oh God, it's going to feel *so good* to finally do her in. At last! Am I *really* going to do it? Now, after all these years? Perhaps I am Electra? Huh. Maybe it is written? She shouldn't have stolen my husband. She shouldn't have ruined my plan.

It's not the *money*. That's not why I'm mad. Inside I'm still that little girl locked in the dark in the attic. Banging on the wooden door, screaming, 'Let me out.' Scared of every creak, every noise. Crying silently. I'm six years old and I don't understand why she loves Beth not *me*.

So, how am I going to do it? Knife? Stairs? Blunt instrument? Or, even better, *swimming pool* . . . That worked well last time. All those years of treating me like

I'm the anti-Christ. All those years of making me feel like I'm the problem child. Possessed by the devil. Maybe she was right?

I peer into her sleeping face; she's out like a light.

I grab the Tiffany's box from my bag and open it up – diamond earrings! I try them on. They're chandelier style with sparkling stones cascading down shining white gold. I check myself out in the rear-view mirror: very Audrey Hepburn. I keep them on. I'll look *fabulous* for my big moment of reckoning.

Monday, 16 October, 2 a.m.
The Bishops Avenue, Hampstead, London

'Here's fine, thanks,' I say.

'I'll help you get her inside,' says the chauffeur. We stagger across the gravel to the front door. I find Mum's key in her handbag and unlock the door. The chauffeur and I drag my mother to the lift.

'I'll be fine now,' I say, pressing the button for the lift.

'Are you sure you don't need a hand upstairs? I'll help you get her to bed.'

'No, really. You've done enough. Get back to the party,' I say.

'OK, if you insist. Goodnight, madam.'

'Bye.' I force a smile and try my best not to look like a killer.

My mother slips out of my hands and flops down to the marble floor. The lift pings and the doors swish open, but I don't get inside. I watch as the chauffeur crosses the hall and leaves through the front door. As soon as his back disappears and I hear the door click shut, I grab my mother by the ankles and drag her behind me.

We're on.

It's quiet. There's no one else around. All the other staff are at the wedding. I need to hurry up. I'll make it look like she drowned in the pool. The autopsy will prove she was wasted. My mum feels heavy, leaden, as I make my way through the house. I kick off my sky-high heels. They were starting to hurt. I pull off my ridiculous hat and chuck it on to the coffee table.

I struggle to pull my mother along the thick-pile carpet. There's a crick in my back and the muscles in my legs are straining. *Great.* That is going to ache in the morning. This is worse than *CrossFit.* I'll have to remember to stretch it out or lactic acid will build and I'll be walking around like a duck. *Hurry up, Alvie. Move it.* But she's heavier than she looks and she's not even *dead* yet. We stop by the French doors that lead out into the back garden. The key goes click in the lock and I swish a glass door wide open. It's dark outside. The sky is black and you can't see the stars through the clouds. The water in the pool is turquoise, lit up prettily with lights.

I grab her by the ankles and drag her out of the house and on to the patio. The security lights flick on. She lands with an inelegant thump. I pause. Will she wake up? She banged her head on the doorstep. I watch to see if she'll stir, but her arms flop out and her head is lolling to the side like a rag doll's. It's fine. She's out cold. I haul her over the tiles to the edge of the pool. I stand and pant with my hands on my knees. That was a *marathon.* All I can hear is the sound of my breath and —

'You're going to kill me, aren't you?'

341

I freeze. The blood drains from my face. It takes me a moment to find my voice. When I do, I say, 'No, I'm not. I'm just . . . getting you some air.'

'See, I told you. You're *bad*. All bad. Go on, do it,' she says.

I don't move a muscle.

'You'd be doing me a favour,' she says. 'I can't live with myself.'

'What are you talking about? You've had too much to drink. Come on,' I say, finding my stride. 'Up you get.'

I grab a sunlounger for her to lie on. The metal legs scrape the tiles.

'My husband is *gay*. I'm past my prime. It's clear that I'm not ageing well. It's getting more and more difficult to maintain my figure,' she says.

'I'm not going to *kill* you,' I say. 'As if.'

'You're just like *me*,' she slurs. 'We all turn into our mothers eventually. I turned into mine. It's a curse.'

'I am *nothing* like you,' I say. 'I'm the opposite.'

I lift her up on to the sunlounger and she kind of rolls.

My mother laughs. 'You always reminded me of myself,' she says. 'Of the *worst* part of me. The dark and ugly fucked-up bit I tried so hard to conceal . . .'

I grit my teeth and close my eyes. She knows how to wind me up. Well, I'm not going to react. I try to do some yoga breathing. What would Tiffany do? But she laughs again and I totally lose it. This is *bullshit*. Why do I have to take this crap? Earth would be better off without her. I'm doing the world a favour . . .

I grab her and drag her to the edge of the pool. Her

hair falls down to the water, sending ripples across the surface. She lets out a scream. She's leaning backwards over the water. I stand above her, panting. The figurine of Mum and Dad falls out from my cleavage – splash. I watch it sink and disappear into the water – down, down, down, down, all the way to the bottom.

'Go on, do it,' she says. 'Go on. You weren't *born* bad. *I* created you.'

'What the hell are you on about?'

I grip her even harder, digging my fingers into her flesh, lowering her into the water.

'*I* turned you into a monster,' she says proudly. 'You're my *masterpiece*. And now my monster is going to put me out of my misery.'

'Say it again,' I say. My voice sounds frightening, strange. My hands are shaking. My shoulders heave and my muscles strain with her weight as I hold her over the water. I shake her and shake her and shake her. 'SAY IT AGAIN,' I scream.

'I *want* you to kill me.'

I look into her eyes. She's wasted. She's not seeing straight.

Why did she call me her *masterpiece*? What does that even mean?

My mother wails like a wicked witch: an eerie sound. She wanted me to be a *killer*. She wanted me *bad*, like she was.

'I am *not Frankenstein's monster*,' I shout. 'I'm not your *creation*. I am my own person.'

She laughs. 'You're a monster, like I am.'

I freeze. I think I hear a noise. I look up but the garden is still. The stars are peering down now through a clearing in the clouds. I shiver. One of the stars is brighter than the others. Is that Tiffany? Is that her soul up there looking down? Is she burning bright like the sun?

'I'm not going to do it. *Fuck you*,' I say.

I refuse to fulfil her prophecy. I wasn't *born* a psychopath. I was misunderstood. I yank her up.

She falls on to the tiles. Her hair is soaking wet.

'Right. Get up. You're going to bed. You've had too much to drink.' I grab her hand.

'No, I haven't,' she moans.

'You have,' I say. 'You're imagining things. You are off your head. And you're talking utter *shit*. You've really lost it this time.'

I help her up again. We stagger back across the patio, my mother draped across my shoulder, leaning on me, *dribbling*. Could I have got it wrong all these years? Is it *nurture*, not *nature*, that made me bad? That corrupted me? That turned me into a killer? Perhaps I wasn't *born* evil. *She* turned me into a monster. Ha. She tried to anyway. She wanted me to be like her. We all turn into our mothers eventually. Isn't that what they say? Well, not *this* girl. Not *this* time. No! Over my dead body. She is finally *proud of me* for trying to *murder* her. That is crazy. That's just *nuts*. That is so messed up.

I'm beginning to understand (although it makes my brain hurt). I was like some kind of psychological experiment. My mother only ever told my identical twin she was *great*. Beth was the good one. She was the angel. She was the golden child. But Mum told me I was her shadow. I was the devil's child. She *wanted* me to be like this. *No one* is BORN EVIL. She knew she'd killed her husband and

344

moulded me to follow in her footsteps. And I have been fulfilling her fucked-up prophecy ever since. Living my life on *her* autopilot. It was my mother's doing! I get it now. It all makes sense. It's *mad*, but that's what happened. She's more fucked up than I thought, and I thought she was *fucked up*.

I open the doors that lead to the lounge and haul my mum inside. 'I'll take you upstairs to bed, but you have to promise me that you won't kill Dad.'

'OK, I promise,' she says.

I study her wasted eyes. I'm not sure I believe her. But I guess I don't have a choice. I've decided *not* to kill her.

'Unless it's in *self-defence*,' I add. 'I hate to say it, Mum, but you should know. He might be *dangerous*.'

'Edwin? Please.' She cackles. We make our way through the living room, my mother leaning on my shoulder and dragging her feet on the carpet.

'It was a long time ago . . . but I know what he did in the eighties.'

'What did he do?'

I sigh. It doesn't matter now. I might as well tell her.

'He stole a painting from a man called Enzo, Enzo Brusca. The painting was worth a lot of money and Enzo killed himself.'

She looks at me, then doubles over in laughter. 'The Da Messina? That old thing? Oh my God. Who cares? Stealing that was *my* idea. Ed sold it and started his fund.'

I gaze at my mother. '*Your* idea?'

'Ed would never have had the balls.'

She's laughing so hard now she is crying. I don't know why I'm surprised. It's *exactly* the kind of thing she would do. Of course it was *her*. Who else? She stole the painting. Dad is just too *nice*.

Nino and I have been plotting to kill the wrong person all this time . . .

And then Nino himself appears (his *ghost*) in the living room. It's the first time I've seen him in *months*. He's looking well.

'Oh, there you are,' I say. 'Been a while. Where've you been?'

I know what he wants. It's obvious. I know why he's come back now. It's *Mum's* fault Nino's dad is dead. I look into Nino's eyes. They are soulless, empty, black. He wants Mum dead. Wants her to pay. This is his big moment of vengeance.

I close my eyes, shake my head. I'm not the same girl as before. There are things I know. I'm not going to do it, even for him.

'I'm sorry, it's over, Nino.'

'Who are you talking to?' asks Mum.

'Shh, no one,' I whisper.

'Alvie, baby,' Nino says.

And I see it now. Nino never really loved me. Not like Tiffany did. It was all just *sex* with him, albeit really good sex. I close my eyes and breathe in deep. I'm a different person. I don't have to do what I've always done. I can decide. I can choose. Every single moment is new. I have my own free will. It isn't written. It isn't fate. This isn't a fucking Greek tragedy. It is time to move on now. Heat spreads from my heart to my throat to my cheeks and I flush. It takes all my strength to say, 'Nino, please don't come again.'

Nino fades away.

I tuck my mother up in bed and leave a night light on.

'Try to get some sleep,' I say. 'You're going to feel *rough* in the morning.'

I tiptoe into the en suite – there's the Samurai sword on the wall and there's the bathtub where Tiffany died – and I head for the medicine cabinet. My hands shake as I open the door and grab a packet of aspirin. I close the cabinet door and tiptoe out into the bedroom. I leave the aspirin on the bedside table with a glass of water.

'Here you go,' I say, but she's already sleeping.

I stand and watch her breathing. Seriously, *that was a close one.*

I grab a piece of notepaper and a pen from inside the drawer. I scribble *Ernie's with Ursula. Don't forget to get him.*

I hesitate then place the note on the table for Mum to see when she wakes up in the morning. I sigh. Poor kid. Poor Ernie.

> *Some things finally*
> *Make sense. So many questions*
> *Remain unanswered.*

I flop down in an armchair and play with my phone. My head's still spinning. *Fuck.* In a desperate attempt to gain some insight into my mother's beyond-bonkers brain, I decide to google 'How do I make my baby evil?' Something else comes up: 'Help I think my baby is possessed by the devil'. I click. There is something called post-partum psychosis. I read. I read and read and read. And I can't stop reading . . . *Oh my God*. It's an actual thing. It happens all the time. It's not just *me*. It's not just *Mum*. There are other 'demon' children. I read the whole website. Then another. And another. It's not that common, but it happens. Sometimes mothers get it. They think their kids are possessed by the devil. They think their kids are *bad*. I've never heard of it before, but this psychosis thing sure as hell explains a lot. I wonder what came first? The chicken or the egg? Did she think I was *born* evil, then try to convince herself that she really wanted me evil? Or was I just a normal girl and Mum made it her mission to create a killing machine? I guess I'll never know.

Perhaps Mum couldn't cope on her own with newborn twins all those years ago and I am the culmination of her madcap delusions. Crazy hormones, sleep deprivation, babies screaming in stereo . . . and, on top of that, she'd just killed her husband. I bet she was *stressed out*. It's a recipe for disaster! She went nuts. She turned Beth into her golden child and I became the black sheep. Or did she believe the whole damn thing? *I* believed it. Wow. That's it. My whole life's right there in that word: psychosis. I wasn't *born a killer*; I wasn't even *born evil*. It doesn't matter which side of my chest my heart is on. Who cares? Who gives a shit if it's on the left? It doesn't mean anything. I have a heart of gold, Tiff said. I have a soul. A *spirit*. I can choose my fate, my destiny. I'm beautiful, like a crystal. I'm not a child any more. I'm a grown-up. A woman. I decide who I'm going to be. I have a *job* for God's sake.

I haul myself up from the sofa and chuck my phone in my bag. I refuse to live in my mother's shadow for a minute longer.

I close Dad's bedroom door and walk along the hall to the lift. I press the button for the ground floor. I lean my forehead on the mirror and rest for a moment, exhausted. Tiredness hits like a tidal wave. Fuck me, I am *knackered*. I close my eyes and feel the cool glass on my skin. It's cold. I'm hot, too warm in my layers of lace. My cheeks feel flushed on my burning face. I'm about to fall asleep right there, when the doors swish open. I step out into the entrance hall and stand there, motionless. I don't feel like going home, not yet. I'm too tired to travel. Instead of heading for the front door, I turn and head for the garden. I tiptoe through the living room towards the French doors. Some fresh air will do me good. I need to *breathe* for a minute. It's been an emotional rollercoaster. I wish Tiff were here, to be honest. Tiffany would know what to do. She was always so grounded. It's like she had all the answers to life, like she had God on speed dial. But I have put my mother to bed and Tiffany would be proud. It's the spiritual thing to do; there's no doubt about it. I don't want to be like *my mum*. I spared her life. Now there's a *first*. I don't have to play *her* game. *I'll* decide if I'm good or bad, or maybe something in between – a shade of grey, a *human being*.

I open up the doors. Poor Tiff. And I'm even beginning to think . . . poor Beth. I never, ever thought I would say it, but she didn't deserve to die. Maybe she wasn't *perfect*, maybe she was a victim too, always under pressure to be the *good* one. The role model. To be fucking flawless. And, yes, she was a *cow*, of course. But I see now that Beth wasn't the enemy. We were both acting out roles that weren't ours to begin with. I can't help but feel a deep sense of regret about what might have been. Beth and I might have been *friends*. Who knows? Like Tiff and I were.

I take a deep breath. Keep cool, carry on. It's in the past. It doesn't matter. Look forward, not backwards. *Hakuna matata*. It will be all right in the end, and if it's not all right, it isn't the end yet.

I step out to the cool of the dawn, the scent of grass and dew. It's sunrise now and the pink sky is filled with cloud formations that look just like an angel's wings: terrifying, majestic. Long, thin clouds resemble feathers in endless swooping rows all along the distant horizon. Sunlight turns them gold. It's stunning. For a moment I watch them moving through the sky. I've never seen a sky like this. It looks just like a painting from the Renaissance, something Italian, something religious. There's a light breeze and the clouds' motion is barely perceptible, but if you watch them really hard, you can see that they're moving, whispering, dancing almost. The sky is sublime. I want to take a picture. I wouldn't even need to edit it. No colour filters. I'm about to grab my phone and take a photo for Insta, when I pause – what if I go to snap it and it disappears? It could vanish at any second. It would never look as good as this on a phone screen anyway. No, I'm not going to take a pic. I'll keep it a secret for me. But Tiffany would have loved it. She was always on about angels and how they left signs in the clouds, white feathers and rainbows to let you know that they're watching you. I always thought it was bullshit. But now, I guess, I'm not so sure.

'Hello? Tiff? Can you hear me?' I call up into the clouds.

What about the other people I killed? Beth? Nino? That nun? Is there a hell? And if there is, will *I* go there?

What if I turn over a new leaf? What if I just kill fish from now on? Fish and a few crustaceans?

I turn my attention to the garden, which is bathed in an ethereal glow. It looks magic in the half-light. Otherworldly. Ghostly. The first rays of sun are piercing through the golden clouds like spears, shimmering silver, almost white, against the dark of the earth. The garden stretches out before me: the statues, the orchard, the dovecote, the rows of flowers, the swimming pool, my old cottage. Birdsong fills the air, and the dawn chorus sounds just like a choir. I breathe in deep and smell the flowers. Other than the twittering, it's silent, deathly quiet. I suddenly feel very alone. It's eerie at this hour.

I shiver and wrap my arms round myself and walk to the edge of the pool. I stand and look out at the water. It's tranquil, as still as a millpond. Its surface is as smooth as a mirror's. I study my reflection and see a face peering back at me, but I feel nothing. I'm numb. Those glassy eyes are mine, I know. But they could belong to anyone. I stand and stare until the face in the water changes to Tiff's.

I close my eyes. *Don't be stupid, Alvie. You're imagining things.*

The scent of chlorine fills my nose. I take a deep breath and lift my arms up high above my head, then dive into the water. It's freezing and the temperature shocks me. I swim up for air and gasp; my whole body's shaking, my skin alive with goosebumps. It's much colder than I'd expected, like a slap in the face. Icy liquid wraps my core and the skirt of my dress weighs me down, the material clinging to my thighs like it wants me to drown. I tread water, panting, struggling to breathe in the bitter cold.

Tiffany's face appears in my mind. She's smiling. Smiling.

Smiling. I killed my friend. I nearly killed my mum. I killed my twin, Beth. Oh, Beth. She's gone. She's gone.

Time slows down.

Stops still.

I sink down into the water. The air escapes from my nose and bubbles rise up to the surface. I watch them float away . . .

- Beth
- Ambrogio
- That priest
- The hitmen from the Mafia
- That mugger in Bucharest
- The nun
- Nino
- The policemen
- Tiff

And I nearly killed my *dad*. Oh God. I'm a *murderer*. It has taken me a while, but it's really sinking in now.

I sit on the tiles at the bottom of the pool under the water. I look up. Dark figures loom, standing at the edge of the water. There are a dozen blurry shadows surrounding the pool. I blink and blink and rub my eyes. I look again. *It can't be!* It's all of the people I killed. They're standing, staring at me. The figures look ghostly through the water. Behind them, the sky in the east is blood red with the rising sun. I catch a glimpse of Beth's face. I stretch out a long pale arm. She reaches down as well, but she's too far away. I can't reach her.

I'm sorry, Beth. I am.

Nino's standing next to her. His eyes are two black

holes. There's a round black void in the centre of his forehead. He turns and walks away.

Goodbye, Nino. Goodbye.

Tiff is there as well; she's shining in a rainbow-light
body. Her golden hair glows like a halo. She looks really
pretty. And there's the nun I killed in Rome still dressed
in her torn black habit. The nun makes the sign of the
cross then reaches down towards the water. She scoops
up water in her hands then lets it fall into the pool. What
the fuck? Is she *blessing* me? What is this? A *baptism*? I
scream and scream at the top of my lungs, but there's no
sound, no nothing. Just me and the dead and cold, cold
water filled with rising bubbles.

Fourth Stasimon

Monday, 16 October, 10 a.m.
Number One Top City Hostel, Archway, London

Dear Miss Faelan,

Congratulations! We are delighted to inform you that you have won first prize in our Poems on the Underground competition for your haiku entitled: 'Summer Emptiness'. A cheque for fifty pounds is enclosed with this letter and your poem will be displayed on fifty London Underground trains. Your poem was selected from among thousands of entries and the judges were unanimous in their decision to award you the grand prize. The judges commented on the raw emotion and astonishing existential angst you were able to convey in such a compact form. We wish you the very best with your future writing career and look forward to seeing more of your haikus in due course.

Yours sincerely,
Mrs J. L. Abrahams
President of the Poems on the Underground Foundation

I reread the letter six more times before folding it back up again and tucking it into the envelope it came in. I yank out the cheque for fifty pounds and blink at the names and the numbers. That definitely says, 'Pay Miss Siobhán Faelan . . .' and that is definitely *me*. I mean, it's not *me*. It's my nom de plume. But it is me, if you see what I mean. And that number is *definitely* fifty pounds. Fifty British pounds just for me! I can't believe it. No one has ever liked my haikus before. In fact, most people hate them. I've lost count of the number of times people (my mother, Beth, the teachers at school, all my former bosses) have told me to stop wasting my time writing poetry . . . but now this. THIS! At last, recognition. Appreciation of my talent. A little fucking vindication. And I'm not even thirty. And to think I believed that, like Keats and Van Gogh, I would remain unappreciated in my own lifetime.

Atchoo.

I sneeze and sniff and wipe my nose. I must have caught a cold early-morning swimming. Man, that was fucked up. I'm not doing *that* again. Things were getting *spooky* . . .

I glance at the time. I'm late. If I don't leave the hostel immediately, I will be late for my shift at the Savoy. I shove the last Pringle in my mouth and wash it down with some water straight from the tap; I don't have time to fuck around with a *glass*. Baby licks my fingers as I dump some fillet steak in his bowl. I fill up his water bowl as well and leave it on the floor in the kitchen.

'Be good, Earmuff. I'll see you later. If you have to chew up some shoes, then chew Bob's shoes, not my shoes. Get it?'

He looks up and licks his nose. I ruffle the hair on his tiny head, then sprint out of the door. I run downstairs and out of the hostel. I'm at the station in under a minute.

'Hey,' I say to the room full of cooks as I barge into the kitchen.

'Oh, hi, Siobhán,' they say.

I yawn.

'Late night?' Jack asks.

'Uh-huh.'

'What were you up to?'

'Er, wedding.'

I wash my hands and pull on my hat and my apron, and grab my knife. I find a nice pink chunk of fish in the refrigerator. I pick up my knife and chop. I sink the blade into the flesh (the fish's flesh, not Jack's flesh). The knife moves like lightning, so fast you can't see the blade. I whistle Taylor as I chop. 'Shake It Off'. That's another good one. It always reminds me not to take things *too* seriously.

'You're in a good mood,' says Jack.

'I just won a competition.'

'Oh? What kind of competition?' he asks, standing next to me at the counter.

'A poetry competition,' I say. I know I look smug, but who cares?

'Wow, you're multitalented,' he says. He elbows me in the ribs.

'Yes. Yes, I am,' I laugh. I can make my own way, my own money.

'Chopping up sushi, writing poems, looking cute in a chef's hat . . .'

I pick up my knife and point the blade at Jack. 'You have no idea.'

My phone rings. It's Mum. I pick it up and say, 'Wassup?'

'Alvie?'

'I'm at work, Mum. I'm busy. What is it now?'

'Ed and I are off on honeymoon,' she continues. 'We're going to the Bahamas and Fiji, the Maldives and Mexico.'

'Is *James* going too?' I ask.

'He is. But not Ernesto. I need you to look after him.'

'*Ernie?*'

'Yes. He's your nephew, remember? I left him at the house with Fifi, you know, Edwin's housekeeper? You need to go and pick him up.'

'*Ernie?*' I say again.

'Yes, are you deaf?'

'Where are you now?'

'On Ed's plane.'

'You mean Percy. How long are you going for?'

She pauses. 'A couple of months? Maybe more . . .'

But her voice sounds strange and far away. *A couple of months?* I can tell when she's lying.

'You're not coming back, are you?'

She pauses. 'No, darling, I'm not.'

The line goes dead then hums.

'Mum? Mum? What the fuck? DON'T KILL ED,' I yell.

But it's too late. She didn't hear. She's gone. I stare at the phone. She's never called me 'darling' before. I don't know how I feel.

She's leaving me my nephew? *What?* I picture his face: his ocean eyes, his cheeky smile, his hair as soft as snow-flakes. She's giving me my sister's son. He's all mine? All for me? *That's* priceless. He's worth more than millions. Not quite a *billion*, though . . .

'Is everything all right?' asks Jack, resting his hand on my shoulder.

I turn and blink. 'What's that?'

He laughs. 'Are you all right?'

'I'm fine.' It's me, Ernie and the dog. We'll be just fine together. 'I'm fine,' I repeat.

'O-*K*,' he says.

'I am. I'm fine. It's all good.'

There is every chance that Mum is going to kill my dad and thereby inherit his fortune. I know there is. I'm not *stupid*. But that doesn't seem to bother me right now as much as it ought to. I guess it's out of my control, my circle of influence.

I take a deep breath and carry on chopping. Everything will be all right. I am going to be a *mum*. I have *two* dependents. I'm a *mum*. A *single* mum. What will I do with Beth's kid? I guess it's time to start hanging out with people who are *alive* rather than dead folk in my head. And Ernie is a *cherub*. I close my eyes and breathe in through my nose and out through my mouth. If I can get away with *murder*, I can raise a *kid*. I mean . . . come on. How hard can it be? I chop, chop, chop with my eyes shut. I'll work it out . . .

'You're so badass,' Jack says, 'doing that with your *eyes closed*.'

'No!' I say. I open my eyes. 'I *used* to be badass. Now I guess I'm just *ass*.'

'What?'

'That came out wrong.'

What I *meant* to say is a little less *An eye for an eye*. A bit more *Turn the other cheek* . . .

'Actually, I have to go. I need to pick up my kid.'

I throw the knife down on the block and untie my apron.

'You're crazy,' Jack says as I walk out of the door. 'You're crazy, but I like you.'

I smile to myself as I leave. 'What's not to like?'

Exodos

ONE WEEK LATER

Monday, 23 October, 10 a.m.
Chancery Lane, London

I carry Ernie in his pushchair up the stairs to the front door, dragging Earmuff on his lead and trying not to trip up. I push through the door and make my way to the waiting room. I park the pushchair by the coffee machine and sink down in a chair. The dog and I gaze out through the window, watching raindrops make snaking patterns as they slide.

'Miss Faelan?' comes a woman's voice.

It makes me jump. I stand up. 'Er, no. Yes, I mean, yes! That's me. I think. OK.'

She frowns.

I try a hopeful smile.

'You *are* Miss Faelan, aren't you?'

'Yes, today I am.' She looks blank. 'It's fine. I am her,' I say.

I chuck the copy of *House and Garden* on to the coffee table and pick up my broken umbrella from the floor. There's a wet patch on the seat where I sat in my damp clothes. It looks a bit like I wet myself, but I didn't – I was just *soaked*.

I pull Baby on his lead and go to fetch the pushchair, then trail the woman out of the waiting room into a narrow hall.

She raps on a door.

I hold my breath. *Why am I even here?*

I read a brass plaque on the door: 'Gregory Firth Solicitors'. And it's a force of habit – I *sweat*. I don't like *law* or *lawyers*.

'Come in,' comes a muffled voice.

'Miss Faelan for you, sir.'

She holds the door open for me and I step inside and sneeze. The office tastes of dust and smells of dying books. An ageing man is standing behind a mahogany desk. He reaches out to shake my hand.

'Gregory Firth,' he says.

'Oh, right, yeah,' I say. 'Siobhán Faelan.'

'Pleasure.'

He gestures for me to sit down on a black-leather chair.

'So why did I have to come in?' I ask. 'What is this about?'

I can barely see him over the piles of documents and papers. Bushy white eyebrows protrude from rimless spectacles.

'As you know, my dear, you are an executor of your father's will.'

'An *executioner*,' I correct.

I sigh. I bet I can guess why I'm here. My father's changed his will, and now my mum will inherit it *all* and I'll be left with *nothing*. Poor me. Poor Ernie. Poor Baby too; there's no way he'll survive on dog food from a *normal* shop. He is used to Wagyu. I slouch back in the leather chair and stare up at the ceiling. I'm going to be poor forever, aren't I? Making other people's fish and scribbling tiny poems . . .

'As you know, your father recently remarried.'

Urgh. 'Yes, yes. I know. *I know.* He's changed his will again, hasn't he?'

'He has. And as an ex–'

'*Executioner.*'

'As an . . . executioner of the will, you will need to read it and sign it. There's only one very *slight* amendment. It shouldn't take you long.'

'Whatever.'

I roll my eyes as Gregory hands me a single piece of paper. At the top of the page it says: *Amendment to the Will of Edwin Forbes.* I bet my mother's already spending her billion-pound inheritance. She'll be kitted out in Versace, dripping with blood diamonds. She'll have splashed out on a solid-gold loo. She'll have bought a super-yacht bigger Roman Abramovich's. She's so *materialistic.* Ha. She's so *unspiritual.* Not like me and Tiffany. I don't want the money anyway. I don't care. I'm over it.

I skim the rest of the page. Blah, blah, blah, blah, blah . . .

I hereby leave my wife, Mavis Forbes, one green ceramic frog from the Northern Song Dynasty, valued at eighty-six million pounds.

Kermit? The stupid frog?

I read the line again. That's it. That is all it says. *What?* I turn over the page but it's blank on the back. *Is this some kind of joke?*

'If you would be so kind as to sign it once you have read it,' he says.

'What? That's it? And the rest of the will?'

'Stays exactly the same. Mr Forbes' fortune will be

divided between yourself and young Master Knightly, when he comes of age, of course, should he still be a minor.'

'Fuck,' I say.

Gregory jumps.

'I mean, *shit*. I'm so sorry. It's just . . . that if I'd known that frog was so valuable, I would have been more careful with it.' He nods as though he understands. 'Actually, no. I probably wouldn't, if I'm being honest.'

I skip out of the lawyer's office whistling 'Love Story'. It's lucky I opened a bank account in Siobhán's name! The sun shines down from a gap in the clouds. There's an actual *rainbow* stretching out across the sky in glorious Technicolor. I laugh out loud to myself. I fondle my leprechaun. I carry the pushchair and the dog down the steps. My mother's not getting *shit*. It is all for me and the kid! Not that eighty-six million pounds is *nothing*. It's a *lot*. I'd say it's more than she deserves, but you know what? She can keep it. I've decided to *forgive* her. I forgive her for *everything*.

What was it Tiff said to me the other day inside my head? *I forgive you.*

That was it! It was *very* spiritual. I read something in one of Tiffany's self-help books about how forgiving someone else actually frees *you*. Forgiveness sets *you* free . . .

'*I forgive you*,' I whisper to no one in particular, to the sky. And you know what? I forgive *myself*.

I suddenly feel lighter.

I flag down a cab on the road. I load the dog and the kid and climb on to the back seat.

'Harrods. And step on it.'

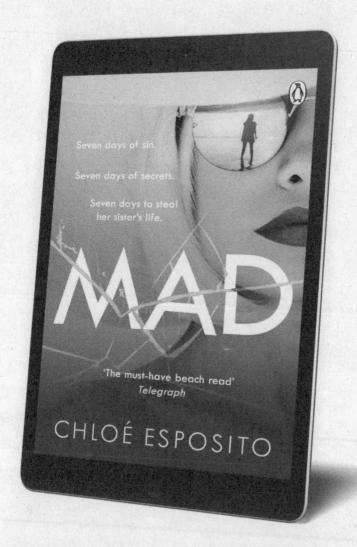

Loved *Dangerous to Know* and want to see where Alvie's journey first started?

Read on for an extract from *Mad* . . .

Disclaimer

There's something you should know before we go any further: my heart is in the wrong place. So is my stomach, my liver and my spleen. All my internal organs are on the opposite side, in exactly the place where they shouldn't be. I'm back to front: a freak of nature. Seven billion people on this planet have their hearts on the left. Mine's on the right. You don't think that's a sign?

My sister's heart is in the right place. Elizabeth is perfect, through and through. I am a mirror image of my twin, her dark side, her shadow. She is right and I am wrong. She's right-handed; I am left. In Italian, the word for 'left' is 'sinistra'. I am the sinister sister. Beth is an angel and so what am I? Hold that thought . . .

The funny thing is that to look at us, you can't tell the difference. On the surface, we're identical twins, but peel back the skin and you'll get the shock of your life; watch in awe as my guts spill out all mixed up and topsy-turvy. Don't say I didn't warn you. It's not a pretty sight.

We're monozygotic, if you want to know; Beth's zygote split in two and I materialized. It happened at the very earliest stage of development, when her zygote was no more than a cluster of cells. Mum had been pregnant for just a few days and then – poof – out of nowhere, I show up, cuckoo-like. Beth had to share her nice, cosy amniotic bath and Mum's home-cooked placenta.

It was pretty crowded in that uterus; there wasn't a lot of room for the two of us and our umbilical cords. Beth's got tangled around her neck and then knotted pretty badly. It was touch and go for a while. I don't know how that happened. It had nothing to do with me.

Scientists think identical twins are completely random. We're still a mystery; no one knows how or why I occurred. Some call it luck, coincidence or chance. But nature doesn't like random. God doesn't just *play dice*. I came here for a reason; I know I did. I just don't know what that reason is yet. The two most important days of your life are the day you are born and the day you find out why.

DAY ONE:
Sloth

My problem's always been failure to give a fuck.
@AlvinaKnightly69

Chapter One

Monday, 24 August 2015, 8 a.m.
Archway, London

From: Elizabeth Caruso
ElizabethKnightlyCaruso@gmail.com
To: Alvina Knightly
AlvinaKnightly69@hotmail.com
Date: 24 Aug 2015 at 08.01
Subject: VISIT

Alvie, darling,

*Please stop ignoring me. I know you received my last two
emails because I put that recipient-tracker thing on, so you
can stop pretending. Despite being at risk of repeating
myself, I would like to invite you, yet again, to come and
stay with us at our villa in Taormina. You would LOVE it
here: 16th-century original features, the smell of frangipani
in the air. The sun shines every single day. There's a pool to
die for. We're around the corner from the ancient Greek
amphitheatre, which frames Mount Etna to the west and the
shimmering Mediterranean to the east. Even if you can only
manage a week – I know you're a slave to that ghastly job – it
would be wonderful to see you. I can't believe you haven't
met Ernie yet; he's getting bigger each day and is the spit of
his Auntie Alvina.*

*But seriously, I need you. I'm begging you. Come. IT'S BEEN
TWO YEARS.*

There's something I need to ask you and I can't do it by email.
Beth x

PS I know what you're thinking and no, it isn't still awkward.
Ambrogio and I have forgotten all about it, even if you
haven't. So stop being a mule and come to Sicily.

PPS How much do you weigh at the moment? Are you still
9 stone 5? A size 10? I can't lose the baby weight and it's
driving me insane.

Fucking hell; she is intolerable.

The smell of frangipani in the air blah, blah, blah, *the ancient Greek amphitheatre* blah, blah, blah, *the shimmering Mediterranean* blah, blah, fucking blah. She sounds like that presenter on *A Place in the Sun:* 'Alvina Knightly seeks a pied-à-terre in the stunning coastal region of Eastern Sicily.' Not that I would ever watch that kind of thing.

I am *definitely not* going. It sounds boring, old-fashioned. I don't trust volcanoes. I cannot stand that kind of heat. It's sticky. Sweaty. My English skin would burn in two seconds; I'm as pale as an Eskimo. *Don't say 'Eskimo'!* I can just hear her now . . . *They don't like that name. It's not politically correct. Say 'Inuit' instead.*

I scan my bedroom: empty vodka bottles, a Channing Tatum poster, photos on a pinboard of 'friends' I never see. Clothes on the floor. Cold mugs of tea. A vibe that would make Tracey Emin's cleaner freak. Three emails in a week. What's going on? I wonder what she wants to ask me. I suppose I should reply or she'll continue to break my balls.

From: Alvina Knightly
AlvinaKnightly69@hotmail.com
To: Elizabeth Caruso
ElizabethKnightlyCaruso@gmail.com
Date: 24 Aug 2015 at 08.08

Subject: Re: VISIT

Elizabeth, darling,

*Thank you for the invitation. Your villa certainly sounds
stunning. Aren't you and Ambrogio and, of course, little Ernie
lucky to have such a splendid home in what sounds like the
perfect location? Do you remember how as children, I was
the one who loved the water? And now you have the
swimming pool . . .*

(and I have the bath with the blocked-up drain.)

*Isn't life funny? I would, of course, love to see it and meet
your gorgeous little cherub, my nephew, but it really is flat
out at work at the moment. August is always our busiest
month, that's why I've been so tardy in responding.
Apologies.*

*Let me know when you're next visiting London; it would be
good to catch up.*

Albino

No matter how many times I type my name, *Alvina*, predictive
text always changes it to fucking *Albino*. (Perhaps it knows how
pale I am and it's taking the piss?) I'm just going to change it by
deed poll.

Alvina

*PS Do send my regards to your husband and give Ernesto a
kiss from his auntie.*

Send.

Elvis Presley's twin brother was stillborn. Some people have
all the luck.

I drag myself up and out of bed and step in a pizza I left on
the floor. I only ate half of it late last night before passing out

around 4 a.m. Tomato sauce all over my foot. A piece of salami between my toes. I peel off the meat and shove it in my mouth, wipe the sauce off with a sock. I get dressed in the clothes that I find on the floor: a nylon skirt that doesn't need ironing, a cotton T-shirt that does. I look in the mirror and frown. Urgh. I rub the mascara away from my eyes, apply a slick of purple lipstick, run my fingers through greasy hair. That'll do; I'm late. Again.

I go to work.

I grab the mail on my way out of the house and rip it open as I trudge down the street sucking on a Marlboro. Bills, bills, bills, bills, a business card for a minicab company, an advert for takeaway pizza. 'FINAL DEMAND', 'BAILIFF'S NOTICE', 'URGENT ACTION REQUIRED'. Yawn, yawn, more of the same. Does Taylor Swift have to deal with this shit? I shove the letters into the hands of a homeless man sitting outside the Tube: no longer my problem.

I push through the crowds in the line for the turnstile, slam my Oyster card down on the reader. We shuffle through the station at 0.0000001 mph. I try to write a haiku in my head, but the words won't come. Something deep about existential struggle? Something poetic and nihilistic? But nothing. My brain's still asleep. I glare at the adverts for clothes and jewellery that cover every spare inch of wall. The same smug, airbrushed model with the same smug, airbrushed face stares down at me just as she does every single morning. She is feeding a toddler in an advert for follow-on milk. I don't have a toddler and I don't need reminding. I definitely don't need to buy follow-on milk.

I stomp down the escalator, push past a man taking up too much space.

'Hey, watch it!' he yells.

'Stand on the right! Dickhead.'

I am a great artist trapped inside the body of a classified

advertising sales representative, a reincarnation of Byron or Van Gogh, Virginia Woolf or Sylvia Plath. I wait on the platform and contemplate my fate. There must be more to life than this? Stale air kisses my face and tells me that a train is approaching. I could jump now and it would all disappear. Within the hour, paramedics would have scraped me off the track and the Northern line would have resumed service.

A mouse runs over the metal rails. It only has three paws, but it lives a life of freedom and adventure. Lucky bastard. Perhaps that train will crush its little skull? It darts out of the way in the nick of time. Damn.

I perch on the shelf at the end of the carriage. A man with a cold sore invades my personal space; his shirt is translucent with sweat. He holds the yellow rail above my head, his armpit an inch from my nose; I can smell his Lynx Africa mixed with despair. I read his *Metro* upside down: murder, drugs, war, a story about somebody's cat. He presses his crotch against my thigh, so I stamp on his foot. He moves away. Next time, I'll knee him in the balls. We stop for a few minutes somewhere in London's lower intestines and then start again. I change trains at Tottenham Court Road. The carriage empties its bowels and we disembark as amorphous excrement. I am defecated at Oxford Circus.

Hell hath no fury like a woman scorned . . .

Bad, the second instalment in the
Alvie Knightly trilogy, is available
to buy now!